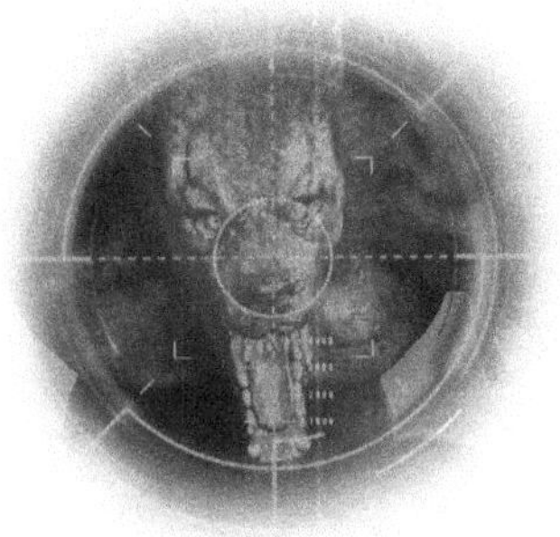

This book is dedicated to

Ghost,

a magnificent black wolf,

who was my brother

my bodyguard

my friend

"Hey, Ghost, how you been, my old friend?

I knew the Lord would bring us together again."

'I have clinched and closed with the naked North
I have learned to defy and defend
Shoulder to shoulder we have fought it out
Yet the wild must win … in the end.'

Robert Service
Songs of a Sourdough

CHAPTER ONE

"We're going to kill Hunter."

The words, spoken with casual indifference, were directed toward two scientists in white lab coats who exchanged confused glances as the chief researcher of Saturn Industries, Professor Scipio Dante, stood over them.

"That's murder, Dante."

The comment came from a scientist on Dante's right, Jack Cronis, who did not otherwise move. He simply held the professor's imperious gaze. He didn't blink and didn't look away. It was as if his words needed nothing more.

Scipio Dante frowned, "To the contrary, doctor, I consider it self-defense." He glanced placidly over the vast laboratory filled with billions of dollars of space-age equipment scarcely to be found anywhere in the world. "Hunter has already killed Luther and Vang. And if another one of us uses the serum, then there is no question that Hunter will track us down and kill us in the same merciless manner. And I, for one, have not come this far in our quest for immortality to have it derailed by some itinerate mountain man."

As if posing for a portrait, Dante added, "We stand at the threshold of a new age when man will no longer be a victim to disease or the degenerate decay of old age. Where we shall be like God, and where good and evil will be thrown into the trash bin of antediluvian ideas whose time has come and gone. Yes, my friends, a superior age has dawned, and it requires a new and superior kind of man. That man and the men with him will lead this world to a new dimension where man, and not God, will decide who lives and who dies."

Mike Pinion, the second scientist, was a thinly built man who looked not unlike a pale corpse in a white frock, asked with a hint of dread, "And just how do you suggest we accomplish this, Dante? Like you said, this man, Nathaniel Hunter, has already killed Luther and Vang and, if you don't mind me saying it, Hunter seems to be pretty good at killing what all of us once thought was unkillable. I don't see why it makes sense for another one of us to take the serum and go after Hunter. In fact, I would suggest that it defies common sense because if Hunter is committed to killing each of us as we undergo the transformation, then what use is there in continuing? As each of us change, Hunter tracks us down and kills us just like he tracked down and killed Vang and Luther. And rather ruthlessly if I may say so." He paused. "I think it's in our best interest to simply continue trying to isolate the genomes that prevent this creature from succumbing to the natural processes of aging and disease. I mean, that's all we really want, isn't it? The genetic secret to its impossibly long life? The life span of a *god*? A life that quite literally defies death and stretches for unknown thousands of years?"

Scipio Dante was the all-powerful owner and CEO of Saturn Industries, the multi-trillion- dollar pharmaceutical global empire that had discovered and illegally mapped out the DNA of what was once the mightiest and most savage predator the earth has ever endured – a specimen that was mercifully dead when it was discovered but whose DNA was easily synthesized from the long-frozen corpse.

It was estimated by on-site anthropologists that the subspecies of *Homo Scimitar* had been entombed within the glacier for ten thousand years, a number arrived at by the depth of the ice surrounding it. It had, in fact, been so deeply buried within the gigantic, continental-wide ice that the body was only discovered by a fissure that occurred for no explainable reason as the research team was setting up camp at the exterior wall. It was almost as if the beast had split the glacier with the power of its will so that it might be free.

Dante seemed unfazed by any reluctance as he answered confidently, "All great scientific breakthroughs require sacrifice, doctor. And if our choice is to sacrifice our dream, or sacrifice the life of Nathaniel Hunter, well, I choose to sacrifice Hunter."

"You're still talking murder," Cronis repeated. "And that's something we've never done, Dante. It's true that Vang killed innocent people when he used the serum. The same thing happened with Luther. But what they did after the transformation can't be classified as murder. They took the serum, transitioned, and lost any semblance of human control. They reverted to the animal's purest form. A creature without a conscience. Without feeling. Without fear. Without mercy. A creature that lives only to satisfy the slightest impulse of its unconscious mind. And, like I say, that's not murder. That's just a tiger doing what a tiger does. But you're suggesting we take this to a new level. And I'm not even sure that it's possible. The instincts of this creature are far too powerful to be focused or controlled. I mean, you're as familiar as I am with its MRIs and brain scans. The rage centers of its brain are a thousand times those of any creature ever discovered. And you're thinking about *taming* that locus so you can focus it on killing one man?" Cronis leaned back. "That's impossible."

Dante confidently responded, "We can conclude with certainty that this subspecies of Homo Scimitar *was* easily the most ferocious killing machine nature ever designed. It will always be earth's mightiest and most savage predator.

There is nothing in the fossil records that can even compare to its instincts, its strength, its speed, its – "

"Psychotic obsession to kill everything in sight," finished Cronis. "An obsession for which it has the power and strength to satisfy no matter what gets in its way. You need to remember that this thing is basically a subspecies of the Sabretooth tiger, Dante. We all know there were a ton of subspecies, but this one turned out to be the long-sought-after missing link between man and beast. You might even say it's the true missing link and not Neanderthal or Cro-Magnon, which were just subspecies of Homo Erectus with no incumbent animal DNA. No. Not at all. This animal was the *real* missing link – the link that has evaded anthropologists since Darwin's theory of evolution hit the ground. And I would suggest that even ol' Darwin would have been shocked at how real his theory has proven to be. But this thing is still more beast than man. In fact, it's *far* more beast than man. It has the speed, the strength and the natural weapons of a tiger as well as a tiger's predatory instinct, so there isn't much in it that you would call 'human' except for a few million strands of hominid DNA, so it's still a tiger. And, technically, a tiger can't 'murder' anybody. Only a human being can commit murder.

"This thing kills because its instincts relentlessly drive it to kill. To destroy whatever gets in its way. And when I say it kills everything and anything in its path, I do mean that it kills *everything* and *anything*! But what you're talking about doing is focusing all the instincts of this phenomenally powerful killing machine against one man for the express purpose of murdering him. And that's not the instinct to kill, Dante. That's cold-blooded, premeditated, capital murder. And that takes *conscious thought* – something this creature doesn't possess. Its killer instincts are far too powerful to be targeted on a single person."

"It's a worthless argument," countered Pinion. "Vang and Luther both tried to kill this guy and he's still around.

He's on top of the ground and I have no idea where the hell they are but they're not alive or they would have initiated the plan, and they haven't. And Vang didn't transform alone, either. He took those three prehistoric wolves with him, so he had a lot of help. And Hunter *still* killed him. And the wolves, too! I got that much from our army contractor." He shook his head. "If Vang couldn't kill Hunter even with the help of three monstrous, prehistoric wolves, what makes you think any of us stand a chance?"

"You're missing the point," Dante countered. "I am not suggesting that *one* of us use the serum to transform and hunt down Hunter. I'm saying we *all* use the serum at the same time and transform together – the three of us working in unison in the form of Scimitar – and focus on Hunter with the express purpose of killing him. Hunter may have mastered the means of defeating one of these creatures at a time. But he will have no experience at battling *three Scimitar* that are all determined to kill him." He paused. "Until now, Hunter has been the predator. Now he will be the prey."

Pinion and Cronis exchanged dubious glances before Cronis asked, "And how can we be sure that we won't turn on each other, Dante? The savagery of this beast is way beyond anything any of us have ever seen. It's really a marvel of evolution – a creature driven only by the deepest, darkest desire of its unconscious mind to kill everything in sight. That's its greatest strength. And its only weakness, really. It has no conscience to restrain it or cause it to weigh the odds of success or failure and maybe wait for a better day. Everything about this animal drives it to satisfy the slightest impulse *now*, and its entire neural network is devoted to killing anything that impedes what it subconsciously wants to achieve." He gestured to a wall of vials as if they were meaningless. "I mean, we all know Vang believed the thought patterns of this animal could be controlled or, at the least, channeled. But I was never very certain of that theory then, and I'm not now. So, if we all transform at the same time, there's a good possibility that we'll all just kill each other."

Dante walked to a safe, opened it, and removed a small rack with three brightly colored tubes that he meticulously placed on the table before them. He continued, "I have made further, and more elaborate alterations, to the serum. Using samples of our own blood, I modified the serum with our separate strains of DNA aimed at the rapid replication of our individual cerebral networks. It is a much more elegant and, I believe, effective approach than Vang attempted. Each vial is engineered specifically for each of us. Yours will work for you alone. Your alteration will not work for me. My alteration will not work for you. But it will work for me."

Dante paused, clearly concentrated. "I am confident this alteration to the serum will not suppress the creature's superior instincts. Nor will it affect its physical superiority and natural skills for hunting and killing. But, to our advantage, I am certain that, with this modification, we will be able to retain just enough of our human minds to focus the full power of this beast on a single objective. And that objective will be to hunt and kill Hunter. And yet, gentlemen, to alleviate any of your doubts, I have added a modest guarantee that ensures we will succeed."

Both scientists stared grimly.

With an air of indifference Dante began, "With the assistance of Colonel Blakely, whom you both know is – "

"Is a cold-blooded killer of women and children," Cronis commented dryly.

Pinion added, "I know Blakely's a ruthless bastard who'd steal his mother's bones from the grave and sell them to buy flowers for a whore. Is there anything else to know?"

Dante dismissed the comments before continuing, "As I was saying, with the good colonel's assistance I have gathered a vastly experienced, lethal army of thirty mercenaries who await us at an abandoned hospital near the mountain Hunter calls home. At no small expense, I might add, I financially secured the facility for this single undertaking and have stocked it with all the essential equipment we will need.

"My plan is to take a leased jet to this base of operations, complete the transformations within secure holding facilities, and test our abilities to channel the power of this beast. Then, if we are successful, we will launch a coordinated attack against Hunter on his mountain. Hunter will have no warning, no time to prepare, and no one to help him. He will be outmanned, outgunned, and alone. We shall have every advantage. And if by fate or some damnable, unforeseen circumstance, a complication does occur, we'll have a mercenary army to finish what we cannot. Either way, Hunter will be dead. And we will be free to consummate our plans and enjoy very, very long lives unaffected by the ravages of disease or time. We will be, for all practical purposes, immortal. And we will finally claim what we have long deserved and have been long denied. Or, as Nietzsche so aptly prophesized, the time will have come for a certain superior kind of man, a man that stands beyond good and evil; this man and the men around him will become Lords of the Earth – the ultimate beast of prey."

CHAPTER TWO

S plitting wood in the back of his modest cabin Hunter heard a car stop at the crest of his clearing. He straightened as he heard a door close and followed the sound of footsteps around the west end of the cabin. Within a few seconds he saw a familiar figure emerge in full view and he buried the long angle of the ax in a log.

"Chaney!" laughed Hunter. "Long time, no see!"

Chaney stretched out arms as he approached, "I thought I'd get a look at God's country in the summertime!"

"Yeah?" Hunter continued to smile. "What do you think so far?"

Chaney stopped a distance from the unstacked pile of chopped wood. "I think I saw three very intimidating packs of wolves on the way up here. Or, hell, it might have just been one gigantic pack. I don't know. That road has more curves than a Tijuana whore. But I know for a fact that I saw three *ginormous* Grizzly bears – I *do* know what a damn Grizzly looks like – and a herd of what I think were caribou."

Hunter laughed, "They're moose. But a lot of people make that mistake. And you only saw three grizzlies?" He grunted. "We got about twenty running around up here. They're probably hunting down in the valley. It's too early for fishing. The trout aren't running."

John Chaney, a former U. S. Marshal, had been Hunter's chief contact during his battle with the initial Homo Scimitar fifteen years ago. The hunt occurred in Alaska at the very edge of the Arctic Circle and had almost killed Hunter, Chaney, and the rest of their safari before Hunter finally took the beast down. But they had survived – narrowly – and for a long time Hunter thought the nightmare was finally over as Chaney ruthlessly shut down the facility where the creature had been created and arrested half a dozen scientists for delving in illegal biological warfare outlawed by literally every country on the planet.

Hunter remembered his relief upon hearing Chaney had thrown everyone involved in the sordid affair in prison because, for certain, Hunter never wanted to repeat the ordeal of hunting a similar beast born so far out of time – a creature that possessed every conceivable strength with no apparent weaknesses. But Hunter had been wrong in wishing for too much too soon because not too long ago he had been asked to again hunt another member of the same species across a decidedly haunting English moor. That, too, ended in a narrow victory with Hunter finally destroying the creature but losing his best friend in the struggle. And something told Hunter that Chaney wasn't here to talk about the good old days. Lifting his shirt from what remained of a tree, Hunter gestured, "Come inside and have some coffee."

The interior of the cabin was nowhere near as spartan as the exterior. Chaney walked to a table and turned on a lamp. "You've got electricity up here?" he asked, a bit incredulous.

Hunter smiled as he poured coffee. "This isn't the dark ages, Chaney. They ran a line across this mountain forty years ago. Course, I had to pay extra for them to lay one up to this place, and any electricity up here is pretty uncertain in the wintertime, anyway, but, for the most part, I find it convenient. I even have a computer and TV so I can keep up with all the lies they're telling us."

They took a seat at Hunter's handmade table and Chaney gazed slowly around the cabin. It was early American pioneer-style with round wooden logs and a roughhewn floor. There wasn't a nail in sight. There were front and back doors, and a large, black, wood-burning iron stove centrally positioned. One wall was stacked with crates of Meals Ready to Eat and another was stacked with five-gallon drums of kerosene. Another wall was a hefty supply of bottled water, coffee, and canned food. A gun safe stood beside the front door. It was open, and with a glance Chaney noted an impressive arsenal of guns and ammo.

Turning his head, Chaney was intrigued that one entire wall was devoted to bookshelves packed from floor to ceiling with volumes on what appeared to be every conceivable subject. Glancing over Hunter's selection, Chaney saw all the classics he was familiar with as well as books on philosophy, theology, logic, physics, biology, archeology, paleontology.

It was the library of a scholar.

"Have you read all them big 'ol books?" Chaney asked with obvious admiration. "That is one helluva private library, son."

Hunter threw an amused glance at the books, "Oh, yeah. I love to read. When I read, I can go anywhere in the world in my mind. Egypt. First Century Palestine. Prehistoric Siberia. In fact, I was planning to start the collected works of Jonathan Edwards tonight. Next to physics and paleontology, seventeenth-century Puritan history is one of my favorite subjects. Did you know that the Puritans invented football? Yeah, Chaney, they did! If not for the Puritans," Hunter laughed, "we wouldn't have a Superbowl!"

He leaned back, "Yeah. People think that the Puritans were all depressing, sour people who dressed in black and killed anything fun. But they loved sports, hunting, fishing, arts and crafts. Hell, they perfected modern farming! But so many people never look deeper than the surface. People see Puritans and decide without really studying them that they're miserable, judgmental people. Kinda like people look at me and decide I'm just a mean 'ol son of a bitch mountain man who kidnaps and barbecues people in my kitchen." He paused. "I mean, how someone looks on the outside is just chance – a twist of fate. Anyone can look like an angel. But you have to appreciate what someone is beneath the surface to know if they're a man or a monster. It takes a little bit of work, a little wisdom, and *a lot* of caution. Because there's plenty of monsters out there and you never know when you're gonna run into one."

Chaney gazed out the window; Hunter's only vehicle was an old Army surplus two-ton cargo truck with oversized tires.

"That's a big rig," Chaney commented. "That your only ride?"

Hunter took a sip. "Yeah. I don't get into town much but, when I do, I pick up all the supplies I'll need for the winter. Sometimes all I'll need for the whole year. I have MREs and emergency supplies. But I mostly hunt and grow my own food."

"So you don't get down to the city much, huh?"

"Oh, I'll go into town two or three times a year to pick up food and ammo. Water. Batteries. Kerosene. Otherwise, I tend to stay up here."

"What's the kerosene for?"

"Lamps." Hunter pointed to six kerosene lamps positioned around the room. "In the winter we might lose power for three months at a time. The stove heats the cabin, but I need kerosene for light." He shrugged. "It's boring to walk around in the dark."

Chaney pointed out the window. "That's a good truck. Made for this kind of terrain. But why don't you have a horse?"

"I've got three of them. But old man Blanchard keeps them at his place lower on the mountain where the feed is better and it's not so cold. He has good fields and a good barn. I helped him build it." A pause. "Yeah, ol' Blanchard is a nice old codger. Healthy as a horse and he's in his seventies. He'll probably outlive both of us." Hunter glanced out the window at Chaney's vehicle. "This isn't good terrain for a horse. It ain't good terrain for a Toyota, either. I don't suppose I've got lucky and you're just here to say hello?"

Chaney sniffed, as if reluctant, before he said, "I came to give you a heads-up."

With the ghost of a smile Hunter replied, "I'd expect you to have a file or something with you." He glanced at the window. "And about thirty more men."

"I don't have enough for a file, so I'll just give you what I got." Chaney leaned forward, cupping his coffee. "After that first incident in Alaska, the FBI planted moles in the mother company of the lab that created that thing. We found out later that the place, big as it was, was really just a small part of a global empire made up of a hundred pharmaceutical heavyweights, entire medical empires that controlled cities and states, industrial giants all delving in space-age technology, and world-wide chains of banking giants. The thing is an octopus. It's called Saturn Industries. And like any other big-ass industrial megalopolis, they have a controlling membership, a board of directors, sky-high, blue-chip stocks in a thousand divisions and who knows what else. But in reality – and I mean on a day-to-day basis in the real world – the whole motherlode is controlled by a single man."

"Scipio Dante," stated Hunter.

Chaney straightened. "How did you – "

"I know Dante," responded Hunter absently. "Known him a long time. In fact, he bought the manufacturing rights to some of the pharmaceuticals I discovered. I even had dinner with him the last time I was in DC."

"Did you know he was this big a shark?"

"Anybody who makes half a billion a year in profits is a player. But I didn't know he was this big."

"Are you in his league?" Chaney's eyes widened. "I mean, you got a ton of money from all those medicines you discovered."

Hunter laughed, "I'm nowhere *near* Dante's league. I've got some money, yeah, but when you're talkin' Dante, you're talkin' *real money*. The kind of money where you can do whatever you want whether it makes sense or not. You just buy it, tear it down, and build another one just like it because you can. Dante is so rich nobody even knows how much he's worth. But I'd estimate he's good for way over a trillion with all his companies and real estate combined. Still, his name isn't on any of it. He's got thousands of front companies, international banking conglomerates, computer empires – you name it – to hide his personal involvement. When you see a list of the richest people in the world, Dante's name isn't even on it. To them he's just another lame billionaire." He grunted, "I've always kind of admired that about him. It hints at humility. But I don't think Dante's humble. I think he's just secretive."

"Well, I don't think you'll admire him for this, either," Chaney stated dully. "We think Dante is ultimately the one responsible for creating that animal we had to cut down in Alaska. And the other one you had to put down in England."

"You heard about that, huh?"

Chaney waved, "Ah, hell, let me get you up to speed. The State Department – this whole thing has been placed in their purview now – made me Special Agent in Charge on all things related to this ball-bashin' fiasco."

"Wait a minute, Chaney. You're a U. S. Marshal. Do the marshals have jurisdiction for a global investigation like that?"

"I *was* with the marshal service," Chaney corrected. "Then I accepted a lateral transfer to the FBI. Truth is, a long time ago, I began in the FBI. But then the marshals saw how I had a gift for manhunting, and so the FBI loaned me out to them for a few years. And, finally, I went back to the FBI not too long after that adventure we had in Alaska, and I stayed FBI until I retired."

"That's a lot of bouncing around."

Chaney dismissed it with a wave, "Nah. It happens a lot with senior federal agents. A guy starts out in Treasury and ends up FBI. Guys in FBI end up with the marshals. It's nothing new. Our current FBI chief was once a Secret Service agent. Go figure."

Hunter laughed, "So how you liking retirement?"

Chaney sighed wearily, "I *was* enjoying it. I got myself a real nice condo down in Florida. Right on the beach. Got my pension. Plenty of pocket change. I eat out more than I eat in. I fix boats to keep busy. It's a zero-stress environment. There's nobody shooting at me or, in this case, trying to eat me. It's a good life. Then I got a call saying another one of these bastards popped up in England and that a lot of folks were getting themselves killed. Well, I left your file with the right people in the London police, but I didn't get personally involved. Maybe I have too much faith in you, but you'd already tracked down one of them. I didn't see why you'd need my help with the other one, so I left you alone."

"That don't sound much like retirement, Chaney."

He laughed, "I don't do much else, but I still keep tabs on this thing. I have special clearance with the State Department to monitor any suspicious activity. And England was more than suspicious. I knew somebody had resurrected that damned program."

"Why'd State pick you?"

"I like to think it's because I've got the most experience. But it's probably because nobody else would take the job." He shrugged, "It's just sort of an overwatch position. I'm not expected to get involved. But if I sense something suspicious, I'm supposed to let the right people know what to look for. That's why I gave the London Metro Police your file. You'd killed one. Didn't see why you couldn't kill the other one."

"Thanks a lot," muttered Hunter.

"No problem. Anyway, about a year ago, after we became suspicious about Dante's involvement in this operation, we planted an agent in his main office. Her job was to keep tabs on Dante best she could from gossip, unusual memos, any kind of suspicious activity – things like that. We wanted more solid information, but it's impossible to bug the place. Dante has the whole facility scrubbed every day. He has an entire department devoted to it. And, frankly, I didn't have high hopes for any of it because our plant wasn't too close to Dante himself. But this week she found something that got my attention."

Hunter blinked once, and slowly. "And?"

Chaney raised hands, framing it. "Last week Dante and two of his lead scientists – guys who specialize in genetic physics and all that Satanic stuff – were supposed to leave for a fishing trip in the Bahamas. Only, they didn't go to the Bahamas. They booked penthouses in all the finest hotels, chartered a yacht the size of the Queen Mary, and *somebody's* staying there because the room service bills are astronomical. But it ain't Dante and his boys. We have twenty people on it and we haven't gotten a single visual confirmation that he's there. Which makes me think he's up here. Near this mountain. And I think he's coming to take your head as a trophy."

Hunter grunted, "That's pretty thin, Chaney. You've got no evidence to think he's up here and no reason to think he would be. Besides, if he was up here, I'd know about it. We don't talk to each other much, but we do notice strangers. And why would he come after me, anyway?"

"Because you've wrecked his plans twice," stressed Chaney. "Listen, Hunter, we both suspect that they're using a serum synthesized from that prehistoric bastard's blood to transform a human being into something *very much not human* because they think this thing's DNA will make their evil ass immortal. Every insane dictator the world has ever known has had the same delusion. They all believed they were gods. Or that they were immortal. Same ol' same. But these guys actually have the means to gain a really, really long life whether they're gods or not. And who cares about being a god when you'll live for a hundred thousand damn years, anyway? But there's always been a catch to their plan, and that's the fact that this animal can't be controlled.

"Yeah, the serum might make them, for all practical purposes, immortal. But it also turns them into insane, homicidal killing machines that their conscious minds can't control. And that's where their plans always go off-track. I mean, really, you can't rightly go around killing everything in sight and live long enough to enjoy immortality, you know? Sooner or later – and usually 'sooner' – someone is going to put an army on your ass, hunt you down, and kill you graveyard dead with a couple of gunships. I mean, this thing is tough, but it's not indestructible. We proved that in Alaska. You proved it in England. So this thing's insane rage to kill everything in sight has always been their main problem. It's the fly in the ointment. A hitch in their getalong. But what if they've solved the problem? What if they've refined this serum to leave room for human consciousness to control or, at least, channel the rage of this animal? Because my contact at Saturn Industries said she'd seen orders lately for twelve tons of tungsten steel bars – the kind of bars that can contain a pissed-off gorilla."

Hunter waited. "So?"

"To build a cage, Hunter! Don't you see?"

"Don't you think you're reaching a little bit, Chaney?"

"Like hell I am!" Chaney almost rose. "I'm telling you this son of a bitch is up to something no-good and I think it's all about killing *you*!" Leaning forward, he slammed down a fist. "I think they've created another one of these things but this time they're keeping it in a cage and they're shipping it to you on a C-130 or some damn thing and they plan to give it your scent so it'll track you down like a bloodhound!" He stretched out his arms. "It's not a bad plan, Hunter! Here you are! All by your lonesome! Your guard is down! Your guns are way over there and everything is nice and peaceful. So here you are, just eatin' supper one night, watching the news, when a big damn monster comes crashing through your back door and tears you to pieces."

"Good lord, Chaney. You're getting all this from some steel bars?"

"And the fact that the beast in England had, at least, the *vestiges* of a human mind. And the fact that they've had fifteen years to perfect this serum. And the fact that you've stopped them twice now. And the fact that Dante is nowhere near the Bahamas and that he's not at his headquarters and he's not at home and none of our people have been able to locate him anywhere in the world. We've also been unable to locate the other two scientists – the ones closest to him on this project. They've disappeared, too. Just like Dante. And Dante has paid a lot of strange bills lately that we can't trace through his maze of banks and holding companies, but it's a lot of money written off to 'classified projects.' Which brings me to this: You, more than anybody else in the world, have stopped Dante from achieving his goal of immortality. And I think he believes that if one of his people transforms again, you'll just track it down and kill it like you killed the other two. So as long as you're in the picture, Dante's plans of running free with an outrageous fortune and living forever and ever, amen, are useless. But if you're taken out of equation, then there's nothing to stop him."

Hunter was unconvinced. "I'm not the only tracker in the world, Chaney. Listen, man, I can name half a dozen guys who can track this thing. It's not exactly 'supernatural.' It just *looks* like it. And then there's you. You've got experience with this thing. You know its weaknesses. And the army put together a pretty good team last time. Why can't they just put together another one? That is, if you're even close to being right about any of this." Hunter thumbed his coffee cup before he asked, "What else you got?"

Chaney rocked back. "What else I got! What else do I *need*?"

"More than *this*," muttered Hunter.

Chaney stressed, "Alright. Three days before Dante vanished, he ordered the liquidation of two trillion in assets. He converted it into cash. Now that's the kind of money that can buy a dozen countries. And if you use it right, it can buy you a world! *This world*! Think of it, Hunter! The power to live forever! Your own world and the power to do anything you want for as long as this damn world lasts. I'm telling you! It's the same damn kind of insanity that has cursed humanity since some genius invented the wheel! There's always been some bastard who wants to play God and rule the world! And he's always insane! And he's always got a private army to take what doesn't belong to him! Hell, that's what brought down Satan! He wanted what didn't belong to him! He wanted it all! But God took down Satan! And you and me are going to have to take down Dante because I think God is going to sit this one out."

Hunter studied Chaney's face before he stated, "And you're convinced Dante thinks he has to get me out of the way."

It wasn't a question.

"Yeah," Chaney nodded. "As long as you're dead and gone, Dante's a free whatever-the-hell he is." He waved angrily, "It don't matter none if you think other people can do what you've done! *They* weren't the ones that did it! *You* did it! So Dante is thinking that if he gets you out of the way, then nothing can stop him!"

With consternation Hunter studied the distant wall, as if checking supplies. "I don't know, Chaney. It still sounds thin. For one thing, I don't think this creature can be controlled enough to focus on a single target. Not with a human mind, anyway. It's too primordial." He sighed. "That's its strength, really. It doesn't know fear or hesitation or remorse. And that's because it has no conscious mind to process any of that stuff. It's just an out-of-control killing machine with the ferocity and instincts of a Sabretooth tiger. And if you compromise that, then you take away its greatest advantage."

"All that might be a *dis*advantage." Chaney didn't budge. "You know that as well as I do. You killed the one in Alaska because you lured it to the one place where it might realize what it was doing. You made it think! You made it hesitate! Just for a second! But that was enough! It gave you the edge you needed to finish it!"

"That was luck," Hunter muttered, a shrug. "I didn't know if it'd work. And I didn't have any reason to think it would."

"But it did work!" Chaney used his hands again as he leaned forward and continued, "Listen! The one in Alaska – its name was Luthor if you don't remember – "

"Oh!" Hunter interrupted. "I remember!"

"Luther was the most primitive form of this animal that we've encountered. We checked on him. He was one of Dante's original team that dug this thing up. Then, without authorization, Luther used the serum synthesized from this creature before it'd been perfected by Dante's mega-billion-dollar research complex. He used the serum in its rawest form and it turned him into an exact replica of the beast. But the second Scimitar that you encountered in England was different, wasn't it?"

Hunter was quiet before, "Yeah. It was different. It was as if he had something like … a plan. It's hard to describe, really, but he was working in cahoots with a human being on some kind of checkmate. And he seemed to be setting all the pieces in place before he made his big move." He gestured. "I never confirmed what it was. Both him and his accomplice were killed before we could get any answers.

Although I didn't have much choice in the matter. It had come down to it. Kill or be killed."

"Was his accomplice one of the daughters? I only got a partial report from a very close-mouthed dude from Scotland Yard."

"Yeah. One of the sisters was working with it. But her own sister killed her about the same time I killed the creature, so we'll never know what their plan was, although it obviously involved some kind of conscious thought from the creature. So, I guess you're right. For the past twenty years they've been synthesizing, or refining, this serum. Perfecting it. Trying to allow space for human consciousness. Although I think that's a mistake. You can have God in the form of a human tiger or you can have a man. You can't have both."

Silent for a long time, Chaney stared at nothing before he looked back. "I know this is thin. I know I don't have anything solid. But I came all the way from godforsaken Salt Lake City to tell you that I think you should take precautions. Or maybe even disappear."

"Nah," Hunter shook his head tiredly. "There ain't no hiding from these people, Chaney. If you're right, and they're coming after me, they'll find me no matter where I go. The best move is to go after them before they come after me. But since all you've got is piecemeal conjecture, and a hunch, I think I'll just wait for them to come to me. If they're coming."

"You'll be alone," said Chaney, brow hardening. "I couldn't sell the viability of this idea to anyone at State, so they wouldn't give me a team. You'll be all by yourself. And I can't even imagine what a man with Dante's resources can bring."

Hunter paused before he said quietly, "I'm never truly alone, although I might look like it." He was silent, then, "I don't control this mountain. But I've got an understanding with what lives here – the wolves, the bears, the eagles, the buzzards, or hawks. We help each other. We watch out for each other. And they have their own ways of telling me when something's not right. So, really, I'll stand as good a chance here as anywhere else. And if I'm forced to retreat, I know every rock and cranny, every ravine and foot trail."

Hunter laughed, "You'd be surprised, Chaney. I knew somebody was coming up the road hours before you got here. Probably about the same time you stopped to ask for directions at the store. Because those wolves consider me part of the pack." He glanced toward the open front door. "You're right. You didn't see three packs. It was the same pack. They were ghosting you. They do it to everybody. They wanted to know where you're going. What you're doing. And they warn each other if they see somebody that doesn't belong up here. Then, about two hours ago, one of the wolves came up to me and just stared, and I knew somebody was coming up the road. I didn't know it was you but I knew it was 'somebody.' And the bears are regular guests around here. Half the time they sleep on my porch. And that's not even mentioning everybody on the reservation that keep track of every mosquito. They know every car that's supposed to be on the reservation, and that Toyota ain't one of 'em. By now the whole res is looking for you." He paused, pensive. "In the woods, the birds tell you when something's close. Up here, if you're part of the mountain, the mountain tells you."

Chaney seemed to accept Hunter's resolve with reluctance. He leaned back in the chair, arms stretched over the table, and sighed, "I figured you'd be like this." He paused. "Well, if you can't beat 'em, join 'em. Come on. Let me show you something."

Hunter followed Chaney to a remarkably well-packed Four Runner full of crates and what appeared to be never-used camping gear. Even with a casual glance Hunter saw that a few of the crates were marked "U. S. Army." Without hesitation Chaney opened the hatch and stretched out a hand as if in formal introduction.

"I bring you the most dangerous weapons in the United States Army's rather extensive arsenal of most dangerous weapons," he stated with a hint of ceremony. Pulling out a small crate, Chaney used a crowbar to open it and lifted a loop of white line. "This is detonation cord. Loop this around any number of trees and hit the detonator, or shoot it, and there won't be a tree on this mountain still standing."

Hunter muttered, "I kinda like my trees."

Chaney lifted an apple-sized device from another crate, which was stacked to the top with similar devices, and held it before Hunter's suspicious gaze. "It is my honor to present to you the M-67 fragmentation grenade. It is the current anti-personnel grenade issued to American infantry. It combines a lethal amount of over-pressurization and fragmentation with a kill radius of twenty feet. Nothing inside that range should survive – not even a prehistoric abomination of a Sabretooth tiger."

With a strange, and somewhat childish, delight Chaney grunted as he hauled out a longer crate and opened it with great splendor before Hunter.

Standing back, Chaney nodded, "The new and improved Barrett .338 caliber M-107A1 bolt-action assault rifle with a nine by twelve night-vision scope. It fires a .338 Lapau with a stainless-steel target barrel that gives it a ten-inch drop at 1,200 yards." He abruptly looked at Hunter. "We got plenty of ammo."

Hunter lifted a hand, "Don't you think this is a little overkill, Chaney?"

"Hell, no!" Chaney angrily responded. "We don't know what that bastard Dante might bring to us!"

"*If he's coming at all.*"

"Just in case! You were a Boy Scout, weren't you?"

"I was *never* a Boy Scout."

"Be prepared! It's the Boy Scout marching song! *I* was a Boy Scout!" As if he'd been holding it for a big finale, Chaney pulled out a series of plastic crates that he laid on the ground. He knelt and opened one and gestured grandly as he raised his face. "There you go! What do you think?"

"Laser beams?" asked Hunter.

"Motion detectors!" Chaney stood, staring down with a nod. "Yes, sir! Place any one of these babies within a hundred yards of this cabin and we'll know instantly if something is moving out there!"

It took Hunter a moment before he lifted a hand to the tree line. "Chaney! This is a wilderness area! There's wolves and bears and cougars and everything else out there! Something's *always* moving! Wolves pass through here every night! Grizzlies sleep on my porch! Those things are going to be going off every five minutes!"

"I'll set the range for stuff that's only five feet off the ground," Chaney countered. "That'll leave out the wildlife. And these things have cameras so we can check to see if it's friend or foe. We got it covered."

Hunter glanced at the descending sun and rubbed the back of his neck. "It's not gonna leave out the Grizzlies. They stand five feet or more at the shoulder. But I appreciate your efforts, Chaney, and concerns. I really do. Come on; I'll help you set 'em up."

CHAPTER THREE

With a deafening roar the beast launched itself against the tungsten steel bars grasping a rod in each clawed hand. It hauled back with the incomprehensible strength of an enraged dinosaur. It violently shook its fanged head bellowing in rage that it could not destroy what had taken Dante's team a month of welding to prepare. Then, finally, it released its death-grip on the bars and slowly stepped back, glaring with red eyes at Dante and Cronis, who stood side by side, watching the shocking display of unbelievable strength.

Cronis commented, "Your new serum, which is supposedly synthesized to calm the creature down, doesn't seem to be working, doctor."

Dante revealed no concern. "It takes time, Cronis. That is why I insisted we come here for the initial transformation. What we could accomplish in a lab setting might be entirely undone by this environment because everything plays a part – the temperature, the elevation, the barometric pressure, the sights, scents and sounds. Right now, the serum is integrating with the animal's neural network to negotiate a controlling measure of Doctor Pinion's consciousness." He shrugged, "Of course, the animal side will initially seize command. I expected as much. But if my calculations are correct – and they always are – Dr. Pinion's human consciousness should assume a significant measure of control within a few days.

And, until then, he will continue like this. Well-fed and safely contained."

Cronis walked to a narrow window and gazed into the modest parking lot. They were in the lowest level of the abandoned hospital – a place which vaguely resembled a World War II bomb shelter – but still allowed a view of the exterior through narrow windows. He commented, "All the trucks are disguised as construction vehicles. Your mercenaries are dressed as plumbers and carpenters. You've got truckloads of pipes and wood. You've gone to a lot of trouble to make this look like a construction site, Dante."

Dante laughed, "Military vehicles invite questions from local lawmen, Cronis. But construction vehicles are self-explanatory to the sheriff and the population. They'll simply think someone has bought this old place and is renovating it for re-opening. And these people will be happy to have another hospital in the area, anyway. I doubt they'll even ask questions. But, just in case, I've established a very visible headquarters in town so the sheriff can get all the answers he wants and not make any troublesome visits."

With a shocking blast of animal might the creature abruptly threw itself against the cage door with earth-shaking force that made the cement floor tremble. It rebounded off the impact to instantly launch itself again into the door, roaring as a single herculean arm lashed out between the bars, black claws closing on empty air.

Cronis had reflexively leaped back from the attack before he even realized he had moved. He felt a lightness in his chest and his heart was racing. His throat was suddenly tight, and it took him a moment to breath before he asked, "Are you *sure* that cage can hold him? Of all the people in the world, Pinion is the last person I'd expect to transform into something like this. That thing can tear the head off a rhinoceros."

"Exactly," muttered Dante. "Everything is at it should be at this phase. The serums are prepared and within some few days we will be perfectly prepared to move."

With a steady gaze Cronis studied the crates of weapons heaped in the underground corridor. Then he studied the makeshift laboratory. It had taken extensive and exacting work to set up a lab perfectly mirroring their work environment at Saturn Industries, but the mercenaries had succeeded with remarkable precision. Still, Cronis suspected a number of Dante's medical technicians also had a hand in the assembly. Some of the machines required an expert touch. He ventured, "Let me ask you a question, Dante."

"Of course."

"If these mercenaries are as capable as you say, then why not let them finish Hunter off all by themselves? There's certainly enough of them. And they've got enough guns. Why utilize the transformations at all? Because it seems to me like we're taking an unnecessary risk. And you've always wanted a zero-risk possibility with experiments. That's why we repeatedly test each integer of a process before we initiate the test."

Dante responded as if he were addressing a league of graduating doctors. "In this case the potential dividends of killing Hunter ourselves outweigh the risks. And I might remind you, doctor, we all have our reasons for why we're doing this. Mine are both personal and professional. As for yourself, I don't know why you have joined me, nor are your reasons important. My single priority is that Hunter is, at last, removed from this equation and the way is made clear for me to consummate my plans. But if you wish to know something of a more specific nature, I simply don't trust anyone else to do the job properly. Not even this team of cutthroats. I want to feel Hunter's blood on my hands, and look down on his body, and know he is dead. He has interfered quite enough in my affairs. He has set my work back decades with his ability to destroy what he cannot begin to understand. He has caused me no lack of frustration."

"We've already mastered the process of transformation, Dante. Luther succeeded beyond all expectations."

Dante spat, "Bah! In his ignorance and impatience Luther only succeeded in making himself a target for the army! He had no plan! He only coveted the physical properties of this creature and the prospect of a long life! Luther's attempt was doomed to fail before he began! I never imagined that someone like Hunter would be the cause of his demise, but I'm not surprised. Because of his lack of foresight, Luther was dead the moment he took the serum."

"What about Vang? Didn't you and Vang work together to synthesize a more workable integration?"

Taking longer to respond, Dante finally said, "Vang also rushed the process before it was perfected. Although we knew what properties had to be altered, the serum was not fully tested. And as you so very well know, doctor, the whole point of science is that you must repeat the same tests with the same results before you can call your experiment a success." He gloomily shook his head. "If Vang had only waited a little longer. But he was impatient, as well."

At the furthest end of the corridor a mercenary disguised as a construction worker opened two steel doors allowing light to flood the darkness. He returned to a van and lifted the back haunch of a bull, dragged it to the edge, and hooked it. Another worker hooked the rear of the huge slab, and they began forward.

"So we just feed him for a few days and wait for him to calm down?" asked Cronis. "Is that the plan?"

"Yes." Dante watched the slow, labored approach. Then he briefly cast a look at the beast before adding, "Of course, I don't envy these men the task. But they are being well compensated. And they were advised beforehand of the potential risks. Of course, now that they are on site, they are not free to leave. No one is free to leave. We must all see it through. The good colonel and his trigger-happy pirates will eliminate anyone who attempts to defect."

"I don't think any classroom orientation could prepare anyone for something like *this*," Cronis said with a hint of horror. "Hearing is one thing. Seeing is one thing. *Believing* is another. And that animal will make you a believer real quick."

The mercenaries arrived and the creature was standing against the far wall watching them with its head slightly lowered. Cronis couldn't determine, from beneath the heavy shadow of its prominent brow, how closely it might have been studying them. The men took a single step toward the cage, swung the carcass back, and then stretched out their arms to throw it against the bars.

The creature exploded from the wall in a movement too fast for Cronis to follow and its arm lashed out between the bars at the same split-second that its clawed hand closed on the forearm of a mercenary. The man's scream was heart-stopping as the beast hauled him into the cage and twisted, tearing his arm away from his body. It was something done in a single second – the attack, the capture, and the kill. It was done as quickly as a man might wave a fly from his face. And just as cold.

With a growl the creature's fangs sank into the arm as the mercenary staggered back. Blood was spiraling wildly and violently from the gaping wound at his shoulder and his mouth moved but no words emerged. He fell onto his back, grasping at the emptiness alongside his chest and, after a moment, he was still.

The second mercenary rose from his side and looked directly at the creature as it feasted hungrily on the arm. Then he unsnapped his holster and placed a hand on his pistol as Dante sternly shouted, "Put your gun away! You are under orders not to harm the creature. Your friend is dead because he was careless. I told you how dangerous this animal can be. Now return to your duties and tell Colonel Blakely to come down here. *Now!*"

With a last, despising glance at the creature, the mercenary slowly turned and walked away. In a few minutes Blakely appeared at the distant opening of the corridor and came stoically forward. He studied the dead mercenary with indifference, then glanced at the creature before removing a radio from his belt.

"Raven to Three-one," he said.

"*Three-one*," was the reply.

"We have a man down in the basement. I want disposal procedures initiated ASAP." Lowering the radio, Blakely focused on Dante. "Do you want me to replace him, doctor? All it takes is a phone call."

"No," the professor shook his head and gracefully stepped back to avoid the widening pool of blood on the cracked cement floor. Then, squinting, he focused on the creature whose rage had clearly not abated. The beast was glaring at them with malevolent red eyes as it impatiently paced behind the copper-toned bars, consuming the arm.

"No, colonel," repeated Dante. "I am becoming more confident by the hour that your mercenaries might not be needed, after all."

* * *

"Don't be wandering off, Chaney."

Hunter had called loud enough, but Chaney didn't respond. Turning, Hunter saw him sixty yards away mounting the last camera five feet from the ground. Hunter had wrongly believed Chaney was closer and was alarmed. He walked purposefully along the ridge and in moments was beside the FBI agent as he removed the laser beam cap.

The machine instantly connected to the reflector.

Chaney cast a quick glance. "Did you say something?"

"Yeah," Hunter said as he collected the last of the boxes and dropped them in a canvas bag. "I told you not to be wandering off."

"What? Because of the animals?"

Hunter nodded.

"I thought you said you know these animals." Chaney didn't remove his stare from Hunter's face. "You said the wolves come up here to warn you." He paused. "You said they sleep on your porch! You said they're friendly!"

"They're friendly to *me*," Hunter clarified. "But they know me. They trust me. They see me every day and they're not afraid of me. But they don't know you, and that's not likely to end well. You might scare 'em, and that's the last thing you want to do with a Grizzly. It'll react the only way it knows how and then you'll be a *dead* ex-FBI agent."

"We do have rifles, Hunter."

Hunter laughed loudly. "Damn, Chaney, you city boys never cease to amaze me. I don't care what kind of rifle you've got! Have you ever tried to shoot a Grizzly that's charging straight down on you?" He shook his head, "Good luck with that."

"What about climbing a tree?"

Grimacing, Hunter shook his head. "I get asked that all the time. For some damn reason, everybody from the city thinks that climbing a tree will save them from a bear. Think about it, Chaney. A bear climbs trees for a living, and it can climb a tree a hell of a lot better than you can. Although it'd probably just knock you out of it."

"What about playing dead?"

"Nah," countered Hunter, "it'd just maul you to death. Tear your scalp off. You'd bleed out in ten minutes." He dropped the last shred of paper into the bag. "A Grizzly has four-inch claws. It's got fangs the size of a Siberian tiger. It's ten feet tall and can weigh as much as a ton. And it's all muscle. Around here, the Grizzly stands at the top of the food chain." A pause. "Some say that man stands at the top of the food chain. But they're never met a pissed-off Grizzly."

As if he were enjoying this wildlife education, Chaney asked, "What about a tiger? Would a tiger stand a chance against a Grizzly?"

"I doubt it," answered Hunter. "A Bengal tiger is about the same weight and length as a Grizzly. And it's got the same arsenal – fangs and claws – but people have tried pitting Grizzlies against tigers before, and the Grizzlies always won."

"Who the hell did that?"

"The Romans. Back when the coliseum was a big thing." Hunter sighed as if he could envision it. "Yeah, the Romans used to throw a pissed-off Grizzly in with a tiger just to see which would survive. The fights were over in seconds. The tiger would leap into the Grizzly and the Grizzly would just grab it with a foreleg and bring its other paw down on top of the tiger's head. The bear would crush the tiger's skull like an egg. Dead in one second. The fights were over so fast, the Romans quit staging them. No sport." Hunter lifted the sack, glanced at the sun. "Come on. It'll be dark soon. We need to get inside."

As they casually meandered down the short slope to the clearing containing Hunter's cabin, Chaney asked, "Just how high are we? The air seems different."

"We're at about ten thousand feet. The air's thinner. But it doesn't get dangerously thin until you hit twenty thousand. That's where you're not taking in enough oxygen to keep your brain alive, so you're basically dying with every breath. Climbers call it 'the death zone.' In fact, I know a guy who climbed Everest without oxygen, and he told me that at twenty thousand feet it was like he could literally hear his brain cells exploding from a lack of oxygen. Or you might get pleural edema. And that's just as bad."

"What's that?"

"It's a buildup of fluid in the lungs. You drown in your own body fluids." He cocked his head. "Yeah, I've had to watch out for it a few times because edema can come on you real quick and kill you even quicker." He pointed toward the summits of higher, surrounding mountains. "If you're up there at the snow line, you can be climbing and feeling great one minute, and then one minute later you can be lying in the snow and can't breathe. That's how fast it hits. No warning. One second you're feeling fine, and in the next second, you're dying. And if you don't reach a lower altitude in a few hours, you won't make it. And then there's cerebral edema. Swelling of the brain. Too much fluid. But if you get cerebral edema, you'll be dead in minutes and there's not much anybody can do for you. They can try and fly you out, but you probably won't make it. That's the way it is with a lot of injuries this high. Even the smallest cut at this altitude can be life-threatening if you don't take care of it. And it comes on you fast. Usually there's no time to get you down to a lower elevation."

"Yeah," Chaney said as they reached what might be described as Hunter's 'back yard.' "I noticed your first-class medical kit. Looks like the same bag EMTs carry."

"It is. I have a working relationship with the sheriff and hospital. Unofficially, I'm a deputy and an EMT. And since they use me to find people who get lost up here, they provide me with an EMT bag. It's got almost everything an ambulance has. Except I don't have a damn ambulance. I have to carry the thing on my back. And it weighs sixty pounds." Hunter threw Chaney a glance. "You don't wanna be hauling sixty pounds of medical gear across those peaks, dude. That gets old real fast."

"I'll bet," grunted Chaney. "How does the sheriff communicate with you?"

"I've got a HAM radio," Hunter shrugged. "It's under those blankets in the corner. And it's pretty reliable most of the time. That's how they reach me. How I reach them.

Otherwise, I don't really talk to many people. I'll see the occasional backpacker when I'm out, but not a lot of people hike this high. I guess you could say I talk to animals more than I talk to people. But that's all right. Animals are more civilized."

The cabin was warm, and they unloaded the gear. Chaney sat at the table where he'd assembled fifteen small remote video screens. Slowly, one by one, he turned them on and found each of them functioning perfectly. Seeming more relaxed, he pointed, "As the light fades, the cameras will automatically switch to night vision. I'll have to change the batteries every morning, but I figured this might be a long-term exercise, so I brought enough batteries to last us a few weeks."

Hunter smiled, "You knew I wouldn't leave?"

"I knew you wouldn't run. You ain't got it in you."

Hunter sat a hot cup of coffee on the table and laughed, "Good thing I stocked up on coffee and MREs. It's a chore going down into town."

"You sure we got every approach wired?" asked Chaney.

Hunter blinked slowly before he asked, "Just how certain are you about this hunch, Chaney? I've never seen you this nervous."

"Surviving is a habit close to my heart." He adjusted the brightness on the laptop he was using to control the trail monitors. "This system really isn't any different from the monitors the Wildlife Service uses. Same technology. But these are built on servos so they can rotate 180 degrees, and these monitors have automatic alarms. If anything walks across the laser, then the monitor starts flashing. So if we've wired every likely approach, it'll be real hard for anything to sneak up on us."

"Again," Hunter asked patiently, "how confident are you about this hunch?"

Chaney leaned back. "Confident enough to leave the heavenly peace and quiet of my beachfront home." He was studious. "You see, I don't think you're the only one Dante holds responsible for his failures. I think there's enough blame there to spread around. So, after he checks you off his list, there's every chance he'll come after *me*. And if *you* didn't have a chance, then I'm as good as dead. I won't last a single day with that thing on my ass. And it can get me in Florida as fast as it can get you up here." He gestured, "I'm banking those rifles might take some steam out of its stride. But I ain't gonna bet the farm."

Hunter bent and lifted one of the Barretts from the box. He checked the bolt action, the safety, the optics before he asked, "You do remember that Luthor was practically bulletproof? I mean, Bobby Jo hit him at a hundred yards with a fifty and all it did was knock him down. He was up and gone before she could get off a second shot."

"Yeah. I remember. That's why I brought steel-tipped explosive rounds."

Hunter stared. "How explosive?"

"Explosive enough to vaporize a man's chest. It's like getting hit by a small hand grenade traveling three thousand feet a second."

"Where the hell did you get those?"

"At Redstone Arsenal down in Alabama. It's an army proving ground. A lot of weapons testing goes on down there. Yeah, the rounds are still in the experimental stage, but the rangemaster told me they'd functioned perfectly so far. He gave me ten boxes and charged them to the FBI. Good thing, too. I sure couldn't afford them."

"Who charged them to the FBI?"

"General George Forge. The base commander."

"I didn't think anybody was backing you."

"I said 'the State Department' wasn't backing me." Chaney clarified. "But Forge was the guy who put together our old team in Alaska. Remember those guys? The team that got vaporized by Luther after he'd liquidated everybody at two separate military installations? Well, ol' Forge had some real good friends on that team. He'd even trained some of them and knew they wouldn't have made a mistake, so he's aware of what we're up against. Anyway, when I told him about the fix I'm in, he invited me down to Alabama and said he'd have the rangemaster fix me up with the most lethal stuff they had in their armory."

Hunter's eyes widened. "You drove all the way here from Alabama?"

"Nah. I had the army ship all the ordinance to Salt Lake City. I picked it up at the FBI headquarters, along with the monitors. Yeah, I been putting this operation together since our mole started noticing a super-abundance of 'classified' projects with Dante's prints all over them." Chaney fixed Hunter with a stare. "I can always tell when Ol' Dante is personally involved."

"How's that?"

"Because he lists practically everything as classified. Even the computer chips. Even the vehicles. And everything he classifies is always ten times more expensive than it should be, which means he's paying some people for developing amnesia. They can't remember what was in the warehouse or what's missing. In fact, not long ago, I arranged for a federal search warrant of Saturn's main warehouse under the cover of a health inspection and found that everything Dante would need to build a mobile command station seemed to have been shipped out. And without any recorded manifests, either. Without any witnesses. Without any paperwork. And the destinations were classified under national security protocols."

Hunter slowly tapped the table, as if considering, before he remarked, "Must be nice to have friends in high places."

"That bastard has *always* had friends in high places," Chaney stated angrily. "I don't know who gave Dante permission to drill in the Arctic Circle, but it had to be someone inside the Department of Interior. You don't just go building weather platforms inside the Arctic Circle without permission. You can start a war with the Russians over crap like that. But I can't find out who's in cahoots with him. I can't even find out who gave Dante permission to keep the body of that predator at his private facility. Something like that should have been turned over to the army or the Smithsonian. The Department of the Interior should have shut down the operation, not facilitated it. But somebody who outranks military oversight okayed it. And I bet they're not doing it for free. I bet Dante is promising them the same thing that he wants for himself. A real long life and all the money in the world."

Hunter observed, "Immortality can buy you a lot of friends."

"So can Fort Knox," Chaney frowned. "And Dante can promise both." He paused from tweaking the computer screens and fixed Hunter with an unblinking stare. "Just what the hell do you think Dante wants immortality for, anyway?"

Hunter shrugged, "To rule the world, Chaney. You said it yourself. It's been the dream of every madman since they invented the wheel. Just to name a few, I can think of Alexander the Great, Genghis Khan, Stalin, Hitler, Mao, and nowadays there's dozens of multi-billionaires who gather at secret places and want to control what the rest of the world says or does or thinks or where they live, where they go, who they can see, how many babies they can have, or what they can eat. They're from every nation and every walk of life but they all share the same insane obsession." He sighed. "They want to control what doesn't belong to them because they fear death."

Chaney didn't blink. "Because they fear death? How's that?"

"God said a man is fated to die once," Hunter stated as if he'd thought it through a long time ago. "And that works for every man and woman. We're born, we die, for dust we are and to dust we shall return. And then there's judgment

Day, where we're judged on everything we've ever done or said, and it's all weighed against us in the last court we'll ever face. At that point, God himself decides whether we die a second time or whether we're allowed to go on to a world beyond this. And that's what they fear. They fear that judgment because they know their deeds are evil, so they're always devising ways to escape it. Basically, they know that when the book is laid open and all they've ever done is revealed, they'll fail with flying colors and bust Hell wide open when they land."

Chaney seemed amazed. "Do you think Ghost is in Heaven? He was, without any doubt, the greatest wolf God ever created."

Hunter smiled sadly, "Yeah. I think Ghost is with God. And, sometimes, I think he's still here with me. Sometimes I think I catch a glimpse of him in the trees. Like he's with me. Still watching over me." He almost laughed. "I believe a lot of things, Chaney. And I believe that one day I'll see Ghost and the Lord at the same time. And I'll be glad when that day comes."

Slowly, Chaney nodded, but then he asked abruptly, "But do you really think that any of these heathens we're chasing actually believes in God? I mean, get serious, Hunter. We are talking about 'below sub-human' refuse that came out of a dinosaur's ass."

"Yeah," stated Hunter. "I do think they believe in God. And that's why they fear death, Chaney." He sat back. "You're right. They don't respect God or his laws. His ways. But they do believe that God exists, and they're scared to death of meeting him. They all know that when all the things they've done – the good and bad – are placed on a scale, they're going to come up short, and then they'll be sentenced to a room without doors. And they won't be measuring their imprisonment with hours or days, but with millennium on top of millennium until time ceases to exist."

There was a long moment before Chaney said slowly, "I didn't know you believed in such things, Hunter."

Hunter shrugged, "Hell, Chaney, you think someone could live like I do, surrounded by the mysteries and miracles of nature, and not believe in God? If I didn't know an ounce of what some call 'formal theology,' there's still 'natural theology.'" He raised an arm toward the ceiling of the cabin, to the window. "The stars in the sky reflect the vastness of God. That's why God put them there. To give man a glimpse of his power. His majesty. Even the most ignorant savage in the most primitive place on the planet can see the power of God at work in creation. You don't have to have an education. You don't have to know how to read or write. Even if you can't see, you can feel the wind. Just like a man can feel his spirit. You don't know where the wind comes from or where it's going, but you can feel it and know it. Why do you think I live up here? It eliminates the meaningless distractions of life. I have more time to think about things that matter. Like how I live, what I do, and where I'm going to spend eternity."

"So why aren't you a monk?"

"Nah, man. I don't believe God ever meant for us to live in temples. God created man to both serve him and to be of service to others. To do what God would do if he were still walking around down here in the flesh. Yeah, God made us to be social creatures, and so I'm social. I'm not as social as *some* people – like you, for instance – but I'm not a monk. I stay social with a half-dozen wildlife societies and I find people who are lost up here almost every month. Why do you think I've got a HAM radio? To talk to God? Ha! I talk to God all the time without a HAM radio. I just use that thing to find out what they might need me for down below." He gazed over the room. "Granted, this life ain't for everybody – no doubt about that – but I like the peace and quiet. And when the snow falls it's like – "

A monitor began beeping and flashing and Chaney instantly sat up to see a colossal black image. Nothing else was visible; the black silhouette filled the screen.

Unconcerned, Hunter asked, "Is that up on the ridge?"

"Yeah! The last one we planted!"

"That'll be Moe," said Hunter without concern. "He's a Grizzly. I've raised him since he was a cub, and he loves to sleep on the porch. When it's snowing, I let him sleep in the house." He nodded to the stove. "He'll get over there by the fire and sprawl out and make more noise than a busted chainsaw."

Chaney looked back to the screen. "Are you sure it's just a bear? That creature in Alaska was pretty big, too."

"Nah," said Hunter, reaching for his cup, "it's not a Scimitar. I would have known hours ago. And so would you."

"How would you know?"

"The wolves would have told us. They'd be howling. Warning each other. And they're quiet as a church mouse, so it's Moe."

Chaney turned his face at a huge thump that lumbered slowly down the long porch. At the door there was a muffled shuffling and a huge groan following by the smothering collapse of what sounded like a furry freight train falling on its side.

"Well," Chaney looked at Hunter, "we can say the front door is secure."

"Yeah. Moe doesn't sense any danger."

"How do you know?"

"Because a bear has the best nose in the animal kingdom, Chaney. A bear can smell a single drop of blood at five miles. No other animal comes close. And he doesn't smell anything unusual, or he'd be reacting to it."

"How about a bloodhound? It's got a pretty good nose."

"A bloodhound has a good nose, yeah, but a bear's nose is ten times better. If there was anything within five miles of this place, Moe would be pacing up and down the porch, sniffing the air every ten seconds, huffing and grunting, working himself up for a fight. He does that when he senses something unfamiliar. And he'd be *seriously* agitated if he sensed that it might be another apex predator. If he detects that, he'll take a stand in front of the cabin and get himself ready for a fight to the death. But he'd still stay close." Hunter was staring at the locked front door. "Moe doesn't go looking for trouble. But he doesn't run from it. He just takes a stand and lets it come to him and then, well, it's the law of the jungle. The strongest survive."

Stretching his arms across the table and leaning back, Chaney observed, "I can see why you like it up here." He paused. "You sure ain't alone. In fact, I think you have more friends than I do. And I live in the city. I'm surrounded by people! But I'm surrounded by people who don't know me and I don't know them. We might as well be by ourselves. And, for sure, none of them would sleep on my porch to make sure I'm safe. They'd rob me first."

Moe's cavernous snoring could be heard through the door.

"Yeah," laughed Hunter. "I think we're safe."

CHAPTER FOUR

Seated in a cushioned chair, Dr. Jack Cronis found it fascinating to watch the creature as it stalked to and fro within the spacious cage. It was clear that the hoped-for arrest of its obsessively murderous mind was not yet complete because with every narrow scarlet glare the beast threw at Cronis, he could literally feel its murderous desires. The hair on Cronis's arms would stand up and his skin would crawl as if from a freezing blast of wind. Cronis had no doubt that the creature would tear him to pieces if it got the slightest chance, and he began to wonder at the wisdom of this experiment.

"It is still too early for any significant change," said a voice behind him.

Cronis turned to see Dante walking forward with Colonel Blakely. Dante's posture was relaxed with both hands comfortably gloved in the pockets of his lab coat. Blakely was carrying a long black rifle that Cronis couldn't identify.

Dante stopped beside the chair, gazing only at the creature as he added, "Are you beginning to have doubts about our experiment, my friend? Do not be unduly concerned. I estimate another day, or perhaps a bit longer, before there's any significant change. In this, the process resembles that of a patient awakening from a decades-long coma. The brain has to reconstitute neglected neural networks.”

Cronis asked dully, “How will we know if it’s working?”

“It will cease pacing,” answered the older scientist. “Pacing indicates agitation. But when Dr. Pinion’s human mind begins to assert itself with more domination, it will become more still. That will signal the beginning of integration. And in another day the transformation should be complete. But the serum only has a temporary effect. It will wear off within the hour, so Dr. Pinion needs a booster. Then the integration will be uninterrupted.”

Cronis rose as Blakely stepped forward, shouldering what Cronis now recognized as a tranquilizer rifle like those used by wildlife officers. Blakely drew down and fired a dart into the creature that roared and instantly ripped the projectile from its neck, hurling it to the side. It took a single step but didn’t launch another futile attack against the inescapable cage. It was as if the beast had somehow accepted the fact that it could not break free from this prison with brute force which was, itself, a sign that it might be learning to reason.

“How do you know whether it received the full dose?” asked Cronis with some dread. “He ripped that dart out awfully fast.”

“The dart administered the full dose upon impact,” answered Dante. “It doesn’t require any time. And that dose should be enough to carry him beyond the required hours to finish the initial stage of integration.”

“And then?”

“And then, my dear Cronis, Dr. Pinion will revert once again to his human condition, and we will eventually test him to see if the initiation of immortality has taken hold.”

Cronis’s eyes narrowed. “And how will you do that?”

Dante shrugged, “We must wait for a few more transformations, of course, but certain faculties should eventually take hold in Doctor Pinion’s human form. Still, the only way to be certain is to slice his heart in half and observe the healing process. If he heals instantaneously, then the process is beginning. If he dies, then we will know we have failed, and that this entire operation has been for nothing. Far worse, we will know that our larger plans to establish a global hierarchy of immortals requires more time and work."

"And you plan to do the same with me?" Cronis asked, eyes widening. "Cut my heart in half and see if I heal up or die?"

"As you agreed," Dante answered with an uncaring glance. "Although, I admit, you did not know the finite details of my plan. But you agreed in principle, and that is enough. And I should remind you once more that the time for deserting the program no longer exists. At this stage there can be no withdrawal. But consider what you shall grasp, Cronis! I shall give you your own kingdom to rule as you please! I will give you an entire nation that will be yours, and yours alone, for as long as this earth lasts! And is that not reward enough for a single moment of anguish?" He shrugged, "But, of course, you will have to accept the rules of immortality."

"Rules?" Cronis asked.

"Yes. A rarely considered truth is that immortality is a curse if anyone is aware that you are ultimately just human. The very power of immortality rests upon keeping the secret of immortality exactly that – a secret. The minions must see us as gods or there will be uncontrollable uprisings which can only be suppressed by the most severe use of force. So if the peasants realize we are only human, the peasants will revolt."

"And why is that, Dante?"

The professor briefly tilted his head as he stated, "It is the same with every revolution, Cronis. Name any war; the French Revolution, the War of the Bolsheviks, the Romanian Civil War, and it's always the same. The insipid have-nots rise against those who have. They tear down the walls of their superiors, their kings, their princes and betters and take their heads. They burn city and crop until they grasp what they have not earned and do not deserve because they are ultimately only cattle and should remain in their place. They are worker bees whose job it is to keep the hive. And they are ultimately expendable because they are so easily replaced. But you and I shall belong to a different reality – a reality where we alone have the power of eternal life. A life where we will never see death. A life where God does not exist. But if the world knows our secret, then they will no longer look upon us as Gods. They will look upon us as men, and men can be destroyed. Then we will no longer have the power to decide men's lives. We'll no longer be able to make the nations tremble. We'll no longer be able to choose who lives and who dies. What nations may rise and what nations must fall. We shall no longer rule all that we behold, which will be all the earth."

Cronis was staring warily at the older man as he cautiously asked, "If your vision is so grand, doctor, then why share it with Doctor Pinion and myself?"

"Because, Cronis, I am wise enough to know the plague of living a very, very long life. And I am ensuring I will not be plagued with it."

"What plague?" asked Cronis.

Dante sighed and fixed him with a flat stare.

"Loneliness," he said simply. "I will not be the only immortal on the earth, doctor. There will, of course, be yourself and Doctor Pinion. But, in time, and through a very careful selection process, we shall recruit others that we will allow to join us. And we shall make them immortal one by one until we become a race of immortals ruling this world in an eternal hierarchy of indisputable and perfect power." He nodded steadily, "Yes. We shall never be alone. We shall never see death. We shall never be judged. We will be Lords of the Earth. And even some nostalgic thought of the Hebrew God will be known as the discarded, obsolete idea of a once ignorant world that God and his bastard son failed to save."

* * *

"Holy Crap," said FBI Special Agent Vernon Sanders as he watched, through the glass walls, as four men in business suits shouted at Special Agent in Charge Mack Johnson.

It was strange that anyone would berate the most powerful FBI agent in the state of Utah. It was ever stranger that they would do it to Mack in his own office. To his face. And with a lot of attitude. Another Special Agent, Jeffrey Gantry, walked up and muttered, "What the hell is going on in Mack's office?"

"I don't know," Vernon answered dully. He didn't remove his gaze from the spiraling confrontation. "You think it was something we did?"

Gantry grunted, "We don't *do* anything, Vernon. This is Salt Lake City. This is the most do-nothing FBI office in the bureau."

Finally, one of the intruders – because of the rank hostility, Vernon considered them 'intruders' instead of 'guests' – leaned over Mack's desk pointing violently in his face and said something that couldn't be heard through the plexiglass partition. Then the four men turned and marched out. After a very long moment Mack simply rose and stood in his office door calmly surveying the thirty-seven agents assigned to his domain. Everyone was pretending to be hard at work. Then he purposefully walked to Vernon and Gantry.

"We didn't do it," said Gantry.

"We weren't even there," volunteered Vernon.

"Relax," Mack muttered as he sat on a corner of the desk. "What do you two rookies know about a heap of military grade weapons shipped to this office from Redstone Arsenal?"

Vernon and Gantry exchanged cautious glances. Then Vernon said, "Do you know John Chaney, boss? 'Cause he's the agent that picked up all the hardware in this big four-wheeler and he mentioned your name when he was here."

"Yeah," Mack nodded, "I know Chaney. We went through the academy together. We were partners in the Houston field office. We busted cartels for three years before they transferred him to the Chicago marshal service and booked me to LA. We kept in touch for a few years. Then he went his way, I went mine. Why?"

"Cause Chaney talked like he knew you," said Vernon. "In fact, he talked like he trusted you. Said you guys put away some real maniacs back in the day. And if you don't mind me asking, boss, just who the hell were those guys that just walked out? Those guys were real assholes if you ask me. They didn't have no right to talk to you like that."

Mack chuckled, "They were NSA, son. Or so they said. They had the credentials. But I don't know. Nothing about this chaos is what it seems."

"Are they looking for Chaney?" followed Gantry.

"Yeah. Real hard. So tell me about this ordinance."

Vernon gestured to Gantry, "Well, we were told by dispatch to report to the warehouse because they received this suspicious shipment of military grade ordinance. But it came with all the proper paperwork, and it was addressed to FBI Special Agent John Chaney. But since Chaney wasn't around, we just locked it up. Then, a few days later, Chaney shows up with the paperwork to claim it. He had all the sheets and signatures, and his ID checked out. He even had credentials from the State Department that said he's got some kind of super-secret security clearance that I'd never heard of, so we helped him load up his stuff and get on the road." He stared. "Did we do something wrong?"

"No," said Mack, "you guys did what you were supposed to do. Did Chaney happen to mention where he was going?"

With a frown Vernon shook his head. "He just said it was State Department business and that all the stuff was detailed for a classified training exercise. But we thought he was really going to raid one of the Aryan Nation compounds."

Mack focused on Gantry. "You were there, too?"

"Yeah," Gantry nodded, "don't you remember that you assigned Vernon and me to work together?"

"Yeah, yeah, I forgot for a second. Do either of you guys remember anything about this big four-wheeler Chaney was driving?"

Gantry tilted his head before he said, "I remember it wasn't government issue. He rented it from some place. Probably the airport." He squinted. "It was a late model pale blue Toyota Sequoia. And I don't remember the tag, but we can get it. We'll just make some calls. Why? Is Chaney in some kind of trouble? I mean, I hope not. I kinda liked the guy."

"This may be the most important mission of your rookie FBI lives," Mack said as he stood off the desk. "Because I think Chaney is in a whole heap of trouble with the wrong kind of people." He took his authority-figure position. "I want you boys to find Chaney and I don't care how you do it. Just find him. But don't tell anyone what you're doing. Just find out if this Sequoia has a low jack and track it. And do it quietly."

Gantry tentatively offered, "There's one more thing, boss." He shrugged, "It might be nothing. But it got my attention, for sure."

"What is it, son?"

"It was in the back of the Sequoia," Gantry continued. "Chaney had a lot of camping gear like he was gonna do some serious backpacking or something. Really, if it hadn't been for the camping stuff, I wouldn't have thought twice about loading up the ordinance. But something didn't make sense. I mean, none of us are gonna camp out on a stakeout, you know? We'll rotate shifts and use hotels." He paused. "It was almost like Chaney was gearing up for a one-man operation where he wouldn't be able to leave his post. But he was also loaded for bear like he was preparing for a fight."

"Just what kind of ordinance did Chaney pick up?" asked Mack pointedly. "Be as exact as you can."

Vernon answered quickly, "Standard issue military hand grenades – the M-67s. He had a crate with two sniper rifles. Armor-piercing explosive rounds. Det cord. A case of C-4. Detonators. Remotes. Trail monitors and video scanners." He stared at nothing. "And there was some more stuff, but I don't remember what, exactly. I just remember being impressed and thinking that he must be going into something real risky. I almost asked him if he wanted any help but – "

"Yeah!" Gantry joined in. "We'd have been glad to help him!"

"But we didn't ask," Vernon finished, "because something about him sort of told me that what he was doing was … well … "

Mack waited. "Was what, son?"

Vernon replied with obvious reluctance; "Well, boss, there was something about the way he was moving. He was real matter of fact, but he was in a big damn hurry, too. And he didn't talk much and that made me think he was doing something that might be off the books." He gazed up at Mack's implacable face. "*Way* off the books."

With a heavy sigh, Mack bowed his head. He was silent before he pointed to each of them. "You two greenhorns are going to get me the location of that Sequoia pronto and then you're going to come to *me* with it. And me alone! Do you understand? You will not tell anyone anything about what you're doing. And if anyone asks, you're on some lame assignment to track stolen cars. And you can consider this the first field assignment that could get you both thrown into Leavenworth. But you gotta get your feet wet sooner or later. It might as well be saving the ass of the best FBI agent to ever came out of the bunker."

With that Mack slapped the desk.

"Get on it!"

* * *

Rifle in hand, Chaney pushed back the curtain peering at the moonlit landscape that appeared stark white against the more distant darkness.

"Would you relax?" asked Hunter from his desk. He was tapping on the computer for any local crimes that defied explanation. "If there was anything out there, Moe would let us know. And he's sleeping like a rock." He turned his face from the computer. "There's nothing out there, Chaney, so calm down. You're making me nervous."

"I thought you didn't get nervous," Chaney muttered.

Hunter grunted, "Who the hell told you that? Most of been an FBI agent." A laugh. "No, Chaney, I get nervous, and scared, just like anybody else. But somewhere along the way I learned that there ain't nobody coming to help me, so it don't do no good to cringe. You just gotta get moving and do what you gotta do regardless of what you feel."

"Simple as that, huh?"

Shutting off the computer, Hunter walked to a recliner, and sat. "The difference between people who live and people who die is usually simple, Chaney. Sometimes it's just luck, but that's one in a million. Most of the time the difference between the living and the dead is that the people who live are the ones who just tied up their wounds, got back on their feet, and kept moving. The ones that don't give up live. The ones who quit die."

Hunter clicked the TV on a local news channel and watched in silence. Finally, he commented, "There is nothing going on, man. I've checked all the local newspapers and all they're discussing is a church social and a house fire. But if we had a mysterious animal attack or some kind of killing, or even just a missing person, that's all they'd be talking about."

"Why don't you use your HAM radio and check with the sheriff?"

"I already did. Buford told me that the only new thing in the area is that somebody bought this old, abandoned hospital down in the valley and they're renovating it. Said he drove by there a few times and all he saw were plumbers and carpenters. Then he stopped by their office in town and they showed him blueprints for the new hospital. But, just in case, he checked their background and said they looked legit."

"Is it an arm of Saturn Industries?" asked Chaney.

"I don't think Buford has the resources for that kind of background check. Maybe the NSA could trace it back that far but, other than them, what Dante wants hidden is gonna stay hidden. But if Buford just saw plumbers and carpenters and truckloads of wood and pipes, I don't think we need to be concerned."

Chaney came across the room and took a seat in the cabin's second recliner – the only other chair. "There's nothing about any suspicious activity?"

"Nothing."

"And nobody's gone missing?"

"Why do you keep asking?"

"Because I'm beginning to think that you might be right," stated Chaney as he checked the safety on the rifle. "I don't think this thing can be controlled enough to not do some collateral damage on its way here. If it encounters something, it's gonna kill it. No two ways about it. This thing is a killing machine no matter how much they try to control it." A pause. "If that bastard was in the area, we'd have dead bodies stretched halfway across Montana."

"Yeah, man, so relax."

"I'll relax when I know for sure that you're right and I'm wrong."

"And what, exactly, is going to prove that to you?"

Chaney nodded, "If we haven't seen anything in a few weeks, I'll get out of your hair. I ain't gonna spend the rest of my days up here when I have a good life in a beachfront home with vodka martinis and naked women." He glanced at the big iron stove. Flames could be seen through the slits. "That thing keeps this place pretty warm, don't it?"

With a laugh Hunter replied, "I have everything anybody else has, Chaney. I have food, a solid place to live, electricity. And if you throw three sticks in that stove it'll heat this entire cabin all night. You wake up in the morning, throw in another three sticks, and it'll keep you warm all day. I don't know why everybody doesn't have one."

"You don't get lonely up here?"

Hunter chuckled, "Lonely is in the mind. If you don't mind being alone, then you don't get lonely." He sighed, "And I occupy myself when I'm not working. I chop wood, read, or fix the cabin. I go down to the valley and tend my horses. I help out on the reservation. And there's never a shortage of mystery around here. A lot of women tend to vanish."

With a hard stare Chaney asked, "What do you mean?"

"I mean," answered Hunter, "that the FBI has demographics for just about every ethnicity of women that vanish under mysterious circumstances. Women who just disappear and never turn up. The FBI has a demographic for how many white women have vanished in the past year. They have a demographic for how many black women have disappeared. They have a demographic for how many Spanish women disappear. They have a demographic for every race and creed of women except Native American women. The FBI has no demographic for how many Native American women go missing every year." Hunter lowered his gaze. "I think it's pretty clear. The FBI doesn't care, which means nobody at the Bureau of Indian Affairs cares. Which means nobody in Washington, including Congress and the president, cares. But a lot of Native American women go missing every year, and nobody knows how many. And nobody knows why. But I have a theory that I've developed from several tracks where I found a handful of them."

"What's your theory?"

"They're being kidnapped," Hunter said simply. "People come across the Canadian border for the purpose of kidnapping a few Native American girls to use for some kind of evil thing. Maybe as sex slaves. Maybe they sell them to the highest bidder – some Saudi prince or whoever – who has a fetish for Indians. I don't know. I found three of them before they were shipped out of the area and got the girls back. But those were the lucky ones. Sometimes I'm not notified for weeks, and by then it's too late for tracks, so there's not much I can do." Hunter pondered it before he added, "Oh, I'll patrol the borders looking for anything suspicious. I'll check all the bars and waterfronts. But that's like searching for a needle in a stack of needles. It's too big a search area and there's too many players. There might not be as many people in Montana, but there's every sort you have in the city. We might not have a New York mafia, but we've got mafia. We've got every kind of evil there is."

"You think they're coming across the Canadian border? What about places like Los Angeles or somewhere in the states?"

"Them, too," nodded Hunter. "I was on one track and found them at a local hotel as they were loading up and I took down the whole crew. There were four of them, and they're in a Montana prison now." He grunted, "They were lucky that day, boy. My shooting hand was off. But, anyway, there's also a big sex ring out of Los Angeles that works this region. I've arrested a few of them. But none of them would talk. They said that if they talked, their lives wouldn't be worth spit. Even in prison. So they chose to do the time rather than give up their handlers. I guess these people keep a tight rein on their Satanic little operation. And, afterwards, we gave what we had to the FBI. But nothing came of it. I guess the FBI had better things to do than find a bunch of missing Indians."

"That's strange," said Chaney, "now that you say it, I can't think of more than two or three cases where I was asked to investigate the disappearance of a Native American." He took a moment. "Most of the time that kind of thing is given to the closest FBI office. And I was working out of Chicago at the time. I remember thinking it was unusual that we'd be asked to investigate the disappearance of an Indian girl from Wyoming. But I was told they wanted someone from outside Wyoming to do the job." He frowned, "We didn't find anything. Nobody would talk. Treated us like we were lepers or something." He stared away. "Yeah, a reservation is its own world, man. Hell, it's its own *nation*. If you don't belong there, and they know exactly who does, they won't even talk to you."

"They don't trust the white man."

"They trust *you*."

Hunter responded grimly, "I've earned their trust. Just like I've earned the trust of every creature on this mountain. They know I'm not here to hurt them, and that's what they're afraid of more than anything. Including ol' Moe out there. We're kinda like family. Moe sleeps here not only because he wants to feel safe. He sleeps here because he wants to make sure *I'm safe*." He lifted his gaze to the window. "And right now there's at least three wolves circling the cabin. I'll show you the tracks in the morning. They'll stay out there all night watching over me like an old member of the pack. Wolves are like that. If a wolf is older, they'll keep him in the center of the pack, and the young wolves will mount a perimeter in case the pack gets attacked. The younger ones don't expect the old wolves to fight. They know that fighting is their job." He was thoughtful. "Wolves are bodyguards that never sleep. And noble. They treat their old ones with respect. The pack won't move faster than the old ones can move. And they treat an older wolf like a father or mother. It'd be nice if human beings were as civilized."

Chaney stared at nothing before he asked, "I'm not doubting you, man, but if wolves are outside, then why isn't Moe growling and stuff? Aren't they enemies? Wolves and bears? I mean, *natural* enemies?"

Hunter laughed, "No, man, they're not enemies – natural or otherwise. The Grizzlies don't bother the wolves, and the wolves don't bother the Grizzlies. They co-exist *peacefully* – which is more than I can say for humans. And Moe knows those wolves, anyway. Hell, everything up here knows everything else. It's like a small town where everybody knows everybody else and they all know each other's business. I've even got names for the wolves. I'll run into one of them on the trail and I'll just say, 'Hey, Lancelot,' or 'Hey, Bandit,' and keep moving. I'll never even look back. I don't have to. And if they start following me, it's just 'cause they're bored and want to see what I'm doing. Sometimes – even after a hard track – I'll look around and there'll be half a dozen of them staring at me. But they'll vanish like ghosts when the med-vac arrives. It's like they were never there."

"So that's what you mean when you say you always know when someone is on your mountain?" asked Chaney. "The animals tell you?"

"Yeah. And I let them know when danger is close. Like poachers. Then I'll go and take care of the poachers."

"How do you take care of those guys?"

Hunter simply waved, "Most of the time I'll just walk up to them and arrest them. I think I told you I'm something like a deputy. Just a different kind of deputy. But I still have arrest powers. Even on the reservation. And if poachers – or anybody else, for that matter – gives me any trouble, well, trouble can work both ways."

"Does it usually end in trouble?"

"Most of the time, yeah. Poachers operate under the mistaken idea that they can't be held responsible by the law for what they do in the deep woods or, even, discovered. But anybody, and anything, can be found. Nothing moves in the forest with leaving sign. Not even a bug. If you look close enough at any square yard of ground you'll see the tracks of beetles, gophers, moles – all kinds of things. You just have to know what to look for."

A rumbling on the porch caused Hunter to turn his head. He rose from the recliner and walked to the front window, pushing back the curtain. He stared out a minute before he remarked, "Moe senses something."

A wolf howled in the distance.

Hunter stepped to his gun safe and lifted a rifle. He looked down as he levered the action, shoving a round in the chamber. He ignored the Barrett sniper rifle that Chaney had brought as he opened the front door and stepped outside.

Shock didn't quite capture the sensation that engulfed Chaney as the door swung wide and he beheld the unbelievably gigantic sight of Moe standing on the front porch. The colossal beast rolled its massive head toward Hunter as he walked outside. Hunter lifted his face to the stars as if listening. Chaney wouldn't have been surprised if he was trying to scent the approach of an enemy.

Hunter stood there for a long time before he patted Moe alongside his head. Chaney heard him say, "It's warm tonight, brother. You stay outside."

With that, Hunter closed the door and put the rifle back in the safe. He left the safe open and now Chaney understood why. Up here you needed quick access to a weapon. After Hunter sat again, Chaney noticed more closely what he'd taken from the safe. It was in a holster, but Chaney could tell it was a gigantic pistol.

Hunter removed it from the holster and began to load it from a box of extremely large stainless-steel shells. He moved slowly, methodically, before Chaney said, "I do believe that is the biggest hand-cannon I've ever seen."

With a laugh Hunter snapped the cylinder shut and handed it to Chaney. "Chaney, you are now holding the world-famous Magnum Research .500 caliber Bushwhacker with a six-inch barrel. Forget Dirty Harry and his .44 Magnum. Forget the Casull .454. *This* is the most powerful handgun in the world, bar none. There is no competition."

Hunter merely watched as Chaney checked the sights and weight as Hunter added clinically, "That gun hits with three times the impact power of a .44 Magnum. It doubles the velocity of most hunting rifles and even hits harder than a 45.70 buffalo gun or a .50 caliber sniper rifle. It is capable of dropping any game on the planet with a single round, and that includes rhinos and giant crocodiles. And if you fire it into something that is normally bulletproof to a rifle cartridge, it'll turn that target into Swiss cheese. No ballistic vest can stand up to it. And neither can the bullet-proof skin of a pissed-off prehistoric monster."

Chaney raised a gaze. "It only holds five rounds."

"The rounds are too powerful for the cylinder to hold six." Hunter laid six speed-loaders on the table and began to charge them with the outrageously over-sized bullets. "And you have to use monster-size bullets or the power of the discharge will tear the lead to shreds. Then you'll just be throwing a lot of pellets downrange. You might as well be shooting a BB gun." He didn't look up from the speed loaders as he added, "But I poured these bullets, myself. They're made out of carbon steel. It should increase the penetration power by about forty percent."

"What's the velocity of this thing?"

"I loaded these for 4,000 feet per second." Hunter turned over another box of shells on the table. "Yeah, I bought this thing not long after that little escapade in England.

It pissed me off how everything I threw at that thing just kept bouncing off it. I mean, rhinos and hippos are *bullet-resistant* but they're not *bulletproof.* And I don't think this thing is, either. We just haven't hit it with the right round. And if this don't do it, I don't know what will. But I think that ballistic hide has a limit. And I'm gonna find it."

"Why didn't you take this thing to Alaska? Or England?"

"It was still in development. Magnum Research had a lot of problems figuring out how to make it work. The cylinders kept disintegrating, and the top strap kept blowing off. They had to come up with a way to fire the cartridge without the whole gun exploding in somebody's hand and killing them and everybody standing close to them."

"How'd they solve it?"

"They added a lot more steel to the cylinder and strap." Hunter looked up, his eyes wider. "*A lot more.*"

Staring at the revolver, Chaney mildly asked, "Got another one?"

Hunter laughed, "Sorry, man. This is the only one I've got. And since I'm supposedly the main meal at this banquet, I'll be keeping it on *me*. But I've got a good .44 Magnum that you can carry. It'll hit a lot harder than that FBI issue." He shook his head, "I hate to tell you, Chaney, but that nine-millimeter won't break popcorn with this animal."

Chaney noticed that Hunter seemed more attuned to the night and kept glancing toward the window and door. Finally, Chaney asked, "What do you think it was?"

Hunter shook his head, "I don't know. But it was down in the valley. If it was close, the wolves would have been making a racket. But that was from a wolf somewhere at the base of the mountain. He was signaling to the others. Warning them."

Feeling stupid for asking, Chaney asked nevertheless, "How do you know he was warning them? Don't wolves howl all the time?"

"Wolves use different howls. Sometimes they howl to find each other. Sometimes they howl to verify a kill so everybody can eat. And sometimes they howl to warn others. And that was a warning. That was a wolf down in the valley. And something spooked it."

"Like what?"

After a long pause Hunter said, "We'll go down to the valley tomorrow and take a look around." He grew more concentrated. "Wolves don't get spooked easy."

Clutching the rifle, Chaney released a deep breath.

"I don't like any of this," he said.

Hunter frowned, "It was a long way off, buddy. It was down in the flatlands. And whatever it was retreated, or we'd be hearing more howls, so it's gone. And, like I say, tomorrow we'll go down into the valley and take a look around."

Dismayed, Chaney shook his head. "This is a big damn mountain, man. I don't know where we're gonna start looking."

"There's only a few trails up this mountain. Nobody can climb it through the bush. A man wouldn't get half a mile. So we'll check the foot paths and horse trails for anything that looks out of place. And, until morning, we'll just keep up our guard."

Chaney sat the rifle on the floor.

Hunter chuckled.

"Relax, Chaney. We've got bodyguards who never sleep."

CHAPTER FIVE

I n the Salt Lake City, Utah, regional headquarters of the FBI, Special Agent in Charge, Mack Johnson, the ASAC, was still laboring at his computer as Agents Vernon Sanders and Jeffrey Gantry unceremoniously entered with a manila envelope. Mack raised his gaze from the screen as a nearby printer began to work.

"What you boys got?" he asked.

Gantry removed a sheet of paper from the file. "It was a light blue 2024 Sequoia rented from Country Rent-a-Car at the airport. Chaney paid for it with a personal credit card and didn't give a return date. We questioned the lady that rented it to him, and she said that he specifically asked for a four-wheel, off-road vehicle."

"They ain't got nuthin' *but* off-road vehicles," muttered Vernon.

Gantry expanded, "She told us that she gave him a Sequoia four-wheel drive with the big engine and that it could go anywhere a backpacker would wanna go."

"Does the thing have a low jack?"

"Sure does," Vernon nodded. "We're tracking it right now."

"Did Chaney have any luggage?"

"We asked," Vernon said with a hint of excitement. "The check-out lady told us Chaney only had one bag and no camping equipment, so we went by the closest REI to see if he'd stopped in, and the manager remembered him. He said Chaney didn't seem to know what he might need for camping, so the manager helped him out. He said Chaney bought nearly one out of everything in the store and paid with the same credit card." He pulled out a sales receipt from the folder. "We got a list of everything he bought."

"Did Chaney happen to mention where he was going?"

"He just told the REI guy that it was high country and that he needed something warm. He bought a North Face Arctic Jacket and – "

"Arctic jacket!" interjected Mack. "It's August! Where the hell is he going? *Tibet*?"

Gantry volunteered, "If you don't mind, chief, we've got a theory that Chaney is going to make an unsanctioned stakeout on one of the Aryan Nation compounds." He regarded the sales receipt before he added, "He bought a pair of really good binoculars – "

"More like a *telescope*," said Vernon.

"– and a stand to mount it on."

With an unconvinced grunt Mack rose and walked to the printer. He removed pages and returned with his head bent. Then he shuffled sheets with practiced efficiency, reading quickly. Finally, he handed the pages to Gantry.

"Find out where the hell this guy is at," Mack stated with no uncertainty about whether they *would* succeed. "His name is Nathaniel Hunter – that's a biographical sketch of him – and Chaney worked with him a few years back to clean up some kind of top-secret situation gone to hell near the Arctic Circle. It was classified then, and it's classified now, so I don't know much more. My *very* few contacts on this only know that a lot of regular army and CIA operators were killed and that it had something to do with biological warfare. But one contact told me that a prehistoric animal from a military research facility was involved, and that Hunter was the tracker hired to hunt it down and kill it.

"I'm not sure where Chaney fits in, so what I need from you greenhorns is this: Find out if Hunter has a place anywhere in our region. Then use the low jack on this four-wheeler to confirm Chaney's location and see if he's moving in Hunter's direction. Because I have a suspicion that whatever happened in Alaska has happened again, but this time it's in our back yard, and I'll be damned if I'm gonna let some government goon bury it again. I'm still waiting for my last source, and he might have something more specific for us, but that's it for now."

"Uh," Vernon began, "just asking, boss. But is there another reason why you think Chaney is headed for this guy's place?"

"The camping equipment," stated Mack. "Chaney ain't no camper. He hates camping. Hell, it took everything I had just to get him through survival school at the academy. A whole week in the woods and Chaney never stopped complaining. And the only occasion I can remember when Chaney was even near the woods after that was the time he spent in Alaska with Hunter. Chaney told me all about it afterwards. We were just in a bar telling lies about how brave we used to be when he said he'd learned more about the outdoors in that one week than he ever knew about the city. And he's lived in the city all his life. Plus that, I got the impression that Chaney considers this guy a good, close, personal friend. So, since Chaney is packed for the outdoors, maybe he's working with Hunter again. I don't know. It's just a hunch. But check it, anyway."

"Holy crap!" Gantry exclaimed, lifting the file on Hunter higher. "Did you know this guy is worth more than seven billion bucks!"

Gantry looked dead at Mack. "Is that *right*?"

"It's right," nodded Mack. "Hunter is some kind of world-famous tracker who's worked in every wilderness area on the planet. And he's discovered all kinds of botanical things that he's sold to pharmaceutical companies – stuff for pain or high blood pressure, cancer treatment, that kind of thing. Chaney told me all about it, and he seemed kind of amazed, himself. He said Hunter lives like some kind of dirt-poor Daniel Boone and he's got all this damn money. So, if Hunter's in our region, I think that's where Chaney's going. This isn't exactly Chaney's neck of the woods."

"Got it," they said together.

Mack nodded, "You boys are doing good. Keep it up and I might make FBI agents out of you, yet."

Together, they beamed.

* * *

Staring at the gargantuan creature as it stood staring at Cronis from behind the copper-toned bars, he could not shake the fear than emanated from the center of his being. It was as if he were looking at the incarnate nightmare of man's subconscious mind, a beast that first gave man a real good reason to retreat from the darkness.

The creature's huge, clawed hands clutched and unclutched convulsively as if it could not restrain the desire to tear through the bars and rip Cronis's arms and legs from his body before the sabretooth fangs clamped shut on his face, tearing him to shreds. It occurred to Cronis that it would probably kill him so quickly that he wouldn't even feel it. By the time his conscious mind realized that he was about to die, he'd be dead. And for no logical reason he thought about death by guillotine and how some theorized that the severed head had surely lived for a few moments after being cut from the body.

Lost in that uncomfortable thought, Cronis was abruptly struck cold by a shadow that fell across the floor before him. The darkness was wide and enormous, engulfing Cronis' entire body, and stretched across the cement to the cage.

Instantly the caged beast raised its face, glaring over Cronis's shoulder. Its fangs separated as if it beheld a god. It took two stumbling steps backwards before it froze, head uplifted to gaze upon what had struck it with such fear and what seemed like respect. And even in the horror of the moment, Cronis somehow knew.

It was Dante – it could be no other – and the insane professor had assumed the form of the beast. And it was standing behind him.

There was no measuring the flood of molten yellow fear that surged through Cronis. There was no logical thought although Cronis was aware that his hands and knees were trembling uncontrollably. There was only a bone-deep horror – the same horror that primitive man must have known when he had stood in the presence of the beast without the uncertain safety provided by the steel cage. The beast literally stood within arm's reach of Cronis and Cronis closed his eyes, surrendering to fate. There was nothing he could do, and Cronis accepted it. He was ready. He had always subconsciously felt he would die like this.

And now he would.

A huge, clawed hand gripped Cronis's right shoulder and with surprising restraint moved him to the side. Cronis didn't raise his face, but he saw the tall, shaggy form of Dante as he stepped within arm's length of the cage.

Dante's cavernous growl emerged from deep within his chest and made the floor tremble. Then he violently barked as if communicating to the caged creature that he was master of the pack. To Cronis's spiraling horror, he instinctively knew that Dante was demonstrating to the beast that he was king, and all others existed only to serve him, and there would be no dispute. He was announcing that he was Lord and all the atoms in the universe were held together by his will, and his will alone. Then Dante's incarnation of the beast lowered its wedged head and stared upon Dr. Pinion as if he could telepathically communicate with the caged doctor.

Dante's head tilted as Pinion stepped forward in a more relaxed posture – a much calmer posture. The creature that was Pinion gazed up at the even more gargantuan shape of Dante and, after a moment, bowed its head. And then, with a gesture of surprising tenderness, Dante reached through the bars and stroked the creature along its head. It was as if he were petting it, or soothing its fears.

To Cronis, the gentle gesture was more horrifying than what stood so close to him. But even within his mind-numbing shock Cronis realized that Dante had transferred his human consciousness into the mind of his version of the creature long ago and that this exercise was simply to see if the results could be repeated.

Without ceremony Dante turned from the bars and stalked across the basement with incredibly long, tiger-like strides until he reached the stairway. He climbed the steps into the false light without any whisper of sound, and was gone.

Only then did Dante realize he had not drawn a breath. His chest deflated and he inhaled desperately like a man who has barely escaped drowning. He was aware that he had a hand flat against his chest as he staggered to the side, putting out an arm to steady himself against the wall. He blinked, trying to clear the bright blinking lights from his sight.

Horror does have a physical form. Cronis knew that now. It was like he had been engulfed in a black lake of liquid fear that smothered and shut down every impulse of his conscious mind. He was dimly amazed that he could move at all. He lifted the hand from his chest and, with effort, made a fist. He did it again to make certain. He realized his breaths were deep and desperate as if he were trying to recover from a grueling race.

Cronis didn't raise his face, yet he narrowly confirmed that the creature was still standing immobile within its cage. Its impatient pacing had frozen into a kind of worship, or awe, and it was staring at the distant stairwell. It seemed almost as if it were awaiting its master's return.

The image caused Cronis to grimace.

For a moment Cronis wasn't certain at all that he wanted to continue with this experiment. Even the thought of calling this an "experiment" caused him to shake his head in disbelief because this was beyond the place where any experiment should go. This was where science should surrender to Nature. Where some questions should not be asked, and the answers avoided for the salvation of your soul. Here they were trifling with cosmic powers that hold the very universe together. Here they were dealing with the unknown powers of the atom and the dark secrets it might unlock. But then, leveling his doubts about escaping this madness by running into the night, Cronis once more remembered Dante's words …

"It's too late to turn back …"

Cronis was certain that, if he attempted to leave, Colonel Blakely would ensure that he was shot dead and buried in this cursed wilderness where no one would ever find him. Then Dante would arrange a convenient explanation for his disappearance to pacify authorities. Dante had done it before. Indeed, the world-famous physician had not reached the apex of his profession without physically destroying anyone that had stood in his path.

Suddenly Cronis felt perilously exhausted and took uncertain steps toward a black cot set up in the basement. He wasn't sure that he could make the short walk and then he sat upon it, pulling up the single blanket. He needed sleep, and he had the hope that, when he awoke, he would realize that all that had seemed to have passed had just been a nightmare. But he knew that it was no mere nightmare.

It was the most horrible nightmare.

Because it was real.

* * *

Kneeling over a trail in the noon-day sun, rifle balanced across a thigh, Hunter studied the ground coldly and clinically. Standing to the side, Chaney turned in every direction aiming the rifle at every bush whose looks he did not like.

"Chaney," Hunter began tiredly, "would you stop waving that gun around?"

"You afraid I'll have to shoot it?"

"I'm afraid you'll shoot *me.*"

Hunter pointed, "Three wolves. Last night. They were making their usual rounds." He stood. "The pack dispatches guards at night so they're not surprised by an enemy. They station them down here and up high. But these were just walking along real relaxed. Nothing to indicate any alarm."

Chaney clutched the rifle. "How can you tell?"

"If they were alerted to something by scent or sight, or even sound, they would have stopped moving." Hunter waved a hand again over the tracks. "There would be shifting or mulling to show where they stood in place looking in a specific direction. But they just kept walking along nice and slow."

"How can you tell they were walking along nice and slow?"

"Because the tracks tell me they were walking along nice and slow, Chaney." Lifting his face, Hunter studied the stark blue sky where vultures were beginning to circle. "But *something* happened last night. Let's see what it is."

Hunter began leading them into the bush and Chaney understood instantly what Hunter had meant when he said no man could climb the slope of this mountain. Without the trail it was a physical and mental ordeal to bulldoze a way through the overgrown bush although Hunter seemed to have a way of sliding through it without visible effort. Half an hour later they were staring at the dead carcass of a large gray wolf.

Eyes narrowing, Hunter raised his face, searching the surrounding forest. He didn't say a word as he walked to the nearby tree line and began pacing, studying the limbs, the ground, all that could be seen. It took far longer than Chaney preferred, but finally Hunter walked back and knelt. He gently laid a hand on the shoulder of the slaughtered wolf.

"Ah," Hunter moaned as he bowed his head, *"Bandit …"*

For a long time, Hunter rested beside the wolf, his hand on its shoulder. His head was bent. Finally, he took a deep breath as if to put away a great emotion. Then he stood, and Chaney saw him wipe something from his face.

"Sorry about your friend," Chaney allowed. "You recognize the track?"

Hunter nodded, "Yeah. It's a Scimitar." He pointed. "It came in through that way last night. Probably to test our defenses. But it must not have been expecting the wolves." He paused, then, "It came up on poor Bandit without any warning and killed him with one blow. Hit him across the neck. But it didn't go any further. It turned around and took the same path going out as it took coming in. And that's a rookie mistake. No experienced predator would do that. It gives you something to think about."

As if he didn't really want an answer, Chaney asked, "So I'm right? It's here?"

"You're right," said Hunter. "It's here."

"Damn! I *hate* being right!"

Hunter took a long time studying the surrounding slopes of thick bush with scattered harbors of trees. Then he grimaced, "There's no mistaking the track. Nothing else leaves a track like that. And this is a big one. Bigger than the one we managed to get up in Alaska. Bigger than the one I tracked in England."

"Great. Well, uh, you're something like an archeologist, aren't you?"

"More like an amateur paleontologist."

"Whatever. What do you really know about this creature?"

Hunter frowned, "You know about as much as I do, Chaney. It's a subspecies of the Sabretooth tiger – there were about thirty of them – and it was one of the meanest predators the world had ever seen until it died out in the Quaternary Extinction. Along with pretty much everything else. It was a time of severe climate change. And a time when human predation reached a zenith. A lot of species got wiped out.

"Now, I say it was *like* a Sabretooth, but it wasn't *exactly* like a Sabretooth. It was smaller, and its jaws were shorter and flatter. It was also leaner and faster and more agile. The Sabretooth was big and bulky and, personally, I don't think it was much of a fighter. It was too heavy. Too slow. It was more like a wrestler. And because it was so big, it'd just wrestle its prey to the ground, bite it, and wait for it to die. But the Scimitar was perfectly designed for fighting. Comparing a Scimitar to a Sabretooth is like comparing a karate master to a weightlifter. Or a jaguar to a Siberian tiger." He paused. "Some paleontologists theorize that the last of the Scimitar might have been the missing link between animal and man. That some of them had rudimentary human DNA. I don't know. It's just a theory. But I wouldn't be surprised if there's not some truth to it. Homo Scimitar disappeared at about the same time man rose up to dominate North America. About ten thousand years ago. It's not really hard to imagine their DNA overlapping in some kind of bizarre twist of evolution."

Chaney pressed, "What about *this* Scimitar? I mean, since this is the one trying to eat us. What are we dealing with?"

"Oh," Hunter continued absently, "well, this one's about seven feet tall and it weighs a good six hundred pounds. It moves slowly. But it's not wounded or lame. Still, it seems to hesitate a lot. It could be checking the surroundings or … "

Chaney didn't move. "Or what! You're killing me, Hunter!"

"It moves like its unsure of itself," Hunter muttered, still staring down. "It moves like it's not accustomed to being in the wild. Or, like, it doesn't know where it's at. It doesn't move like the ones in Alaska or England. They both had some kind of internal compass that always told them where they were. But this one is different. It's like he's lost … or something. He moves more like a man, which it is, really."

"Does that mean anything useful to us?"

"Everything means something useful, Chaney. People think tracking is something that happens below the waist. That it's just prints on the ground. But half of tracking happens above the waist. Rustled branches. Dew wiped off a leaf when there's no tracks in sight. Hair scraped on the bark of a tree. A handprint on a rock or a stump. Put it all together and it tells you what the thing is thinking. It tells you what's in its *mind*. So everything it does, from head to toe, is useful. And if you ignore a single thing, it can come back and bite you."

Hunter seemed to involuntarily clutch the rifle with his left hand. "This thing was acting like it was lost. And I've never seen that with one of these animals. Even in total darkness, their sense of scent leads them to their prey. In a lot of ways, they're like wolves. Or big cats. A wolf hunts by both sight and scent. And this thing is the same, so it shouldn't have hesitated back there. It shouldn't have stopped up here. It should have kept moving all the way to the cabin. But it didn't. It was acting like it didn't know where it was."

Pointing his rifle at the print, Chaney asked with admirable resolve, "What else can you tell about this one?"

Hunter shrugged, "That's about it. I know he's a lot bigger than the others. But it's also a lot more cautious. You're right. Luther was the purest form of this animal. He didn't even think about it before he attacked. He just attacked and to hell with the odds. And the one in England was more cunning but, in the end, he was still more animal than man." He paused. "But this one is in a visible conflict. I can read it in how he moves. Its instincts are telling it to do one thing. Its conscious mind is telling it to do another. It's like it's got two minds. It can't decide what to do. It doubts itself. And that could be an advantage."

"How could that be an advantage?"

Hunter continued, "It's like they want the instincts of this beast, but they also want to control it with a human mind. And that's impossible. With every attempt to make it more human, they make it weaker. They dilute the very thing that makes it so dangerous. If this one was the purest version of this beast, he would have kept moving. He would have known exactly where he was. Only a man would get lost and hesitate."

"That's reassuring," muttered Chaney. "But, somehow, I don't think this is going to be a cakewalk. I don't care how confused it is." He scanned the woods. "And I'm guessing that these things learn from their mistakes. That's why they've come after you first. They want you out of the way because every time they set another one of these things free, you track it down and kill it. And they've had enough of that. They've had enough of *you*."

Hunter's voice was resigned. "I don't think reasons matter, anymore, Chaney. It's here, and we have to kill it just like we did before."

"I don't give a damn what its reasons are!" grimaced Chaney. "But you're right about one thing. We gotta kill this animal before it gets away from us again. I mean …" He lifted the rifle and swept it down, "… we gotta put this thing in the dirt because there's *no way* I'm going through the hell we went through in Alaska again! This is the last one I'm gonna hunt! We find a way to put this one down! And then I go after Dante! Proof or no proof!"

Hunter fixed Chaney with a gaze. "How do you know they don't already have a hundred of these things?"

Chaney briefly closed his eyes before he said, "God Almighty, I hope not. But, maybe, with this dead maneater's body, we can get a full shutdown of Saturn Industries. And I mean a full and complete shutdown of every facility! Dante might be powerful, but I've got the power of the Secretary of State and the National Security Agency. And when I give them the dead body of a seven-foot-tall killing machine with the fangs and claws of a Sabretooth tiger they're gonna *have to* comply with my request. I'm gonna tell them everything I know whether they're read-in or not." He hesitated. "Secrets are what gave these maniacs all they needed to perfect this monstrosity. Well, the time for secrets has passed. I'm gonna tell the *world* about this!"

Without expression Hunter stared at the track.

"If we live to tell."

CHAPTER SIX

Mack Johnson lifted his face as an FBI agent knocked on the frame, struck in his head, and asked, "Got a minute, chief? There's somebody who says he's here to give you some kind of paperwork. We x-rayed it and checked it for pheromones. It's sterile. Nothing but paper. He says you're expecting it."

"Show him in," muttered Mack.

Without a word a burly, tall man wearing a beaver-skin cowboy hat strolled into the office firmly holding a yellow folder. Without a word he laid the folder on Mack's desk, turned, and walked out. Again, without a word.

With a sigh Mack opened the folder and removed the slender report. It wasn't more than ten pages, but as Mack started to read, he began to understand the true scope and danger of what Chaney had confronted in Alaska.

It was incredible. Every detail of the covert military action, authorized by the president, was accounted for with names and the manners of death and notification of next of kin right down to what weapons and ammo they'd been issued. It was the kind of red-lined report never meant to see the light of day and it was only through Mack's single source in the NSA that he was able to get his hands on a copy.

As Mack examined what had been done to this man that had been transformed into this prehistoric creature – some kind of missing link between man and beast – Mack easily understood how dangerous such a thing would be and what kind of threat it would pose to the world. And that included man *and* animal.

It was a creature with no consciousness and no mind as one might understand either. It was phenomenally molded in the most perfect way for killing. Its strength, speed, its tiger-sized claws and fangs and its sheer rage all made it the ultimate predator. It was bulletproof and it had been estimated by scientists that it could kill a Siberian tiger with its bare hands. Or break the back of a Grizzly. There was literally nothing the beast could not accomplish in its mission to destroy anything in its path. And then Mack reached Chaney's account of how Hunter had lured it into a cave that held the fossilized bones of its ancestors, how that had temporarily disoriented it, and how Hunter had used that moment to ambush it with what was, perhaps, the only weapon in that battle that could have destroyed it. The report described in technicolor the frantic final fight between the man-beast and Hunter and how Hunter had, in the end, taken its head.

Mack blew out a slow breath, "Probably the only way to be sure." After pondering, he added, "I've have driven a stake through its heart." He tossed the report on the desk as Gantry and Vernon jauntily came through the door.

Gantry excitedly lifted a map. "I think we got him!"

Ignoring the red-lined report, Gantry spread the map of Montana on Mack's desk and pointed to a place circled in black. He added, "This is where Hunter is at!" He waved at the ceiling. "This guy's got a ton of homes! He's got a penthouse in New York! An apartment in DC! He's even got a place in Siberia! But we made a phone call to the local sheriff up there at Cut Bank, Montana, and he told us that Hunter's been at this place for five months and that, as far as he knows, he's still up there. Said he talked to him today, in fact."

Mack asked, "Up there?"

"Yeah," Gantry continued, "Hunter lives on top of what the locals call 'Wolf Mountain' because it has so many gray wolves on it. It's near Cut Bank, Montana, at the edge of Glacier National Forest and it's about thirty miles from the Canadian border. And this guy, Hunter, is like some kind of wilderness officer. He's also a deputy – sort of. And the sheriff got real serious when he told us that. Then he told us he's the chief pistol packer in his county and that we needed to let him know if we have any business on his gravel."

Mack mused, "Never heard it put like that." He stood. "Alright. Get your bags. We're going on a field trip." He picked up the phone. "I want a helicopter on the roof in five minutes and a Lear jet prepped with a flight plan for Helena, Montana. Scramble a team from Hostage-Rescue and tell them to meet us on the flight deck."

As he hung up, both Gantry and Vernon were staring.

"We get to go, too?" asked Vernon.

Mack impatiently threw up a hand. "You boys are damn FBI agents, aren't you! And you two greenhorns need some trigger time instead of pushing paper! Neither of you have ever fired your piece or even threw down on somebody!"

As Gantry quickly removed the map from his desk, Mack again noticed the NSA file and suddenly it seemed far more threatening.

His voice was grim.

"Well, this should give you plenty of both."

* * *

It was later in the day when Cronis recovered enough to enter the remarkably well-equipped office Dante's men had prepared on the second floor of the abandoned hospital. He found the doctor in human form working placidly at his desk. He was wearing dark slacks, a dark shirt and his customary white lab coat. He was scribbling notes when Cronis walked through the door and Dante put down the pen with a smile.

"Good afternoon," he said, leaning back. "I hope I did not cause you any alarm with my intrusion."

"You gave me cause for plenty." Cronis took a seat. "How long have you known that this process of conscious integration was possible?"

"For the past year," Dante relied with surprising candor. "I perfected the serum for myself and, just for safe measure, tested it in a setting where I would be restrained. Since the transformation is determined by how much serum one absorbs, the change can be a matter of hours or days. Or even weeks. And I theorize that if one were to overdose on the formula then it would kill the test subject. But there is also a possibility that it could transform him into something that we wish to avoid at all costs. It might transform him into a creature ten times more powerful and far beyond any means of control."

Dante folded his hands; it was almost as if he'd been secretly dying to tell someone about his genius. "At first – regrettably – the transformation was merely bestial. I would simply awaken to find myself naked and caged. And, so, I continued to synthesize the DNA strands. And then, at last, I isolated the genomes that controlled the central nervous system of the beast and added tiny fragments of my own DNA until the integration began to achieve the hoped-for results. Of course, it took many, many unsuccessful attempts at merging my conscious mind with the primordial power of the beast, but I could determine that with each attempt I was steadily approaching success.

"Still, it was only after another forty transitions that I was finally able to remember details of the occurrence. Also, I must say that I returned to human form each time with a little more of the creature's innate physical characteristics harbored in my DNA." He chuckled, "Believe me, doctor, it was a thrilling process. But a process without a path. I was simply shooting in the dark. But after the last transition – not including the one I invited last night – I finally absorbed what this experiment was created to cause in the first place. Watch this carefully."

Before Cronis could object, or even comprehend, Dante drew a scalpel from his coat. He laid his left hand flat on the desk and with his right hand stabbed violently downward into the back of his hand. Grimacing at the pain, Dante drew the scalpel up and out the top of his hand, between his fingers, before ripping the blade free.

Cronis grimaced, "*Jesus …*"

Dante blinked unsteadily.

"The pain is quite remarkable," he gasped. "But now – if you will – watch this incision closely."

As Cronis watched, the wound running along the back of Dante's hand quickly began to close. It started at the wrist and within seconds the incision was completely healed. Dante took a cloth and wiped blood from his hand before displaying it like a trophy.

As if teaching rudimentary anatomy, Dante continued, "You see, doctor? I have permanently absorbed a measure of this beast's power in my human form. I have altered my own DNA so that its healing faculties are now part of myself. And soon I will absorb even more of its amazing abilities. But by hard experimentation I have learned that it requires a long series of transitions which must be closely monitored and controlled with the most exacting precision. And most importantly, everything must be accomplished in a tightly controlled setting. Without sufficient safety measures, the beast would escape containment and then would where we be? Or too much of the serum could be administered and consequently kill the subject. Or, as I theorize, it might turn him into a hulking monstrosity that cannot be stopped by any measure of force. That is why I gave Doctor Pinion only enough serum to initiate the most fundamental transition."

He regarded his watch. "And the good doctor should be returning to his human form any minute now, so let us see how he fared."

Dante led Cronis down the short stairway to the lowest level of the building. Although he should have been amazed that the mercenaries had the boiler working, Cronis barely noted it. He was too focused on the cage. And when he saw what was within it, he didn't feel the rush of adrenaline that he had expected. Instead, he felt like he had expected to see this all long. There was no shock or even surprise.

It seemed like everything was as it should be.

On the floor of the cage Dr. Pinion lay in human form. But at their approach the doctor struggled to his knees and, after noticeable effort, raised his face. His arms hung limply at his sides. His breathing was ragged. Then, with a shocking lack of caution, Dante unlocked the cage and stood in the entrance.

"Come, doctor," said Dante calmly, "you're all right now. The transition is complete, and you are, again, yourself. Come forward. There is nothing to fear." He pointed, "Cronis, be a good man and fetch that chair and blanket."

As Pinion emerged from the cage and tiredly took a seat wrapped in the blanket, Dante merely stared as if doing a cold visual diagnosis. He stood with hands in the pockets of his lab coat, glasses perched on the edge of his nose, face slightly bent. "Well, doctor," he began, "I know this may seem like a strange question, but what do you remember?"

As if struggling to form words, Pinion managed, "It's … hard to describe." He hung his head for a long moment before looking up. "I remember rage. I remember hunger. But I also remember wanting to be free. And then I remember something that … that stopped the rage. Like I was being controlled by a higher power." He shook his head. "Some things aren't very clear. It's hard to describe."

Emboldened, Cronis grabbed a blood pressure sleeve and placed it around Pinion's arm. He pumped it up and placed two fingers on Pinion's wrist, staring at his watch. Then he removed the sleeve and commented, "Pulse is steady and strong at eighty-two. Blood pressure is within normal parameters. There's no indication of residual stress."

"Indeed not!" Dante laughed. "My guess is that Doctor Pinion will be feeling better than ever after he gets a little rest!" He cordially placed a hand on the doctor's shoulder. "Now you must eat, doctor. You have consumed quite a few calories during the transition."

Mike raised a confused gaze. "Is that it? I'm done?"

"You are done for now," smiled Dante. "And we are almost prepared to finish the task for which we've come. But, for the moment, you must rest and eat. And tonight we'll go into the field to accustom you to a harsher environment." He beamed over Mike's human form. "I do love it when the results of an experiment are repeatable. It happens so rarely."

Cronis stepped back as two guards came to Mike's chair and helped him stand. Then they walked him to the stairway and ascended. As they were gone, Dante turned to Cronis with an abruptly severe expression and with a thrill of fear Cronis noticed his hand outstretched toward the open steel cage. Then he noticed that Dante held a vial filled with yellow serum in his remaining hand.

Dante's voice held no mercy.

"Shall we, doctor?"

* * *

Mack took a stand in the hanger before six black-clad commandos from the Hostage Rescue Team and the diminutive, suit-wearing shapes of Gantry and Vernon who looked like dwarfs encircled by machine-gun wielding orcs.

"Alright," Mack began, "gentlemen, we are going face to face with something that killed more than forty United

States Rangers and ten covert CIA operators the last time it was confronted with military resistance, so make no mistake: We are challenging the greatest physical threat you have ever faced and as of this second you have a standing green light to use any level of force you deem necessary.

"We are hunting an animal, gentlemen. But it is an animal with a human being's insane mind. And even though it's just an animal, be advised that it made mincemeat out of more than forty heavily armed commandos the last time it was threatened. It has the instincts, strength and speed of a tiger with the fangs and claws to match. It also walks upright like the stuff you only see in nightmares. And there's evidence to suggest that it's ballistic-resistant, which means it might be as bulletproof as a hippo or rhino. Beyond all that, there are a lot of factors that we don't, and won't, know until we confront it. And then we'll have to adjust quickly, or we'll die a lot quicker. The only thing we are absolutely certain of is that this animal is loose somewhere in the state of Montana and confidence is high that we have a close fix, so watch your background, make good shots, and *do not* stop shooting until it goes down! Mount up!"

Exchanging fearful glances, Vernon and Gantry followed the HR team to the Lear and Vernon asked quietly, "Have you ever used your gun, Jeffrey?"

"I've never even pulled it!" gasped Gantry.

Vernon ran a few steps seeming to wrestle with his own thoughts and fears before he managed, "This is a hell of a way to start."

* * *

Although it was nearing dusk, Chaney was attuned enough to the wilderness surrounding the cabin to notice the furtive gray ghosts moving from tree to tree along the ridge. He glanced at Hunter who was sitting placidly on a nearby log, bolt-action Barrett positioned on his hip. Hunter was so calm he might have been watching ducks in a pond.

Walking over, Chaney asked, "You think it'll come for us before dark?"

Hunter shrugged, "Each one is different. You never know. But the wolves are close, and I don't hear any warnings." A pause. "Still, it came up on Bandit last night quietly enough not to spook him, and dropped him, so it knows how to move without making a sound. It knows how to kill like lightning. And it knows when to retreat."

"How do you know that?"

"Because the wolf we heard last night wasn't Bandit. Bandit was killed before he knew what hit him. What we heard was the howl of another wolf that must have seen what happened and got clear so it could warn the others. And that's when this thing decided to retreat, so I'm guessing that it's going to rethink its strategy before coming up here."

Hunter's eyes narrowed. "Yeah. Right now the whole pack knows there's an enemy around, and they're all alert. But they won't go after it alone. That's why you keep seeing so many wolves. They're sticking together. And they'll attack it together the same way they attack a hostile bear. All of them at the same time. But they might be biting off more than they can chew because this thing's a lot stronger than a bear. It's even stronger than the other two Scimitar. I'm thinking we might even be dealing with the leader of the pack, which means these insane eggheads probably did accomplish what you've been alleging, Chaney. They might have found the means of instilling a human consciousness into this thing. At least, enough to make it cautious, which is an advantage the other two didn't have. And I hate to say it, but I could be wrong. Instead of making it weaker, that could have made it twice as dangerous."

Chaney took a moment. "Well, which is it? First you say that would make it weaker and now you say it could make it stronger?"

"It makes it weaker to a point," Hunter explained patiently. "To a point, it depends on the will of the person who undergoes this transformation. It's the same with hunters or trappers. Some hunters are just cold-blooded killers who aren't much more than animals themselves. And some are civilized men who hunt with a code of honor. They respect what they're hunting. They play fair. And if whoever has done this to himself has some kind of personal code of honor, then maybe his nature might get in the way of this thing's insane determination to kill everything in sight. But if he's just a cold-blooded killer as a man, then he'll be just as cold-blooded in the form of this animal except he'll have a sense of caution, and that'll give it an advantage it's never had." He grimaced, "We're not gonna know until we meet up with it."

"Do we have anything *like* a plan?" Chaney asked not even bothering to conceal his nervousness. "I mean, we got the cameras and all, and these rifles, and grenades, but all that stuff is really just a roll of the dice." He sighed. "What I brought was the best I could get. But frankly, I think it'll take a gunship to stop this thing. And my chances of getting some gunships up here are less than zero. Hell, *I'm* not even supposed to be here! I'm probably out of a pension when I get back. But if I get off this mountain alive, I really don't think I'll care. And, by the way, you can keep the rifle. I didn't exactly get it through official channels."

Hunter laughed as he hefted the rifle. "It's a good piece. What'd you say the range was on this thing?"

"It's got a thirty-inch MOA at 1,400 yards. And these rounds will vaporize whatever they hit. Even if this thing is as bulletproof as ol' Luther was in Alaska, I think it'll feel this round a lot more than that bronze alloy Bobbi Jo was using."

"I'm looking forward to finding out," Hunter said steadily.

Chaney studied him for a moment. "Are you *enjoying* this? I'd think you'd be a little bit afraid! Like me!"

Hunter laughed, "Chaney, I live in a world where something is always trying to kill me, so I'm used to fear. Some people think the wilderness is a peaceful, beautiful place to appreciate Nature. To enjoy the flowers, the trees, the animals. But let me tell you; Nature is not peaceful and it's not your friend. Nature is indifferent to whether you live or die. Nature doesn't care. Everything in this wilderness is being hunted or it's hunting and killing. The second you walk into that tree line, you're being hunted, so a certain measure of fear is your friend. You need to always remember: Nature feeds on the weak. It feeds on the wounded, the tired, the old, and the young. But it also feeds on the strong with something stronger, so nobody, and nothing, is safe." His voice hardened. "Safe don't live up here, Chaney. It never did."

Chaney just watched as Hunter continued like a man with first-hand experience; "To stay alive in the wilderness you have to be more animal than man, and animals use cautious fear all the time. It's what keeps them alive and what keeps us alive, too. I mean, sure, you have to use every advantage you've got as a human being – your rifle, your pack, everything you've got – but you can't forget your animal instincts. I've done it my whole life, and the one thing I've learned is that everything out there is trying to kill me, so I'm always prepared. I'm always on guard. I'm always ready to fight." He gazed dead into Chaney's eyes. "The only thing that shouldn't be afraid in the deep woods is God. Everything else should carry a rifle."

After spending a long time gazing at what seemed like a rather inhospitable place now, Chaney asked gravely, "Are you planning to die up here?"

Hunter frowned and shook his head, "No. Every mountain man eventually comes down from the mountain. The cold starts to get to him. His eyesight begins to fade, and then he can't shoot anymore. His body breaks down a piece at a time. It's just old age, but it happens to us all. Most of the original frontiersmen went down to a town in their later years. Even ol' Liver Eatin' Johnson went down to a town and became a marshal, and it'd be hard to find a mountain man with his credentials. He was a legend in his own time. Then there was James Beckworth. He was as tough a frontiersman as you'd ever find, but he died down in the flatlands in Pueblo, Colorado. And Jim Bridger – maybe the greatest mountain man of them all – died on his farm outside Kansas City. And that's as flat as it gets. So all mountain men eventually come down from the mountain after old age catches up to them and leaves them more vulnerable to the elements, wears down their joints, and they can't shoot worth a damn. It's just a matter of time. And I'm already showing signs of age."

"What's wrong with *you*?" asked Chaney.

"Ah," Hunter rolled his shoulder, "I've got arthritis in both my shoulders and the cartilage in my knees is wearing out. My back can't carry what it used to. At least, not as easy as I did. I can't stand up to the cold like I could. Winter gets to me a lot easier now so, yeah, old age is setting in. I'll probably be going down to a town in the next five or six years. I'll deed this land to the county so they can make it a ranger station. They need one up here." A pause. "Yeah, this was a chapter of my life, and I like to think I made the most of it, but nobody can stay up here forever. We all come down from the mountain, in the end."

"Just how old are you, Hunter? It's hard to tell."

"I'm fifty-three," Hunter answered without hesitation. "But it ain't the years, Chaney, it's the milage. And I've got a whole lot of miles." He turned his face to the adjacent ridge and pointed, "Forty years ago I got it in me to hike from that ridge all the way down to Colorado. I was gonna take an old trail cut by Hugh Glass, one of the first mountain men. Yeah, ol' Hugh stayed up here just a bit too long and got killed up on the Yellowstone by a tribe of Arikawa. But he did what he loved right to the end. Anyway, when I was still a kid, I wanted to follow one of the first trails Hugh blazed down the Rockies. I was only twelve years old, and didn't have a clue what I was doing, but I had my backpack and a week's worth of food. Not much to go on. But, worst of all, I didn't have any experience.

"I made it as far as Wyoming before I was starving to death. I didn't even know what was good to eat or what would kill me, and I didn't have a rifle. I didn't know how to track or hunt or trap. And I had just about given up. I was exhausted, starving, and sitting all by myself beside this trail when an old man came walking by. He had a big white beard and sure looked like some kind of mountain man. He was holding a trap in one hand and fresh game in the other. He just stood there, staring at me as if he was deciding whether I was worth saving. Then he said, 'All right! Come on!' and took me to his cabin. It was a real rough place built out of logs, but it was solid. And warm. He was a trapper. Made his living trapping.

"Anyway, he told me I could leave any time I wanted, but I'd be a dead little mountain man if I did. And I wasn't all that smart, but I knew that I had no idea what I was doing, so I stayed with him for three years and he taught me everything he knew. He taught me how to track, how to shoot. What was safe to eat. How to find good, fresh food in the winter. How to skin and make clothes from the skins. And, most important, he let me keep for myself what I trapped, so I skinned and sold the game I bagged and built up a pretty good road stake. And, finally, when I was ready, I picked up my trip. But by then I had a good horse and tac, a good pack mule, and rifle. I reached Colorado in a couple of months and then I came back here. I passed my GED and began working with law enforcement to find people who get lost in these hills and, after a while, I gained a reputation.

I began to get asked to track people in other states. Then other countries."

He gestured wearily, "I found out it was all the same. A wilderness is just a wilderness. A jungle is just a jungle. Different animals, same kinds of threats, but things are mostly the same. So I built up a name for myself and it eventually turned it into a business. Big companies would pay me ridiculous amounts of money to find teams of their people lost in the desert or the Amazon. Funny thing is that I would have found their people for free, but I wasn't going to turn down an absurd amount of money, either. Then I discovered a local herb used by Australia aborigines for pain and sold it to a pharmaceutical company. Did the same thing in the Amazon. And by sheer accident I came across a flower used by Bedouin tribes for birth control. The women chew it after sex, and it keeps them from getting pregnant. And boy howdy, son, *did that one sell*! I guess you could say I've made real good money off birth control. I don't even look at my bank account anymore. But there's got to be a couple of billion in there."

"Where you gonna go when you leave this mountain?"

There was a slight, uncaring motion. "Hell, Chaney, I've got places all over the world. Got places in Paris and Rome. London. A penthouse in New York." He hesitated. "I kind of like New York, by the way. I like the opera. Then I got a nice town home in DC because I like to visit the Smithsonian, and they'll let me take things home so I can study them. I even have a little hut in Siberia. But I'll probably make Hawaii my main place. I have a house that's on the beach, and it's a safe distance from the closest volcano. Or neighbors, for that matter. It's quiet, and I don't want much else."

Chaney spent a long time staring into the surrounding trees, occasionally catching the flash of a gray shape dashing between the Ponderosa pines before he offered, "Well, you know, there's another possibility. We could both die up here.

Because, right now, it don't look like there's any guarantee either of us will be leaving this mountain alive."

Hunter chuckled, "Come on, Chaney. Be positive. We've got a lot on our side."

"Like what?"

"Well, we've got these two super-rifles you picked up. We've got hand grenades and a while suitcase full of detonation cord. We've got enough ordinance to hold off a small army. And both of us have seen this thing in action. It's not like we're rookies. We know how it moves. How it attacks. We know its weaknesses and – "

"*What weaknesses?*"

"What weaknesses! Hell, Chaney, it's got a lot of weaknesses! Its number one weakness is that it's *stupid*! I've killed two of them because they were stupid! I mean, sure, they know their way around a forest or jungle. They've got perfect instincts. Even better than a tiger. But if you put it in unfamiliar surroundings where it doesn't have any instinct to rely on, you can get the best of it. The one thing it doesn't do too well, is think."

Chaney was staring. "Again: We got some kind of plan?"

"You could call it that. I'm thinking about the det cord. If I'm right, it doesn't know what det cord is. To him it'll be nothing but string – a tripwire – something he can tear through without even trying. I'm thinking we rig a trap, let him walk into a whole spider web of det cord, and once he's wrapped up, detonate it. I don't care how tough he is, he won't survive that."

"But we'd have to know exactly which way he's coming. I didn't bring enough of the stuff to wire the whole mountain."

"How much you got?"

"We got three boxes. About three hundred feet."

"How big does it blow?"

Chaney calculated, "Well, det cord is synthetic C-4, which is basically TNT, so it blows pretty big. If you wrap a strand around any of those trees up there, it'll blow the tree clean in half. It's primarily used to clear landing zones. They wrap it around a bunch of trees and then blow out an area for helicopters. It's also wrapped around cement support pillars to knock down buildings. But those pillars aren't moving with the speed of a tiger. If this thing runs into a web of det cord, it won't need two seconds to get clear, so it'll take some real quick reaction on our part to blow it at the right second."

"You think det cord will do it?"

"If it's wrapped up in det cord," Chaney considered, "well, *yeah*. The problem is gonna be getting enough of it around him. It's not like the son of a bitch is gonna sit still for us to wrap him up. I mean, there's nothing wrong with your plan except the doing of it. How we gonna get it to stand still long enough?"

"The oldest trick in the book, Chaney. *Bait*."

With an agonized groan Chaney rocked back before exclaiming, "No! I *knew* you were gonna come up with some crazy-ass plan like this. You're gonna get us both killed! What are you gonna do? Set out some bait and *lasso him*?"

"I'm thinking the rage it has to kill me – if you're right – is gonna overrule its instincts and better judgment." Hunter was studying the ridge behind the cabin. "The most guarded approach to this cabin is that ridge. The trees up there are the thickest and, like a tiger, it'll want the most concealment. Because right now I think it's studying us. Same as a tiger would do because this thing has the same instincts as a tiger right down to the ground."

Chaney's face twisted in confusion. "A tiger has a weakness?"

"Sure, a tiger has weaknesses. For one, tigers don't chase prey. They're too big. Too heavy. It takes too much out of them, so this thing is gonna scout out the area until it decides on the closest point for an ambush – a place where it won't have to charge across open ground. A tiger hates open ground, and that's a weakness, because it sets limits on how it can approach its prey. And I'm thinking this thing is the same."

"You're betting your life on a theory?"

"It's all we got," Hunter answered. "Some say the Sabretooth tiger was nothing like a modern tiger. But I disagree. I think a tiger is a tiger. Look at your average house cat. Leave it outside long enough and it kills exactly like a Siberian. It'll sneak up on its prey and pounce on it from ambush, grab its throat, and choke it to death. A cat is a cat. Instincts don't change. So I think this thing is gonna do the same thing. It'll try and sneak up on us."

"You're gonna have a real short-lived regret if you're wrong."

"I don't think I'm wrong," Hunter stated. He stood, "Come on. Let's try and rig up some kind of fly trap."

Chaney followed.

"It better be a helluva fly trap."

CHAPTER SEVEN

S tanding safely outside the cage, Dante and Pinion observed the bestial shape of Dr. Cronis pacing impatiently on the far side of the bars safely contained within the escape-proof pod. There was no question, from its hulking frustration, that it would kill them like dogs if, God forbid, it escaped.

"Is that what I was like?" asked Pinion weakly.

Dante answered without interest, "You were actually much more frustrated, doctor. I was eventually forced to use a type of telepathy to calm you in your altered state. But, afterwards, you adjusted quickly enough. And now I believe you are safe to accompany me tonight when we take a closer look at Hunter's little fort."

Pinion turned toward the professor. "Was that what you meant about a harsher environment? We're going outside? The two of us?" He pointed, "What about Cronis?"

"The good doctor has not yet stabilized, and there are too many complications for any missteps, so we cannot risk taking him with us tonight. It's a very delicate task, and I myself did not fare well in my last survey of the mountain where Hunter lives. I had a very unfortunate, and unexpected, encounter with a wolf. And, although I ended it quickly, others sent a signal that we were close – a signal that Hunter surely recognized. It was a regrettable failure. But I believe we shall do much better this evening.

I have devised a plan where we may bypass the wolves and begin our reconnaissance much closer to Hunter's home where there is far less chance of detection." Dante turned as Colonel Blakely entered the basement. "Ah! Colonel! Is everything in order?"

Blakely nodded, "Everything's ready. I've posted men on the mountain to let us know when traffic gets scarce. I don't know when you want to leave, but we can be moving with five minutes notice."

"It will be several hours," answered Dante. "We will not go until dark. And the men who will accompany us?"

"They've been exposed to the transition. There shouldn't be any problems."

Dante mused, "Just curious, colonel. But what was the reaction among the men at the death of one of their brothers-in-arms?"

"No reaction at all, doctor. I hate to remind you, but they're not soldiers. They're mercenaries. They're in this for the money. And as long as they get paid, and get out of here like you promised, they're not going to care how many of the others get killed. It's all about the money. And a successful escape, of course. Are those choppers on standby?"

"Indeed, colonel." Dante was the steel soul of confidence so much that Pinion was almost inspired, himself. Dante continued, "I have procured three Sikorsky long-range helicopters – at great expense, mind you – equipped for this mission. After we conclude our business with Hunter, the men will load onto the transports and I have a secure facility where they will transition to their new, and quite flawless, identities." He waved, "Their money will be automatically deposited into their foreign accounts."

Blakely's stare hardened. "And *my* fee?"

"You shall obtain what you contracted for," answered Dante with an abruptly Cimmerian stare. "You shall receive *exactly* what you contracted for. And the rich province you desire shall be yours until the end of time." He continued to hold the colonel's gaze. "I shall fulfill my obligations, colonel, as long as you fulfill yours."

Blakely's tone hardened.

"Then that mountain man is as good as dead."

* * *

The airport at Helena, Montana, was the closest base for the Lear's required landing space. The HR team unloaded the cargo and set up a table in one of the hangars as Mack sent Vernon and Gantry on errands until they had rented enough vehicles. When Sanders had mildly inquired why they should do all the fetching – they sure could use a little help – Mack explained that it wouldn't do to have BDU-clad commandos at the desk of rent-a-car agencies and he didn't want local law enforcement to get wind of this operation, anyway.

When the two of them walked up to Mack after securing the last vehicle, Vernon gasped, "That's it, chief! It took us a while, but we got all three Humvees! All four-wheel drive and gassed up and fluids and tires are good! We checked everything twice!"

"Good boys," Mack nodded. "I'm proud of you. Now, get over to the table, get something to eat, and get dressed up like a couple of grown-up commandos." As they began to walk away, Mack called out, "Wait a minute, boys."

They turned.

"Have either of you even fired your piece since the academy?"

Exchanging glances, they shook heads.

"All right," Mack added, "then leave the rifles alone. Don't even pick one up. I don't want you shooting anything you're not supposed to. Jeffery, you're driving the second Humvee. Vernon, you'll be driving the third. I'll drive the first. We'll leave the HR guys free to use their rifles in case we encounter a not-so-welcome party."

"Uh," Gantry hazarded, "boss, is this what you meant when you said we could end up in Leavenworth?"

"No," Mack stated brusquely, "we haven't got to that part, yet. But, believe me, it's coming, and you'll know when it gets here. And so will everything else on that mountain. Now hurry up! And get yourselves one of those piss bottles! We won't be taking any breaks!"

At the table piled with ammo magazines, rifles, ballistic vests, BDUs and a large pot of stew, they quickly shed suits and donned commando gear. As Gantry was tightening his web belt and shoving extra magazines in every pocket, Vernon asked, "Hey, Jeffrey, what are we gonna do that can get us thrown into Leavenworth?"

Jeffrey glanced up.

"I think we already did it."

"What did we do?"

"We mentioned Chaney's name."

* * *

"This is the craziest damn thing I've ever done," managed Chaney as he secured more detonation cord around Hunter's position. "And I've done some pretty damn crazy things." He cast a glance at the wide-open space where Hunter planned to wait after dark for the beast to approach. "You do know it could just leap over all this stuff, don't you? And if we rig any more of it, the thing might notice the det cord and get suspicious."

Hunter glanced up from where he was carefully piling scrap metal at the base of the detonation cord's tie-down. "I'm more worried about whether it'll come into this clearing at all, Chaney." He brushed off his hands and lifted the Barrett. "If the wolves start up again, there's a good chance it'll just retreat like it did last night. This thing's not too bright, but it knows a warning when it hears one. That's why we have to make this as tasty as possible. As risk-free as we can. We have to make it so easy, it can't resist."

Casting a glance over the clearing where there was absolutely no cover from an attack, Chaney remarked, "Well, this is pretty damn easy. There is *nothing* between you and that tree line. The cabin is a good fifty yards away, and even if we slam the door in its face, that wood door will hold it for exactly zero seconds. You might slow it down with a few rounds from the Barrett. But I wouldn't bet the farm."

Hunter laughed, "I thought you said this explosive round would vaporize it."

"I said it would vaporize *a human being*. I didn't say what it would do to a damn prehistoric monster. We are dealing with the Great Beyond here, Hunter. Didn't you say that the one in England was different?"

"Wasn't *that* much different, Chaney. As far as the physical goes, it was a lot like Luther. Big. Fast. Fangs and claws. Meaner than hell. The one in England was just a little bit smarter. Which makes me think this one is gonna be even smarter than that. I mean … I don't know. But I think it's a safe bet."

"Huh," grunted Chaney. "Well, you been right about this thing so far. I ain't gonna bet against the house."

"No sense in underestimating it, Chaney. I was hunting a tiger once in India and I had set up what the locals call a 'bagha fall.' It was just a deadfall with stakes coming out of every side covered up at the top with a thin layer of bamboo. I had it perfectly concealed. I baited this Bengal Tiger with a dead goat hung out over the pit. But when that Bengal showed up, it stopped right at the edge of the pit and looked at where I was concealed in a tree. It knew where the pit was. It knew where I was. Hell, I don't even know why it bothered to show up. It knew it was all a trap. Then it leaped up, grabbed the goat in its teeth, and landed safe on the other side of the pit. One of the most powerful things I ever saw. I was so mesmerized by what it'd done, I forgot to take a shot. Then it just walked into the woods with the goat in its mouth like it'd done it a thousand times."

Chaney hadn't moved. "Did you ever get the tiger?"

"Yeah," Hunter sighed, "I eventually got him. I had to, really. It had killed six villagers and it was probably going to kill the rest of them." He took a second. "Most tigers do everything they can to avoid people or villages. But this one had lost half its teeth to a bullet. It'd lost its ability to take down its usual game. And since it's a lot easier to kill a human being than a water buffalo, it was a maneater now. It sometimes happens with large predators. They get injured or lose teeth or get sick and then they start preying on human beings. And it's sad that they have to be put down, but that's the way it is. And tigers are hard to hunt; I'll give them that. But, in the end, they don't stand a chance. The right man is the ultimate predator in any jungle."

"That's what scares me most," stated Chaney. "This thing *is* ultimately a man. All the scientists we arrested told me that this thing had human DNA just like you said. *But they confirmed it*! They kept repeating how it was the true missing link between animal and man! How it was half-human even 10,000 years ago when it was running around killing everything in sight. That's why they didn't have too much trouble synthesizing this serum. It's really not all that different from human blood. But then somebody got the bright idea of keeping the animal part of its DNA viable because of the long life span that it could generate in a human host. And, no, sir, they couldn't let *that* get away. The chance to live forever was too great a temptation even if it had a whole trainload of risk behind it. So, they did it, anyway, and put the entire world in danger. That's a mad scientist for you, boy. To hell that half the world is gonna die. Let's do it, anyway. At least the six of us, who happen to be the only inoculated people on the planet, will survive."

Chaney turned his head to see that the sun had almost disappeared behind a very distant ridge. He remarked, "Night comes fast up here."

Hunter straightened, "Yeah. It'll be full dark in about half an hour. It's time for you to go inside and do what we planned. Leave the back door open with the lights on and set up a shooting bench. If I miss, maybe you'll still hit it."

"And you'll be a dead son of a bitch leaving me to fight this thing alone," observed Chaney miserably. "Course, I don't think I'll live long enough to get mad about it."

* * *

Pacing relentlessly behind the bars, the creature paused and once more tested the strength of its enclosure. But it did not launch itself at the cage. Rather, it reached up and pulled experimentally at the copper-toned steel.

A red haze like the scarlet surface of a sea with a rage as deep as that sea made its eyes glow like boiling blood as it stood without moving. Something was piercing its mind like infinitesimal streaks of white – *lightning*! – compelling it to think. There was something strange in the tiny bolts of electricity cutting through its brain. It was like an invasion. Like something corrupting its purity.

It had never known corruption. It could remember millennium of slaughter. It could remember thousands of years of savagely killing and hungrily feasting. It could remember all the visions of all the time its world changed from red lakes of fire into cliffs of ice disappearing into the distance. Each vision was alive in every cell of its mind, every fiber of its being. Not that it recognized time any more than it recognized anything else. No, it only knew its own desires, its own lusts … and the blood.

Yet even in the primitive bestial brain that controlled what little it had ever decided through conscious thought, it sensed that this invasion was something unnatural to itself. It knew it was unnatural because it had so rarely paused to think.

It had never hesitated to pursue what it wanted to pursue. It had never hesitated to consider the extensive black claws protruding from its monstrous hands or the fangs distending from its jaws. It had never considered anything but killing.

Somewhere in its cellular memory it remembered clinging to the neck of a gigantic thing and tearing out its throat as the creature bellowed in fear and pain. It remembered clinging to its neck and tearing at it with fang and claw ...

And the blood ...

But something was different now that made it difficult for it to find itself. Like another force was reducing it. It straightened, trying to establish the strength that it knew so well, but a ghost was smothering it. A ghost that it could not escape.

Baring fangs, it stalked forward. Despite this white specter spreading through its mind, it still knew the bloodlust to kill. It knew the lust so well that it could already taste the blood. And knew it would not be denied.

Soon it would kill.

And kill ... and kill ...

* * *

Colonel Blakely motioned for two commandos to step back as he placed a hand on the rear on the trailer parked in a lookout area along the road leading past Hunter's house.

Blakely had pulled the truck onto an overlook because it was only a scant mile from Hunter's home. It had been decided, and not by him, that there was less chance the wolves would give warning if the creatures began so close to their target. Indeed, without climbing up the mountain slope through the ubiquitous wolf pack, there was even a chance the creatures might come upon Hunter with no warning at all. At least, that was how the inscrutable Dr. Dante had reasoned it. And far be it from Blakely to dispute with the hand willing to grant him eternal life and the most depraved kingdom the world would ever know.

A traitorous colonel already wanted for espionage, Blakely had, at first, balked at taking this job on U. S. territory. His specialty before this high-risk stunt had been with overseas operations because he had tremendous respect for American law enforcement and his face was on every Most Wanted list on the internet.

He had a self-preserving fear for American lawmen because they were always more cunning than one expects and fiercer when confronted than their reputations allowed. And Blakely certainly had no desire to tangle with the military arm of the federal government, which would surely be here if they had any suspicion that such a highly illegal experiment involving a weapon of mass destruction was occurring on American soil.

If the authorities knew what was being processed in the basement of that hospital, they would shoot first and never ask questions at all. Then they'd set fire to the place before bulldozing it. And, just for good measure, they'd lay a solid block of cement on top of it and establish a military guard that would be present for as long as this world should last. But that would only be *after* they arrested the scattered survivors and put them in permanent cells at Guantanamo Bay because creating a doomsday weapon like this creature was a crime absolutely outlawed by every nation on the planet.

Even China and Russia weren't reckless enough to create an abomination like this. If it escaped, it would be as much a threat to them as it would be to the entire world.

And to think that the fury of this mindless killing machine could be channeled so that it would kill Hunter, alone, was the depths of insanity. It lived only to kill, and it wasn't particular about what or who. Blakely already understood that much. So, as far as he was concerned, to create this creature at all was akin to suicide.

Ignoring his trembling hand, Blakely opened the rear of the trailer.

Inside, the trailer was a black pit like the surface of the ocean beneath a moonless night. A sliver of moon cast faint illumination across the commandos and the overlook but the inside of the trailer was a deep block of inky, impenetrable blackness.

Blakely heard the hoarse, bestial breathing before he saw the image and a split-second later a gargantuan shape broke the plane of darkness – a shaggy, wedge-shaped head – before the creature slowly emerged. It rose out of the solid wall of black like some monster rising from the depths of the blackest surface of the sea. It came inch by inch, slowly, as the huge shoulders emerged, and then its gorilla-chest and the tigerlike hind legs were visible. It walked on its back legs like a man, making it more manlike than beastlike. Nor did the colonel fail to notice the stark white, distended fangs or the black claws that threw back the light.

Unaware he was retreating as the beast advanced, Blakely somehow still managed to lift his hand and point toward the tree line on the far side of the two-land road. He opened his mouth to speak but he could form no words.

Beholding the beast without the safety of steel bars restraining it was altogether a far more shocking experience than gazing upon it through a cage. In this moment there was nothing to stop it from lashing out with that blinding speed and taking Blakely's head off at the neck and then killing the other guards before they could fire a shot.

The beast dropped heavily to the ground landing as a second shape emerged from the darkness of the van. It, too, seemed to come cautiously into the starlight and then it leaped forward to land beside the first, more enormous creature. The larger beast turned its head for an instant as if communicating something to the smaller one and, without casting Blakely another glance, they took one step and leaped cleanly over the road to land in the distant bush where they vanished into the trees.

Only then did Blakely release a breath. He wiped sweat from his face and bent, hands on knees, before he managed, "All right. Jack the truck up and drag out the spare. Take one tire off the back to make it look like we're changing tires up here. Nobody's gonna think twice about us if they come by." He leaned against the van. "Now we'll just wait for them to they get back. Then we'll load up and take 'em to the base."

Neither guard moved.

Blakely raised his face.

"Move it! I wanna get out of here when those freaks get back!"

* * *

Seated on a log he'd been chopping for firewood, Hunter suddenly lifted his face to the forest. His eyes narrowed as he searched the darkness along the ridge. After a few moments he saw wolves moving randomly. They displayed no signs of alarm.

Outside the open door where Chaney was poised with a rifle, Hunter scanned the long wall of darkness encircling the cabin. Sensing some kind of shift in the night, Hunter took a step forward, lifting the rifle. He listened for the wildlife that could not be seen – the birds and multitudinous smaller creatures that made such a racket after sunset, and it seemed as if the noise had suddenly grown just a tiny bit less. It was as if something had scared all of them at the same time and they were doing what they instinctively did when frightened.

They were silent. They were hiding. And they would remain silent and hidden until whatever spooked them had passed. And with so much of the forest falling silent at the same time it was curious to Hunter why the wolves were still behaving as if there was nothing to fear. Some were merely pacing idly along the wood line.

Hunter glanced at Moe who was sleeping soundly beside his post. Moe had come out of the woods an hour ago, saw Hunter, walked over, and collapsed on the ground beside him, instantly falling asleep. But not even Moe had been roused by anything in the night.

It occurred to Hunter that perhaps this prehistoric animal was not perfectly silent at all. Perhaps there was another factor to explain why the wolves hadn't detected it.

Wolves and bears typically ignore scents they're familiar with. And if this creature was close, and they recognized the scent of man or machinery, then they might not react with alarm. They might assume it was just the scent of another man, or the scent of another wolf cloaked in the smoke of a campfire. There could be a dozen reasons why they might not react, and Hunter was angry that he hadn't considered the possibility before now.

Maybe he was already too old for this.

But the rest of the forest was indeed quiet as if something unknown had passed their way. Then two wolves on the ridge suddenly leaped up from their resting positions and spun facing the slope to Hunter's left.

Scanning slowly and acutely, Hunter clicked off the safety on the Barrett. He knew he had an explosive round already chambered, and he didn't need to check the Bushwhacker again. The rifle was loaded with five big, dangerous rounds.

Simply from habit Hunter counted the rounds he could fire before reloading. He had five in the rifle and five more in the Bushwhacker. And although experience suggested to Hunter that there was simply no way any natural creature could charge through so many devastating rounds, he reminded himself that this animal wasn't 'natural.'

Hunter didn't even glance at the detonation cord because it was behind him and checking it required him to take his eyes off the ridge. And setting the monitors five feet above the ground was an early warning system easily bypassed by an intelligent creature. All it had to do was crawl until it reached the edge of Hunter's home.

If the rounds Hunter was holding didn't, at least, slow it down, he'd never outrun it to the all but useless defense of the cabin where they'd wired the back porch with a substantial length of det cord. But such a lethally close detonation, should the creature walk into it, would level the entire cabin, of course, leaving them all in the open – if they survived at all – and that would throw them into a truly desperate face-to-face fight.

That wasn't a scenario Hunter wanted to endure. In a perfect world, he'd see the beast and drop it with one round from the rifle. In an all-but-doomed last stand he'd draw the Bushwhacker and put five rounds of .500 Magnum into it at close range. But, at this moment, neither of those scenarios seemed probable. Reluctant to admit it, Hunter had to accept the fact that the most likely outcome would be that all the rounds combined wouldn't even slow it down and it'd survive to rip his arms and legs off.

It continued to feel strange to Hunter that he had seen and sensed nothing. His life had been saved time and again by his animal instincts. And this was no different. Most apex predators quickly perfected the art of silent stalking, but all those skills are useless if the prey has a sixth sense that alerts them to danger even when it makes no sound, and Hunter had long ago developed keen senses for detecting threats.

A sudden explosive howl from the wood line made Hunter turn with the rifle leveled at the black line of forest at the top of the ridge. The wolf's agonized cry was gone as quickly as it came and then the other wolves were cautiously moving in that direction. They were slowly creeping forward as if closing the final steps on an unsuspecting prey. They would step and pause, faces uplifted and eyes darting, before silently stepping again.

Hunter didn't need to look to know that every wolf in the vicinity was now on full alert. There were no gray, ghostly shapes slinking between trees. There was no sound. It was like the entire forest was holding its breath in a paralyzing, frozen fear.

In the sea of silence Hunter clearly heard Chaney's voice from the porch where he had emerged from the cabin. Even Chaney could sense the change in the forest and wouldn't be confined to the structure any longer. And Hunter knew all too well that the FBI agent wanted a shot at this thing, too.

"The ridge!" whispered Chaney.

"*I know*!" Hunter grimaced. "*Get back inside*!"

Hunter could practically see leaves moving in the distant darkness of the ridge. He wasn't even looking for shapes. He was watching for the darkness to deepen between the trees and then he'd take a shot with the rifle whether he could identify it or not.

At this point, hitting it first was the best – if only – option. At least they'd see if these experimental rounds had any effect or – and Hunter tried not to worry – whether they'd work at all. If they didn't even discharge, then Hunter would be left with the revolver. And he didn't like his chances with that because what a .500 Magnum could do to a block of cement was no true measure of what it could do to a bullet-resistant, prehistoric cannibal.

As if from nowhere an idea occurred to Hunter and he mentally counted the spare rifle cartridges on the bandoleer slung from his shoulder. Then he leveled the rifle, aiming at the largest tree on the slope, and fired.

Beside Hunter, Moe roared and twisted.

The explosive round worked just as Hunter had hoped. It hit the oak tree and exploded in an eruption of splintered wood and flame bright enough to light up a big section of the ridge. And in that frantic, fleeting split-second, Hunter glimpsed and then heard the injured scream of an image crouching in the shadow. It was so quick as to not even be there. But it *was* there. It had only been visible for a tenth of a second, but Hunter saw it clearly enough.

It was regrettable that the Scimitar had moved so fast Hunter hadn't been able to track it for a second shot. But as the round had hit the tree, the titanic shape of the beast had twisted away from the explosion with a scream. And for the briefest split-second, the creature glared at Hunter with a plain expression of shock. Then it made a quick move and was gone.

Moe was grunting and swaying, preparing for battle.

Hunter continued to watch the tree line.

It had vanished, but Hunter knew that it now had an idea of what it would face down in this clearing. It would be more cautious now, and that was a disadvantage. The less it knew about what awaited it, the better Hunter's chances of taking it down. But now it would be even more guarded, and that multiplied the threat. But throwing some light on the situation had seemed like a good idea, and Hunter had no regrets. Without looking at the rifle, he shoved another round into the magazine. The reload left him with nineteen rounds in the bandoleer and he'd use every one of them if he could cut this creature down. He'd shoot it until he was out of rifle rounds and then empty every round from the Bushwhacker into its skull.

Then he'd burn it.

Leaping forward at the same time, the wolves suddenly charged away from the tree line and down into the clearing.

Hunter leveled again and fired the rifle at a tall Ponderosa Pine. The tree had no branches at the base and the rich tar of the pine would set the tree on fire in seconds, casting the entire ridge into the light. The explosion was exactly what Hunter had hoped, and he instantly worked the bolt on the rifle preparing for a fast second shot. But what he saw caused him to hesitate.

He swung the rifle left and aimed at the now-visible creature. Then Hunter saw another horrifying image and shifted aim to his right.

Adrenaline erupted in Hunter's chest.

Clearly in the fast-burning flame, Hunter saw *two* Scimitar standing upright on the ridge staring over him. The fire was burning energetically into the pine and there was no mistaking it. There were two Scimitar. And they were setting up intersecting angles of attack. They were coordinating with intelligence and precision.

This wasn't the attack of an animal.

This was the attack of a soldier.

Hunter shifted the rifle to target the largest beast and, as he put his cheek to the stock, it disappeared into the pitch black between the trees. Hunter instantly swung aim to the second beast, but it was already gone. There was nothing on the ridge but a tall Ponderosa Pine burning to submerge the whole glade in wavering orange light.

"Holy shit!" Chaney cried from the porch. Hunter risked a glance as Chaney stepped forward, pointing violently. *"Did you see that?"*

Hunter grimaced.

Yeah, he'd seen it. He'd seen it all too well. And it was something he hadn't prepared himself for – not mentally or physically. And all of a sudden the weapons he was holding seemed very, very inadequate. Hunter had the impression that he was waving a stick at a Grizzly charging down on him.

Moe ran forward to charge up the ridge.

"*No!*" shouted Hunter. "Moe! Come here, boy! Come on, Moe! Yeah! That's a good boy! Come on back now! You're staying inside tonight!"

With a last, angry glance at the ridge, Hunter abandoned his post and walked toward Chaney, who was staring in obvious shock at the ridge.

Chaney pointed at the trees with the rifle. "Did you see that?" he repeated. "There's two of the them! Two of them, Hunter!" He turned haplessly to his left and right before, "We gotta get outta here, man! Or we gotta call the National Guard or the NSA or something! We gotta call the damn Army! *The real army!*"

Shouldered by Moe, Hunter walked over the det cord not caring whether it blew up under his feet or not, and into the cabin. He collapsed in a chair at the table and spoke wearily to Chaney, "Leave the door open. I think they're gone, but I'd rather see 'em coming if they're not." He hung his head in exhaustion, drawing deep breaths. "Moe will stay inside with us. If they come back, he'll hear them before we do. And now that he knows something's out there, he'll have his guard up. They won't get close again without Moe warning us."

Chaney was still standing where he'd been.

"*That's it?*" he shouted. "Did you see the size of those things? We need to call in the army, man! This is serious! I mean, I can see the two of us taking down one of those things with all this ordinance! But I can't see us taking down *two of them* with less than a damn gunship! And we ain't got a damn gunship!"

Gravel crunching on the narrow drive leading to the cabin caused Chaney to turn, tightly lifting the rifle closer. He ran to the edge of the door and glanced out. Then he slid down the back wall until he could see the drive and risked a glance.

Headlights had stopped twenty feet from the cabin. It was three pairs of headlights in a row of military precision and Hunter thought the vehicles were Humvees. Chaney leveled the rifle using the corner for support as a door opened and a big man walked into the glaring illumination. Fully visible, the man lifted both arms as he shouted, "Chaney! It's me! Mack!"

Standing close, Hunter saw Chaney's face soften in confusion. Then Chaney slowly lowered the rifle as if not believing what he was hearing. Finally, after glancing at Hunter, he called out hesitantly, "Mack? Is that you?"

"Yes, it's me you dumb son of a bitch!" Mack shouted, dropping both arms. "You gonna make me stand out here all night after I done drove halfway across Montana to find your sorry ass?"

With another glance at Hunter, who shrugged, Chaney lowered the rifle and called out, "You picked a hell of a time to visit, Mack! But come on up if you're loaded for bear! We got plenty for you!"

CHAPTER EIGHT

S till waiting at the outlook, Blakely reasoned that nothing could have shocked him more than the image of the two creatures emerging from the blackness of the trailer, but he discovered he was wrong when the first beast leaped the two-lane road to land, scattering gravel, directly beside him. One second later the second beast crashed onto the plateau.

From reflex alone Blakely had spun and reached for his pistol but the largest creature merely stood before him breathing heavily and staring down with a malevolent red glare. One side of its head was badly scorched. Blood ran in rivulets from its gaping jaws, and the shaggy fur was charred to reveal blackened skin beneath. Blakely was afraid to even look at the second beast. He had already seen more than he could process.

Without waiting for what might seem like instruction, Blakely reached over, undid the latch on the truck, and threw up the panel. Without words the first beast leaped into the darkness and the second followed. When they moved deeper into the black interior, Blakely quickly pulled down the door and secured the latch.

Only then was Blakely aware that he was faint with adrenaline. He took a moment to compose himself before motioning impatiently to the guards still standing in what seemed like shock beside the rear tire.

"Hurry up!" he shouted. "We ain't got all night!"

* * *

Introductions were not even exchanged as Hunter, Chaney, and Mack took seats at the kitchen table. Mack had barely cast Moe a glance. It was as if the senior FBI agent was accustomed to sharing a cabin with a Grizzly.

It took Chaney exactly two minutes to explain to Mack what had transpired before his unexpected arrival. Hunter was amused that Mack heard every word without the slightest indication of skepticism. In fact, it seemed like the FBI man had anticipated exactly what Chaney so grimly detailed.

The Hostage Rescue commandos were stationed in a secure perimeter around the cabin. Two of them had ventured into the forest and returned with reports of scattered tracks that they couldn't identify. It only took Hunter three seconds before he confirmed the tracks belonged to a Scimitar. Then he assured them that he'd track the creatures out in the morning, but it was too dangerous to venture into the pitch-black forest. If these creatures had the night vision of a cat, they had every advantage in the dark.

Mack was the very soul of an ultimately unexcitable senior field agent of the FBI. As Chaney unraveled the story, Mack's weathered face remained grim and implacable so much so that Hunter could not imagine that visage ever expressing surprise. If Chaney had told Mack that they had been attacked by Martians armed with laser beams Mack would have just nodded, as if he expected as much.

The youngest two FBI agents who had joined the HR team in the light of the still-burning pine, seemed like fish out of water. They followed the rescue team's every move without asking a word and it was obvious that this was their first time in the field. Chaney noticed it, too, because he finally asked, "You bring a couple of greenhorns, Mack?"

Mack sniffed, and said, "Them boys have gotta get combat experience at some point, Chaney. I can't think of a better way for them to do it than hanging out with the likes of us." He rubbed snot from his nose. "Ah, man! It's cold up here! A lot colder than I thought it'd be for this time of the year."

Hunter laughed.

Mack continued, "Yeah, I was sort of expecting you to be neck deep in something like this, Chaney. I read the file on Alaska." He looked at Hunter, nodded. "That was good work up there." He glanced around. "You know, I was sort of expecting you to live in a fancier place, Hunter. Hell, I was expecting you to live in a bunker! One would come in handy right about now."

Hunter muttered, "This fight will be settled outside. And a bunker wouldn't do you any good. They'd find a way in."

"How do you know so much about Hunter?" asked Chaney.

"Ah, hell, Chaney, the NSA has a file on you and Hunter three inches thick. Since that ball-bashin' fiasco began in Alaska, they've kept tabs on both of you. They've monitored your contacts in the scientific community. Your friends, your enemies. They even got a psychological profile on Hunter from the Behavioral Analysis Unit. Damndest thing I ever read. I ain't never read anything as damn crazy as his file. Is it true you got a mansion on the beach in Hawaii but you prefer to live in this old run-down place?"

"It's solid," shrugged Hunter. "Keeps the rain off my head."

"Not much for hula parties, huh?"

Hunter responded easily, "I like the peace and quiet. So, what are your orders on this, Mack?" He studied the agent's face. "Or do you have any?"

"I ain't got none," Mack stated, flat. "This is a command decision. I haven't cleared it with Washington and there's no use trying. They'd never okay this stunt. They'd leave both of you to die. I saw that much in the Alaskan file."

"You keep mentioning this file," Chaney noted. "I never saw a file on what went down in Alaska. How'd you get it?"

"*Illegally*," stressed Mack. "If anybody knew what kind of favors I called in to get that file, I'd be burned at the stake. Hell, if they could, they'd make it *retroactive*. They'd fire my ass and date it for last week. But that file makes it clear that you guys stepped on a lot of expensive toes up there. Somebody had big plans for this animal." He grunted, "You both know that this debacle was sanctioned from the top, don't you? This mad scientist had the backing of the president and about a dozen world leaders from the get-go. It wasn't until the damn thing escaped and started killing American servicemen, and it looked like it'd go on killing until the end of time, that the president short-sheeted the original plan and sent in Hunter to make it go away. They all knew that if this crazy-ass super-predator reached a town and left a trail of blood that would fertilize the Sudan, then their whole operation would all go public, and nothing would cover it up. And that's the one place they didn't want it to go. The government might have paid for all this, but it sure wasn't a government-sanctioned project. Congress wasn't involved. No oversight committee knew about it. No, sir. This was the work of the nameless elite."

Mack leaned back. "Make no mistake, Chaney. They didn't order you to kill that thing because it was out of control. They didn't give a damn about how many bodies it left in the dirt. They ordered you to kill it because the whole thing was about to go public! And they knew that, after all the question-asking, especially with scientists that can't be trusted to keep a secret, this blood-soaked affair would go wide and that'd be the whole ball of wax. Some would go to jail, some would fall on their sword, and some would run to non-extradition countries. And then some would be killed by their buddies for messing it all up."

Chaney scowled, "Did you happen to see what their original plan was?"

"*Was!*" exclaimed Mack. "*It still is!* They've never abandoned their plan, Chaney! They still think this creature holds the secret to a life as long as 'ol Methuselah's! I mean, the existence of this thing makes the idea of nuclear bunkers obsolete! Why in the hell would you hide underground for three years when you'll heal up instantly from radiation poisoning, survive any injury, and just keep booking? What kind of malignant, megalomaniacal, power-mad homicidal bastard would walk away from a dream like *that*?" His eyes widened. "I wouldn't!"

"You would if you got a good look at what this thing can do, Mack. You ain't seen that monster in action. And, believe me, it only takes once."

"I haven't seen it in action," Mack agreed, "but I've seen the file on it. It was a badass back in the day and it's a badass now. Only, this ain't back in the day. The time for this animal has come and gone and, frankly, I don't think this old world can survive it twice. The Ice Age was the only thing that stopped it the first place. I got no idea what can stop it now. And, so, I came to help you two put it back in the grave. Where it shoulda' *stayed*!"

"There's two of them," stated Hunter, no expression.

Mack nodded at what was apparently old news. "I'd say there's *three*. The one up here right now. The one in Alaska. And the one in England. I got a mention of what went down in England, too. My NSA sources are good." He stared hard at Hunter. "If you don't mind me saying, I think that bear came in awfully handy with those dire wolves or whatever the hell they were. My source might be a great spy, but he's not an archeologist."

"Paleontologist," muttered Chaney.

"Whatever."

"You don't understand, Mack." Chaney's voice assumed a lower level of fatigue. "Hunter's telling you that there's two of them *up here*. Right now! They were here tonight, and we managed to drive 'em off but, believe me, they'll be back."

"They were testing our defenses," commented Hunter without tone. "It's instinctive for an animal – any animal – to test the defenses of its prey before they attack. And apex predators are experts at it. One of the reasons they live to an old age in a jungle that doesn't forgive a single mistake is because they don't just rush in. They'll study you until they know you better than you know yourself. They'll know what time you wake up, what time you go to the bathroom, what time you go to bed. They'll know where you're gonna be at a certain time of day and whether you normally have someone with you or if you carry a rifle." He glanced at Mack's surprised expression. "Yeah, Mack, they know a lot about weapons. And they're good at luring you to where you don't normally carry one and where you're normally alone. And that's when they'll hit you. When you're most defenseless."

Hunter stared along the wall before he added, "These two are trying to be different from the others I've tracked and killed. They're trying real hard to control the rage of this animal with their conscious minds. I'm sure they've tinkered with this serum so that they'll retain a measure of their human consciousness. To be smart. To pick and choose their prey more carefully. But it won't work. The power of this creature can never be controlled. They can try, but they'll fail. Hell, they're already failing. They just don't know it. Because they didn't use any caution tonight. They were going to attack me in the glade, and not even a starving tiger would have done that. This creature's rage to kill overrules anything and everything that would make an apex predator hesitate – that would make *any animal* with a sense of caution hesitate. Either one of those freaks would attack a battalion without a second thought." He grimaced, "They're trying to control what can't be controlled. They've signed their own death warrants with this insanity."

Mack asked, "Does the thing actually believe that it's unkillable?"

Hunter frowned, "Yeah. It believes it. But it's not unkillable. It's just hard to kill."

Mack seemed to absorb the news with a lot of consideration. Then, finally, he asked, "Do you think I've brought enough men?"

The question was directed at Hunter, but Chaney answered, "If you haven't brought a gunship, you haven't brought enough men." He shook his head, "I'm sure that file was thorough, Mack, but you can't really appreciate the scope of this threat until you've faced it. This ain't just a pissed-off prehistoric asshole. This is a genuine monster! Even in its heyday, surrounded by the T-Rex and crap, it was *still* a monster. Ain't that right, Hunter?"

Hunter gestured vaguely, "T-Rex was extinct 93 million years before this thing even came on the scene. But you're right. If T-Rex had been around, I'm sure this animal would have just considered it another meal." A pause. "I don't think it has the mind to know fear. At least, not in its original form. And I don't know what these crazy scientists have done to it, but we can bank on it not being too far removed from its true nature. It's the ultimate predator and I don't think any kind of science can take that out of it."

"I think that's why they want it," offered Mack. "It's the perfect weapon."

"No," Chaney objected, "they only want what it can give them – a really long damn life. But because Hunter has put two of them in the ground, they want to remove him from the situation so they can finish their plan."

"And what would that be?"

"I don't know," shrugged Chaney. "Maybe one of them is crazy enough to believe he can rule the world with all that physical power. But immortality and perfect health aren't gonna do you much good if you've got the best tracker in the world on your ass, especially when he has a proven track record of putting freaks like you in the grave. And I don't know how much good a long life is gonna do you if a whole world wants to arrest you for illegal biological warfare, so they've got to have a bigger plan that just living for a real long time." He seemed to study the table before adding, "Only one thing is for sure. They're not doing all this just so they can live forever in misery. There's a bigger picture. And I'm betting it has something to do with ruling the damn world." He hesitated. "It always does. It's a motive as old as the hills and there's no sense changing it now. Ruling the world will always be the maniacal ambition of the criminally insane for as long as the insane shall last."

After a moment Mack stated, "Well, let's concentrate on the two that we've got up here right now. Anybody got any ideas? Because I'm not really one to just sit around waiting for the next attack." He lifted a hand toward the door. "We've got six heavily armed, experienced operators dying to take a shot at one of these things. Why don't we go after *them*?"

"With two rookies tagging along?" asked Chaney. "This hunt won't be for the faint of heart, Mack. And if those HR operators don't have combat experience in a war zone, even they're gonna be at a disadvantage. Trust me; I was a combat vet before I joined the FBI. I'd seen my share of hot action. But even I was taken off-guard by the scope of that thing.

"I'll send the rookies back down the mountain and put 'em in a hotel," Mack remarked. "I didn't know things were gonna be this bad."

"Just bring 'em along," stated Chaney, dropping his head.

"They don't have any experience, Chaney."

"Neither did I before Iraq, Mack! Neither did you! And those two boy scouts have to get baptized somewhere, somehow. You said it yourself. And we're veterans. We can keep 'em out of harm's way if everything goes to hell."

Mack frowned, staring at nothing.

Hunter commented, "Mack is right. Tracking them to their lair is the smartest play. But we don't know where they've gone to earth. And, in human form, they look just like anybody else, so they could be anywhere. A hotel. Somebody's home. A rental. Hell, they could be in an RV at one of a thousand parks around here. For all we know, they're somewhere in Glacier National where there's nothing *but* RVs and trailers and hotels. But one thing is certain. Letting them pick the time and place to attack is not what we want to do. If nothing else, we should make ourselves scarce." He paused. "They came here for me, so I have to come up with a plan that makes them think they're getting what they want."

"So you're the target," stated Mack. "I figured as much. I mean, I knew their primary target wouldn't be Chaney. If they wanted Chaney, they'd just ambush him at his beach house. I don't think they'd consider sand dollars and jellyfish much of a deterrent." He glanced at the gun case. "What else you got?"

"Just what you see," said Hunter.

Chaney asked, "What'd your boys bring?"

"Remington 700s. Glock nines. Flash bangs. CN cannisters. I did make sure we had a Remington 870 Marine Magnum for each man and they're loaded with slugs. And, right now, I think a shotgun is what they need. That slug is a solid ounce of lead going down range at a thousand feet per second. That's *got* to knock it down."

"Don't bet on it," Chaney said morosely. "A nine won't even break its skin." He paused. "I don't know about the Remingtons. I don't know about the slugs. But I wouldn't bank on either one tearing through its skin. The one we fought in Alaska was hit point blank with a fifty and it just jumped up and ran off. Not a drop of blood. So these things might not ultimately bulletproof, but they're pretty damn close."

"*Nothing* is ultimately bulletproof, Chaney. If you get a big enough gun, you can shoot through *anything*." Mack glanced at the heavy Bushwhacker that Hunter still wore in a cross-draw holster. "You think that thing can bust its hide?"

"I don't think its gonna give me any choice," Hunter remarked. "But I think this pistol has a good chance. And as far as your guys go, I've got a collection of hunting rifles that I use for elk and moose. I've got a .458 Weatherby, a .600 Nitrous, and two .300 Winchesters. Your men can help themselves."

Chaney offered, "I've got a crate of M-67s. A grenade might cut it up. But there's no telling. We don't really know the true strength or weakness of the enemy. And that's always the first rule. Know your damn enemy."

Mack: "Well, all we've got are M-4s, shotguns, and Remingtons, which are good enough for human beings. But I'm not sure what kind of ordinance you need for a prehistoric damn serial killer." He seemed crestfallen. "Is there a gun store below?"

Hunter remarked, "There is. But whatever you'd find this time of year will just be blind luck. They might have something for elk or Grizzly. But I can't guarantee any ammo. Ammo's been in short supply lately." He sighed, "Ah, this thing's gonna be over before we can get more weapons, anyway. I'm surprised they haven't already attacked us again. I must have hurt one of them worse than I thought. And they've never been hurt before. It's a new experience. Right now, they're licking their wounds. They thought they couldn't be hurt. Now they've found out that they can be. They're re-assessing their original plans."

"What do you *think* they're going to do?" asked Chaney.

"They've retreated to see how long it takes to heal up." Hunter spent a moment staring out the open door. "They've fallen back to come up with a new strategy." A pause. "You gotta remember that they're scientists, and none of them are used to this kind of conflict. They're off-balance right now. But once they confirm that they'll heal up from an injury, they'll get their bearings. And that will make them more confident. They might just decide to ditch all the stalking and take us in a rush. I wouldn't doubt it. And something tells me we shouldn't bank on any assumptions we have about them."

Chaney stared before, "What do you mean?"

"I mean, we think that there's two of them," Hunter answered. "But what if there's three? Or four? Or what if there's a whole pack of them – twenty or thirty – and they'll come at us next time with all they've got and all we've have are a handful of men with what are largely ineffective rifles? It'll be like the Alamo or Custer's last stand. It'll just be a matter of time before we're overrun. So I'll say it again; the best chance we have is to ambush them in their liar. If we can find where they've gone to earth, we can take 'em by surprise when they're in human form."

"That's a gray area," muttered Mack. "You're talking about killing an unarmed human being, Hunter. That's plain ol' murder."

Chaney responded angrily, "Would you rather they change back into monsters before we shoot 'em, Mack? Because I can tell you right now that that didn't work out for us too good in Alaska! We never did have a chance to confront him when he was human but, if we had, I would have just shot his human ass graveyard dead and wrote it up as self-defense."

Mack lifted an uncaring wave, "Ah, hell, boys, I'm not particular about how we end this thing as long we end it without – *especially me* – getting killed." He looked hard at Hunter. "How do you reckon they got this high without you knowing they were out there?"

"Transport," Hunter said simply. "Somebody brought them up here in a van or truck. Or maybe even an RV. They probably got out at the overlook and bypassed the wolves.

Then it's a short trip to this cabin. It'd take them less than an hour, so there wouldn't be an alarm. I don't see how else they could have done it."

Mack's tone was annoyed. "That would – very unfortunately – mean they've got some capitalistic help."

"You mean mercenaries," stated Chaney.

"Not just any mercenaries, buddy. A guy like Dante doesn't hire gangbangers knocking over local seven-elevens. He's gonna hire the best. Guys with skill sets, trigger time, experience in special warfare. Veterans. The kind of guys that are probably wanted in a dozen countries for illegal snatch and grabs and occasionally mowing down a church full of women and children." Mack scowled. "Needless to say, gentlemen, we may find ourselves outgunned."

Chaney ventured, "You certain that you can't call for backup, Mack?"

"Chaney, I already told you. They want what this creature can give them. They've wanted it all along, so they're not gonna care about a few dead FBI agents who got themselves killed in what they'll call 'an international dispute.' They'll put our pictures on a wall, give our next of kin a plaque and a flag, and that'll be it. Our names won't even make the news. They'll just say 'a bunch' of us got shot dead. End of story."

Hunter had been studying the night during the discussion, and then he spoke, "They're not going to stop until we give them what they want."

Chaney stared. "What are you saying?"

Hunter fixed him with a deadly gaze.

"I'm saying we give them what they want."

* * *

As the rear of the panel truck noisily opened, Colonel Blakely stepped spritely to the side to avoid the slouching, primordial shape that descended to the ground. The creature didn't even deign to cast Blakely a glance as it moved down the short stairway to the basement of the once-abandoned hospital. Yet, as it passed the colonel, Blakely saw that its head wound had changed. The skin was already healed.

Seconds later the second creature followed in the steps of the first and then it, too, was lost in the darkness of the vast subterranean chamber. Releasing a huge breath, Blakely motioned to the pale mercenaries, "Clean this thing out. Hose it down. I don't want hairs or spit or footprints or anything else that can connect us to those things. And do the same thing every time we take them out."

A mercenary asked, "We're gonna have to do this *again*?"

"I ain't the shot-caller," said Blakely. "I take orders, same as you. Why do you ask?"

The mercenary pointed to an empty lot. "Because I think I know a better way to get them high without so much exposure on the road."

Blakely concentrated. "The Sikorsky?"

"Yeah!"

"Never work," Blakely shook his head. "No sane pilot would take off with those two freaks stowed in the bay. It's crazy enough that we're *driving* them up there! You haven't seen what one of them can do! And if either one of them went ape, we wouldn't be able to restrain it. It'd tear that chopper apart and kill every one of us stone dead. Yeah, I told you this might be a suicide mission, boys, but you signed up for it, and there's no turning back. Not for any of us."

With a deeper, steadier breath, Blakely turned and descended the steps to the basement where he found the assistant scientist, Pinion, leaning against a wall. He was once again in human form. Unlike Professor Dante, who still towered above them in bestial shape glaring at the creature in the reinforced cage. The imprisoned creature mimicked every move that Dante made as it stared up with worship.

Even the thought of such sentiments between these fell creatures made Blakely shiver with revulsion. But he had his instructions, and he was bound to fulfill them. If he disappointed the stone-faced doctor, Blakely was certain that he would not be given the reward he coveted so greedily. For there was no substituting any amount of money for the prize he would win once he completed this mission.

He would have his own nation that would live or die at his pleasure. He would build his own army, his own emerald city, his own palace. And all who looked at him would tremble before they knelt. Riches would be his, and all the pleasures a man could look upon and desire. He would withhold nothing from himself.

As Blakely lifted the stocky tranquilizer rifle to inject the caged beast with a booster of whatever compound Dante had prepared, the thought came to him that he, too, must undergo this ungodly transformation to achieve the immortality he had been promised. But the inevitable anguish made little difference to him as he aimed at the creature's neck.

No difference at all.

He fired.

CHAPTER NINE

The azure morning dawned very, very slowly. It was as if the night was reluctant to surrender its remorseless grip. Crouching along the road leading over the mountain, Hunter pointed, and six Hostage Rescue Team commandos bent to study the displaced gravel.

"This is the impression of a pretty good weight landing real hard," Hunter remarked. "There's no print, but the gravel is depressed and scattered." He looked around. "A van pulled in here last night. It came from the valley. It stopped here. Then something – I'm assuming it was one, or both, of them – got out of the back. Then they made a straight line for my cabin. It's just over that ridge. That's how they bypassed the wolves. And they guessed we'd have motion monitors and crawled beneath the cameras."

Chaney asked, "I thought the wolves would let you know when someone was coming up the road."

"It's hit and miss," shrugged Hunter. "If they don't like the look of you, they'll let me know. But they don't alert on every car or hiker that comes over the mountain. This is a main road into Canada. A lot of truckers use it coming and going. A lot of hikers use it for the same reason. The wolves alert on some visitors – they have their reasons – and ignore the rest. I've never put much thought into it because I'm not at the cabin that much." He motioned to the vast landscape. "I spend almost all my time up there. Most of the people I rescue are up above the snow line." He studied trees on the far side of the road. "But there's no question that these two leaped the road and landed over there."

Mack: "How do you know they didn't just walk across?"

"The impressions on the far side are too deep. That means they jumped from right here. But there was no reason to jump." Hunter grimaced. "They're being extra careful. More careful than they have to be. Which might be good."

Chaney asked, "How can that be good?"

"It might mean they're uncertain of themselves. I mean, sure, they command the speed and strength of a Sabretooth. But they're not experienced at using all that speed and strength and they don't know their limitations." Hunter stood. "A big predator conserves energy. It doesn't make big moves unless it's attacking. Most of the time it just creeps along. Or doesn't move at all. It just rests. But leaping over this road took a lot of energy that an experienced predator would never expend unless it had to. Normally it'd just walk across the road to conserve strength, which means they don't understand the physical limits of this creature. And it does have limits. They just haven't run into them, yet."

Chaney commented sullenly, "What kind of limits could they have? Didn't you see the size of those things?"

"That's not what I mean, Chaney. By instilling a piece of their human consciousness, they may have suppressed too much of this creature's instincts. In trying to exert some kind of human control over what is very much *not human*, they may have taken out the part that makes it so dangerous – the instincts that give it every advantage. And if they've weakened that, then what else could they have weakened? I mean, I told you before, Chaney. You can have a tiger. Or you can have a man. But you can't have both at the same time because then each of them will be less than they are alone."

Mack was gazing alertly down the road. "Now what?"

"We go back to the cabin," said Hunter, and began walking. "I'll check with Buford again for any unusual activity, but I'm betting these things are holed up in a safe place by now. The best thing we can do is find out where that place is, and then we can attack and maybe finish all of them at once. Otherwise, we've got nothing."

Chaney sighed, "'Nothing' sounds a lot better than what we've got."

* * *

Now in human form once again, Cronis took the report of last night's battle against Hunter with considerably more concern than either Pinion or Dante. Seemingly unperturbed by the encounter, Dante remained sedately reclined in his office chair while Pinion assumed an exhausted position on the couch.

Standing in the middle of the office, Cronis asked Dante, "Are you saying that you can remember everything that happened?"

"Yes," Dante nodded. "I can vividly remember every nuance of the encounter, doctor. I have assumed human consciousness within this beast for several evolutions and now my mind is quite awake when I undergo the transition."

Cronis was quick to respond. "I thought you said you didn't gain conscious control until your last transition."

"That is true. But I was *aware* of my actions before then. Last night, however, I was in complete control, and I remember every detail." Dante cupped his hands, fingertip to fingertip. "I was taken by surprise when Hunter used an unusual weapon. It not only shocked me. He managed to wound me."

"Wounded you!" Cronis stepped closer. "I thought you said that this new synthesis would make us immune to injury!"

Dante glanced up. "Calm yourself, doctor. We made a mistake. That is simply a bane of science. And since we are dealing with forces capable of holding the universe together or tearing it apart, there will inevitably be missteps. But miscalculations have forever been a part of great scientific breakthroughs. For example, it took Edison, the Wizard of Menlo Park, over six hundred attempts before he found a longer-lasting filament for the lightbulb."

"To hell with Edison! Edison wasn't being shot at! Our *lives* are in danger, Dante! And you said this would be like shooting fish in a barrel! And now you're saying that Hunter *surprised* you with something? *With what?*"

Dante was ice as he slowly explained, "Hunter was well prepared for another encounter with the Scimitar, doctor. Indeed, it seems he has been preparing for quite some time. Doubtless, Luther and Vang left him with quite an impression. He has procured for himself armaments that could conceivably injure – or even kill – any one of us after transition. That is why we must carefully reconsider our initial plans."

Releasing a weary breath, Cronis sat heavily on a stool. Finally, he asked in a decidedly calmer tone, "And just what do you suggest?"

Dante shrugged without concern, "Our original plan was to simply ambush Hunter at his cabin and kill him. But, as I said, he was unexpectedly prepared for that. So, we must lure him away from his stronghold and into the forest where we will have every advantage. And then we will most certainly finish him."

"What about the wolves? That bear? The animals that Hunter controls?"

"Hunter does not 'control' those animals," Dante retorted with obvious disgust. "Hunter and the animals 'cooperate' with each other, but they are all just base animals. And even without benefits of the serum, we are more powerful than some uneducated, backwater mountain man living in a log cabin in the middle of nowhere." He frowned, "You overestimate our enemy, Cronis. Hunter is no apex predator. He is a *relic*! A man born out of time! He is a phantom of when men lived by musket balls and tomahawks. He stinks of leather and blood and dirt. He is a reminder of an age when men first emerged from caves to eat grass like goats. Despite the futile help offered by his friends, Hunter will be easy prey once we isolate him. And then we will destroy him. Completely. And once Hunter is dead, then the last, remaining hero of that meaningless age will be gone."

Eyes glinting red, Dante lifted his chin.

"Gone!"

* * *

"I've heard some crazy ideas in my life, but this is the craziest."

Methodically packing a leather pouch with supplies, Hunter didn't even look as Chaney paced the cabin after his comment. Hunter had been listening to Chaney's objections since he told them he'd go deep into the woods and bait these maneaters into stalking him.

Hunter explained that the beasts probably wouldn't return to the cabin because they didn't like the exposure. Again, he stressed, they're ambush killers. They want concealment until the last moment. Also, he was confident that he'd wounded one. How badly, he wasn't certain. But if it'd been wounded, then it'd be much more careful with its next attack, so Hunter had to make the opportunity irresistible. And nothing would be as tempting as the sight of Hunter alone in the deep woods.

The fact that Chaney, Mack, and the Hostage Rescue Team would be overshadowing Hunter's planned position apparently did little to ease Chaney's fears. Nor did the fact that the most experienced big game hunters on the team were loading up with Hunter's heaviest elk and moose rifles. Or that Mack had decided to take Vernon and Gantry along, after all.

Mack reasoned that the rookies might never get an opportunity like this again – to learn what high-stress combat is all about. But this was a conflict where a single mistake can get you killed, and they'd have to learn quick. Then, after listening to Mack explain the alarming situation to the rookies, Chaney had to give them credit; no, they had no experience, but they didn't hesitate to volunteer. And, in the final analysis, no one involved in this stunt had any experience hunting 10,000-year-old monsters that once terrified the earth.

No one except Hunter.

Chaney looked again at Hunter. "You say these things won't come for you as long as you're at this cabin. Well, isn't that a good thing? That gives us more time to find out where they're hiding! Then we can ambush 'em! You know? Like hunters! We'll take 'em by surprise!"

The fact was not lost on Hunter that Chaney was certain, after they killed Hunter, they'd be coming after *him*. And although Chaney was no coward – in fact, Hunter considered him one of the bravest men he'd ever known – Chaney was vividly aware of his limitations. He was an FBI agent with a phone book of high-risk arrests under his belt. He had taken down traitors, KGB assassins, suicidal terrorists, hitters from the Aryan Nation, and the most psychotic, dangerous serial killers on the planet. But he was no hunter, and he knew next to nothing about the outdoors. A trip in the wild, for Chaney, was a weekend in Vegas.

"Chaney," Hunter stated patiently, "I have already told you before now. They could be in any one of a hundred billion places. They look like people, although they're not. But they're the only ones who know that, so nobody is gonna look twice at 'em. They could be someone's next door neighbor and no one would have a clue that they're one of the most vicious predators the world has ever known."

"*I know that*!" exclaimed Chaney. "But we are *severely* outmatched! Because I'm betting those other two scientists who disappeared with Dante have both changed into these animals with him! I can feel it in my bones! And that makes three of them! That's why we've got to find all of them while they're still human and kill them before they can change!"

Hunter stopped with the pack and raised his face, "And where you gonna start looking, Chaney?" He extended arms. "Where? You're got Glacier National Forest to the west. That's a hundred thousand hotel rooms and condos. Forty miles to the north, you've got Canada. That means searching every house on the Canadian border where you don't even have jurisdiction. And what about the RVs that can relocate every day? And what about all the private homes of the rich and famous? There's hundreds of them in Glacier. How long do you think it'd take you to get search warrants for the private homes of half the senators in Congress? And what about the fact that you've only got six experienced men to help you search an area the size of Los Angeles and their only backup is these two boy scouts? It'd take you ten years to even begin a search, Chaney. And this thing will be over in a day."

Chaney had ceased pacing but, for some reason, he looked to Hunter like he was still moving. Hunter wrote it off to the probability that he was attempting to put on a much calmer demeanor although he wasn't succeeding.

Turning, Chaney stated, "Mack! What are the odds of us getting some help?"

Mack responded with his first hint of frustration, "Chaney! You have got to accept the fact that we are *totally* on our own and that's the way it's going to stay! The odds of us getting help are less than zero. We are in No Man's Land, buddy. We are on the Titanic as it goes under for the final time. We are in a bomber over enemy territory with all engines flaming out. Mayday, mayday, coming in hard."

Chaney simply stared.

Mack broke open a double-barrel shotgun that he'd removed from Hunter's gun safe. Hunter had sawed it down to twenty-inch barrels. Mack removed the shells, examining them. "Twelve-gauge slugs. I'd like to see it survive *this*."

He reloaded, snapped it shut, dropped a handful of slugs in his coat, and laid the shotgun across his lap as he added, "Since you've never seen the report, Chaney, I think you should know that the Anchorage office called for backup when you guys were on the shady side of dead. Everybody knew you two were up a real mean creek. The report even had early copies of your obituaries in case they were needed. But any effort to help you was shut down from the top. And I don't mean, 'from the top of the FBI.' *We* were ready to go. I mean that it was shut down from *the very top*."

Mack gripped the shotgun more firmly as he leaned forward. "Someone in Washington shut down all FBI efforts to send in a chopper to evac you guys the hell out of there. And we had a whole army of heavily armed FBI agents jumping up and down ready to try. Even the damn army was on standby with an entire company out of Anchorage. But Washington pulled the plug on every bit of it. They pushed you into traffic – live or die. And if we call for help now, I promise we'll get the same response." A pause. "No response at all."

Chaney asked in a sterner tone, "Are you telling me Washington knew how desperate things were in Alaska and they cut us off?"

"They cut you lose without a second thought," Mack nodded. "You gotta get it through your head, buddy. These people want this creature *alive*. They don't want a dead Scimitar. They want the walking, talking embodiment of their dream. So, all you did with your all-go U. S. Marshal gunslinging in Alaska was just piss off a lot of very rich people who wanted to claim whatever the hell this creature can supposedly give them. And they're still pissed at you about it because, let me tell you, presidents come and go. Members of Congress and bank CEOs are replaced every day. Some big firm on Wall Street goes bankrupt, another takes its place. But the people who *own the big money* don't change. And it's a family thing. If you ain't born into it, you'll never be part of it. Because these people keep a tight rein on their New World Order, buddy, and they're not going to share it with a bunch of peons like you and me. You got in the way of their plans when you stomped ol' Mr. I'm-Gonna-Live-Forever into the grave up in Alaska and that pissed them off. And these people are *not* the forgiving type. So, to sum it up, *that* fiasco brings us to *this* fiasco. Now, once again, they have what they imagine is a chance to snatch victory from the very jaws of defeat. And the only thing stopping them is you guys. Again. The same thing that got in their way in Alaska is in their way now. And they're not about to let you two mooks beat 'em twice. So make no mistake, my friend. If we all die a horrible death, they won't give a damn. And they'll find a way to keep it quiet because this creature isn't just their meal ticket to a 'better life.' It's their meal ticket to *eternal life.* And they're gonna have it if they have to kill every one of us."

Mack laughed grimly, "Think of it, Chaney. As long as someone is ultimately doomed to die, they're irrelevant. They're peons. Peasants. Cannon fodder. Fools digging their own graves. And these maniacs don't see themselves as peons or peasants or fools. They see themselves as kings beyond any known standards of right or wrong or good and evil. They're beyond all that pedestrian nonsense that keeps people like you and me stomped down and broke. And they're not about to let some dime-store son of a bitch FBI agent mess up their dream again. So, are we alone in this? Yeah, buddy. We are as alone as it gets."

Slowly turning his face, Chaney saw that even Hunter had been vaguely affected by Mack's dismal summation of their situation. Then Hunter merely raised his brow, with a sigh, and continued loading magazines for the Barrett with the deadly little explosive cartridges. Chaney noticed six speed loads prepared for the Bushwhacker.

One thing was clear; Hunter wasn't going down without a fight. But whether he would live long enough to fire those rounds was another question. Chaney remembered how fast the creatures had disappeared last night. He'd forgotten they can move faster than the human eye can follow. Then he wondered if they'd retreated from fear or strategy. If they had retreated from fear, then this trap might not be in vain. Nor were the rifles and the grenades and extra guns. But if they retreated only to make another plan, then this was a dice roll.

Chaney was not, by training, disposed to dealing with combat situations that were evolving off-the-cuff. In the Marshals and the FBI, they had always crafted a fool-proof plan to take down a dangerous subject, although nothing was ever 'fool-proof.'

In this 'relative' quiet before what was certain to be a fiasco of a fight, Chaney was reminded of words that an FBI veteran had shared with him on the takedown of a dangerous international terrorist. The old federal agent had said, *"No plan survives the first thirty seconds of combat, so you have to be ready to improvise. All the planning in the world ain't worth spit if the plan goes to hell. Sometimes you just gotta shoot from the hip ..."*

Hunter left his gear on the kitchen table and walked to a closet. He rummaged before removing camouflaged hunting overalls that covered his entire body. Chaney glimpsed that it was fully insulated and remarked, "How cold does it get out there this time of year?"

"It'll be about 40 degrees tonight," Hunter answered absently. "Unless a storm comes in. Then it'll drop to freezing."

"*Is* a storm coming in?"

Hunter glanced out the window. "Nope."

Chaney looked out the same window. "How can you tell?"

"The birds are too high. Birds fly low when a storm's coming in." Hunter zipped up the body suit. "Ants go back to their mounds. Chipmunks go back to their holes. Lions stay in their dens. The whole forest seems to know there's a storm coming before man does. Even with all our science, we're always the last to know."

"Huh," Chaney grunted, "I've never seen a low-flying eagle."

"Eagles are an exception. An eagle has telescopic vision, so an eagle can see a storm coming thirty miles away. Then an eagle will just lock its wings and soar until it pops out on top of the storm. It'll hang around at twenty, twenty-five thousand feet until the storm passes. Then it'll come down."

"How does it breathe at twenty thousand feet?"

Hunter continued, "An eagle has air sacs in its chest that function like oxygen tanks. When an eagle is low, it'll fill up its sacs with oxygen. Then, when it goes high, where there's no oxygen, it'll breathe the oxygen it takes with it. It can stay up there all day breathing its own air supply. And it won't have to fly around. It'll just lock its wings in place with these notches it has in each shoulder. Its wings will stay at a fixed angle without any effort. Then it'll just ride the thermals. It can glide all day without working its wings a single time. It could do it forever, but it'd eventually run out of oxygen and have to come down."

Without looking away, Chaney said, "You're gonna miss this life, aren't you? I think you're more at home here than I've ever seen anybody at home anywhere in the world.

I've seen princes who weren't at home in palaces as much you are in this wilderness."

"Well," quipped Hunter, "you know what they say."

"Home is where the heart is?"

"Close enough."

Immobile, Hunter closely studied what lay on the table.

His gun belt had the .500 Bushwhacker in a cross-draw holster on his left hip and six five-shot reloads on the right. The .338 Barrett lay across the top. He had eight five-round magazines, plus individual rounds, in a bandoleer. He had a bowie knife on his right side and a crossbow with a full complement of four-edged, broadhead bolts strapped to his backpack. He seemed in every way the frontier equivalent of a modern SWAT officer. Chaney didn't know exactly what Hunter had stuffed into his black backpack, but he did notice that a large roll of detonation cord and seven M-67 anti-personnel grenades were missing.

Hunter pointed toward a distant ridge.

"If you take a place on that ridge," he said with exact precision, "you'll be able to see my campfire. I'll be in a little coolie that's on the other side. But don't come closer than two hundred feet. If you get closer, they might catch your scent." He motioned toward a large bonfire that he'd begun. "Before you go up, stand in the smoke of that bonfire for about ten minutes. Cloak your scent as best you can because animals aren't alerted to the smell of a campfire. Like oil or gas, they smell campfires all the time. The smoke will cover your human scent, so you should be good as long as you don't come too close."

Mack presented a scoped Remington.

"Do you think this will hurt 'em?"

Hunter remarked, "I don't know. They're all different." He leaned on the table. "The only common weakness I've ever seen is that they're all vulnerable to edged weapons. That's why I'm taking the crossbow. I'm got a suspicion that these bolts will cut through its skin where a bullet can't."

He concentrated. "When I cut off Luther's head in Alaska, there wasn't the same resistance to the bowie that there had been to a bullet. The blade cut through his hide the same as it would slice through the skin of a lion or tiger."

Chaney morosely observed, "The main problem with hitting it with an edged weapon is living long enough to do it."

"How come you're staying so close to the cabin?" asked Mack.

"I'm not going to retreat too far into the woods because I don't know how well these things can track." Hunter paused, squinting at the ridge. "I'll stay close enough for them to smell smoke from the fire and see the light of the camp. Now, before it gets true dark, I want each of you to take up positions in the shape of a horseshoe around my location. Leave a wide-open space between me and the road because I think they'll come in the same way they came in last night. And I don't want you between them and me."

"What makes you think they'll come in the same way?" asked Mack.

"Because the creature that killed the wolf in the valley retreated the same way it came in. An experienced predator wouldn't do that. But these things aren't experienced. And since that route up from the road has worked for them before, I think they'll keep using what works until it doesn't." Hunter gazed into their faces. "You'll have to pick spots on high ground. Get up in a tree if you can. And if there's not any good climbing trees, try and get to the highest rock where you still have a clear view of my position. I doubt that I'll get a clean shot at them as they come in. But you'll have the high ground, and you ought to be able to see them circling me, so don't hesitate to take a shot. I guarantee I'll need the help."

Slinging the rifle, Hunter bent and lifted the backpack with a cable-strong hand. He gazed around the cabin for a moment before he slowly remarked, "Well, if this is the last time I'll ever see this place, it's been a hell of a party."

CHAPTER TEN

Again in human form, Cronis regarded Dante with cautious doubt as they sat in the basement of the hospital. They had been planning tonight's excursion for an hour – since Cronis had reverted once more to his human condition – and they still remained in disagreement over the best course of action.

It was bad enough that Hunter was using unheard-of military ordinance in an experimental rifle. And it was twice as bad that Hunter had recruited help as if he somehow anticipated this move by Dante. That complication had offset their efforts all morning and into the afternoon because, if Hunter had recruited one shooter, what confidence did they have that he hadn't recruited a hundred? That single consideration opened a world of possibilities, but the unavoidable conclusion was that Hunter was no longer alone.

Factor by factor Dante's well-laid scheme of ambushing the mountain man when he was alone and off-guard had been derailed by Hunter's animal instincts or just sheer, blind luck. And Cronis was inclined to believe it was instinct.

Dante took a seat on a desk and began, "If my analyses are right, then we are prepared to launch a final attack. Even though Hunter does have a weapon capable of wounding or, perhaps, killing one of us, it's unlikely he'll have a chance to use it since the mercenaries are coming with us to neutralize that advantage."

"Who says that's his only advantage?" asked Cronis.

Dante crossed arms and assumed his characteristic stand. "You have been wary of this mountain man since the beginning, Cronis. Why is that? Hunter is uneducated. He uses the weapons of Daniel Boone or Davy Crockett or some equally dead frontier peasant of the past. He is a throwback to a time that no longer exists. Hunter is no more than a reminder of an extinct age that was conquered centuries ago by men who mastered the power of the human mind. Why do you consider this Neanderthal such a threat?"

Not replying immediately, Cronis simply gazed at Dante's arrogant posture. Then, finally, he said, "Because men like Hunter survived in an age where a man lived or died by nothing but his wits and his physical strength, Dante. Men like Hunter survived blizzards with nothing but the hide of an animal they killed with their bare hands. Hunter is a man out of another age, it's true, but you should consider what age he comes from.

"Hunter doesn't come from an industrial age where men were puppets and slaves to an infant understanding of mechanics. Men in that age were weak to begin with, and the industrial age just made them weaker. Hunter belongs to an age where men survived the most violent forces of nature with nothing but the power they had within themselves. And if you think that this 'backwoods mountain man' is out of moves, Dante, you better think again. Because I'll bet my life – in fact, *I am* betting it – that we haven't seen the last of Hunter's tricks. Just like he killed Luther and Vang with traps they didn't see, Hunter always has a last move. And it's always something you don't see. You say Hunter is doomed because he's up against a force he can't comprehend. But you better be careful. It could be the other way around."

Unceremoniously breaking the dubious sanctity of the meeting, Colonel Blakely walked through the door reporting without preamble, "I've got twenty men ready for tonight, professor. I'm leaving five men with the extra trucks and five inside this building to safeguard the explosives. I need to confirm, sir, what is the status on the Sikorskies?"

Dante straightened before stating, "The Sikorskies have stopped for refueling in Helena. Afterwards, they will relocate to an unused airstrip not ten minutes flight time from this hospital where they will await my notification. The commander has informed me that, because of the proximity of the nearby road, they're only willing to be on the ground at this location for ten minutes. Can you manage that?"

"I'll tell the men," Blakely nodded and began to turn away before pausing and glancing over the basement. "Are you still certain on the secondary protocols?"

"Yes," Dante nodded curtly. "You are to detonate explosives that are guaranteed to very thoroughly destroy any trace of our presence here. Nothing is to be left behind. Is there anything else, colonel?"

"No," Blakely shook his head. "I'll have men establish the final charges once we leave for the mountain."

With Blakely's exit the room was eerily still before Dante added, "We will proceed from the outlook where we began last night. I'm sure they haven't yet discovered how we got so high on Hunter's mountain without alerting the wolves." He grunted with contempt. "Wolves, indeed! I would prefer a yelping chihuahua! And that Grizzly bear is of no use to them, either. Any one of us could kill it with a single blow."

Cronis watched without expression as Dante rose and placed his hands on a wooden stand holding the variously colored test tubes. Behind the tubes was a translucent flask much, much larger than the diminutive tubes, and it was filled to the top with serum of the same color that Dante used on himself. There was a single flame beneath the flask. The observation prompted Cronis to ask, "What's in the flask, doctor?"

"What?" Dante asked before glancing behind himself. "Oh. That. Well, since I had a bit of time, I distilled enough serum for myself to last several decades, should I need it. Which I don't believe I will. Once we have absorbed this creature's immortal traits, we can dispense with the transitions. We will be immortal in human form, which was the goal of this experiment from the beginning."

"Just out of curiosity," Cronis pressed, "I know you mentioned this once, but what would happen if you drank that entire flask all at once? I see that it's synthesized for your use, and not either of us."

Dante laughed, "Well, I would most certainly die, doctor. No human being could survive the molecular disintegration and reconstitution affected by so much serum ingested all at once. And if it did not kill me outright, then it would surely transform me into a permanent version of a creature that has never existed. In fact, I am prone to say that, should I miraculously survive the experience, it would transition me into a creature ten times more powerful than our current transformations. Perhaps even a hundred times more powerful." He gestured, "But that is academic, Cronis. I have no intention of destroying myself. The flask is merely to equip myself with enough serum to manage future, and much safer, transitions."

For the first time in the discussion, Pinion spoke. "I know that you say this is highly unlikely, professor, but what if one of us is killed tonight when we're in transition?"

"Then your body would eventually re-transition to human," answered Dante without hesitation. "The transformation remains viable in direct proportion to the oxygen level of the subject. Without a consistent supply of oxygen, the transition terminates." He lifted his head as he added, "But there is no cause for unwarranted concern, doctor. With the physical attributes of this indestructible predator, there is no realistic chance of death. At most, one of us might sustain a temporary injury. But, as long as we remain breathing, even the most severe injury will heal in a matter of moments."

Dante seemed to relish any opportunity for a lecture as he added, "You see, gentlemen, the same molecular power that provides this creature with its incredible life span is the same dynamic that mobilizes its healing power. In fact, what is aging but the body's loss of the ability to heal? Each day the human body suffers the death of millions of cells. It is a natural process because human DNA is encoded with a limited life span that, until now, could not be altered without destroying the genomes of the DNA itself. But as we've discussed on many occasions, what if human DNA could be re-coded to program a longer life span? Because of an alteration in our DNA, what if our cells were programmed to heal as quickly as they died? Then, as you know, there would be no such thing as old age, doctors. There would only be a sublime existence that must be measured with millennium and not decades. This has been our endgame all along. And with Hunter's death we will play our last move in this deadly game of chess."

Pinion: "When do we leave?"

"We will leave early. Hunter and his companion will expect us much later in the night, but I intend to catch them unaware by attacking at sunset. The mercenaries shall depart first and assume their designated stations, and then a vehicle will take the three of us to the vicinity of the cabin." Dante added almost as an afterthought, "I doubt we will have a repeat of last night. That was unfortunate. But Hunter took us by surprise. I underestimated him. And I won't make that mistake again. And then it will be check. And mate."

Cronis stated quietly, "It might be a little early for a victory lap, Dante."

Dante turned. "Really. And why is that, doctor?"

"Because Hunter's a pretty good chess player, himself."

Hunter continued to listen to the forest as he secured hand grenades to trees and rocks and rigged tripwires with fishing lines. After setting one grenade in place, he would carefully straighten the pin and leave it positioned along one of two likely paths into the ravine. As soon as anything hit the tripwire, the spool on the grenade would be released and the explosion would shred the ravine with shrapnel.

There was only one way to enter this narrow gulch. It was little more than a small animal trail that ran along the east side of the gigantic rock walls hemming the ravine between two slopes. In the dark, even starlight couldn't penetrate the thick canopy of trees overshadowing the trail, so negotiating it at night required very slow, careful work even for a creature that had a Sabretooth's power to see in the dark.

A renowned biologist once told Hunter that cats don't have night vision as most would define night vision. He said they can't actually "see in the dark," but neither do cats see what most people would consider darkness. Rather, a cat sees things in shades of gray even in the darkest night. Nothing is unseen, but neither can a cat see at night as it can see in the daylight. The scientist explained that a cat possesses a kind of "spectral vision" that sees the most pitch-black night in alternating shades. Where a man sees only darkness, a cat will see a depthless vista of various grays.

The conversation explained a lot to Hunter because he had always assumed cats could see in the dark. It seemed like a logical conclusion since he had repeatedly witnessed cats negotiate the most difficult terrain in the darkest night. He had never imagined that they possessed a kind of "hybrid night vision" unknown to any other species.

Hunter recalled that the same scientist told him that bears couldn't see in the dark any better than a human being

– something Hunter had long suspected. The only reason a bear can negotiate the dark with more skill than a human being was – again – its nose. If a bear were blind as a mole, it would unerringly find what it sought by its nose alone.

Hunter didn't bother to check the angle of the sun. He still had an hour of daylight before the surrounding summits brought early night.

In this ravine, light cut through the canopy only in pencil-like beams separated by patches of green-black gloom, and at night it was all a solid sea of black, so whatever traps he was going to secure would be quite invisible. Not even the Scimitar would be able to pick out a thin, transparent fishing line concealed beneath black moss.

Hunter didn't wonder whether the creatures could find a way through the granite fangs of this ravine. If their vision was the same as any other cat's, they would easily negotiate a path along the main trail where Hunter had set tripwires for four of the grenades. Even if they detected the first wire, Hunter had set another grenade where they would most likely step. He had set the last two grenades dangerously close to where he would be waiting. There was every chance the blast would kill or, at least, injure him beyond his ability to fight, but it was worth the risk. They wouldn't be expecting him to set explosives so close to himself. It was a dangerous move, and Hunter grunted at the thought.

Dangerous moves were all he had.

He knew that the Scimitar would, of course, be searching for traps. They were inexperienced, not stupid, and would quite probably retain a veneer of human caution, so Hunter had rigged up lesser traps that they would easily detect further up the trail – traps they would avoid, and which might lull them into an unconscious confidence. Then, when they were certain that they had bypassed all his tricks, they would enter the last of the trail which was laced with six hard-to-see trip wires made of fishing line.

As he walked back and conjured up a roaring bonfire, Hunter knew it was unlikely he'd survive this. Without even attempting to resist the impulse, he lifted his face searching for any of Chaney's men taking sniper hides in surrounding trees that ran atop the crest of the slope but saw nothing. They were already so well concealed that Hunter couldn't see them. Or they hadn't even begun.

Hunter heard his own voice.

"Don't take too long, Chaney. Time is a luxury we don't have."

Once more Hunter turned to the site he'd selected for his last stand. Sheer granite bluffs rose on either side hedging him into a very narrow canyon of rock. He studied the walls. The cliffs were coated with ice-cold water unclimbable even to a cat.

The trail behind him was his only possible escape if things went the way he feared because, quite simply, there was nowhere else to go. Since the trail leading from the overlook was certainly the path they'd follow to reach him, escaping along that course wasn't an option. And, for certain, he couldn't climb out of here in a hurry. Only a mountain goat could scale those cliffs fast enough to avoid a fight.

The thought that he'd be able to fight the creatures on the jagged floor of the ravine occurred to Hunter and he immediately dismissed it. He'd be lucky to survive five seconds of close combat with one of them. So, if Chaney and his men didn't lay down some devastating cover fire, Hunter estimated he'd be dead in seconds. He simply had no advantage.

An advantage …

The thought captured Hunter's mind, and he gazed around the ravine. Surely, he thought, there was *some* kind of advantage. He just had to find it.

He'd already set up the grenades and that wasn't anything he cared to change. But he still had two hundred feet of det cord in his pack. As an afterthought, Hunter gazed up the embracing cliffs to estimate the chance of precipitating an avalanche in this narrow gorge. He saw a section of loose rocks and decided an explosion of the C-4 cord was worth the risk. In any case, he'd rather die in an avalanche than being torn limb from limb.

Slinging the rifle over his shoulder, Hunter removed the dangerous white cord from the pack and studied the surrounding ground. He wanted to bank the force of the explosion to somehow amplify the concussion. The space had to be narrow and hemmed in by granite so the shock waves would bounce back at the source. If Hunter's calculations were correct, that would increase the power of the blast ten-fold.

When Hunter was once working in a war zone to track a missing missionary, a veteran military officer explained to him that most people were killed by the concussion of an explosion and weren't even touched by shrapnel. The expert explained that the sound of the explosion liquified a victim's internal organs and killed them without even breaking the skin. And since Hunter had been searching across minefields and boobytrapped trails, he'd remembered the lesson well. He'd avoided tight spaces, like inside a bunker, where the concussion of a blast would be concentrated by the cement walls. He'd walked parallel to trails always keeping a tree at his side to disrupt the shock wave of a blast. Granted, it wasn't much of a defensive gesture but, as they say, "any port in a storm."

A shadow flickered beside a tree at the top of the ridge and Hunter didn't need to raise his gaze to confirm what he knew. Someone had briefly leaned out from behind a trunk, making the tree seem wider for a split second, before concealing themselves again. Hunter knew it was far too early to be one of the creatures, so it was Chaney and his men taking positions.

If Chaney was still at the cabin, the transmitter he wore would have been useless inside the rock walls, but since Chaney seemed to be at the top of the ridge, Hunter decided to take a chance. He pressed the mic fastened to his collar and quietly asked, "Chaney? Are you guys taking positions?"

The reply was instantaneous.

"Read you, Hunter. Yeah. We're getting into position. You have any preferences on where you want us?"

Searching the ridge, Hunter replied, "Station three men on each side of this coolie. There's a fallen tree about fifty yards down that acts as a bridge, so they can cross over. I want you and Mack with the clearest view of where I'm at right now. That explosive round from the Barrett might be the only thing that will hurt it. And put those two rookies somewhere along this trail that leads from the outlook so they can warn us when they're coming. Otherwise, I'm rigging this place with grenades and C-4."

"Copy that."

Finally, Hunter laid the C-4 in the most concealed site he could imagine and, when he stepped back, he was satisfied that the cord would be invisible in the dark. Even if the creatures somehow noticed something amiss, it would only seem to be a vine Hunter had used to wrap the cord from tree to tree. He removed the detonator from his pocket. There was a single red button and Hunter familiarized himself to finding it by feel. At most, he'd have the uncertain light of the fire, but he anticipated finding the small remote without looking. He imagined he'd be too busy dodging the sweeping, monstrous blows of the beast to take his eyes off it.

Is there anything more you can do?

The last of his plan would be to protect himself as much as possible from the effects of the blast. The grenades, although they were close, weren't the greatest danger. The detonation cord was another matter. Hunter had literally surrounded himself with the lethal strands of C-4 leaving very few avenues for evading the concussion.

Also, there was a critical complication with the detonation cord; it was all or nothing. Hunter had no means of detonating "a piece" of it. When he pushed the button, or shot it, the entire strand would blow, and it would knock down half a dozen trees and send rocks ricocheting through the ravine with enough velocity to cut a man in half. Gazing around now that the cord was rigged, Hunter searched for the most likely place to survive the blast.

Trees were all but useless. The granite shards sent flying by the explosion would slice clean through a tree trunk. And Hunter didn't consider distance a viable tactic. If he was close enough to signal the detonation, he would be close enough to get killed by it unless he was behind solid cover. Finally, he settled on a large boulder resting forty feet from the fire. It was heavy enough to protect his body from the effects of the blast and sloped enough to run up before he dropped on the far side.

After clearing out small, jagged rocks on the back side of the boulder, preparing a place for his landing, Hunter took a moment and stared over the site. He saw nothing that made him feel comfortable or confident. Rather, he had the impression he was standing in the middle of a giant fly trap trying to lure in a man-eating fly. And then the trap would close on them both.

He frowned as he walked toward the fire.

Not a bad analogy.

* * *

Standing beside Mack, Chaney gazed deep into the gorge where Hunter was calmly and unhurriedly stoking the fire. If one did not know Hunter was waiting to be attacked by three super-predators from hell, they would have assumed he was simply settling in for a peaceful night in the woods.

"What do you think?" Chaney asked uneasily.

Mack briefly closed his eyes before he sighed, "I don't like it. He's rigged that ravine with enough grenades and det cord to obliterate a tank. The concussion alone could kill him." He paused. "But I understand what he's thinking, and I agree with him. I'd rather die by my own hand, too, rather than getting torn apart by one of those things."

In a swift move Chaney unslung the .338 Barrett and checked to make sure a round was chambered. "It's hard to believe," he added morosely. "This explosive round goes 3,000 feet per second. It can disintegrate the door of an armored car. It can vaporize bulletproof glass. And there's a fair chance it might not even penetrate the hide of that thing." He made an indistinct sound. "This is crazy as hell, Mack."

"And we are neck-deep in it and sinking fast."

Chaney continued, "We hit it with everything we had in Alaska, and it just smiled at us and kept coming. Bobby Jo slowed it down with that solid bore shot she carried in her .50, but nothing else seemed to affect it."

"What about fire?"

Chaney paused. "Fire?"

"Fire, Chaney! Like setting the whole damn forest on fire!"

Chaney blinked tiredly before he muttered, "We never tried that. There was no flame until the very end when Hunter set that pool of oil on fire." He waved at the foliage. "It was a last-chance move. We didn't even know if fire would hurt it. That damn thing really did seem indestructible. I mean, until Hunter took its head."

Mack grunted, "I read that part in the report. Gutsiest move I ever saw, no lie. It's hard to believe Hunter pulled it off."

"The only reason Hunter could do it is because he wore it down the same way it'd been wearing us down. Hunter used its own tactics against it. Good god," Chaney closed his eyes with a pause, "*that* was a hell of a fight."

"So he wore it down, huh?"

Chaney nodded, "And he put it in the one position where it might hesitate before it finally killed every last one of us. *That* was a high-risk move! Believe me! We were in a cave, so there was no place to run. I won't lie. It looked bad. I've been scared in my career, but I've never been as scared as I was then. Not before or since. And I never thought I would be again. Until last night." He hesitated. "Makes you doubt yourself."

Mack's voice revealed no doubt or disappointment. "Ah, you got plenty of stones, Chaney. You remember ol' Mickey Russell down in Houston? You planted Mickey all by your lonesome, and he was a maniac. So don't you ever doubt yourself, old son. I'd choose you for my backup man any day. And I'm betting that Barrett with these dynamite rounds will, at least, hurt the damn thing – if not blow it to smithereens."

After a moment, Chaney began, "I've already briefed the guys, but I'll do the same with you, although you probably know it already." He continued with tighter control, "You won't see the thing until it chooses to let you see it, Mack. Until then, it'll stay camouflaged by the forest. Like Hunter says, it's an ambush killer. But when it moves, Mack, you'll have to track the thing fast while it's attacking. And it moves like lightning. That's no lie. Have you ever seen a pissed-off tiger charging at you with the intention of eating you alive?"

"No," said Mack. "Thank God."

"Well, it's the same thing except this bastard is even faster. And it moves like a man. On two legs with its arms reaching out to grab your ass. It scared the shit out of me the first time I saw it coming after me! And if it breaks that wall on Hunter's far side, it'll cover that distance in less than two seconds. That's all the time you'll have to hit it. And, if you miss, you won't get a second shot. And then it'll be over. That fast."

Mack didn't seem shaken as he answered, "Maybe ol' Hunter has a few tricks of his own, Chaney. He's not exactly a greenhorn at this. And I know he's not just sitting down there waiting for this thing to show up. He's got a plan. I mean, even if we weren't here, Hunter would still have some kind of plan to survive this. I haven't known the guy for a full day yet, but it don't take long to size him up. Hunter wakes up to survival, eats survival, goes to sleep with survival. And he wasn't rigging those trees with Christmas lights. He was rigging them with det cord. So I don't know what his plan is, exactly, but Hunter ain't betting all his cards on *us*." With a frown he nodded, "Smart. I wouldn't, either."

Suddenly, and revealing no tension or fear, Hunter calmly stood and shouldered the rifle. Then he simply walked into the darkness of the ravine.

"Where's he going?" asked Mack.

"He's probably going to set more traps." Chaney paused. "He's big on traps. Some kill. Some capture. He knows them all."

Mack mumbled, "What do you think his chances are?"

Chaney sighed.

"Better than anybody else would have."

CHAPTER ELEVEN

Colonel Blakely's unwelcome presence intruded upon Cronis' moment of quiet contemplation. Cronis had been attempting to prepare his mind for what the night might deliver on his already tortured soul, but with Blakely's endless comings and goings, it was a futile exercise. And when Blakely entered the basement on this particular occasion he seemed distinctly agitated, and that captured Cronis's attention.

Cronis asked, "Are you quite all right, colonel?"

"I'm fine," Blakely responded impatiently. "Where's Dante?"

"I thought he was with you."

"I ain't seen him in an hour." Blakely futilely glanced up and down the basement. "Damn! We've got a problem!"

Cronis regarded the colonel with something like interest. "Really. I thought everything was in order for tonight."

Blakely didn't seem in a mood to respond. But to hell with it. He responded, "It was. But we've had a couple of defections."

"I'm shocked," Cronis said very insincerely. "Which men?"

"The two that took them up the mountain last night. They hit the woods, and it'll take twenty men to hunt 'em down. And I can't do that. With all that's going down tonight, I can't spare twenty men." Blakely stood in nervous frustration. "I don't know how the professor is gonna react to this. But I don't think it'll be good. He might even hold *me* responsible. And I ain't got time for that crap."

Cronis revealed nothing as Blakely asked in a harder tone, "All three of you are supposed to change into those things tonight, right? Before we take you up the mountain? You change into those things down here and then you load up in the truck?"

"That's the plan," answered Cronis. "What's the problem?"

Blakely shook his head, "The problem is that the only living men who have seen those things have chosen to ruin their careers and walk away from a big payday rather than stay on this base. The problem is that those things scare the holy crap out of any sane man and I don't blame them. Only four men have seen them. One is dead and I almost joined him. Yeah, for real, I almost died, myself, the first time I saw one of those things up close. And now the two men who saw what I saw have run off. And I don't know what the others are going to do when they get a good look at what you people are capable of becoming. I tried to prepare them for it. But *nothing* can prepare you for it. By the time a man believes what he's seeing, he's dead or he's running naked through the woods. And where the hell is the damn professor?"

"Calm yourself, colonel," intoned Dante as he entered the chamber. "And worry not that two of your men have chosen dishonor over victory. I anticipated as much and planned for such a contingency. But good old-fashioned greed should suffice to reinforce even the most severe reluctance to complete our task." He gestured toward the door. "Go and advise the men of tonight's plan and of these meaningless defections. They are no matter. And it is best that you tell them of this cowardice before they discover it themselves. And, also, inform the remaining men that I have doubled their fee. Now they shall each receive six million dollars. Their money and new identities will be waiting for them when we complete the mission."

Blakely stared as if he wasn't certain whether even that amount of money was enough to keep the mercenaries from scattering.

"This new world you're intending to make," he began, "you'll need security, won't you? I mean, uh, won't you need a loyal force of personal bodyguards?" He gestured, "You'll never be able to relax if you don't have something like 'a royal guard,' professor. You'll need bodyguards that you can trust with your life no matter what. Good men! Like presidents have! Or kings! Or sultans! All those guys! You'll need guards you can trust with your secrets. Men who are loyal only to you and damn the police! Damn the military! Damn all of them! And a royal guard like that ain't easy to find, professor. You might want to think about it."

Apparently amused, Dante sat on a corner of the desk. His folded hands rested demurely on a knee as he regarded the colonel with a spectral smile. "I assume you are speaking of the brave men who have brought us thus far?" he inquired.

Blakely raised and dropped hands. "We've been with you from the first!" he added more earnestly. "We know the truth behind this thing, professor. And if you'll just reward each of us with a piece of what you have, I think every one of them will be with you 'till the end. And that's the truth, sir." He paused, breathing more heavily. "There ain't a man alive that can resist what you're selling."

Dante laughed.

"Sin is easy to sell, colonel, and men have always been willing to pay for it with their soul." The smile that lighted Dante's severe face was both bitter and calculating. "You are correct, colonel. I will, indeed, need a royal guard. And so! It's decided! Tell the men they shall have both fortune and eternal life if they finish this mission. Then they will share in an immortal kingdom that shall have no end."

* * *

"You want me to climb *this tree*?" Vernon stared wildly at Gantry with the words. He lifted the gigantic Remington 700 rifle. "*Holding this rifle*? Are you nuts, Jeffrey?"

"Mack told us to climb trees and be lookouts, Vernon."

"You climb it!"

"I can't climb it holding that rifle!" Gantry responded. "I'm gonna find a high rock or something."

"Then that's what I'm gonna do, too! I ain't breaking my neck trying to climb that tree with this cannon!"

"Damn," Gantry shook his head.

Vernon continued, "I don't know why we're way out here, anyway. How are we even gonna see them way up here? Did anybody think about that? No! Nobody thought to tell us how we're supposed to see two Super-Godzillas walking by us in the dark."

"I've got the night vision goggles, Vernon."

"Night vision don't see through trees, Jeffrey! I mean, I don't know anything about this stuff. Not really. But even I know that much. Hell, I'm so bad at this stuff, they made me go through survival training three times before they passed me. And I still don't know if I really passed or they just felt sorry for me. I didn't sign up for this."

"Good grief, Vernon. *Nobody* joins the FBI to fight monsters and giant squids and aliens and crap. Do you think I'm crazy? I'm a tax attorney! I haven't climbed a tree since I was twelve. So just climb it, will ya? And shut up. I want us to be in place before it gets dark. And if you keep talking, somebody out here is gonna hear us."

Vernon stood on the slope and stretched out his arms. "Somebody out *here*?" he repeated. "Just who the hell is out *here*? Do you not realize that Hunter lives out here precisely because there's nobody out here?"

"You're killin' me, Vernon." Gantry bowed his head. "You're killin' me …"

* * *

Hunter finished carving a stake with his bowie and stuck the knife in the log serving as a bench. He tested the point.

Yeah. Sharp enough. It was the last stake in a bungee pit – an old Indian trick. Once a person's foot plunged into the concealed hole, the stakes would cut into him as he tried to pull his foot out. It was only a fatal trap if the stakes were poisoned, but it would definitely slow down a pursuer. Even a prehistoric one.

Hunter had no intention of simply sitting here and letting one of those things ambush him from the tree line. The trees hemmed him at less than twenty feet, both left and right. If it charged at that distance Hunter would barely have time for a single shot and, although he suspected that the explosive round from the Barrett might indeed injure the beast, it'd do Hunter no good if the round didn't blast it into pieces.

Calculating, Hunter imagined that the crossbow offered the best chance of success. He had killed two of these things and they had both been vulnerable to an edged weapon. Sure, they were supremely resistant to bullets just like a hippo or rhino or crocodile, but they had the same weaknesses, as well. In truth, a bullet-resistant skin was not an unknown thing in nature, and this wasn't the first time Hunter had been confronted by it. But he suspected that that Kevlar skin had the same weakness as a Kevlar vest.

Ballistic vests defied bullets because the Kevlar fibers of the vest spread the force of the impact across a wider area and diluted the bullet's penetration power. The only situation where a bullet proof vest couldn't negate the power of a bullet was when the round was simply traveling so fast that the vest didn't have the millisecond required to disperse the force. And the same weakness could be exploited against a vest with a knife. The blade didn't give the fibers the nanosecond required to spread out the force of an impact, so bullet proof vests were useless against a knife. That's why criminals, unfortunately. carried ice picks. An ice pick would penetrate the bullet proof vest of a police officer when a bullet would fail. It was also why there was a sorely known rule in the criminal underworld: Always carry an icepick.

Hunter had long ago decided that he'd make this camp the location of his "last stand." And because he knew this small ravine so well – when he was a kid, he used to play here – he could see in his mind the best places to pick the creatures apart as they made their way down the gulch. He had eight bolts for the crossbow, all four-bladed and razor-sharp. The blades were cut backwards against the angle of the shaft so that it was almost impossible to pull from prey. They had to be cut from the carcass.

Imagining the beast hit by a bolt, Hunter could see in his mind the rage it would experience as it did massive damage pulling the shaft from its body. If it was intelligent, it'd leave the shaft in place and cut it free later. But he didn't think they were that smart. Instead of waiting, it'd rip the bolt out of its body causing a gigantic amount of tissue damage. There was no question whether the beast was strong enough. Yeah, that thing was easily strong enough to rip the shaft out of its body tearing chunks of flesh with it. But that strength was also its weakness. It would use its own great strength to do itself infinitely more damage.

He needed six locations for a series of ambushes, and he needed a path of retreat along the ridge of the ravine. He'd hit and not even wait to measure the damage before retreating fast along the cliff and dropping into his next ambush site. He'd have time to hit them once at any site before he'd have to run. He wouldn't have time to riddle them with bolts from a stationary position because, once they saw him, they'd attack.

He had to keep moving. Fast.

Hunter reasoned that he'd be fortunate to hit them with all eight bolts before he reached his last place of ambush. Then he'd be out of time. But he encouraged himself with the thought that the trail was also rigged with bungee traps and hand grenades and, finally, a long strand of C-4, and that was his last trick. After that, he'd only have the rifle and whatever uncertain damage he could inflict with the explosive rounds.

As Hunter considered all he'd set in place, he was not truly optimistic. He did not suffer from some kind of latent PTSD because of his past encounters with the beasts, but he could recall in living color the sight and smell of flames and blood and the struggles he'd experienced against these creatures in the past. In his mind Hunter could still feel the horror of his battle in that Alaskan cave – a horror that provided him with a panoramic view of the ancient battle between prehistoric man and earth's greatest predator.

Hunter closed his eyes at the image.

He liked to think of himself as beyond feeling when it came to killing. He had tracked and hunted his entire life. He understood that the wilderness provides as much as it takes. There is no guarantee in the deep woods. Everything is prey. Everything is a predator. The strong feed on the weak. The weak feed on those that are weaker. And, all the while, Nature merely watches. And there is no favor. You survive or you die by your own strength and there is no such thing as mercy. These were the laws Hunter had accepted from the beginning. And blizzards, crippling wounds, animal attacks, snake bites, broken bones and near-fatal infections had endlessly reinforced the laws to him all his life. Nature was never slow in treating a living thing as coldly as it would treat a stone.

Hunter was aware that some counted him a hard man. And, being honest, he had to admit that he was. He didn't expect mercy, and he was surprised when he gave any. But perhaps, he thought, he did show mercy when he could because Nature had never shown any to him and he knew how terrible that could be.

In a way Hunter sometimes regretted that he had only survived by cold, hard strength. In a deep, internal place it seemed to extinguish any kind of joy leaving an emptiness that knew only how to move, to fight, to kill.

It was the life of an animal.

Hunting, always hunting …

Often Hunter had wondered about the undying spiritual bent that still resided in his soul. Perhaps it was because that was the only piece of himself that the subhuman harshness of Nature had not yet extinguished.

Certainly, he considered himself a spiritual man, although he was not educated in such things. He did, however, admire those who were. Sometimes, reading his bible late into the night, Hunter had sometimes pondered that he would have been content being a "man of letters," as it were. But that wasn't the cards God had dealt him, and suffering had taught him a long time ago that it didn't do any good to complain.

Nothing was going to help him but himself.

Standing, Hunter slung the rifle and lifted the crossbow. The bolts were secured to the bow leaving his hands free to keep the weapon ready.

Glancing around once more, Hunter nodded.

"Okay … let's do it."

* * *

Cronis stoically watched as soldiers loaded into three vans stationed outside the hospital's derelict emergency entrance and it occurred to him that it was a bit strange they'd had no visitors at this construction site since they'd arrived. Not even the sheriff had made an unannounced inspection to ensure they were proceeding according to codes.

He concluded that the people of this mountain community simply tended to mind their own business and cared nothing for what anyone else might be doing. Perhaps that was how they maintained their sanity in a community where ten houses in a row might be using cardboard to insulate themselves from the cold. Also, it was clear that the people of this scattered township – if it could be called that – faced an endless and exhausting struggle to survive in the harshness of this environment, so they probably had no emotion left for the lives of others.

Still, Cronis had observed curious details upon approaching the property that made him think some kind of unnamed benefactor was assisting the poor people of the area. Even from the window of the helicopter Cronis noticed an impressive multitude of convenience stations with impossibly low gas and food prices.

He'd seen a medical clinic very ably equipped with what looked to be brand new ambulances. Four cars in the parking lot suggested that it was also well staffed. But, most striking, Cronis's attention had been captured by a large business along the main road offering construction materials at fire sale prices. There was no way that, at those prices, the business was making a profit. Then, quite absently, Cronis thought of Hunter, and knew the mountain man was probably doing his best to help those in his community in his anonymous way.

It was a shame to kill a man who did so much good for his neighbors. But it only took one thought to make Cronis harden his resolve to finish this task. The possession of eternal life and the power to remain beyond the distress of old age, sickness, or disability was the endless desire of every man. It had been the dream of man since the very beginning when Adam and Eve sold their souls to be like the 'Most High.'"

There was something about that old, worn-out fairy tale that made it seem more real to Cronis in this moment than it had ever been before, and he didn't have any inclination to lessen it with logic or his better nature. He was in this now for the possession of eternal life. It was all he cared about. And concerning whatever mistakes he'd make along the way, he was certain he'd have centuries to forget about them.

* * *

"It's gonna be dark real soon," said Vernon.

Gantry looked from the scope of the rifle that he'd laid across the boulder, which both of them had selected as an ideal observation post. "I know it's gonna get dark real soon, Vernon. I'm standing right beside you. Why do you insist on stating the obvious?"

Vernon followed with, "Do you think these things can see in the dark?"

"Chaney told me they can't see in the dark. He said that they can see better than a person, but they don't have night vision, and they don't have heat vision – or whatever that's called." Gantry dragged up the goggles. "And we've got night vision! One of the HR guys gave it to me! He said we'd need it after sundown!"

Still staring over the crest of the slope, Vernon asked, "He only gave us *one*?"

"Well, how many pairs of googles do we *need*? You use the night vision, and I'll stay on the rifle. This scope don't have night vision, but the HR guy said it amplifies ambient light, so you point them out and I'll get them in the scope."

"Wait a minute!" Vernon objected. "We're not here to shoot one of them! We're just supposed to let Mack know if we see 'em coming! Nobody said anything about getting into a fight with them! I don't think they want us to do that!"

"Then just let me know if you see one," Gantry said patiently. "I won't shoot unless one of them sees us and charges like a lion does. Then I'll have to shoot."

"Then you better get ready to shoot," came a voice.

Gantry and Vernon spun to see Hunter poised on the downslope of a higher boulder. He gestured to the sky behind them. "You're on top of a boulder with both your heads sticking up against the sky. So, unless boulders grow human heads, they're gonna see you real quick." He motioned for them to follow. "Come on."

Literally following in his steps, they trailed Hunter fifty yards along the ridge until he stopped and stated, "This'll do. You've got trees behind you to conceal your outlines. You've got seventy yards of clear visibility of the trail. There's no way they can get past this spot without you seeing them. And below you is a hundred feet of rock that they can't climb too fast. It'd take 'em half an hour to get up this face." He looked around, nodded. "It's a good spot. And even if they do see you, I wouldn't be too worried. They're not after you."

"How did you find us?" asked Vernon.

"I heard your yakking." Hunter stared over them before he said, "Listen up, boys. Here's a tip about hunting and stalking. Don't talk while you're doing it. Don't get on your cell phones or radios. Don't give Mack or Chaney an update. They don't want an update if nothing is happening. And don't move. At all. Piss in your pants. The secret to stalking is not being seen or heard while you're doing it."

"We've never done this before," volunteered Vernon.

"Really."

Gantry asked, "Why don't you stay with us?"

Pointing, Hunter said, "I'll be eighty yards down the far side of the ravine. I'm gonna hit them with a bolt when I get a clear shot. And you'll be close when it happens, so you'll hear a lot of commotion. But don't panic and start shooting. You might hit *me*. And don't run off. You'll be safer where you're at." He motioned to the bluff. "Just stay along in here. You'll be behind them, and they won't be looking for what's behind them. I'll lead them down the ravine away from you, and when you're sure they're gone, tell Mack they're coming. But until then, just hold quiet and don't move. And you'll be alright."

With that, Hunter began to turn.

"Wait a minute!" gasped Gantry.

Hunter paused.

"Shouldn't we have some kind of wilderness call to let the other one know we're in trouble? Like a bird call or something?"

"Do you know any bird calls?"

They exchanged glances.

"No," they said.

Shaking his head, Hunter walked away.

"Don't worry. You'll be in screaming distance."

* * *

Cronis glanced over the hospital's empty parking lot.

Twenty grim faced, heavily armed soldiers had departed a half-hour ago. They'd be at the base of Hunter's mountain by now. In another hour the killers would be stalking paths through the overgrown green foliage and moist black gloom of the ravine.

Dante had done a layman's job of explaining the topography of the landscape to him although Cronis was certain the professor had missed critical details. Still, Cronis wasn't overly concerned. His long sojourn as the beast had taught him that the creature had all the necessary instincts to instantly know its surroundings.

He remembered how Dante had told him that he had somehow become lost the first night he set out to stalk Hunter's home. He told them about his unfortunate encounter with the wolf and how he had retreated because of sensory overload and confusion. But the professor had adjusted the serum to compensate for that unexpected neural weakness and now the potion was as close to perfect as it was likely to become.

Cronis had learned a great deal about the nature of the beast before he transitioned back to human form. Even now he could feel the all-but-superhuman strength in his hands and shoulders and legs. And after such a long transition, he was certain that his body had absorbed a measure of its superior physiology. Contemplating the nature of the beast, Cronis was inspired to wonder how it ever became extinct in the first place.

It was certainly made to endure any kind of injury, and it was virtually impervious to the elements. Cronis did not believe that any amount of heat or cold could conquer it's all but unlimited native ability to endure the harshest climates. But then he remembered they had found it frozen inside a continent-wide glacier that dated to more than 10,000 years B.C. and accepted the fact that a deep enough cold could, indeed, stop it.

"Maybe the only thing that stopped you from destroying the whole damn world was the Ice Age," he muttered. "I don't doubt it."

"Are you ready for the evening, doctor?"

Cronis turned without surprise.

He had been aware of Dante's steps on the stairs several moments ago and chalked it off to the latent instincts of the beast merging with and enhancing his human senses. Absently, Cronis wondered how much of the beast's nature had already taken over Dante's mind since the professor had undergone the molecule-shredding transformation countless times. Cronis grimly recognized that he would know for himself soon enough.

"Did I interrupt your thoughts?" Dante smiled as he approached. "If so, please pardon my intrusion. But now that we have a moment, I want to say, doctor, that I do understand if you have any misgivings. I must say that I, myself, had misgivings when I began." He nodded, "Yes, I was haunted by this relentless fear that I might be challenging Mother Nature or recklessly tampering with the unknown powers of the universe."

Dante laughed as he stopped beside Cronis, placidly staring at the setting sun. "But then it dawned on me, doctor. Why should I dread doing what I have always dreamed of doing? Why should I fear doing what I am trained to do? For that matter, why should I deny myself anything? Why should I withhold from myself whatever my eyes or my pride desire? Because there is no such thing as right or wrong in science, doctor. There is only what we know and what is not yet known. And since we are ultimately unencumbered by any obsolete, archaic understanding of good and evil, we should confidently command the power of life or death. We should decide the fates of both men and nations because we are the only ones rightfully qualified for the job. We should confidently raise up kings or bring down kingdoms. We should even dare to improve on Nature itself because we possess the power to do so."

It was obvious that Dante reveled in the glory of his own mind as he continued, "When I began my career as a physician, Cronis, I operated under the impression that it was my responsibility to heal the sick. But I found one facet of that understanding endlessly frustrating. You see, I could give my patients an easier life. But I could not give them *more* life, for the length of days was supposedly decided by God, alone. Yes, I could make their life more enjoyable. But I could not give them more days to enjoy. And I was always bitterly disappointed with that. In my admittedly naïve youth, I even toyed with a Frankenstein-like approach to death in my ambition to overcome the power of it. But I quickly realized the futility of that approach, and so I contented myself with merely creating new pharmaceuticals that vastly multiplied my fortunes, and I forgot about my once noble ambitions. And through a multitude of mergers and alliances I built for myself an empire of enormous power and wealth. But in accomplishing all that, Cronis, I found that I had discarded my most cherished dreams somewhere along the way. I had callously cast off my higher ideals of improving life and concentrated on merely extending it for a few meaningless days or weeks. I became nothing more than a shrewd chemist and a merciless negotiator, a cunning corporate lackey skilled at taking advantage of those far less intelligent than myself. Instead of becoming a great physician, I became just another capitalistic cannibal on that carousel of fools. And I was shocked at how far I had fallen.

"Indeed, failure seemed to be my miserable lot in life. To make for myself a fortune and then die and leave it to someone else – an ending so tragic that it should be biblical. And then some years ago – to my great surprise – the Scimitar was discovered within that glacier and all my dreams were resurrected as if by a volcanic eruption. I was so overpowered by the rebirth of my ideals that I personally oversaw every analysis of the Scimitar's incredible properties. Yes, Cronis, all that you are part of today began quite by accident. I was never a mad scientist. I was merely a discontented one who wanted more for my patients than science could provide. And then I realized that the innate properties of this creature did not only provide the cure for every disease known to man, but could overcome death itself."

Cronis observed, "But you say you're not going to share it with everybody."

Dante shook his head once, "No, doctor, I shall not share this great gift with just anyone. Those I deem worthy of eternal life shall have it. And those I do not deem worthy can have what their all-powerful God sees fit to give them – a lonely life filled with endless suffering that ends far too quickly in an agonizing death. They can keep their lives of bitterness and disappointment and pain. My ideals are higher, and I shall have them. And if I must cast God and his faithful children upon the trash heap of useless and obsolete ideas whose time has finally ended, I will gladly do so."

"You're playing God, Dante. Do you think you're qualified?"

Cronis shrugged, "I can scarcely do a worse job than God has done, himself."

"A lot of people have been killed in this, Dante."

"So! The number of my dead are *nothing* compared to the mountains of dead that God heaps upon the earth every single day of every week! And if God finds it so moral to kill a million people, I see nothing wrong with me killing my meager share. Clearly, when it comes to killing, I cannot even compare to God! God is a killing machine! And since life obviously means so little to God, you might even say I'm 'contributing to the cause.'"

Dante's argument was so crazy, Cronis couldn't even find a way to debate it. He shook his head, "Well, I guess you've finally reached your goal, Dante."

Frowning, Dante said, "Not yet, doctor. Those doomed to die still have one hero who stands in our way. But soon Hunter will be as dead as his God created him to be. For it is written, from dust to dust. And then my dream will begin."

Suddenly uneasy, Cronis asked, "What dream?"

Dante lifted his chin.

"To be like the Most High, Cronis. What else?"

CHAPTER TWELVE

T he narrow ravine was a killer's dream for premium ambush sites and Hunter considered more than a dozen of them before settling on six narrow spaces between fallen boulders that littered a trail running along the top of the cliff. He would be shielded from view and at the same time the path below him was unobstructed by branches.

Running fast, Hunter familiarized himself with the terrain of each site and tried to calculate the required steps and seconds between shots. He understood that, once it began, he'd have to lure them into the flattest part of the trail when he'd rigged the grenades. He'd already straightened the pins on the M-67s and loosened them so that the faintest pressure would finish pulling it, sending the spool spinning, and in three seconds the anti-personnel weapon would envelope the ravine with shrapnel, flame, and over-pressurization.

As he made use of the rapidly descending sun, Hunter was acutely alert to the wildlife surrounding him. The birds would be first to inform him that something unknown had entered this area of the forest. But there would also be the scattering of other creatures. Ground-dwellers would go scurrying for their holes and squirrels would take to the trees. The entire forest would come alive the second someone set foot in their home.

Hunter abruptly lifted his head, but, at what, he wasn't clear. Something had happened in the distance that must have been close to the road. He stood, staring, but saw no flights of fowl. Still, there was something. It was like a silence had fallen far up the trail – a silence that had not been there before.

Any change in the forest foretold some kind of danger. Wolves and deer could be scrounging for food, ravens and squirrel could be idly foraging for berries and even bear and bobcat could be finishing a carcass. But at the first indication of the most minute change – a scent, a sound, a shadow – and all of them would cease moving. And in the next moment they would disappear like ghosts. And although Hunter couldn't see it, he knew they'd all ceased moving. That was the first alarm to danger.

Hunter tried to catch a scent, but he detected nothing.

They were far away – probably still close to the road. It would be half an hour before they could bull a path through the thick jungle of Rhododendron banking the far edge of the forest. But, after that, they'd be able to make good time.

He didn't have long.

He returned to the first ambush site – the one closest to the road – and subtly eased back against the rock wall, leaving himself a good view of the trail and leaving the path along the crest open. He certainly didn't want to be standing on the only escape route if a startled deer came charging toward him. A deer is far stronger than a man, and if either of them were going to be injured in the collision, Hunter knew it'd be him. He didn't even have to consider what he'd do if a terrified bear came stampeding along the narrow trail. The choice of leaping from its path was no choice at all; he'd have to risk the fall.

Some dangers could be calculated and prepared for with vague plans, and others had to be dealt with on the spot with pure instinct and reflexes. Hunter didn't even consider glancing over the edge of the enclosing bluff. It was a hundred feet straight down and anything more than twenty would more than likely break a leg.

Continuing to acutely listen, Hunter heard a faint stampede approaching that only an experienced outdoorsman would detect because it wasn't the classic ground-shaking likened to buffalo. Rather, it was a subdued rustling easily mistaken for the wind rattling branches and leaves. It was all but undetectable, but it was there.

A deer charged over the small rise to Hunter's right and he flattened himself against the wall immediately angling to avoid the rack of antlers that cut the chest of his jumpsuit. His arms were straight out, and the crossbow was as much a part of the wall as Hunter himself. Then the deer was gone as quickly as it had appeared.

Hunter remained flat against the wall, awaiting another approach, but there was nothing, and he finally relaxed, resuming his watch. But he didn't relax his vigilance; all animals, even bears, had an uncanny manner of charging without sound.

Although he didn't glance at the sun, Hunter knew that he had about fifteen minutes before it was true dark and that somehow didn't fit with what he expected from the creatures or, more importantly, what he had experienced. Upon every occasion, the Scimitar had waited for full dark before launching an attack, so it was far too early for them to enter the woods. Then he remembered that Chaney said Dante had recruited a team of mercenaries to "clear the way" for the creatures.

Ignoring caution, Hunter keyed the mic: "Something's entered the woods up here, Chaney. I don't know. but I think it's your shooters. *Don't* hit them right off. If you hit them before I can hit Dante and his guys, it'll scare them off, so wait for me to move first."

A moment.

"Copy."

Hunter considered whether this intrusion might be an innocent troupe of hikers exploring the gorge and he instantly felt a thrill of alarm. The very last place on the face of the earth they should be at this moment was inside this ravine, which was about to become a bloodbath where no one, and nothing, would be safe. But, worst of all, there was no manner by which he could confirm or disprove his suspicion. He'd have to wait and see what emerged from the dark moss of the leaf-curtained trail.

If it did turn out to be hikers, Hunter would have no option but to descend from his ambush site. In good conscience he couldn't let them stay in this area when he knew everything in this ravine would soon be wounded or dead. But if he descended, then, needless to say, he'd be critically vulnerable. And it'd be a lose-lose decision because climbing the sheer granite of this rock face again might take more time than he'd have.

Barely easing forward to gaze up the path, Hunter confirmed that nothing was visible. And his slight movement – so small as to not be there at all – was cloaked in shadow and silence, and he did it without thought. It was done by habit. By reflex. For he was accustomed to stalking and was reflexively immobile to the point of even suppressing his breathing. And although he was still adrenalized from avoiding the buck, he slowed his heartbeat by inhaling deeply through his nose and out his mouth. And, within seconds, he felt his heart slowing.

Hunter had learned how to slow his racing heart when he was just a kid climbing cliffs or running down deer on foot. And, throughout his life, he'd sometimes been amused at how many times the skill had proven useful. He'd been bitten by a rattlesnake once and slowed his heart rate to little more than thirty beats a minute as he made his way to the hospital; the slow circulation had prevented the venom from spreading through his body. And as he got even older, he discovered that every involuntary action of the human body could be ultimately controlled by the mind. It was a control that been critical in surviving both heat and cold and even agonizing pain. And all it took was the power of his mind – and practice.

After a half-hour, a green silhouette emerged on the far side of the ravine; a man clad in jungle BDUs. He held a black semiautomatic rifle – it was an M-4 – and his face was painted in green-black camouflage … *Sally pack, grenades on vest, two smoke cannisters, a bandoleer with magazines, pistol, knife, machete, microphone in left ear, gas mask pouch outside right leg, first aid kit outside left leg …*

So, Dante had, for certain, hired outside help to guarantee success. There was nothing surprising about that. Just frustrating. Because it meant that Hunter would have to wait even longer for Dante and the other Scimitar. The primary danger is that one of the commandos might stumble into one of the traps Hunter had rigged and then Hunter's entire plan was finished. They'd retreat, Dante and the others would call off the attack and return to wherever they came from, and Hunter would have to play this whole thing out again.

He watched the mercenary knowing there'd be ten to twenty more easing in relative silence toward his camp site, and then Hunter noticed how this point man was carefully avoiding the main trail where there was more likelihood of tripping a trap.

So, they were experienced jungle fighters and, realizing that, Hunter released a very slow breath of suppressed frustration. While he was relieved that they wouldn't be triggering any of the grenades, their jungle savvy would also make them harder to hit if they fell back in some kind of tactical retreat.

Experienced soldiers don't just "run for the hills" when they retreat. Instead, they fall back ten to twenty feet at a time covering one another with ground fire. None of them would ever turn away from the attack site without six more throwing a ton of lead down range to reduce the chance of someone getting shot in the back.

Hunter had seen it play out a hundred times; veterans retreated in small increments, and in teams with each team covered the trailing group until they gained safe distance from the kill zone. Then they'd break the thread formation and reposition in case of a pursuit launched by the enemy. It was suicide to merely 'retreat' or 'run for it.' There was no safe way to evade pursuing rifle fire if they didn't fall back in an orderly fashion. In fact, veterans never used the word 'retreat' when they described the tactical moves of a battle. Instead, they called it 'falling back for a better tactical position.'

So quietly as to not speak at all, Hunter keyed the mic. "Chaney? Copy?"

A moment.

"Copy."

"Men in fatigues. Heavily armed. Quarter mile."

"Copy. The rookies count twenty. Heavily armed. We will wait for you to engage. No Scimitar yet. Out."

Hunter was familiar with the fact that a perfectly executed ambush was incredible difficult to accomplish. This was not the first surprise attack he had orchestrated; he had ambushed both animals and men all his life. But he had never staged an attack that had so many moving parts. And none that he would personally guarantee.

A thousand things could go wrong with this, and Hunter took a moment to consider a few of them. One, the FBI rookies could make a mistake and reveal their position. And Hunter didn't know much about the FBI operators Mack had brought, but he suspected they knew very little about jungle fighting. Even if they were ex-soldiers, they would be veterans of desert warfare and not war in thick foliage and trees. The nation hadn't engaged in jungle warfare since Vietnam, and anyone old enough to have been in that conflict was too old to be here.

Hunter calculated what he could.

If the mercenaries below him continued to move at the same pace, they'd reach the campsite in roughly half an hour and, if they had thermal vision, they'd detect Mack's men regardless of their concealment. Then a premature firefight would ensue, and the walls of this ravine would amplify the sounds of gunfire like a speakerphone across this entire mountain range. And regardless of whether the creatures had entered the trail, they'd certainly hear the chaos, know they'd lost the advantage of surprise, and quickly fall back. And although this plan wasn't fool-proof, Hunter was skeptical about whether they'd get another chance half this good.

Clearly, Hunter realized, Dante was willing to do whatever was required to see him dead before sunrise. Then, with him dead, there would be far less – if anything – standing in the way of whatever demented dream Dante possessed for the rest of a vulnerable world. Still, Hunter thought with regret, he should have anticipated the worst possible scenario. He should have expected the old man to bring weight.

Hunter did find some respite in the fact that he had taken the trouble, and the time, to set scattered fires along the base of the ravine. Although certainly suspicious in nature, and likely to slow any impetuous attack, the fires were the only means of seeing what might be moving along the shadowed path.

He had carefully scattered the bonfires so that no patch of trail was in total darkness. There were twenty in total allowing illumination for the entire trail, and all were stoked with enough wood, and built in a very specific manner, to burn until sunrise. If the soldiers took the time, they could extinguish each fire as they passed. But experienced soldiers would also suspect the sites as likely traps and subsequently avoid them altogether, which was exactly what this point man was doing.

Realizing his oversights, Hunter quickly tried to play out every possible combat scenario in his head. If he was hit with something that he was totally unprepared for, and had to retreat into the forest, he had no delusions about his chances. No matter what he did, three Scimitars backed by twenty experienced gunfighters would catch up to him and kill him in a matter of hours. And he had no weapon that could kill one of the Scimitar so quickly that it wouldn't still be able to tear him to pieces – something it was more than capable of doing in seconds. To kill it so quickly that it didn't rend him limb from limb, Hunter needed a rocket launcher. And, of course, Chaney didn't bring the one thing they needed most.

"Hunter."

Hunter keyed the mic and whispered, "Copy."

"Three! I repeat! THREE Scimitar just passed Vernon and Jeffrey! Copy that? THREE! *Confirm if you copy!* THREE!"

It took Hunter a moment to wrap his mind around that even though he'd been expecting it. Despite his control, his heart rate exploded to the point where he was breathless. But in the same split-second he was also a little relieved that there weren't even more. In some dark quadrant of his mind, he had feared that they might come with a whole platoon of Scimitar – *fifty* of them. And he wondered why they hadn't.

He keyed the mic: "Three. Copy. Out."

Mentally reviewing obstacles in the path of the beasts and the handicapped ground speed of a cautious approach, Hunter calculated he had ten minutes before all the commandos passed his ambush site. And since it would be impossible to hit more than one of them before he'd have to retreat to the next site, he desperately hoped all the mercenaries would be past this location when the Scimitar arrived.

He mentally reviewed the status of his weapons. The crossbow was drawn, and the four-bladed bolt was locked

tight in the cord that could fire it at 400 feet per second –
the length of a football plus another thirty yards. And the
shaft was tipped with carbon steel, razor-sharp blades which
provided his best chance of inflicting a debilitating wound.

He tried not to think about the possibility that they might
be invulnerable to the bolts, too. At some point in this show,
he *had* to get a scrap of good luck. It just wasn't possible
that *everything* could go wrong at the same time.

In the dismal moment, Hunter bowed his head and
tried to think of something encouraging. He considered
that, yeah, the hide of this bastard was real tough. It was
like armor. But the crossbow had been invented to punch
through armor and had made plate steel all but obsolete in
the Middle Ages. Even fired from as far away as 400 yards,
the thick, fast-moving bolts would tear through a coat of
English armor like tissue paper leaving a knight dead on
the field before he even reached the battle. The crossbow
had been so terrible an innovation that it literally decided
the course of medieval history. Entire nations regained their
sovereignty from merciless invaders and even relatively
defenseless city-states had resisted assaults and gained
victory over superior numbers with the mastery of this new
weapon that single-handedly leveled the fields of battle. It
had, in fact, been the ultimate weapon of war for a hundred
years until the invention of the cannon.

Hunter lifted his face.

And he had the rifle.

Hunter had it zeroed for a hundred yards, but at this
diminutive distance it wouldn't make any difference. He
wouldn't even need the scope. There was a twenty-round
clip of explosive rounds in the magazine, and Hunter
had twenty more five-round clips in the bandoleer. Then,
finally, he had the .500 Bushwhacker on his belt – a five-
shot revolver with one shot being powerful enough to drop
a charging Grizzly. Hunter felt that the formidable weapon

should give him some sense of comfort. He was troubled that it didn't.

It was Hunter's savage instincts that made him sharply focus on a dark patch of foliage concealing the depth of the path below. He stared without blinking, his hand tightening on the crossbow, as the dim outline of a Scimitar began to emerge into the light of the fire.

It was six feet tall with huge, sloping shoulders infinitely more powerful than any human being. Its arms were longer and incredibly muscled in hunched circles with overly large hands. The long fingers ended with curving black claws. Its body was completely covered in shaggy dark hair and its long, wedged head was led by a wide snout that hung open to reveal jagged white jaws glowing red in the flames.

It took a cautious step from the black-green wall of forest.

Moving ever-so-slowly, Hunter silently shouldered the crossbow. He didn't know when he would fire. He would fire when instinct told him to fire. In the moment he was relying on instinct, reflex, and experience. This was not the time to let his mind ruin things.

The beast slowly turned its head to the right, the left.

It fully emerged into the light of the flame and cautiously began to make its way along the trail. It used no care at all in placing its steps. It set a foot on mud or rock with equal disregard. It stalked twenty yards from the curtain of black, and when it was as near to Hunter's hide as the trail allowed, Hunter fired.

The bolt solidly struck its chest and the beast straightened with a roar of agonizing pain. The entire ravine was filled with enormous, thundering horror as it reached up instantly to tear at the black shaft protruding from its chest. Hunter dove to his left and was running along the crest of the ravine. He didn't look to see whether the beast succeeded in tearing the bolt clear of its chest. His mind was already in the combat zone of beast against beast and his main priority was reaching the next ambush site before it did.

As far as Hunter could think in his frantic rush across the broken slate, he calculated that the creature would explode in a berserker-attack. It wouldn't retreat now that it was wounded. It would want to kill what hurt it. But the faster it moved, the more careless it'd become. It was Hunter's hope to make it so enraged that it'd charge blindly into the tripwires which would detonate the grenades and maybe the blazing, slicing shrapnel would cut through its hide like knives.

Ignoring the possibility of mercenaries seeing his movement – there was no time – Hunter dropped into his second ambush site.

He was completely shielded from the trail as he shoved his boot in the cocking stirrup and used both hands to pull back the lever of the bow, drawing the string; the crossbow was so stout that it took a man's entire strength to arm it.

Hunter had two quivers attached to the bow because each quiver only held four bolts. He ripped out a second bolt and delicately laid it in the firing grove. Almost in the same move he raised the stock to his shoulder and used the scope to spot the trail.

He tried to slow his breath.

Breath slow … breath slow …

Slow it down …

He heard it coming a full ten seconds before the creature charged into view. Hunter noticed immediately that it wasn't the one he hit with the crossbow. This one wasn't injured, and it wasn't as large as the first. It tore through the leafy black foliage like a man might tear through a paper curtain, advancing in bounds.

Hunter fired.

The bolt hit it low in the torso, and it bent with the impact before it straightened and spun toward Hunter's position. Almost instantly it fixed a red glare directly on

Hunter and its white fangs opened in a murderous roar of revenge. Then, with a single brutal move, it ripped the bolt clear of its chest and threw it aside before exploding into an attack.

Hunter moved as it moved, and they raced along the corridor of the ravine. Hunter was high and the beast was low. But there were more obstacles along the base of the cliff – deadfalls and boulders – that slowed the Scimitar's rush, and Hunter made it to his third ambush site before it was directly below him. He moved like lightning to charge the crossbow, almost losing a quiver in the process, and lifted it to prepare a shot.

A hideous fanged face erupted over the edge of the cliff directly in front of Hunter as a gorilla-like arm lashed out. Again, it was Hunter's savage instinct that saved him as he violently twisted away and he somehow fired the crossbow from the hip.

Three images blazed in what Hunter simultaneously saw in his mind.

One, the bolt hit the creature dead-center in its chest. Second – as if in slow motion – Hunter saw the curving black claws in vivid detail as they swept past his throat and Hunter knew they would hit him. But they didn't. And he didn't know how they missed. It was as if his body knew exactly how far back to twist away so that the claws didn't rip his throat out. And it wasn't a conscious thing; it was as if his body, alone, reacted in a way that saved him because, in Hunter's mind, the great, sweeping blow had killed him. And third, at the impact of the arrow, the beast screamed in agony and fell away. And it was doomed to fall all the way to the ravine floor. It was too far from the cliff face to grasp root or rock.

Hunter didn't watch it fall.

He was already running.

In less than ten seconds Hunter dropped into his next site. He risked a single glance over the edge to ensure the beast hadn't reached this ambush like it did the last one, but he saw nothing and charged the crossbow even as a deafening explosion erupted in the darkness of the ravine's path; a wide circle of fire expanded, hit both cliffs, and rose in twin waves of iridescent flame. And from somewhere within the reverberating sound of the detonation Hunter perceived yet another bellow of pain.

At that very second gunfire broke loose at the campsite and Hunter knew Chaney and the others had opened up on the mercenaries.

He dropped into a crouch and shouldered the crossbow. He was at the very edge of the cliff in clear view of the path because concealment was of no more use. They were aware of what he was doing and – basically – where he was. And if they could reach him, they would. But the sheerness of the cliff made speed-climbing impossible.

Ignoring what was clearly a fierce firefight not a hundred yards to his left, Hunter focused on the depths of the ravine. There was no guarantee now that they'd remain on the path. The detonation of the first grenade might inspire them to hug the cliffs. But Hunter was somehow certain they were still coming. Squinting, he spied where he'd rigged the second grenade. Then he spun his face to see the approach of a wounded Scimitar.

This one was moving more carefully along the far wall of the ravine. It was hugging the rock. Staying clear of the path. The image was uncertain, but Hunter sensed a higher level of intelligence in how it was advancing. It acutely searched for where it would place every step.

This wasn't animal instinct.

This was human caution.

Thinking fast, Hunter focused on the grenade. On its current path, the beast would bypass the tripwire. Tightening the stock of the crossbow into his shoulder, Hunter relaxed his neck and put his eye to the scope. He turned the dial to increase magnification. He set the crosshairs dead on the

M-67 concealed within the branches. He waited until the beast moved to where it stood less than ten feet from the grenade.

He fired.

The bolt knocked the grenade from its perch and – by sheer chance – it landed not two steps from the feet of the beast. The Scimitar looked down and then seemed to recognize the threat, and Hunter saw it whirl away a split-second before it was engulfed with the blinding detonation. Hunter glimpsed a black silhouette swallowed by consuming flame, heavy simian arms uplifted to protect its face and chest and sensed that it was roaring although nothing could be heard within the concussion of the grenade.

Gunfire continued to rage at the end of the ravine and Hunter hurled the crossbow aside. He unslung the rifle because he knew what was coming.

The creature charged back the way it had come. With two steps it was moving with the speed of a tiger. It surged forward and leaped hard as it attempted to clear a fallen tree. But, as it reached the apex of its jump, Hunter fired the rifle. The round hit it squarely in its back and exploded, somersaulting the Scimitar in the air. Then it completely disappeared from view, landing on the far side of the fallen trunk, shielded from a second shot.

In the lightning-fast mindset that comes only in combat Hunter sensed that both creatures had retreated. Moving with far more instinct than thought, Hunter was already running along the cliff toward the campsite as another explosion erupted in the depths of foliage where Hunter had placed a grenade. But it hadn't been tripped by one of the Scimitar. It was blown by one of the mercenaries retreating from the furious rifle fire that Chaney and the others were throwing from the top of the ravine.

Suddenly, jungle-clad figures still holding rifles were rushing beneath Hunter and he knelt to gain aim. Hunter set the crosshairs of the rifle on a soldier that seemed to be limping from an injury, and fired. The explosive round hit him in the chest and detonated in a tremendous blaze of fire and blood that dropped the man where he stood. Ragged shreds of his ballistic vest floated down like confetti.

The others continued to retreat in a riot and Hunter managed another shot before they vanished into the distant undergrowth and that man, too, was blasted almost in half. Then more soldiers charged along the far wall of the ravine – a second wave – and Hunter hit two more before they all cleared the deadfall and Hunter lost all opportunity for another kill.

At the campsite, the shooting had ceased.

Hunter considered pursuing the mercenaries up the gorge until he quickly calculated all the factors and decided to hold steady. He had grievously injured at least two Scimitar, but nothing assured him that they were incapacitated beyond the ability to fight, and experience had taught him that a wounded lion was twice as dangerous. Then there were at least ten mercenaries, probably wounded and decidedly enraged, running pell-mell up this narrow passage and they would have a hair trigger to kill anything they saw. And last – as if Hunter needed yet another reason not to pursue, there was chaos in his camp.

The greatest danger was that Chaney and his men would descend into the ravine and accidentally set off the detonation cord. Then someone on Hunter's own team would be killed by a trap Hunter had rigged, himself. And Hunter hardly had to consider the fact that he still had to retrieve the two hapless rookies. They would be lost out there in the dark.

No …

No choice at all, really.

He let the remaining mercenaries escape.

Hunter made a quick way to the camp and reached the perimeter in time to see Chaney and Mack leading four HR commandos toward unmoving bodies surrounding the campfire. Hunter extended an arm, shouting, "Chaney! Mack! Stop! I've got it wired!"

Chaney raised both his rifle and face at the words, but upon recognizing it was Hunter, lowered aim. He extended an arm toward the men behind him, gesturing for them to stay where they were.

With only a glimpse, Hunter noted four dead bodies at the camp, but he assumed there were more. It took him two minutes to finally pick a cautious way down the bluff, and he didn't hesitate as he walked to the concealed strand of detonation cord. Five minutes later he had the cord safely looped and shoved into his pack. Then he straightened and motioned to Chaney and Mack, "Okay! That's it!"

Chaney approached, still tentative, to the camp's bonfire before he asked, "What about the grenades?"

"They're further down," Hunter managed, catching his breath. "I'll defuse them, too, so you can search for bodies. I left a few for you."

Hunter dispassionately gazed over the dead.

Clearly, Chaney had hit one of them with the Barrett. There was nothing left of the man's chest. There were scorch marks on what remained of the vast hole blown through his ballistic vest and his torso was simply gone. Liquified organs were visible across surrounding rocks.

Grimacing, Hunter analyzed the damage that had been done and knew almost instantly that it was nowhere near enough. This was a narrow victory, but not devastating enough to deter another attack.

Chaney asked, "What happened on your end?"

Hunter coughed, then, "I wounded at least two Scimitar, but it might have been all three. Hard to tell. I hit them with the crossbow, and one with the rifle." He raised his brow as he added, "The crossbow worked. The bolts cut through their hide like a knife. And I got one of them with a grenade – the same one I shot with the rifle. So you can say I wounded them pretty badly. But I don't think I killed

any of 'em, so I'm figuring they'll be healed by morning."
He pointed up the ravine. "I hit four of these guys about a
hundred yards up. They're dead. Believe me. And I can't
say how much damage the rifle did to that last Scimitar, but
I hit it pretty solid. Then he dropped out of sight."

Chaney spent a moment staring into the depths of the
gorge. "Setting those bonfires was a good move. It gave us
something to work with. It would have been a lot tougher
in the dark." He stared back. "You sure you hit one of them
with the rifle?"

"Yeah."

"But you don't know how bad?"

"No."

"Well, hell," Chaney began dismally, "I'd like to have
known how much damage these rounds do to those things."
A pause. "How far up is the rest of this bunch?"

"Not far." Hunter turned and pointed, "I'll defuse the
remaining grenades, then you can search the bodies." He
stared over the dead. "These guys surprised me. I was
expecting them to retreat with a little more discipline.
I expected them to retreat like veterans. But they came
running out like they didn't have any training at all. It was
just every man for himself."

"I think that explosive round had a little something to
do with it," commented Chaney, and pointed to what was
left of a human carcass; the mercenary's chest and head
had been vaporized. His arms lay on separate sides of the
ravine. "He was the first one I hit. I was a little stunned by
the result. I'll have to tell General Forge these new rounds
work fine."

"Oh, yeah," Hunter agreed. "Okay. Keep the guys here
until I defuse the grenades."

As Hunter disappeared into the jungle gloom, Mack
stepped next to Chaney, both staring over the dead
mercenaries.

Mack muttered, "What's our body count?"

"Well, we got six and Hunter got four," Chaney responded. "Ten or eleven, I guess. Enough to make them think twice."

"Ten casualties ain't enough to stop 'em, Chaney. You know that. They'll be back."

"Yeah," Chaney agreed, "they'll be back." He sighed, "Damn! I was hoping to get some answers from these clowns! Maybe find out where they're holed up. Now we don't know any more than we did. Ah, hell … *cais le guerre.*"

Staring down, Mack asked, "What about my boys?"

"Hunter's gone after them. They'll be lost out there."

"Huh," Mack grunted, "that guy is solid, ain't he?"

"As the Rock of Gibraltar, man."

* * *

Blakely was utterly horrified to the point of staggering as a nightmarish shape savagely tore its way free from foliage on the far side of the highway and crossed the road in shambling, uncertain steps, its clawed hands clutching, unclutching.

Glistening black in the thin white starlight, the nightmare image looked like it had been dipped in blood. Its chest was slick with a crimson sheen that descended in rivulets and clots onto the smooth pavement and its demonic eyes gleamed with evident pain.

Involuntarily backing up, Blakely realized he had raised a forearm across his chest as if to defend himself. Then the creature gestured with sharp impatience for Blakely to open the back of the truck. As it reached the port, it didn't leap into the opening like before. Instead, it rolled onto the smooth steel floor of the van with a groan, and even in the scarce light Blakely saw the gaping wound in its back.

Within seconds another of the creatures emerged from the woods limping and holding a forearm across its torso, and then the laborious movement of loading into the truck with a wounded moan was repeated. Blakely somehow knew the third one would soon follow and it would be equally injured, and he was right. Within thirty seconds the last one came stumbling into view. Blakely balked at the tremendous wound in the center of its gigantic chest directly between the twin shields of its pectoral muscles. He wasn't able to assess the cause of the wounds, but he didn't care. As soon as it climbed very slowly into the back of the van he threw down the door and latched it.

Leaping into the cab, Blakely used trembling hands to pull the van onto the road, hearing his own nerve-wracked voice …

"God Almighty … Get me out of this … "

CHAPTER THIRTEEN

C haney and Mack were warming themselves outside the cabin as Hunter emerged from the darkness with Sanders and Gantry in tow. Then ghostly images of Hostage Rescue operators began to take shape in the shadows until they stood in the light. Hunter gestured at the two FBI rookie agents with, "Here you go. Two brave young men who did a real good job. Safe and sound. Congratulations, boys. You got your first kill."

Vernon looked from one to the other. "But we didn't kill anybody."

"You were part of the team that did!" Mack nodded curtly. "Now you boys can consider yourselves veterans. Just like me and Chaney." He lifted a water bottle in something like a salute. "Welcome to the A Team, boys! You did us proud! Why don't you get some food and water and rest up? We all need to relax for a bit."

"It's not over?" asked Vernon.

"No, son. This is hell and gone from over. Go on. Get some food and water. You gotta keep your strength up."

A moment later, inside the cabin, Vernon and Gantry began to excitedly tell Mack about their time as lookouts. To his credit, Mack listened attentively, allowing an occasional nod, as they described how laying on top of that rock had been such a high-risk mission. Nor did they fail to incorporate how horrifying it was to see all three "monsters" walking past them in the dark, and Vernon was sure to add, "That was the scariest thing I've ever done!"

Mack nodded, "You two did good." He lifted a plate, "Here. Have some of this pemmican. You need to eat. You burned up a lot of energy out there."

Hunter picked up his pack and carefully placed grenades into it before closing the top. When he stood, he grimaced, causing Chaney to ask, "You all right, man?"

Hunter lifted a hand to his throat as if searching before dully answering, "Yeah. It was close. But it missed. Somehow."

Mack resumed his commander bearing. "Are those things the same thing you faced in Alaska? Or England?"

"Yeah," Hunter nodded and turned his head to gaze back at the darkness. "Same thing. But there's three of them. And they're working together. And that's not natural."

"Why's that?"

"Because these things are a lot like tigers. And tigers don't work together. Tigers don't even like each other. They hunt alone. They kill alone. You'll never find two tigers coordinating an attack. And these things might be prehistoric, but they're still tigers, so they might be further along with this metamorphosis than we thought."

"If I remember right," Mack began, "you said that the one in Alaska could talk. I mean, it could talk like a human being."

"Yeah," Hunter nodded tiredly, "it could. And Luther, up in Alaska, had something of his human mind. He could talk. But he was still ruled by the animal. He hunted like an animal. He killed like an animal, but ..." He paused, "... these things are hunting like soldiers. They're using military tactics. They approached with a point man, and the other two stayed back in case the first one met resistance. And when their point man got hurt, the one behind him took his place. Just like a platoon of soldiers would do. I thought I saw the same behavior at the cabin when they seemed to be coordinating an attack. I wasn't certain. But I am now. Whatever these people have done to this serum, they've altered it in a way that allows them to keep a whole hell of a lot more of their human intelligence than the other two."

"That might be good," offered Mack. "If they're smart, maybe they'll back off and go home and we won't have to see this thing through."

Chaney shook his head, "No way, Mack. I mean, I wish to God you were right. But I think Dante's in too deep. He's in this, now, up to his neck. Dante didn't come all this way, spending all this money, not to finish it. Plus that, he can't move on with his master plan, whatever the hell that is, unless Hunter is dead. And he knows it." He paused. "Yeah, we might have got the best of them tonight. But don't expect a repeat performance. Right now, Dante and his men are regrouping. Coming up with a better plan. They underestimated us tonight. But I don't think they'll make the same mistake twice."

Vernon raised a hand, "I got an idea."

No one spoke until Mack patiently asked, "What is it, Vernon?"

Vernon glanced at each of them before he tentatively asked, "Why don't we do the same thing they do to a bear?" He stared. "I mean, people step in bear traps, don't they? Even if they're as smart as a human being, they can still step in a bear trap, right? So can't we rig up some sort of bear trap for them so they'll fall into it?"

It was finally Chaney who said, "Not a bad idea, kid. But we don't even know which way they'll be coming. And there's a chance some random hiker could step in it." He very slowly released a deep breath. "I'll give you kudos for the idea. But it's too random. We're gonna have to figure out something else."

Grimly, Hunter stated, "Well, they won't be coming back tonight, so we can get some rest. I hurt every one of the things pretty bad, so right now they'll be licking their wounds. But we'll see 'em again tomorrow night. And their gun hands, too. So we need to change this game."

Chaney asked, "What are you thinking?"

"I'm thinking we go after them instead of waiting for them to come after us."

"You're saying we hunt *them*?"

Hunter's entire aspect seemed to darken.

"We got lucky tonight," he began. "But one of these times we're gonna make a mistake. Or they're gonna get lucky, or smart, or both, so standing around waiting for a repeat performance isn't a plan I want to be a part of. Right now, they have the advantage because they're picking the time and place. I'm saying we take that from them. We pick the time. We pick the place. And hit 'em when they least expect it."

Chaney: "You said earlier there were too many places to search. You said that searching for them was a lost cause."

"A *random* search is a lost cause. But if we know exactly where Dante is, then that's a different game."

After a tired sigh, Chaney asked, "And how do you suggest we move it from a random search to a focused search? To do that, we'd have to know exactly where Dante is, and we don't know that. What? You got an idea?"

"*Somebody* knows where he's at." Hunter gazed steadily at the darkness outside the window. "So we make them lead us to Dante."

"Uh huh," Chaney mused. "And how do you suggest we do that?"

"How did they know I was down in that ravine, Chaney? Why did they send soldiers straight to where I'd built a camp and not to the cabin? Because they knew where I was, man. They were betting they could beat me with numbers but that didn't work because they didn't know your men were at the top of the ridge. And why is that? Why didn't they know you and your guys were up there? It's because you got there late, Chaney, and they didn't have any intelligence on you and the Hostage Rescue team. But they knew *exactly* where I was. So how'd they know?"

Chaney said nothing.

"Who controls military satellites?" asked Hunter.

Mack answered, "Spooks."

Hunter nodded, "Someone in covert ops has targeted your team, Mack, so if you can find out who told them where to find me, we'll know how to find them. Because they're communicating with Dante. It could be by computer or phone – I don't know – but if they can reach Dante and tell him my location, it's some kind of covert government system. All you have to do is figure out which one. And who's doing it."

Chaney bowed his head and whispered, "Son of a bitch … We've been betrayed by our own people. Again. Just like Alaska."

"We can't do anything about Alaska," stated Hunter without a shade of mercy. "But this is a whole new ball game. And I think we should hack their play book."

* * *

Carnage in blood-red light inhabited the basement of the abandoned hospital as Blakely descended to behold three monstrous shapes all in various states of scarlet-soaked posture leaning or laying across the floor. It was as if they had been thrown together into a meat grinder and emerged with gaping, ghastly wounds.

The largest Scimitar pushed away from a blackened pillar and walked toward Blakely and the colonel's heart skipped a beat. Then the creature moved past him to the stairway and ascended. A second Scimitar, the one with the smoking, scorched wound between the blades of his back, suddenly arched and growled and, to Blakely's astonishment, slowly began to transform back into what appeared to be a human being.

And then he *was* a human being.

The Scimitar was Doctor Cronis. And even as Blakely stared, the doctor's gaping wounds began to heal until they were gone. Not even a scar marked where they had been. Cronis slowly reached out, lifted a towel, and began swiping blood from his body. His teeth were bared, as if in the last vestiges of pain, and his breath was slow and heavy like a man recovering from running a brutal obstacle course.

Blinking and light-headed, Blakely reached out to lean against a wall. He saw a chair and pulled it up, collapsing.

A moment later the third scientist was human, as well, and the two doctors walked with obvious effort to separate beds where they sat, faces contorted with effort. It was a half-hour more before Dante descended the stairs dressed in his customary garb. The professor appeared perfectly normal and acutely studied the two physicians. His mouth formed a grim line as if he did not approve.

"Come now," Dante stated, "it wasn't that bad, was it, gentlemen?" He walked to a position between them. "You didn't really expect this primitive mountain man to be an easy target, did you?" He turned at Blakely. "Colonel! How many men did we lose?"

"Ten. And, considering the circumstances, I can't promise that I'll be able to replace them." Blakely drew a deep breath. "And that leaves us shorthanded. I don't know if we have enough men to finish this."

"Not at all, colonel. As I anticipated everything else, I anticipated this, as well. We still have more than enough men to finish this mission. But we have done enough for tonight. Today we will rest, and later I'll reveal the final stage of our operation. Personally, I'm inclined to consider tonight an encouraging success."

Pinion gasped, "How can you consider *that* a success!"

With a steel smile Dante explained patiently, "Because we survived, doctor. We communicated effectively in the chaos of combat, even when injured, and managed a successful escape without revealing our base of operations. We killed two of their men, thus reducing their will to fight. We confirmed that the power of the Scimitar is indeed subject to intelligent human control without sacrificing the prehistoric advantages of strength, speed, instincts and healing! And that is a resounding success!" He gazed between them. "Surely you didn't think Hunter would be so easily eliminated, did you? He is the ultimate predator, gentlemen, and he is far more difficult to kill than any normal man."

"You said our armor would stand up to modern weapons," Cronis groaned, bent forward, head bowed.

"Exactly!" agreed Dante. "That is why we were unexpectedly wounded!"

"Explain."

"Because Hunter was not using a modern weapon, Cronis. He was using a medieval one. A weapon no longer used in modern warfare and considered a child's toy by modern armies. Hunter survived tonight only because he reached into his bag of tricks and pulled out a sling whereas another man would have pulled out a rifle. He survived precisely *because* he is so primitive. It was blind luck, my friends. And luck is no substitute for strategy. He will not be so lucky again."

Cronis said a slow voice of exhaustion, "You're saying you anticipated this? How in the hell could you anticipate that?"

"I did not anticipate *how*. But I did anticipate losses. Yes, doctor, I knew Hunter was the most dangerous prey. And if he somehow got wind that we were coming – and, as it happens, he did – then he would pull something unexpected from his bag of frontier gimmicks. You must remember that Hunter did not live to be old without first becoming wise.

But do not let yourselves be troubled. We still have our resources, and they will keep me informed if there are any more changes."

As if he were already standing atop Hunter's body in the coliseum of this wilderness, Dante added, "You must remember, my friends, that this entire night is yet another brick in the wall that will lead us to the pinnacle of our dreams. I have labored night and day for twenty years to perfect the immortal power of the Scimitar. And now that it is indeed perfect, we need only eliminate the one danger that stands between us and our final victory. Then we will have what gods have. Eternity shall not even exist for us. The past and the future will just be concepts. There will be no past. There will be no future. There will be no beginning. There will be no end. Time itself will be only an obsolete, irrelevant idea for the weak and foolish. For us, there will only be a continuous present that will last until the end of this universe."

From his forgotten perch in the dark, Blakely, alone, spoke.

"Amen."

* * *

Chaney had expected a bit more surprise from Mack as he explained what he suspected concerning a traitor in their ranks. But, seated once more at the cabin's kitchen table, Mack merely stared with his customary deadpan expression until Chaney finished.

"Well?" asked Chaney. "What do you think?"

"It can't be an elected official," Mack muttered. "Elected officials – politicians – come and go like flies. It has to be someone who was in power when you were betrayed in Alaska, and they're still in power. That means it's a career foot soldier and he's either FBI, Marshals, CIA, or NSA –

God only knows. But it's got to be somebody with the juice to change the task of a satellite. And that narrows the list."

Hunter looked up. "He's not FBI or a marshal or even Department of Defense. Dante wouldn't risk trusting a lawman. This is a *spook*. He's CIA or maybe some loaned-out, off-the-books military. But he doesn't answer to any chain of command. He's got his own pocket of government money and he only answers to himself. And nobody monitors his work. He works alone. And he can do whatever he wants without interference."

At a sharp sound outside the window Hunter stood staring into the dark. Then he picked up the rifle, checked the chamber, and walked toward the door. He spoke over his shoulder, "Stay here. Don't go outside."

Mack sniffed angrily, then, "Only somebody with the authority to change the trajectory of a satellite could keep up with us in this wilderness. And that means it's some nameless career goon who's been at the top of his game for twenty years."

"If they've shanghaied a satellite, why didn't they know the HR guys were out at the gulch?" asked Vernon.

"Because satellites don't stay in one place," answered Chaney. "Hunter went out there earlier in the day, and the satellite caught him. But then the bird moved on before the rest of us went out, and it didn't catch us because it was somewhere over China by then. That's why Dante didn't know we were there."

Mack added, "This guy is like an invisible tick dug deep inside our intelligence and he just keeps going from dog to dog. From president to president. He doesn't get replaced with each administration because he's not important enough to replace. He doesn't attract attention to himself. He never does anything bad. He never does anything good. He's just a faceless cog in the wheel. Nobody suspects him of anything because he's not important enough to suspect. And to even have a chance at stopping him you'd have to fire everyone at the CIA, the NSA, the State Department and the White House all at the same time and you *still* might not get him. He's probably some computer geek who's been hanging in there since the Cold War. But he's not a mover or shaker. He's more like a painting that nobody ever looks at. Nobody ever thinks that boring-ass painting is bugged and has been for the past two decades."

Dismally shaking his head, Chaney sighed and leaned back in his chair. He stared at nothing for a long time before he asked, "How did you ever get the file on this in the first place, Mack? I mean, I never got a file on this. I knew there *was* one. Somewhere. But I didn't know who had it or where. How the hell did you get it?"

Mack was obviously reluctant to discuss it, but, finally, he allowed, "My source is inside the NSA. Somebody who used to be with the FBI. I trained them as a rookie. And they're good at this skull and bones stuff. They know how to get a file in a way that nobody notices and nobody can trace. Like I say, I trained them." He pointed. "I trained you, too, you know."

"The hell you did!" grunted Chaney. "The only thing you ever trained me to do was piss in a thermos on a stakeout. Like *that* took a lot of training." He took a moment. "I've never seen you keep the identity of a source so close to your chest."

"They're kind of special to me, Chaney."

It occurred to Chaney that Mack must have a really important reason beyond the usual 'confidential informant' spiel for protecting his source. Then it came to him.

"It's Rachel," Chaney stated flatly, and without doubt. "I knew it." He sighed, "I bet you never taught her to piss in a thermos."

In what wasn't exactly 'a surrender,' Mack said slowly, "My daughter moved up in the world, Chaney. She left the FBI in the dust, joined national security, and now she's a computer whiz at the NSA with a security clearance that puts you and me to shame. Your security clearance and my security clearance couldn't open a bathroom at the bunker where she works. Hell, they wouldn't even let us in the building."

With a slow blink, Chaney commented, "I believe it. But how do you think this thing got so classified without somebody asking questions?"

"You been out of the game for a little bit, Chaney. Some things are the same, but a lot of rules have gotten more complicated in the last few years." He waved at nothing. "And it's classified because some fool in this new administration labeled it as 'classified.' With this new president, they just call it classified and put it in a box and nobody asks any questions. These days, asking questions is a real dangerous thing. It just is what it is and people leave it alone." He grunted, "It doesn't matter if it's a bunch of prehistoric monsters running around killing folks, a giant octopus, zombies, a bent Congressman or a UFO kidnapping entire towns. These days, any damn thing can be classified if some nameless administrative goon puts the label on it. And nobody is gonna ask a single question. That's what gets you into trouble. And nobody wants trouble."

Chaney almost laughed, "I always liked Rachel. She had grit. You taught her well, Mack. That girl worshipped the ground you walked on."

"All little girls worship their old man," Mack shrugged. "When I told her what I was up to, she dug into it herself without my asking. I didn't know about it until she contacted me in a way that let me know she couldn't contact me. And I just sort of guessed the rest. Then, on the same day, a big cowboy walked into my office and laid down a file with no name. I tagged him for unofficial CIA from the get-go, and it made sense. It figures she would use a source outside the NSA. And that was it. I haven't spoken to her about it, and I won't. Ever. So we got what we got. And there ain't no more."

Gantry, who'd been keenly listening to the conversation beside Vernon, asked, "What if we could penetrate NSA security to see who re-routed the tour of the satellite to take pictures of this site? Would that help?"

Chaney straightened, staring.

Gantry put a hand on Vernon's shoulder. "I swear! Vernon can do it! Can't you, Vernon?"

Vernon was staring at Chaney. "Uh …"

"Vernon was at MIT before he dropped out to join the bureau! Didn't you specialize in complex algorithms, Vernon?"

Vernon managed, "I …"

Mack said patiently, "I know Vernon was at MIT, Jeffrey. I have a real big personnel file that says Vernon was at MIT. Says it in big letters. But that doesn't mean Vernon can hack the frontline defenses of the National Security Agency, which happens to have the most iron-clad, no-nonsense, eat-you-alive security shield in the world."

"Uh," Vernon finally said, "actually, it's doable, boss." He stared at each of them in turn. "I mean, if they find out, then I'm toast. I'll be sent to Leavenworth for a very long time. So, now I know what you were talking about. But it's all just numbers, really. Anything can be beaten because they all share the same basic algorithms that make codes possible. All you have to do is find the piece of code that shows you the right connection." He raised his hands, framing a solid cube. "I mean, you'll *never* get in through their frontline defenses. That's impossible. But if we can find Dante's connection, then maybe I can piggyback on it to look for who, exactly ordered the re-tasking of a satellite."

"That could be a lot of people," Mack muttered grimly. "Dante works in coordination with a dozen top secret U. S. agencies, and they all have their own satellites. And if we go mucking around inside a system that monitors every single coded letter in the whole damn universe, we could be discovered real fast."

Again, Vernon raised his hand.

Exasperated, Mack threw up his hands.

"Speak, Vernon! You don't have to raise your hand!"

"Uh," Vernon began very humbly, "that could actually be an advantage, chief."

"How?"

From nowhere, Chaney asked, "You gave up MIT for *this*?"

Mack: "Forget that, Chaney! Vernon! How could that work to our advantage? What are you talking about?"

Vernon scooted to the edge of his chair. "If we can get in through one of Dante's Saturn connections, then I can piggyback on the access code of literally anybody in his system. I can 'commandeer' his contact. And if somebody notices us poking around, any trace will go back to whoever the code belongs to."

Chaney stated, "But we don't know which system to browse."

From the darkness, Hunter walked forward, laying the Barrett stock-first on the floor, and moved into the kitchen. He spoke as if he'd been present for the entire conversation. "Why don't you just ask your daughter who she got the file from, Mack?"

No one spoke until Chaney asked, "How'd you know what we were talking about?"

"You kidding?" Hunter laughed. "I heard you before I left the tree line at the top of the ridge. Sounded like you were hollering at each other."

"We were," muttered Mack.

"Hunter has a point," suggested Chaney. "Why not ask Rachel?"

"You've lost your damn mind, Chaney. I'm willing to see all of us go to prison for the rest of our lives but I'm not willing to see Rachel do a day. No way I'm involving her." Mack seemed to grow angrier. "And whoever has managed to stay hidden for the last twenty years keeps a close eye on his accounts. He's gonna know if somebody's poking around."

"Huh," grunted Hunter. "Jesus always used to put somebody in a position where they'd have to tell a second lie to cover up their first. But they couldn't admit the first because the crowd would stone them to death. Maybe you should try something like that."

Vernon asked, "And how do we do that?"

"Can you hack into Dante's personal computer at Saturn?" asked Hunter.

"It'll be difficult, but I think so."

"Okay. Then look into his Saturn emails and pick out the ones that are encrypted because Dante and his NSA guy aren't using open lines. And leave some kind of bug in Dante's Saturn computer – a way to trace where the messages are forwarded." Hunter shed the camouflage jumpsuit as he continued, "It shouldn't be too hard. Just highlight all the encrypted messages Dante sent and received just before he came out here. If I'm right, the last person he was in contact with will be his satellite buddy."

"And then what?" asked Vernon.

"Knowing this NSA guy's identity won't help us, but knowing his encryption code will. And the first message that comes through Dante's Saturn computer with that encrypted code will be forwarded from Dante's Saturn computer to wherever Dante is currently at. Can you isolate the longitude and latitude of a message beamed into whatever computer system Dante's using in this area by just following the destination of the code?"

Vernon nodded, "Yeah. But what makes you think he'll take the message?"

"Scare him," said Hunter simply.

Everyone stared.

Chaney asked, "Scare him?"

"Sure." Hunter checked the revolver. "You want to find Dante, right?"

Mack nodded.

"So scare him." Hunter scanned their faces; none of them understood. He laughed as he added, "Look, owls hunt at night. But not even an owl can see shapes at night. The prey has to be moving because they see movement, not shape. So an owl makes a big call that scares the crap out of everything in the forest. Everything jumps. Everything moves. And when it moves, the owl sees it. Then the owl swoops down and takes it. So, scare the hell out of Dante and make him move. Then you'll have him. You'll know where he's at."

Chaney asked, "And just how, exactly, do we do that?"

Hunter stepped forward, "First, hack into Saturn Enterprises. I'm sure it won't be a piece of cake, but it'll be a lot easier than hacking the NSA. Get into the email system of Saturn's chief of security. Send him an email that tells him FBI agents were in the building today poking around and asking a lot of questions about whatever contacts Dante might have with government resources. The FBI is trying to trace a traitor. And make it sound bad. Scare the bejesus out of the security chief who will then, in turn, scare Dante when he answers his burner phone."

"Can't we just trace the burner phone?" asked Gantry.

"No," said Chaney, "we don't have the number."

"What if he sends it to Dante's encrypted computer?"

Hunter shook his head, "Dante would never share this stolen encryption with some flunky security chief. Dante will have a burner phone with him. It's the same trick poachers use to avoid getting caught. So, Dante's security honcho will call Dante's burner phone to give him the bad news, and that will scare Dante into contacting his man at the NSA. And we can't trace that because we don't know that number, either. But when Dante contacts his NSA man, he'll use the encryption system. And tracing his satellite man's message back to Dante should give us Dante's location since you'll already know what the encryption looks like."

Vernon: "That's assuming a lot."

Hunter almost laughed, then, "Liars are all the same. So Dante will cover up his first lie with a second. He'll contact his NSA man on his encrypted computer telling him to set the satellite back like it was. And, like I said, we can't trace that. But then the NSA man will undo what he's done and he'll contact Dante through his Saturn computer using the encryption to tell him that it's done. He'll have to so they can keep their lies straight. And if you can follow the encrypted message forwarded from Dante's Saturn computer to his laptop, then we'll have Dante's location." He gazed at Vernon. "I mean, *if* you can trace a message from Dante's Saturn computer to whatever computer he's using locally."

"How'd you learn so much about computers?" Mack asked absently.

"I don't know a thing about computers," answered Hunter. "But I know people."

Chaney asked, "Did you even bring a laptop, Mack?"

"I did," stated Mack. Bending from the chair, he reached into a briefcase he'd retrieved earlier from the Humvee. "I kind of thought this might come in handy. Don't ask me why. But after learning you were involved, old buddy, I figured this would probably get complicated." He presented the military-grade laptop to Vernon, who stood and walked forward. "Will this do the job, Vernon?"

"Wow!" Sanders whispered, "this is an enhanced Toughbook with artificial intelligence sequencing. Holy crap. Nothing but the best, huh?"

"Can you get into Dante's system with that?"

"Yes, sir!"

"Get on it, then. Let me know when you're in and I'll give you the message we want you to send his security chief."

"You got it!"

With Gantry behind him, Vernon sat on the couch.

Chaney watched as the rookie FBI agent opened the laptop and began hacking like nobody's business. He didn't ask for a password or code. He just started typing like it was his own computer. And, not strangely, it did look like it belonged to him. He said, "Jeez, Mack. How come they gave a super-computer like that?"

Mack shrugged, "Hell, Chaney, it's standard issue these days for an ASAC. Everybody's got one. You been out of the field too long, old son. Things have changed since you decided to go skinny dipping with naked hula dancers. What's it like down there, anyway? Plenty of Mai tais and a lot of somethin-somethin?"

"I ain't done much somethin-somethin' lately," Chaney answered, glum. "I spend all my time fixing boats."

"Yeah? Got yourself one?"

Chaney leaned back. "It's on my bucket list. But to tell you the truth, Mack, I ain't been working too hard on it the last couple years."

"Why not?"

"Ah," Chaney began, visibly bothered, "I always knew that thing up in Alaska wasn't finished. This dinosaur business has been bad luck for me since day one. Even after we wiped up that crew at the lab, I knew something bigger was behind it. There's just no way that little ol' lab could have ram-rodded all this. They didn't have the stones. I mean, I never suspected it'd be some kind of titan like Dante but …" There was a long pause. "You know, Mack, I guess I'm still – incredibly – kind of naïve. But I figured somebody like Dante would have made his fortune honestly. Like, by *not* by killing people. That's so sixties. Reminds me of the Gambino family when they were killing each other like dogs. It seems Dante would be a little slicker."

"I keep telling you that the world has changed, Chaney. It ain't like it used to be, old buddy. Back in the day, you and me *knew* who the bad guys were. I mean, even if they *looked* like good guys, we knew. Nowadays, it's not as easy to tell. Half the people at the NSA are traitors and the place leaks like a twenty-year-old Plymouth. The military is full of buck privates going Postal with classified military secrets. And most of the top brass at the bureau has been bought and paid for by Nazi oligarchs. And they sold themselves *cheap*! That's the insulting part! They didn't even demand good money to betray their country! Back when some of the old FBI guard were selling out to the KGB, they at least had the dignity to demand top dollar. Now a top agent's loyalty can be bought and sold like a ten-cent cigar. Almost makes you ashamed to carry the badge."

Unexpectedly, Hunter spoke to Mack from the kitchen, where he was making sandwiches. "I'd have to say some of the finest people I've ever known were line agents with the FBI." He walked to Sanders and Gantry and presented them with a plate of four thick sandwiches. Then he added, "You boys worked hard tonight. Hunting monsters is a tough business. Eat up. You need your strength."

Returning to the kitchen, Hunter continued, "Yeah, Chaney saved my life up in Alaska more than once. I owe him. And look at yourself, Mack. You come here to save both of us and you're putting your life on the line doing it. I can't say I know that many FBI agents, but I can say the ones I do know have accounted for themselves. I owe both of you."

Hunter laid another plate piled with roast beef sandwiches down for the four surviving Hostage Rescue team members. "You boys eat up. There's plenty of food. And there's beer in the fridge."

"Ah," said one HR commando, "thanks, but we can't drink on duty."

"Duty went out the window when we got here," Mack said miserably. "We're on our own time now, boys, so whet your whistle. But don't get too happy. We might still need you on a trigger." He regarded Hunter. "You think those freaks are done for tonight? I mean, that's why we're relaxing, ain't it?"

"Yeah," Hunter answered, putting his feet on another chair. "They're done for tonight. I'm figuring they've never been wounded that bad and they've gone to ground to see how good that healing power holds up."

"What about your bear?" Mack followed the question with a glance at the door. "He still around? I kinda liked him."

"Yeah. He's up on – "

"His name is Moe," Chaney contributed.

Hunter laughed, "Moe is up on the ridge, so he'll let us know if anything approaches. And as long as we don't hear the wolves, we're good, so go ahead and eat. You need the calories. And that's pemmican. Try a chunk of it."

Chaney picked up a palm-sized square. "What's pemmican?"

"You don't know what pemmican is?" Mack asked. "Hell, Chaney, even I know what pemmican is. Knew what it was when I saw it on the table. My old granddaddy used to make it for fishing trips."

"I ain't a mountain man like you, Mack."

"Ain't but one mountain man in this old place," Mack answered, solid. "And thank God he's on our side."

Chaney continued, "Okay. Fine. So what the hell is pemmican?"

Hunter laughed, "It's a mix of tallow, jerky, and berries cooked up in Worcestershire Sauce. I have my own recipe. I mix in a little hash for pain. Go ahead and try it. It ain't half-bad if I say so, myself." He cut a slice for Chaney as he added, "Yeah, pemmican was an old standby for the frontier Indians and mountain men. It's easy to make and stays good for a year in any kind of hot or cold. It's loaded with all you need to keep moving no matter how hot it gets and gives you enough calories to stay warm in the worst kind of cold.

I always carry a block with me. It's saved me more than once."

Chaney took a bite, chewing thoughtfully. "You're right. This ain't half bad."

"I liked it the first time I tried it," said Hunter. "And, up here, you need it. The cold burns a lot more energy than city people realize. If you're not experienced with it, you don't notice it. But your body does. That's why people up here have a routine. It doesn't matter if they don't feel hungry or thirsty. They eat when they know they need to eat. And dehydration is a lightning-fast killer at anything above ten thousand feet, so people drink plenty of water whether they're thirsty or not." A pause. "Up here, survival is an art you cultivate."

Chaney called, "How's it going, Vernon?"

"Still working on Saturn," he replied. "Wow. This guy has government-level encryption. He's serious about his secrets."

"He's seriously *insane*," stated Chaney, and looked at Mack. "Why do you figure somebody like Dante – who's got it all – would risk his life on this? I mean, what more can a man ask for than all the money in the world, power, women and his own good health? Sure, Dante's no spring chicken, but he's still running around digging up dead dinosaurs. Hell, that's more than I can do. I wouldn't last one day up in the Arctic."

"You lasted a whole week," Hunter said absently.

"That was twenty years ago, Hunter! I was a young man then! And that was *before* I spent twenty years chasing this demonic conspiracy across the damn world. And, like they say, it ain't the years, it's the milage." Chaney released a deep breath. "I done got too old for this. There's no denying it. Jumping fences and doing my half-ass MMA routine with bad guys twice my size is a young man's game. And I ain't young. Not no more."

"We're *all* gettin' a little long in the tooth for this," Mack said glumly. "I guess the only upside is that I do things the easy way now. I don't waste time fighting with some kind of Andre the Giant and get myself put back in the ER. I'll just shoot his ass and write it up as self-defense. That's the danger of messing with an old guy who's just hangin' in there. His bad heart won't let him fight and he's too old to run. He'll just shoot you and let a jury decide. And if it goes bad, it don't matter too much. A life sentence to me don't mean what it used to."

Chaney almost laughed, "I thought you were gonna retire to your daddy's old farm and raise tomatoes."

"Nah," Mack shook his head. "Farming's too much work. I thought about it, but getting up early and working all day in the burning sun would be too much for me. No, buddy, when I retire, I'm gonna do just what you're doing. I'm gonna get me a place down on the beach and spend the rest of my days by the pool." He grew contemplative. "I might occasionally do some P.I. work as long as nobody's gonna be shooting at me. But that's about it. I'm tired of people shooting at me. I just want peace and quiet."

"I'm in!" shouted Vernon.

Chaney erupted from his chair and was instantly beside him, staring down. "What do you have, Vernon?"

"I'm scanning for the security chief, but each division has its own separate code, so it might take a while." He grimaced at the screen. "You know, this is remarkably similar to an algorithm used by the State Department. It's like this guy has access to all kinds of government encryption. Do you think he's part of an agency we don't know about?"

Chaney stated, "That's a loaded question, Vernon, but the answer is yes. He's got government help. But we don't know who or why."

"I can tell you why," commented Hunter. "For the same reason everybody else is helping Dante." He opened a beer, took a sip. "It's because Dante has promised them the same thing he'll possess when this is over. It's like you said, Chaney. What do you give the man who has everything? He's already rich. He's got money, women, power – plus wine and song to make his heart merry, as it says in the Bible. But, most importantly, he's beyond the law. Nobody can touch Dante because he's got too many friends in high places. And they're not protecting him because they like him. They're protecting him because he has something they want more than anything else in the world and he's the only one who can give it to them. They're not in this together out of loyalty. They're in this together out of greed."

Vernon asked, "Greed? For more money?"

Chaney answered, "For more *life*, kid." He laughed without humor. "Yeah, all Dante's money doesn't do him any good if he dies, like everyone else, and leaves it all to whatever fool follows him. Seriously, what good does it do a man to gain all the money in the world and then die and leave it all to somebody else? Dante's learned his lesson well. Animals die, men die, so what's the difference? You come naked into this world, make a fortune, and then leave it so someone else can take all the glory you built for yourself.

"I mean, if that's the way it is, then what makes man any better off than an animal? The answer is that there's not any difference. We all go to the same place, in the end, and that makes everything we do in this world meaningless. It makes money meaningless. It makes morality and power and happiness meaningless because it's here today, gone tomorrow. But what if you could cheat that equation and never die and never surrender all you possess to those who haven't earned it?" Chaney grunted, "Well, then, that's a different game where the only move is to cheat death and keep it all for yourself."

Vernon followed, "Is that what Dante's doing?"

"It's close enough," Chaney nodded. "Just stay on that encryption, kid. Get us into Dante's files first because I know exactly what I'm gonna send this security chief to scare the Holy Ghost out of him. I'm gonna give him a Come to Jesus message that he's never gonna forget no matter how long he's in Leavenworth."

Hunter laughed out loud, "I think you're enjoying this, Chaney." He shook his head. "I never figured on that."

"Why not?" Chaney walked into the kitchen and removed a beer. He popped the cap and took a sip before, "I've lived with this nightmare for twenty damn years and that's twenty damn years too long, son. So if Dante wants to take us out, and there's no way we can avoid it, then let's give him a fight he'll never forget. I still got one good fight left in me. What do you say, Mack?"

"I'm in," nodded Mack. "No reason to get all dressed up and not go to the dance." He looked at the Hostage Rescue team. "What do you say, boys?"

They all lifted beers in the pact.

"Alright," said Chaney. "Well, then, that's it. When we find where Dante's at, we go in hot. And, one way or the other, this'll be over. And we'll all be dead, or Dante will be dead. And you know what? Something tells me that I'm gonna miss this stuff. There's just something about fighting for your life that makes you feel more alive."

Gantry's words were dry.

"It's the 'alive' part I like."

CHAPTER FOURTEEN

Entering the surprisingly well-equipped office, Cronis observed Dante adding a tiny measure of serum to the over-sized flask. It was already filled almost to the brim and Cronis vaguely wondered if the professor was preparing for something unforeseen.

"I see you're hard at it," commented Cronis, taking a seat.

"You know what they say about idle hands, doctor."

Dante set the tinier tube once again on a burner and adjusted a valve leading from a cauldron; the setup was crude by laboratory standards, but Cronis was aware Dante had reduced the process to its simplest, most efficient method. At this point, the older physician could probably synthesize the serum from Biscuit.

Cronis asked, "I was wondering what our next move might be. Given it much thought?"

"Indeed, I have," answered Dante, and took a chair, himself. "I am waiting for a reply from a colleague of mine. I decided last night that events mandated a change of plans and that we could use some help."

"What kind of help?"

"Don't worry yourself with the particulars, doctor. Leave the details to me. But I have decided that Hunter has entirely too much help. And that makes the consummation of our plans ten times more difficult. Also, since we have already lost the advantage of surprise, we must isolate him and force him into the open."

"I thought we tried that last night."

"Last night was a ruse of Hunter's. I foresaw that, too, of course. But I incorrectly assumed we had the advantage in numbers. So many guns on our side would eventually have overcome Hunter's abilities with a rifle. And no man could resist even one of us in our altered phase in open conflict. But my sources were not complete, so I made a miscalculation – a mistake I will not repeat. The next time I confront Hunter, it will be man to man, so to speak. Then this contest will end the only way it can end, and we will finish our plans in peace."

"I don't think Hunter is going to cooperate." Cronis read nothing in Dante's face as he added, "The mountain man is more cunning than you give him credit for, Dante. If you'll look at what he's done, he knows a lot more than you seem to recognize. He killed Luthor with a combination of psychology and brute force. Couldn't have been an easy thing to do. And I'm not sure how he killed Vang but –"

"Vang walked into a trap," frowned Dante. "They were both deceived, and so they are dead." He took a moment. "Yes, Cronis, Hunter is more than meets the eye. And you are wrong. I have always been aware of that disquieting fact. But we must remember that trapping prey is what he has done all his life. He knows every artifice in the book and probably invented some himself. That is why I have never assumed Hunter was one of those faceless minions that shoot deer in the winter. Quite to the contrary. I believed from the beginning that Hunter is the most dangerous prey because he is also the most intelligent. We have learned by experience that he has almost supernatural senses in the wild. We have seen with our own eyes how the animals cooperate with him so that he cannot be taken unaware. Despite my stated contempt, I am not certain that he does not hold some kind of mystical power over them. Indeed,

I doubt very little when it comes to this man. But we have the advantage, Cronis. That is something I wish you would remember."

Cronis leaned back. "After last night it's difficult for me to see any distinct advantage, doctor. The soldiers might have been ambushed by the FBI – that was something we didn't foresee – but Hunter wounded each of us by himself. And he did it in the woods where we should have had every advantage over him."

Dante's expression was indulgent. "You miss the point, Cronis. We have the advantage because Hunter wrongly believes he can repeat the victories he claimed over Luthor and Vang. And we have given him no reason not to think otherwise. But he is making a mistake."

"What mistake?"

"Hunter is still fighting us as animals, and not as men. And that is a mistake. You see, when Hunter destroyed Luthor and Vang, it was because he hunted them like the animals they had allowed themselves to become. They fought him like animals and so they died like animals. And they deserved to die like animals because they did not use their greatest weapon."

Cronis paused before, "Their minds."

Dante laughed, "*Of course!*" He continued in his mirth before resuming, "Don't you see, Cronis? Hunter is hunting what he knows. But he only knows what Luther and Vang had become. He does not know *us*. He does not know what *we* have become! Yes, yes, of course, he is aware now that we have brought soldiers. But Vang also brought help in the substance of three prehistoric wolves – wolves of no small repute, I might add. Any single one of them would have destroyed the small contingent Hunter has with him in his cabin. But we have much more than brute strength. Of course, we have that, as well. But our greatest weapon is our intelligence. And our intelligence no longer deserts us when we undergo the transition. Hunter is assuming that we will behave in the same manner Luther and Vang behaved. And that will be his undoing."

Revealing his consternation, Cronis responded, "I thought we *were* using our intelligence, Dante. We were using military tactics. We were separated so that Hunter couldn't hit us all at the same time. One advanced while the other two covered him. And yet Hunter still managed to ambush all three of us with that crossbow. I still can't believe he took all of us down with a child's toy. And then he hurt us with bobby traps that even the soldiers avoided. Think about it. None of the soldiers got blown up by one of those grenades. You didn't see any of them coming out of those woods missing an arm or leg. The only ones who got hurt were us."

Dante answered, "They didn't come out of the woods wounded because they didn't come out at all. We did lose ten men in that exchange, and it is quite possible that one of Hunter's traps took, at least, some of them out of the action. And please mind your tone, doctor. We must maintain discipline. But you are, nevertheless, correct" He took a moment to calculate. "Our intelligence was incomplete, leaving us to unknowingly walk into a trap. Yes, this is what happens with insufficient information. And that is why I am taking steps to ensure that the same misfortune does not befall us twice."

Cronis sighed. Then, "Just what are you thinking, Dante? Because we can't do the same thing again. Even I know that. And I guarantee that the soldiers won't cooperate in another frontal attack. And they're right. It's suicide to attack that cabin in the open field because if we attack that cabin again, Hunter will call in help from the wolves and bears and we'll be fighting the whole damn forest. And, even if we win, we're going to leave a trail of dead bodies all the way back to the lab. Any investigator worth a damn will put it together that we're using this hospital and trace it back to our real identities so that, even if we make it out of here, we'll still be hunted down." He leaned forward. "This is not what you promised, Dante. You said this would be over in a day and we'd be back in the lab before anybody knew we were gone. But this has turned into a damn medieval siege, and I can assure you that any more gunshots at that cabin is gonna bring a whole flock of cops down on this place with a whole helluva lot of people asking a whole helluva lot of questions."

"That is precisely what I am trying to avoid," Dante responded. "An intrusion by outside forces that has been, thus far, avoided. And we must make sure that we continue to avoid it. The good colonel set the explosives for the lab, so they remain in place. And we will use them if we must. But not yet.

"Indeed, laws have been broken, and our footstep here is becoming obvious, so we must bring this to an ending, and so I've summoned someone to help us nullify Hunter's advantages in the wilderness. He will soon arrive and play Hunter's own game against him. And at that point I am calculating that Hunter will prefer to take his chances in the open field. He will retreat into the forest. He will attempt to use his vast experience, his instincts, tricks, traps – his sheer animal strength. But no man ever lived that could defeat the predator who is arriving to deal with Hunter. Also, as I have stated, Hunter is still not prepared for the human mind that guides our combined attacks, and so we have that advantage, as well." Dante seemed to relish the moment. "And when Hunter dies, the most despised reminder of a world damned by its futile and meaningless existence will be gone. Yes, Cronis, this great champion of the lost will die as he has been doomed to die from the beginning. And the most despised part of his world will die with him. And his death will serve as the foundation of a new world that is not made impotent and useless by the futility of its own temporary existence – a world where we become more with each moment. More in scope, more in knowledge, more in power. *That* is the destiny denied us by a jealous God. You see, my friend, death is God's way of controlling his greatest creation. It is the means by which he ensures that his creation does not rise up to rival him. To be like him! To know both good and evil! But we *will* know! And then we will take the power of death away from God. And when we have done that, we shall take the rest of his world."

Glancing at the laptop, Cronis asked quietly, "Are we waiting for something, Dante? Something that you, maybe, forgot to mention?"

Dante's gestured, "It's a small matter."

"Let me be the judge of that."

With a shrug indicating how unimportant it was, Dante said, "My colleague has sent for someone that we should expect at any moment. He made the arrangements last night after I informed him of our unfortunate first encounter with Hunter." He examined his watch. "Yes. Barring any unforeseen mishaps, he should be here within the hour. And tomorrow night he will lure Hunter into the woods and end this matter."

Cronis scowled, "And just who is this famous 'predator' who is equal in every way to Hunter? I didn't think such a man existed."

Dante smiled faintly. "Hunter is not the only legendary tracker in the world, doctor. There is another who is, as one might say, Hunter's opposite number. But I would propose that he is Hunter's superior. Of course, this man exists on a higher tier than Hunter. Hunter saves people and animals and only kills when he absolutely must. This man, however, operates at the opposite end of that spectrum. His reputation is more worthy of a butcher than a conservationist. In fact, he is wanted in more than twenty countries for poaching. And it is said that he has almost single-handedly driven the Bengal tiger to extinction. His hatred of Nature is actually quite remarkable. And, exactly like Hunter, he is hard to kill. I have sent for him only as a precaution, mind you. But should the rest of my plans fail, I assure you that he will not. He is the ultimate failsafe that Hunter cannot escape."

"You're betting a helluva lot on this man."

Dante's eyes widened. "Hunter is renowned for his ability to survive. But so were a thousand men and women throughout history who were claimed by the forces of nature. Bold explorers who froze to death. Famous mountain climbers who finally met their match on some nameless rock. Brilliant scientists, like Madam Curie, who died by the work of her own hand. The world is filled with many famous heroes who died precisely *because* of their skills, Cronis. And Hunter will be no different. He worships Nature. But he is about to discover that Nature does not worship *him*. To Nature, Hunter is nothing more than another meal. Nature equally consumes the sick, the old, the stupid, the wounded, the weak. Hunter knows all this. But now he is going to discover that Nature also consumes the strong. And that there is one master of the wilderness far more skilled and stronger than he is."

* * *

"Vernon, are you getting any closer?"

The question, asked by Chaney, smoldered with impatience. Nor did Chaney, standing over Vernon looming with angry tension, do much to help the situation. Sure, Chaney knew these 'computer things' took time. But Vernon had been working on this for five hours and he hadn't even cracked the code protecting Dante's emails.

Vernon replied without raising his face, "This is a lot harder than it looks, Agent Chaney. Dante is using an encryption system that rivals the one used by the National Security Agency. In fact, I think he *is* using the NSA's system. And he's revoked access to his past emails, so I've been trying to get into his cache through an automatic backup command. But it's tricky. If I try the same thing three times, and it doesn't work, the system will permanently lock me out. It could even alert Dante that somebody is poking around. And that'd be a disaster."

"Can't you try it with another handle?"

"It'll track the IP address and that can't be changed."

Glancing down, Chancy saw that Vernon was rapidly typing in one command after another. He didn't know, exactly, what he was doing, but it was easy to determine that the kid was working hard. Frowning, Chaney walked back to the table where Mack and Hunter were casually chewing on pemmican. He sat.

"You two seem nice and relaxed," he said.

Hunter offered him a bite.

"I've had plenty," muttered Chaney. "Tell me something, Hunter."

"What's that?"

"Have you ever tracked something you couldn't find?"

"Sure," Hunter replied without shame. "A lot of times."

"Like what? I thought you were the best tracker in the world."

Hunter laughed, "There's no such thing. There's a lot of trackers who are as good as me." "Yeah, tracking is an art. It's a science. Some use more art, and some use more science. Some are savvier about wildlife, and others hunt by pure instinct. I've known Innuits who could tell you which direction a polar bear took when the polar bear was in the *water*. I've known anthropologists who could tell you where something is holed up without even looking at the first track. They could tell you where it's at just by what they know about the species. That's half of tracking right there."

"What is?"

"Getting into the mind of what you're tracking. Anticipating what it'll do when you lose it, which happens a lot more than you'd like. Sometimes I'll be dead on a track, everything working together, and then it'll just vanish. Right in front of me. No tracks. Nothing high. Nothing low. It'll be like it just flew away. So I'll have to try and get into its mind." He waved a hand at the empty air. "Where did the thing go? What's it trying to do? Is it trying to get home? Is it looking for food? Is it fishing? Hunting? And if it's hunting, what's it hunting? And if you can figure all that out, then you can try and track what it's hunting, and maybe you'll pick it up again."

Chaney observed, "Sounds to me like you found all of them. Eventually."

"No," Hunter shook his head. "I was tracking something once in West Virginia. It was way up in the hard hill country where even deer hunters wouldn't go. The ground is too dangerous. It's too far from a road, so if you get hurt up there, you're on your own. You'll freeze to death before somebody stumbles over you. Anyway, I was up there all alone when I came over some real strange tracks. I'd never seen anything like them. I didn't know what kind of animal would make them. But I was curious, so I started tracking it. If nothing else, I wanted to see what the thing looked like. The tracks were clear as day in the mud, and I followed 'em for a good six miles through some real mean country."

"What'd they look like?" asked Mack with genuine interest.

Hunter frowned at the recollection, "Well, it was bipedal. It had three big, separate toes. No webbing. A wide heel. Four long, nonretractable claws. It had a claw on each toe and a heel claw. And it was big! Big like a man! And heavy. Then I reached a stand of trees and … well … they just quit. It was like the thing just disappeared. I checked the trees, but I didn't see any sign of it climbing out, so I never did find out what it was. And I've never seen tracks like that again. But I've always thought it was some kind of unknown species that's been out there all this time, and it just hasn't been discovered yet."

Meditative, Hunter added, "Yeah, they're always finding creatures like fish and whatnot that they think have been extinct for tens of millions of years. And then somebody will find one on their porch or catch one on a hook. And that happens a lot more than you'd think. Just because the world thinks something's extinct, it don't mean it's extinct. It just means nobody's seen one in a while. They even have a name for biologists who spend all their time trying to find so-called lost or extinct species. They're called 'cryptozoologists.' There's so many people doing it, they had to give them their own name."

Gantry had wandered over, leaving Vernon by himself, and scanned various photos on the cabin wall. "Is that what you do?" he asked.

Hunter glanced at a photo of him posing with a research team in the alps. It had been taken in the winter, and it showed. They were surrounded by mountains of snow and ice and everyone in the picture was crowded beside Hunter.

Hunter laughed, "Yeah. That's from a trip to Pakistan. That team paid me a lot of money to help them explore the legend of what Native Americans call Sasquatch."

Vernon looked up. "The Abominable Snowman?"

With a shrug Hunter continued, "I don't believe the thing is up there, but the money was good, so I led them around for a few months. I did what I could to help them. I've been on several expeditions to locate species thought to be extinct and, to my surprise, we've found quite a few of them. But they didn't find anything on that trip to make me think there's a snowman up there. What they thought were apelike tracks in the snow turned out to be snow leopards. The wind moves the tracks and makes it appear to be a creature walking on two legs. Photos can be deceiving. You have to be there. You have to study the terrain, the wind and a dozen other factors to understand the track."

Gantry: "Do you know if it was *ever* up there?"

"Oh," Hunter said slowly, "I don't know. Maybe a hundred years ago there might have been some kind of descendent of Australopithecus up there. It's not impossible. But man has been encroaching on its territory for centuries, cutting off the food supply, and food was scarce to begin with, so if any were ever up there, they died out for the same reasons most species die out."

"What's that?" asked Chaney.

"Lack of food. Because man took away their hunting grounds. Same with the California Condor. That condor was one of the greatest species on the planet. It was genuinely prehistoric. And then they built a ton of hydroelectric dams and flooded their hunting grounds and now the condor is extinct in the wild. And it'll be the same for the tiger in a few decades. Forty years from now there won't be any tigers left in the wild. You'll have to go to a zoo to see one."

He seemed to grow remorseful, "The last time I've killed a tiger was when one was preying on a village in India. It'd killed eleven people. The villagers tried to kill it. The army tried. Other professional hunters gave it a shot and failed. Then they hired me and so I tracked it down and killed it. But I felt bad about it. It wasn't really the tiger's fault. Man had cut off its territory and food supply. What did they expect the thing to do? Lay down and die? No, it's gonna fight. It's gonna try and find new territory and a new food supply. But sometimes it goes bad, and the tiger starts preying on people. And that's where I had to step in.

"At first, I tried to trap it. But that didn't work out. That tiger was smart. And experienced. I guess he'd seen just about every trap in the world, and he knew what to avoid. But even if I *had* trapped it, I would have still had a big problem. I mean, after you trap it, what are you gonna do with it? No zoo would take it because it was a maneater, so where you gonna put it? A single tiger needs a thousand acres of jungle and there were too many roads and cities and people. It's a shame. Tigers have been here for tens of millions of years. They were here first. But so that man can make more space for his meaningless stuff, the tiger has to die."

Mack observed, "What about all the laws protecting tigers?"

Hunter frowned, shook his head, "Laws don't do you any good unless you can enforce them. Yeah, there's all kinds of laws protecting endangered species and yet six species go extinct every day. It's ironic. They think they're protecting tigers by labeling them an endangered species, but poachers don't care. A tiger skin will get you ten thousand dollars on the black market. And if you've been changing tires for a dollar a week, that's a lot of money. The truth is that most of your busiest poachers all come from the poorest families. They don't actually hate the animal. They just need the money.

"It's the same with poachers everywhere. In the Congo, park rangers have a standing order to shoot poachers on sight. No arrest, no trial, no jury. If a ranger even *sees* you near an elephant, he'll kill you. But even with all the laws against poaching, species go extinct at the speed of light every day of the week. White rhinos. Black rhinos. Asian elephants. Leopards. The Harpe eagle. The Bornean Orangutan. The Black Spider Monkey. The Mountain Gorilla. God, I can name fifty species not long for this world. We starve most of them to death. We cut off their hunting grounds so that they start to prey on cattle. And then every time they kill a cow, they're hunted down. Hell, the animal didn't have that much of a chance to begin with. But with every Tom, Dick, and Harry taking a shot at them for killing a cow, I'm amazing there's *any* tigers still left in the wild. Even now, the only island in the entire world where a tiger can be found is Sumantra. Tigers on the mainland have been hunted to the point of extinction. And as long as people pay top dollar for the skin, it's only going to get worse, so it doesn't matter how many laws they pass. Killing leopards or tigers or elephants is not even a sport, anymore. It's genocide."

"You've spent your whole life in conservation," Chaney said. "Are most trackers like you? Conservationists?"

"No. Some of the best trackers in the world, unfortunately, are poachers. There's a Russian hunter – a guy named Roska – and he must have killed over a hundred leopards. He stalks them on foot, and he's good. That's his specialty. Killing leopards. And they say he's the best hunter in the world. But he doesn't just hunt leopards. He's killed a lot of tigers, rhinos, elephants, gorillas and I'm pretty sure he killed the last Caspian Lion, which was a truly noble species." He grunted, "With all this awareness about the planet, there's still a big market for illegal skins, horns, ivory, teeth, paws. Whatever can be salvaged, there's a market for it. The pelt of a leopard is worth a fortune. The horn of a black rhino is worth its weight in gold."

Mack asked, "You know this Roska?"

"I know him," nodded Hunter. "Had a few run-ins with him over the years. He's a real dangerous man."

"Is he as good as you?"

Hunter grimaced, "I've tried to track him a few times. Never caught him." He was silent before adding, "He's good. He knows as much as I do about covering his tracks, so every time I've gone after him, it was a stalemate."

Vernon shouted, "I'm inside Dante's emails!"

Leaping to his feet, Chaney seemed to "beam himself" to the rookie's side. "What ya got, Vernon?"

"Just his emails." Vernon peered at the screen. "Wow. This guy sure has a lot of encrypted messages from government officials. He's even got his own government clearance! No wonder he's using NSA hardware!"

Chaney demanded, "Locate names of senders and run them against staff at the National Security Agency, the CIA, and NASA."

"How will I be able to tell who they work for?"

"Just take your best guess."

Vernon's fingers were flying over the keyboard as he remarked, "I'm glad me and Jeffrey didn't come for nothing."

Clapping him on the shoulder, Chaney laughed.

"Kid, I'd adopt you if I could."

CHAPTER FIFTEEN

It was mid-afternoon when the aura of the basement seemed to become somehow subdued. There was an unmoving sense of dread that hadn't been there a moment ago, and Cronis stood, staring at the stairs.

Shadows appeared on the steps and then Dante's tall shape came down the steps followed by the wide, imposing shadow of someone else.

Both men stood in the lab gazing over the room.

"Doctors," Dante began, "allow me to introduce a very special acquaintance and a man you may soon admire." He stepped aside, lifting an arm. "This is Baron Manfred Roska. He is a noble descendent of Orthodox Russian aristocracy and is a contemporary, and rather fierce competitor, of Nathaniel Hunter."

Cronis focused on Roska.

He was more than six feet tall and built like a professional weightlifter. His chest was as large as a barrel and his arms were thick and longer than most. He had abnormally large hands. His eyes were a piercing pale blue and his face was unmistakenly marked by savage claw marks. Four very visible scars trailed down the left side of his forehead to his eye before continuing across his black beard and off his chin. His hair was long and as black as his close-cut beard. And although he wore an obviously expensive suit, it seemed like a disguise. And introducing him as a contemporary of Hunter was all Cronis needed to understand he was a legendary hunter in his own right.

As if in polite greeting, Roska nodded once. But the glint in his gaze didn't falter. His eyes were lifeless ice that seemed to read and judge everyone and everything at once. And he clearly had little regard for what he was observing.

Roska turned to Dante. "Could we get on with it, doctor?"

"Of course!" Dante responded and led him up the stairs. When they were gone, Pinion turned to Cronis. *"Who the hell is that?"*

"A butcher," replied Cronis. "He's some kind of legendary poacher and Dante is going to use him to kill Hunter." He sighed, "But I think Dante still wants to kill Hunter himself. The Russian is just here to lure Hunter deeper into the forest."

Pinion gazed around the room before blurting, "Mercenaries. Three Scimitar. And now some kind of great Russian hunter – a dude that I don't really like the look of, by the way. I mean, good god, there's no way Hunter can survive this. I wonder if Hunter has any clue how much trouble Dante is going through to see him dead."

Cronis remarked in a detached tone, "I imagine Hunter has an idea, although this Russian may be something he doesn't expect. But I don't think Hunter will be taken by surprise. From what we've seen in Hunter, I don't think the guy *ever* lets his guard down."

Casting a gaze at the long lab table, Cronis counted six available tubes for himself and an equal number ready for Pinion. Steady flames of twelve tiny burners were keeping the solutions warm and viable. And for a moment he wondered how he'd fare if he simply drank one tube and took his chances at escape. He'd have the strength and speed of the beast, which would easily be enough to get past the soldiers, but then what would he do? He would essentially be marooned in this No Man's Land without resources or Dante's incalculable support. And Cronis knew without question that Dante's wealth and power were all that would see this through to a successful end. It took him only a moment to decide that his best chance of survival, not to mention claiming the prize he so passionately craved, would be in backing Dante's play – whatever it was.

The thought that Dante's next move might prove to be alarmingly dangerous almost made Cronis laugh. They were so far past "dangerous" that something "alarmingly dangerous" would be a welcome change. But Cronis likened it to standing on a battlefield with bullets flying past his head. It didn't do any good to worry about it. They either had your number or they didn't, so he might as well consign himself to fate.

After a moment Pinion observed, "It's funny how Dante can wax eloquent about bringing down the Lord God Almighty with all this power, and then he goes and hires some butcher of a hunter to help him do it."

"Yeah," Cronis agreed, "but I've already broken almost every rule in my book. I might as well break one more."

"Which rules have you broken?"

"Never mess with Mother Nature. Never challenge a trillionaire. And always have a back door in case you need one. And I've broken all three. First, we are definitely messing with Mother Nature. And even thinking about challenging Dante, which I have, could be the last mistake of my life. And there is no back door in sight. We are in this now and the only way out is over Hunter's dead body."

Pinion bowed his head before he asked dimly, "What's the new rule that you're breaking? I mean, that *'we're'* breaking. Cause I'm in this, too."

Cronis frowned.

"Never trust a man to do God's job."

* * *

Unexpectedly, Vernon expressed more frustration reading the emails than he'd shown breaking the security code. Finally, he lifted his face to all three of them as they huddled at the laptop. "Okay," he began, "I've highlighted the most commonly received encryptions, and the last encrypted message Dante answered before he vanished. It's the same one, so that's probably our man. I guess it's time to scare the bejeepers out of Dante's security chief."

Mack leaned closer, "I want you to type this! Exactly! Send a message that says, 'Very critical situation. FBI at Saturn questioning satellite orbit in hunt for possible actions involving treason. FBI will be back with search warrants.'"

Vernon continued to stare. "That's it?"

"That's it, son. We just need Dante to contact his NSA man. Then his satellite man will get back to Dante through his Saturn computer and it'll be forwarded to Dante's laptop. Are you ready to trace the transmission?"

"You bet."

"Go ahead. Send it."

In seconds Vernon finished the message and sighed heavily, "This might take a minute. This security guy uses saturations of encryptions."

"How long?" asked Chaney.

"It doesn't matter," said Mack. "Just make sure you watch Dante's computer for a reply from his NSA man. Now, you do clearly understand the plan, don't you, kid?"

"Yeah," Vernon nodded, "you want me to watch Dante's email, and when there's a reply from the NSA guy, I'll trace the message forwarded from Dante's Saturn computer to the location of Dante's laptop. Or whatever he's using. I'm guessing that you're thinking he's somewhere close, so I'll load local coordinates and maps to speed up the process."

"Good man." Mack clapped him on the shoulder. "Let us know as soon as you get something. Jeffrey, you check every message to make sure there's no mistakes. An extra pair of eyes won't do any harm." Standing above them,

Mack glowered with obvious pride. "I knew you boys were ready for the field! Now, let's finish this up so we can pay Jekyll and Hyde a visit."

Together they wandered back to the table, taking seats. Chaney watched Vernon a moment before he said, "I knew those boys would come in handy."

Mack guffed, "The hell you did. They offered to help you when you were in Salt Lake and they told me you didn't give 'em the time of day."

Chaney seemed to resent the remark. "Well, damn, Mack. That wasn't because I didn't trust them. But I was coming up here. And this is the last place I'd want to be if I was a rookie. But now that you've brought them up here, anyway, we might as well show them the ropes. Give them some trigger time. 'Cause there ain't no school for this side of police work. Never was. And, as it turns out, looks like they'll learn a lot hanging out with a couple of old-timers like you and me. They might even learn that things can get pretty complicated in the field and all the lawbooks in the world can't help you."

"Yeah," muttered Mack, "this one is off the books, for sure."

Chaney continued, "This is the side of law enforcement where there ain't no laws and you just have to go with your gut. For example, there ain't no laws against turning yourself into a man-eating monster and playing God. I mean, my god, who'd ever think of making one? But that's where we're at. We got 'strange,' and then we got 'stranger.'"

The 'strange' comment prompted Mack to look at Hunter as he asked, "Was that thing in West Virginia the strangest thing you ever tracked, Hunter?"

"Oh, god, no," Hunter answered without hesitation. "I've been asked to track down a lot of strange things."

Chaney asked, "Like what, exactly?"

Seeming to search memories, Hunter stared into space before he said, "I guess I've been asked a hundred times to investigate a Dogman sighting. They used to happen a lot more than they do now. But I still get requests."

"What's a Dogman?" asked Mack.

"Nobody really knows," scowled Hunter thoughtfully. "But I have to say that eyewitness accounts of the Dogman are all remarkably similar. I mean, they're so similar, it makes you wonder. Bottom line, all the witnesses describe a Dogman as anthropomorphic. It's like a man. They say it walks on two legs like a man, but it's covered with hair like a wolf, and it has fangs, claws, red eyes. Basically, if you lived in the Middle Ages, they'd be describing a werewolf."

"You get this a lot?" followed Mack.

"I used to get sightings pretty often, Mack. And most of the reports came from Middle America. Especially Michigan. Yeah, Michigan used to be a hotbed for Dogman sightings, but it's slowed down in the last few years. It's strange because I've listened to a lot of witnesses who claim to have seen things like Loch Ness or giant snakes or Rakes or people that fly, and they all give different descriptions. But eyewitnesses to the Dogman all give the same description. They say it's big, tall, covered with hair, walks on its hind legs, has the head of a wolf, and howls. It sounds a lot like Anubis, that Egyptian god of the dead that has the body of a man and the head of a jackal. Or, maybe, what you'd see in a werewolf movie. Some witnesses don't even try to sugarcoat it. They'll just come right out and tell you they saw a damn werewolf. And they can be pretty convincing, too! They can make you think twice. I mean, I've never seen one, and I don't think they exist, but the people who think they saw one sure believe."

He grew pensive, then, "Course, I've got less doubts these days about cryptids. I used to not believe in cryptids at all despite the fact that I've been asked to track Bigfoot a thousand times. But I've never seen any evidence for Bigfoot, so I've never had any reason to think one of them was out there. I mean, if I see evidence, then I'll be pretty much open to anything. But I've never seen any evidence for Bigfoot or a Dogman. No tracks. No fibers. No blood. One guy even swore that he'd put a bullet in a Dogman. But I looked over the ground, and there was no blood. Nothing. But, since Alaska, I'm not quite as skeptical as I used to be. I'm a lot more open-minded. Where I used to just be cold and logical, now I'm a lot more curious."

Chaney frowned, "Why do you figure so many people think they've seen this Dogman-thing?"

"I think it's a subconscious fear that survives in our DNA," Hunter answered thoughtfully. "Hell, maybe werewolves did exist once, and our body remembers that on some kind of genetic level. That might explain man's instinctive fear of the dark. And that's a fear going all the way back to Neanderthals, who had good reason to be afraid. There were plenty of apex predators out there looking to make him a meal."

"Huh," Chaney grunted, "so why ain't you afraid of these things? If we've got this fear in our DNA, then you should be afraid, too." He stared before added. "Hell! *I'm* afraid! I'll admit that right now! And I barely saw that thing on the ridge the other night!"

"I guess I'm just used to it," Hunter remarked slowly, "Shit, I've seen a lot of strange things in the deep woods, Chaney. I could explain some of them, and then there were some that I couldn't explain. But the thing is, if you spend any serious time in the wild, you're bound to eventually see something you can't explain. Sometimes it's a species that *should* be extinct but isn't. And then, sometimes, you run into a situation like we've got here – a man-eating predator that can tear a Grizzly's head off. And at that point what you believe doesn't matter. You'd better kill it before it kills you."

Chaney leaned to look past Hunter. "Vernon! How's it going?"

"Still waiting!" called Vernon.

After gazing at Mack for a moment, Hunter stated, "I take it you didn't even try to make any of this official? Not even for the HR guys?"

Mack shook his head. "No. I could see from the file that they had every chance to help Chaney up in Alaska and somebody with real juice shut 'em down. I've said it before; they don't want this thing dead. It's worth more to them alive."

"What will they do if they find out you're interfering?"

"God only knows," Mack answered, gloomier. "If we're lucky, they'll just recall us. But considering how much someone wants this experiment to succeed, they'll probably send us to Guantanamo. No judge. No day in court. Not even a day in a military court. We'll all be put in ten- by-ten-foot cells until we die." He cocked his head, "That's the way it is when you catch a spy or a traitor because neither of them have any rights. Hell, according to the Helsinki agreement, you can just execute a spy on the spot. You can shoot him graveyard dead the second you catch him, and you're within the law. And you can still punish a traitor by putting a bullet through his brain on the battlefield. No trial. That's been military law for more than two hundred years and it's not likely to change."

Hunter observed, "But we're not spies, man. And, as far as I know, none of us are traitors. If anything, we're *victims*. And none of us went looking for this fight. It came to *us*. And why would they throw us in Guantanamo when all we've done is kill a few prehistoric predators that shouldn't be running around in the first place?"

"That's the beauty of calling someone a spy," Chaney stated. "It doesn't matter if it's true. Once you smack the label on them, they don't have any rights. It's as classified as any other high priority military secret and that's the end of it. Hell, we've got Russian and Chinese spies in Leavenworth right now that we've held for thirty years without trial. And we'll keep them for the rest of their life or until somebody decides to trade one of them for one of ours. That's how the game works. If you get caught, your government denies your existence. You're on your own until you get traded." He paused. "But when you really think of it, it's all counterproductive. They capture one of ours. We capture one of theirs. They trade one of us. We trade one of them. It's really kind of stupid. Why capture them at all?" He paused. "Better than killing them, I suppose. And we might need one to get our own back. And, believe it or not, that's called 'keeping up foreign relations.' But if we kill these Scimitar, they're not gonna put us in prison. They're gonna kill us because we destroyed their sacred cow."

"Well," Hunter reasoned, "somebody has to have real serious pull if they can withdraw a full-blown FBI team from the field and put them in front of a firing squad. Who the hell has that kind of power?"

"Seriously?" Chaney's eyes widened. "Only about a hundred people at State, the White House, the NSA, the CIA – even the FBI itself. You may be a big yahoo in the jungle, Hunter, but you're talking about my world, now. I know these people. And I'll tell you right now that the upper echelon of political power-players at any of those agencies have no respect at all for the Constitution or Bill or Rights or even the law. They're all got their own, personal agenda and a lot of them are in league with the Devil. I mean, you really think the President of the United States actually runs this country? Let me tell you, son; the president is just a figurehead. He shines a seat at the White House and, bottom line, presidents are bought and sold every day. The real movers and shakers – the ones who decide who lives or dies – are the money men who control world-wide banking empires because money, and not presidents, control nations. One word from any one of the leading money men in the world can crash a country's economy or keep it from crashing. And *that's* why Dante is so dangerous. Dante *is* one of the money men who can bring down a nation or save it. And players like Dante make their own laws. I mean, do you really think Dante gives a damn about any Helsinki Agreement? About American law? About *any* laws from *any* country? No, man. Dante is the river of darkness that supports every ship of state on the planet. And the only law he lives by is his own."

Unable to restrain his anxiousness, Chaney rose and walked halfway across the kitchen before turning back. "Listen, Hunter, do you think Dante is dangerous because he can change into a monster with superhuman strength and speed? That's *nothing* compared to what Dante can really do. The real danger Dante poses is that he can bring down the wrath of this whole world on our heads with one phone call. And let me tell you: There is not a wilderness on the planet that can protect you if he does. If Dante gave the word, he could turn the Amazon River Basin into the Sahara Desert. So, one thing is for sure. Dante didn't turn himself into a godforsaken monster because he wanted more power. He already has the power." He dejectedly shook his head. "No, Dante is playing for something bigger."

After pausing, Hunter finally said, "I saw it in Alaska. I saw it again in England. They both had the same agenda."

"What agenda?" asked Mack.

"They want to live forever," Hunter said simply. "Or something close to it. Dante wants what he believes is eternal life. Something money can't buy. It's the same thing the other two were playing for and failed. But I think Dante learned from their mistakes."

Mack asked, "What mistakes?"

"Dante learned that he can't make his dream live by brute force alone. The other two put too much faith in the Scimitar's strength. But because they were alone, they were hunted down and killed. But because Dante is a genius, he's trying it on a whole new level. He's learned that just one of them, regardless of how powerful it is, can make his dream live. But all of them together might be able to pull it off. And when they've eliminated everyone they consider a threat to their new, eternal lives, they'll conquer whatever's next."

"We've talked about that," commented Chaney dismally. "Yet another maniac who wants to rule the world. God, I get tired of these guys. It makes my little ol' beach house look better every day. Hell, I don't even want a boat anymore. The simpler, the better." He sighed. "But when a mortal man thinks he's god, then, of course, he wants to rule the world. And that's the problem. It's always the problem. And it always ends in a disaster."

Mack fixed on him. "What disaster?"

"It's always a disaster when a man tries to sit on God's throne."

* * *

Looking decidedly better than the last time Cronis laid eyes on him, Colonel Blakely entered the basement laboratory and motioned. He had obviously taken the past hours to gather himself. He showed none of his earlier shock.

"The professor wants to see you," he stated.

With unhappy expressions Cronis and Pinion rose from their seats. In moments they were in Dante's workspace and once again saw the gigantic Russian hunter as he laid an arsenal along a table. The legendary killer appeared distinctly different from his earlier, civilized self. He was dressed in green camouflage hunting garb.

His coat was clearly made from a leopard's skin and was magnificently crafted, but he had attached something like foliage to it. And although one would have thought the sight of a leopard skin coat would be out of place in this forest, the pattern seemed to strangely blend into the array of green and black so that it was almost invisible. But it was clearly a leopard, and Cronis knew it was a trophy Roska had with nothing but a knife.

The rest of him was similarly disguised so that Cronis could easily imagine him walking unseen through any forest in the world. Only his boots deviated slightly from the pattern; they were knee-high and made of a dark brown material that looked far more resilient than leather. At his waist he wore a belt adorned with pouches and a long, wicked-looking knife. Before him on the table was a very large black rifle and a bandoleer of magazines. When Roska turned, Cronis saw his bearded face was painted black and green. The Russian studied them as if they were insects he had never seen.

"I will ask you about your encounter last night," he stated in the coldest manner. "Which of you did Hunter wound first?"

Pinion cast an alarmed glance at Dante, who nodded, "It's quite all right, doctor. The baron is aware of our arrangements. You may speak freely."

Pinion inhaled deeply before he said, "He hit me in the chest with an arrow. I think it was from a crossbow. It cut through my skin. And quite easily, really."

"Did you get a good look at Hunter?"

"No. I never got close to him."

"What happened?"

"He was just too fast."

With that, Roska seemed to consider. "Interesting. It seems my old adversary is still a predator. Good. So much the better." He fixed Cronis with a stare that the doctor felt deep in his chest as he asked, "And you, doctor?"

Cronis blinked. "Yeah. I got close to him."

"What happened?"

"I managed to scramble up this rock wall and tried to kill him. I missed. Mike is right. Hunter's fast. He's like a cat. He was only a few inches from me when I tried to hit him but he managed to evade me. Then he shot me."

"Shot you with what?"

"A crossbow. But he also had had lot of hand grenades rigged along the path. He hit one of them with an arrow and it blew up right beside me. I had to retreat. And while I was retreating, he shot me in the back with that damn rifle."

"You didn't manage to hit him?"

Cronis scowled, "No! Like I said. He was too fast."

"I see." Roska turned from them to the table, resuming what he was doing. "You say he shot you. It was my understanding that the hide of these creatures is bullet proof. Did the bullet wound you?"

"Yes."

"Expatiate."

Cronis sighed before, "The bullets he's using aren't normal ordinance. They're explosive. They're some kind of military round and it explodes like a hand grenade. I don't know how it hurt me, but it did. It took me a while to heal up. In fact, it took me a few hours."

"Yeah," Pinion threw in. "I almost forgot about that. He shot at us with the same kind of bullet the first night I went out with the professor. He missed me but he almost blew Dante's head off. Those bullets are seriously deadly, man."

"Can you remember anything else?"

Pinion asked, "Like *what*?"

"Like *anything*. Tell me about his weapons."

"I didn't get a good look at his weapons," Pinion admitted. "But I was never really close to him. I don't know anything else."

"You don't know how much you don't know," stated Roska. "Were there fires burning in this ravine?"

"Yes."

"Did Hunter build a fire to lure you into his camp?"

"Yes."

"Did you approach this camp?"

"Yes. But we didn't reach it. Hunter ambushed us along the way. But the soldiers made it to the camp."

"It wasn't a camp. It was a trap. And those fools were not soldiers. They are weekend warriors who are no match for Hunter. How long did the gunfight last at the camp?"

Cronis glanced at nothing. "Oh, I don't know. A matter of minutes. I do know that some of the … others … were coming out behind me. But Hunter hit them with the rifle. Blew them in half, really." He seemed shocked as he added, "One shot from that rifle will blow a man clean in two. I've never seen anything like it."

"How many of the others were behind you?"

"Twenty men moved into Hunter's trap and then the FBI agents ambushed them. After that, half of them came running toward me. I don't think they expected an ambush." Cronis paused before adding, "I sure as hell didn't."

"And Hunter killed all of them?"

"I don't think so. But I don't know. I was trying to retreat."

"Then he's no longer using his old lever-action weapon," mused Roska. "He's using a semiautomatic rifle with military-grade rounds. Yes… this tells me much." His eyes narrowed as he fixed on them. "Did you happen to see a large black wolf?"

There was a long pause and finally Dante stated, "I killed a wolf on the night that I went to reconnaissance Hunter's cabin. It seemed to be guarding the mountain. Along with others. A whole pack of them, in fact."

"What color was the wolf?"

"White and gray."

"Then Ghost is no longer with Hunter," grimaced Roska, teeth bared. "Now Hunter is vulnerable."

Cronis managed, "Oh, make no mistake. Hunter is guarded by a large pack of wolves and they'll fight to the death to protect him, so if they think you mean to hurt Hunter, that entire pack will come down on you like the Wrath of God."

"Our intelligence reveals that there is also a bear," Dante volunteered. "A Grizzly bear, I believe, although photos cannot confirm. In any case, it's obvious that Hunter has an ample number of animal compatriots. I don't know if he can actually 'command' them, but one could say they 'cooperate' with each other."

"The other creatures are meaningless," Roska said coldly. "But the great black wolf was not of this world. His power was supernatural. And he is gone. That is all that matters." He lifted the rifle and turned to Blakely. "I will accept transport to the base of the mountain but no further. Advise my driver."

Blakely nodded, "Of course."

"And one more thing, professor." Roska's black stare condensed and froze on Dante. "You will do well to remember your promise to me about eternity. Or Hunter's head will not be the last I take in this world."

Hesitating, Dante swallowed.

"I'll remember."

CHAPTER SIXTEEN

Evening was settling and this day had just dragged on too long for Chaney, who continued to nervously pace the floor while casting an occasional, impatient glance at Vernon. To make Chaney's wait even more intolerable, Vernon wasn't doing anything but staring at the laptop while munching on a square of pemmican. Beside him on the couch, Jeffrey was snoring peacefully, rifle cradled across his chest.

Hunter spoke, "Chaney, would you settle down?"

"I can't help it! I wanna get this guy!"

"You're a veteran agent. You've been on stakeouts before."

"This is different!" snapped Chaney. "I've never gone after a shape-changing serial killer before!" He lifted hands. "God has no mercy! To bring this to me now when I'm in the twilight of my years! Why couldn't God have given me this challenge thirty years ago when I was young and full of beans?"

"Because we were *stupid* when we were young and full of beans," muttered Mack from a chair. "Chaney, back then neither of us had the stones to do what we're doing now. We'd have turned it over to the supervisor and filed a report. Worse! We'd have followed orders and shut up! It took thirty years in the field to prepare either of us for *this* suicide mission! Hell, I can't say I'm ready for it *now*!"

A gunshot cracked on the ridge behind them, and Hunter was on his feet. He didn't move toward the door or window but stared at the cabin's ceiling as if he could read what was on the hill through the timbers. His breathing slowed, stopped. He tilted his head, listening, and suddenly Chaney was aware of the wind sounding through the trees.

Fixing a gaze, Hunter walked to the back door. He stood behind the frame and risked a narrow gaze at the ridge. Unable to prevent himself, Chaney also moved to the back door and stood behind Hunter's shoulder, staring out. Then there was a blurry movement at the top of the slope and a large furry shape that Chaney recognized came rolling down the rocks. It landed slowly at the base and lay there, and Chaney knew it was dead.

"Moe," Chaney heard himself say.

Hunter was staring unmoving at trees along the ridge. Then he turned and walked to the chair. He lifted the Barrett, threw on his leather coat and bandoleer, and stated curtly, "Stay in the cabin. Don't take a shot at anything you see because it might be me."

He moved toward the front door.

"Who's out there?" asked Chaney with concern.

"Someone good enough to sneak up on Moe."

"Someone as good as you?"

"Or better."

"You know that he killed Moe to get you outside, don't you?" said Chaney. "You're doing exactly what he wants."

"Stay away from the windows. Don't go outside."

Hunter was gone.

Gantry had awoken to the gunshot and was walking forward with Vernon beside him. "Okay," he began, "what did we miss?"

"Keep your head down!" called Mack. He was holding his rifle, his back against the wall. He kicked the door closed and said in a low voice, "Everybody get your rifles and stay away from the windows. Now it's a siege."

Vernon's laptop began beeping. The sound caused Chaney to exclaim, "*Now* it gets back to us! Good god! Nothing in this happens when you want it to!"

On his hands and knees Vernon crawled back to the laptop. Instead of taking his seat on the couch, he pulled the laptop off the footrest and set it on the floor. He studied the screen for a minute before he called out, "Chaney!"

"Yeah!"

"There's a message here with a coded name! I don't know who it's from, but it might be what we're looking for!"

"What does it say!"

Vernon leaned close to the screen reading carefully, "It says, 'All things restored. Terminate exercise. No further intelligence will be forthcoming." He stared before quietly adding, "This says the message has been forwarded to Dante's laptop."

"Get us a location."

"I'm on it."

* * *

The laptop on Dante's desk began flashing. Rising from a chair, Dante walked to it, stared down, and stoically pushed a button. He squinted as he slowly digested what he read, then he said in a strangely subdued tone, "Doctor Cronis? Would you please be so kind as to fetch me Colonel Blakely again? I would be most appreciative."

Cronis didn't like venturing out among the heathen, but he was in no place to refuse what was, in essence, an order and not an uncommonly polite request. He stuck his head out the door, didn't see what he was looking for, and left the relative safety of the building. He walked up to three of the mercenaries and stated, "Find Colonel Blakely and tell him the professor needs him in the building right now. It's not a request."

After exchanging brief hand signals and, curiously, not words, one of them walked toward another building on the property.

Cronis took the moment to observe the façade they were maintaining. From the narrow view available from the basement window, he had failed to see that every man above ground was wearing the clothes of a contractor. There wasn't a rifle in sight although Cronis was certain that the weapons were only concealed. Huge stacks of pipes and bricks and wood were mounted on every side of the abandoned hospital as if to shield it from view and suddenly Cronis felt even more isolated than before.

The persistent temptation that he might yet escape this horror – an impulse weakened by his passion to still succeed – all but vanished when he saw a large cement truck slowly turning beside a deep pit. It would be nothing for them to kill him and bury him beneath forty tons of concrete. And to think that any agency would dig up that much concrete to find his dead body in this godforsaken wilderness was laughable. He was no longer confident that he could escape if he transformed. A close look at surrounding obstacles and so many remaining soldiers made even that much uncertain.

Cronis looked up as Blakely approached. He appeared to have been deeply committed to another task as he asked, "What is it, doctor?"

Cronis lamely motioned toward the open door. "Dante wants to see you in the office. I don't know why."

Following the seemingly harried colonel into the building, Cronis carefully assumed a still, quiet position far from Dante and Blakely. Finally, Dante finished typing into the laptop. Then he fixed on the colonel. "It seems our time here has come to an end, colonel. Tell the men to begin loading up all equipment that might be traced to a manufacturer or hospital. You may leave all the construction materials. But pack all medical supplies regardless whether it seems important to you. Even an empty test tube has an identifying mark, and can be traced. How long will you require?"

Obviously confused, Blakely motioned haplessly at the building. "It'll take a little time, doctor. You've got tons of equipment here. If you want every piece of it packed up, it'll take us all night. This isn't a MASH unit. This is, like, a real hospital."

Cronis noted the very large flask filled with Dante's serum bubbling over a flame.

"Then you must begin immediately," Dante stated and sternly pointed to the flask. "But no one is to touch what's on that table. I will pack what is in this office myself. And make certain the men are clear on that. It is inviolable. They are not to touch that flask or anything on that table."

"I'll make it clear enough," Blakely answered, and stared. "What about our deal, doctor?"

"The conditions of our agreement haven't changed. You will get what you have been promised. And so will the others. But we must create another opportunity." Dante gazed randomly across the office before slamming a fist down into the desk. "Damn his luck!"

Even if Cronis had possessed the courage, he wouldn't have voiced his thoughts. He'd never seen Dante angry. He'd never even seen the older physician frustrated by repeated, failed experiments. In Cronis's experience, Dante seemed forever in control of every tendril of emotion and thought. And to observe someone known for their iron control to seemingly lose even a tiny bit of it was fairly alarming.

With a curt nod Blakely walked out the door and began shouting. Cronis ignored the sudden, hurried activity outside the building as Dante leaned upon the desk. With anger burning in his gaze, he focused on the white brick wall. There was something about his posture that hinted at defeat. But his words, when he spoke, were murderous.

"It's not over," he grated. "It's said that if you want to catch an outlaw, then you send an outlaw. Well, if you want to kill the greatest hunter in the world, then you send the greatest hunter in the world."

He bowed his head.

"Roska will draw Hunter deeper into the woods. That is why he is here. To lure Hunter away from his friends – animal or otherwise."

Cronis stared. "And then?"

"And then I kill him."

* * *

Inside the tree line Hunter ran straight along the ridge never giving the shooter a clear line of fire. The Ponderosa Pines were crowded along the ridge and so it was simple to disappear, and the slope was steeply angled, so Hunter could also use the terrain for cover. He moved fast for a quarter mile along the ridge and then placed his back against a boulder and risked a furtive glance. He didn't expect to see his attacker, and didn't.

The bullet that struck two inches above Hunter's head caused him to violently twist away from the slab. Hunter had grimaced at the impact and took a moment to make sure no slices from the stone had cut his forehead because that was critical; no man can fight effectively if he's half-blinded by his own blood.

Yeah … that was close.

This guy can shoot.

He was somewhere downhill from Hunter's position and had made the same mistake almost every shooter makes at this altitude. When you are shooting uphill at sea level, the bullet will rise according to a tried-and-true formula that you can run on a calculator if you guesstimate windage. But at this altitude, with less air pressure and less barometric pressure, the bullet always rises more than it would at a lower altitude. It usually required a good hunter three to four warmup shots to get a feel for it, which meant this shooter hadn't taken the trouble to fire acclimate aim. He had fired cold-bore, and it had cost him a kill. Moe was probably killed at close range and so elevation had not been a factor.

Hunter spent a moment thinking furiously. He never assumed anything, but there were some elements in this that he felt he could calculate with fair accuracy. One, this was an experienced hunter because it was almost impossible to get close to a bear on foot. Also, based on the angle of his shot, Hunter knew his assailant was somewhere on the southern ridge. For a moment, Hunter considered risking another glance but then decided against it because this guy was a dead shot. He had only missed because he'd failed to compensate for the reduced air pressure and that wasn't a mistake he was likely to make twice.

Or, the thought occurred to Hunter, his attacker was primarily trying to drive him deeper into the wilderness. It was a possibility. And if that was their plan, Hunter would oblige. He'd take them to where he was strongest.

Hunter didn't even try to conceal his tracks. He left slide marks and prints in the mud and reached up to snap branches or rustle leaves leaving a trail a child could follow. He tried to create the impression of a man fleeing in a panic although he didn't think this shooter would buy it. In fact, he had a feeling that this guy knew him. He also recognized that this guy was good – perhaps even a rival. But this one didn't hunt a species to save it from annihilation.

He hunted for the trophy.

At the base of the slope was a stream and Hunter made quick time as he moved up the hill to where the creek emerged from a cave. After checking to insure he was guarded from a sniper attack, Hunter moved into the cave, careful to leave his tracks barely visible.

He didn't make it too obvious. Instead, he made it appear that he was injured and in retreat. And if there was blood, it might be deceptive enough to fool even an experienced manhunter. He took his knife and sliced a small cut on his forearm and spread the blood to make it appear like he'd retreated into the darkness of the cavern. In the moment Hunter wished he'd also left a few drops of blood along the trail, but it was too late for that. In any case, this guy wouldn't have trouble tracking him.

After leaving a believable blood trail into the darkness of the cave Hunter searched the ground. It was convincing enough. Then he was back in the sunlight and angled right. It took him only a moment to find a place between two large rocks that offered a bird's view of the cavern, and Hunter took a sniper's hide.

If this worked, Hunter would at least know who was stalking him and, like anything else, the more you know, the better your chances. It was almost two hours before birds lifted off trees along the stream and a half-hour later a massive, dark shape came into view. He held a large semi-automatic rifle at port arms.

He was wearing a leopard skin coat.

Roska.

Hunter recognized him instantly.

"Huh," he grunted, "well, we dance again."

Hunter had long despised Roka and the Russian held Hunter in equal contempt. They had never worked together as guides or on any rescue team or anything else that required cooperation. Roska had always hated Hunter for his devotion to animals and Hunter had always scorned Roska because he saw animals only as trophies.

Roska knelt cautiously on a single knee, rifle ready, squinting into the darkness of the cave. He reached out and touched a drop of blood. Then he lifted his face, turning in every direction, searching.

Yeah, thought Hunter, Roska was anticipating an ambush. And he wouldn't be prone to underestimating Hunter in the same way the Scimitar underestimated him because their bestial transformation into prehistoric form somehow clouded their intelligence. It dimmed their consciousness, reducing them to machines of brute force devoid of higher tactics. Instead of out-thinking Hunter, they trusted that their superior strength and speed would carry the day. But tactics were decisive. Because strength is useless if you can't touch your enemy. And no creature is fast when it's knee-deep in mud or hanging from a cliff.

Without breathing, Hunter watched.

Hunter was, of course, tempted to just shoot him. That was by far the easiest way to deal with this. And, indeed, Hunter wanted to drop him where he stood. But he had to know that Roska was alone. He had to make sure none of the Scimitar had accompanied him. And Hunter wouldn't know that unless Roska entered the cave alone. If the Scimitar were behind him, he'd wait for them and send one the creatures into the dark because the Russian would suspect a trap. But once Roska entered the cave, there'd be no chance for a clear shot.

Hunter's plan, if Roska chose to pursue the blood trail into the cavern, was fluid. Hunter could simply toss a hand grenade into the opening; the concussion alone would probably kill the Russian, although that wasn't guaranteed. Or Hunter could build a fire in the entrance and suffocate him, but that would be far riskier. To build a large fire in that entrance would require exposure, and Roska was a sharpshooter.

Hunter had heard a story of how Roska had stood his ground and dropped a rhino charging straight at him with a single round. He hadn't panicked, hadn't run. The Russian had stood his ground and cooly dropped an enraged two-ton rhino with a single bullet. To make it even more impressive, there is no such thing as a lucky shot if you're firing at a rhino thundering at you. All you have is the horn and shoulders and a rhino is heavily armored. Also, dropping a rhino with one shot required a large caliber rifle. A bolt-action rifle – a .418 or better. But the rifle Roska was carrying wasn't designed to kill big game.

It was designed to kill human beings.

After a long moment spent peering into the cave, Roska rose and stepped back from the entrance. He looked around and began piling wood in the entrance. He wasn't going to risk going into the cave. But neither could he risk Hunter being inside it and perhaps leaving him alive, so he was doing to Hunter what Hunter had considered doing to him. He would build a fire and fill the cavern with smoke.

Hunter smiled as he watched. Within minutes Roska had enough wood for the job, and in seconds he had a raging fire blazing at the entrance. Some of the smoke drifted up, but most of it was drawn into the cavern, which meant there had to be another exit. And while Roska worked, Hunter shouldered the rifle. He calculated distance and looked down to turn a dial on the scope. Watching, and taking time to think, it occurred to Hunter that every time he had tracked Roska, it had ended in a stalemate. But that had been when Hunter was tracking Roska. It had not been when Roska was tracking *him*.

Hunter set the stock in his shoulder and raised aim and then a thought struck him as his finger curled around the trigger.

Roska had to know where Dante was hiding. The Russian had to know where *all* of them were hiding. The thought made Hunter ease off the trigger as he weighed the odds of capturing Roska alive and forcing him to reveal Dante's location. It was only half a plan, but it was enough to compel Hunter to shift the rifle.

Could he ambush Roska?

Was it even possible?

Roska had the skills and instincts of a tiger but, on balance, Hunter thought he could lure him into a trap. Lowering his eye to the scope, Hunter fired into a tree beside Roska's head, and the Russian reacted violently, diving behind a boulder.

Hunter turned and made a fast way through the woods. He was careful to leave an occasional sign to ensure Roska didn't lose the track, but not so obvious that the Russian might suspect a trap. Hunter moved up a stream, knowing Roska would suspect such a move. The Russian would walk beside the water, searching for prints that would indicate where Hunter stepped back onto the bank. Hunter waited until he reached a fallen tree partially blocking the creek and left a single, tiny smear of mud on the trunk.

It was so faint that no normal hunter would see it. But Roska would see it. It would stand out to Roska like bright flashing lights indicating the direction of his prey. It would be as obvious to him as a road sign with an arrow pointing uphill.

After moving another quarter-mile, careful to leave only the tiniest mistakes in his wake, Hunter finally found what he sought. It was a narrow, open finger of ground hemmed in by canyons on each side. It was impossible to stay within the treeline and cross it. There were deep canyons on either side and the trees ended where this naked outcropping of ground began. Roska would have to leave concealment – something he'd be loath to do – but there was no other way to cross this narrow passage.

Moving fast, Hunter wrapped six feet of detonation cord around the base of a tree at the far end of the passage. He picked a tree leaning toward the crossing. He hoped Chaney was right and the det cord would explode at the impact of a bullet. Then he retreated higher on the slope, found a sniper nest, and settled in to wait.

Far faster than Hunter anticipated, Roska came into view on the opposite side of the clearing. Hunter could faintly make out the darker shadow under concealment of the trees. And then everything stopped. Hunter didn't move. He barely breathed. He stared at the unmoving shape of Roska and knew the Russian was debating whether to cross the narrow sliver of ground.

There was no good move. Roska would have to break his own rules to follow Hunter's track to the far side. He would have to emerge from the protection of the trees, and that was one rule that should never be broken. There were other important rules for tracking, but not leaving the tree line was paramount. To leave safe concealment exposed you to others, man and animal, and made you vulnerable.

Hunter knew he could shoot Roska when he was in the open, but Hunter wanted answers. And he would get no answers from a dead Russian.

He suspected that Dante had promised the same gift to Roska that he was promising everyone else. But Hunter wanted to know where, exactly, Dante was holed up and what the maniac intended to do with this new, great power. And if Hunter failed to kill Dante at the end of this, then he could at least cripple whatever empire the insane scientist planned to lead. Either way, this was war. And if Hunter never did anything more, he would fight for the rest of his life to destroy Dante's kingdom and the evil that had spawned it.

Roska had moved. It was slight, but it was there. Hunter had seen the glint of a scope in a flash of ghostly light that penetrated the canopy of trees. For a moment Hunter couldn't determine what Roska was aiming at. Then he knew; Roska was aiming at the detonation cord. He had spied it from even that great distance and deduced Hunter's trap.

The detonation cord was never intended to kill Roska, anyway. Hunter only intended to use it to further convince Roska that Hunter was fleeing into the wilderness, so it didn't matter whether Roska detonated it.

After another moment, Roska fired the rifle and the explosion was spectacular as it blasted the aspen cleanly in half and, already leaning toward the gorge, the tree fell slowly, almost hauntingly, across the narrow plain of ground. Roska waited another three minutes, minutely searching the slope for any sign of Hunter, but Hunter knew his concealment was complete. Roska didn't see him.

Then, in a move that should have surprised Hunter, but didn't, Roska exploded in a dead run across the ground. He used the fallen tree for cover as he leaped branches, staying close to the trunk. The tactic protected him from a sniper attack on his right side but left him exposed on the left. Not that it mattered, Roska was moving far too fast for a cold bore shot. Then the Russian was across the passage and into the trees again. Crossing the glade was the only move he could make if he was to stay on Hunter's trail, so he had accepted the danger and done it as fast as he could and, once again, he was concealed.

Hunter smiled as he turned. Without making a sound he delicately picked his way down the slope. At the base was another stream and he used it to move uphill again. Roska wouldn't see his tracks beneath the water, and he had no dog for scent, so he would lose Hunter's prints. But Hunter didn't want him to lose the tracks just yet, so Hunter occasionally left the most minute sign on the edge of the stream.

He wanted to question the Russian, and that meant Hunter couldn't use any of the rounds Chaney had given him. Any of the explosive rounds would turn Roska into a kindergarten finger painting and Hunter was determined now to take him alive. At the top of the crest, where another stream emerged from the cliff, Hunter spied a thick stand of trees. It was less than forty feet from the headwater.

Careful to leave no tracks, Hunter made his way to the stand and knelt behind them. He didn't eject any explosive rounds from the rifle because he didn't have any regular rounds to replace them. Instead, he removed the Bushwhacker and laid it alongside a tree using his left hand to stabilize. He clicked back the hammer of the pistol to avoid making the sound when Roska was close.

Hunter aimed along the red pistol sights. He had a short and unobstructed line of fire to the entrance of the stream. But first he had to lure Roska closer.

Hunter kept reminding himself that killing Roska was not part of his plan. As much as he wanted to drop Roska where he stood, what was coming was far worse than some legendary poacher looking for revenge. Roska was just a beast in human form that enjoyed killing anything weaker than himself. Far worse, Scipio Dante was a monster who would inflict death upon tens of millions and destroy nations.

Debating the wisdom of this very risky decision, Hunter spent a minute contemplating how to lure the Russian to this location. There was a slim chance that, not being able to track Hunter in the deep woods, Roska had decided to retreat. But Hunter doubted that he would. Roska was too proud to give up so easily. And any man that can stalk a tiger on foot doesn't give up because he temporarily loses sign.

He begins to circle the last track, and enlarges the circle every time he comes around, hoping to find a sign of how his prey tiger left the area. It was the same tactic Hunter used when he lost someone that he was tracking. He would go back to where the prints were sure and then he'd begin circling until he came across fresh sign indicating a direction.

In many ways Roska and Hunter were identical, and Hunter had long recognized that. What separated them was not skill, but something more profound; it was the very purpose for their existence. Roska was a killer and regarded humans with the same cold indifference with which he regarded animals. No life was sacred to him because he was the ultimate predator and lived only for the kill. While Hunter was, first and foremost, the living embodiment of mercy. Hunter's skill was an extension of his spirit, of all that he was, and his heart compelled him to save life, not take it.

Roska lived for trophies.

Hunter had never taken a trophy in his life.

Calculating all that was likely to happen, Hunter raised the pistol and fired a single round into the air. Roska would certainly hear it and follow. Afterwards, Hunter pulled back the hammer again and eased into the growing shadow of a cliff.

Roska would, of course, suspect a trap, which meant he'd approach from the most protected area. Gazing around lazily, Hunter saw that every direction was a shield of massive aspens. Roska wouldn't have any trouble finding a safe approach. And, if he was already close, he'd be here within minutes.

Without looking at the sun Hunter knew it was an hour before full dark. And, with darkness, Dante and the rest of the Scimitar would attack, so he had to get back to the cabin as soon as possible. But not before this.

Hunter didn't move as he waited.

He had spent half his life waiting for the beast to come up the trail in the first faint light of dawn, so he could kill it. Or lethally watching the jungle gloom until the tiger revealed himself in the cover of night, so Hunter was accustomed to waiting. He was conditioned to using patience far past the point when another man would quit the hunt. In the stillness, Hunter became part of what surrounded him. An eagle landed on the rock beside him and Hunter still didn't move. Then Hunter saw a shadow move along the ridge, and knew.

His plan was to fire a single round from the Bushwhacker into one of Roska's legs, crippling him. Then he could disarm and question the Russian. And if Roska bled to death before Hunter got his answers, well …

Death comes for us all.

CHAPTER SEVENTEEN

Dante's appearance in the basement of the hospital carried a dark aura that the elderly professor did not care to conceal. Bearing a small black case in his hand, he approached Cronis and Pinion with a forthright smile and laid the case on the desk. Watching carefully, Cronis said nothing because he knew Dante could hardly wait to speak.

"Tonight is the end of our troubles," the physician began. "We have one more night to kill Hunter before we must abandon this venture. But the plan is perfect. Roska will drive him deep into the wilderness, and I shall kill Hunter myself. And then, my friends, we shall initiate our plans unmolested by inferior minds."

"Inferior minds?" Cronis asked. "Not to rain on your parade, doctor, but Hunter's so-called inferior mind almost put our so-called superior strength in the grave last night, so I think it'd be productive if we regarded the man with a little more respect."

"With Roska luring Hunter so far from his cabin and his friends, we should have no problems tonight," Dante replied. "But you are right, of course, doctor. It's too early to consider this venture a success. In fact, I will not personally consider this mission complete until we have Hunter's body on a slab. And I do look forward to the autopsy."

"We're not going to leave his body?" asked Pinion.

"No," stated Dante, flat. "A skilled physician will quickly deduce that Hunter's wounds were not caused by a bear. And while they will certainly not suspect any of us because we appear to be nothing but human, questions will nevertheless be raised. And we cannot afford questions at this delicate juncture."

The professor strolled across the room, hands in his lab coat. Then, staring down, he said, "In a way that seems quite strange, I almost regret doing what we are about to do. Hunter is a relic of a bygone age, it is true. And perhaps it was indeed an age of heroes. Or perhaps it was simply an age when degenerate beast-men ruled the earth to the sufferance of them all. In any case, he is a man out of time. But he is a legend to this age.

"If there were any justice, Hunter would have been born a thousand years ago when a man lived or died by his strength and skill alone. In that world Hunter would have been a king. He would have commanded armies and, perhaps, a nation. His servants would have written songs about him. They would have created temples and statues immortalizing his victories. But, as nature would have it, Hunter was born in an age that believes Nature is merely something to be conquered or destroyed."

Dante hesitated, then added, "You see, gentlemen, man no longer respects Nature, and that will be Hunter's undoing. Because it means that the world no longer respects *him*. Yes, the time has come and gone when men respected Nature or those who protect it. Now we brutalize, and twist, and blast Nature to pieces to make it conform to our will. We rape Nature in order to make room for more roads and towns and expendable villages for all the meaningless peasants who inhabit them. And what does not cooperate with us, we destroy. Oceans are choked with human debris. Wastelands stretch to the horizon because pollution has reduced them to poisonous deserts or radioactive graveyards. Millions die every day from the chemicals they consume in their food.

Indeed, we are destroying the earth, and ourselves, far faster than we are rescuing it from man himself." He paused. "But that is the old world, and not the new world that we will forge with the strength and power of immortality that we command. All we need to do is kill Hunter, and we can begin."

Although Cronis was aware that his words would fall on deaf ears, he said, "I don't think we'll get rid of Hunter this easily, Dante. He's already beaten all three of us at the same time, and that was when we had the soldiers with us. So even if Roska can lure him into the woods where he'll be alone, we shouldn't underestimate him."

"You are so certain?" asked Dante, amused.

Unfazed, Cronis stressed, "This man has hunted every apex predator on the planet for thirty years, Dante, and he's prevailed, so he knows a thing or two about stalking dangerous prey. And to think we have an advantage is presumptuous at best and suicidal at worst, so if we go after Hunter tonight with the attitude of how 'we can't be beat,' I'm betting that all three of us will be dead by sunrise." He stared. "Hunter is no fool. He knows exactly what we're doing. He knows we're trying to drive him into the wilderness where his friends can't help him. And you think he isn't prepared? He knows. And, believe me, he's prepared. He's always prepared. And he is far from beaten. He probably has tricks up his sleeve that we can't imagine. Because Hunter is the strongest survivor, Dante. He's the fiercest fighter. It's what he does. It's *all* he does. And even with our combined strengths and Roska's bloodless hate, we're still amateurs in a game of death that Hunter mastered a long time ago."

Dante dismissed the argument with a contemptuous gesture. "I speak highly of Hunter, but he is, in the end, only a barbarian. A savage. There was, indeed, a time when Hunter might have been king over some ignorant horde of peasants. But that time, as I said, has passed. Now Hunter is nothing but a useless relic of an age when men lived only for food. When they worshipped superstition instead of science. When the eternal fate of the human soul was considered more valuable than the pleasures of life itself. When men still measured the meaning of their lives in years. And not millennium."

Dante turned back, walked over, and opened the portable physician case. He removed three color-coded tubes and delivered them to Cronis and Pinion while keeping one for himself. He added, "I have made an alteration in the serum which allows for a significant increase in durability and healing. It will also extend the transformation process to facilitate the rapid manufacturing of new tissue and critical blood elements." He nodded, "Yes, we were each wounded in our last encounter. And I do not anticipate us succeeding in our current attack without sustaining additional injuries. But the longer we remain in transformation, the more rapidly we will recover, so this new transformation will continue for a much greater duration. And the longer it lasts, the more perfectly we will heal."

Dante opened the test tube in some kind of salute.

"To a world ruled by strength. And not superstition."

Dante consumed the full dose and Cronis raised his tube to the light, staring at the dark scarlet liquid that seemed to move with a will of its own. He peered into it as if he could see the prehistoric power in the alien molecules that appeared so deceptively harmless.

He grimaced as he wondered of what kind of madness was about to befall them because no action where you challenge the very power that holds the universe together could end in anything but the most deserved death. Yet the dream they stood in reach of claiming was a temptation that could not be resisted.

He drank the elixir.

* * *

A bullet struck the tree three inches above Hunter's head and Hunter had spun, pistol leading, aiming at the ridge above him.

It was too late.

Roska, standing on the crest, already had Hunter in his sights. Hunter might get off a single round, and even hit the Russian, but Roska would put one of those massive rounds through Hunter's chest and that would, without question, be the end of it. Even if Hunter managed to kill the Russian, there was no way Roska would miss at this range.

Hunter tossed the pistol.

"Did you think I would fall for the same trick twice?" smiled Roska. "I thought you had more respect for me, Nathaniel."

Roska was the only person who ever called Hunter by his first name, and Hunter didn't know why. Nor did he care. It was clear that Roska was in the mood to talk before they consummated this ballet, and that was good. The longer Roska talked, the more time Hunter would have to come up with a plan to turn this around so, considering the circumstances, it was critical to keep him talking for as long as possible.

"Well," Hunter replied casually. "it's been a while, Roska. I sorta figured you'd be getting old and slow by now."

"Old, yes. But I don't think 'slow.'" Roska waved the rifle instructing Hunter to move up the ridge. As Hunter walked forward, the Russian added, "I have followed your career since our rather unfortunate encounter in Africa where you left me as a feast for dogs. And I suppose you are not shocked that I survived your gunshot to my leg. I have survived far worse. And some years ago I heard that you were killed in Alaska by one of these strange creatures.

But then, unfortunately, I heard that news of your death was more wish than fact."

Hunter reached the crest without a rifle or pistol and simply stood, arms at his side. He merely stared until he asked, "And now?"

"That way," Roska motioned with the barrel.

As Hunter began walking along the ridge, Roska continued, "You see, my task was not to kill you, Nathaniel – as much as I would enjoy that. No, my duty was to merely draw you away from your friends. To lead you further into this wilderness."

Hunter nodded, "I don't suppose you'd be inclined to tell where to find Dante and the others?"

"You will see them soon enough. I believe the good doctor wants to kill you himself. He told me that you have caused him quite enough pain."

"You doing this for money? Or is this personal?"

"How insulting of you. I care nothing for money. I hunt only for the trophy." Roska added with pleasure, "And you are the greatest trophy of all."

"There's no honor in this, Roska."

Roska laughed loudly before stating, "You are a lion, Nathaniel. You have always been a lion. And, indeed, a lion is the king of beasts. They are the strongest. The proudest. They know their place in their world and valiantly defend it against all challengers. But often, in defending their world, lions die. They die fighting. They die nobly. But they still die." He seemed to relish his thoughts. "I, on the other hand, have always been a jackal. And I shall live longer than you because I defend nothing. I live only to prey upon the world and claim my trophies. But I will live, and you will die, so I guess the old adage is true."

"What old adage?"

"Better to be a living dog than a dead lion."

They continued in silence until Hunter finally asked, "Was it really necessary to kill the bear?"

"I had to lure you outside. And I was aware that you would come to the aid of your friends, which moves me to say that I have always been intrigued by your affection for meaningless animals incapable of returning your sentiments." Roska chuckled, "An animal worships its master, Nathaniel, and you are not its friend. You are not its brother. It knows you are an alien creature and so it thinks of you as a god. But it does not love. It knows only survival, and so it worships what it believes is stronger than itself, which also means that men rule only by deception. But when an animal finally realizes how weak man truly is, then it is man that becomes the prey, and the animal becomes the hunter. Yet you have somehow managed to avoid that mistake all your life, which also brings me to ask, where is the truly great black wolf that used to be at your side? He was worthy of respect."

"He was killed by one of the same animals that hired you," said Hunter plainly. "But he's always with me."

"He is dead," said Roska. "We live. We die. There is nothing else."

"I guess Dante is going to relish killing me himself," Hunter commented idly. "Well, it shouldn't be too hard. I don't have a rifle. I don't have any backup. I'm all by myself with three Sabretooths hunting me. It doesn't get much easier than that."

With surprising candor Roska stated, "I do not agree with the ethics of this doctor. I do believe in fair play, and this macaw tactic is not sporting. But I am being exceedingly well paid in more ways than one, and so I will do as I'm told. And I don't mind saying, Nathaniel, the world will be a lesser place without you. You and I might have been enemies, but I respected you. You were never one of those corporate guides leading fat bankers into the bush so they could harvest a great species worth any ten of them."

"I always wondered why you didn't join me," said Hunter. "What I do is a lot more interesting than killing cats. How many leopards have you bagged now?"

"My trophy room now holds two hundred and three."

"Why leopards, Roska?"

"Because leopards are the ultimate predators, Nathaniel. And they are the ultimate prey. Do you know the skill it takes to stalk a leopard when it is stalking *you*?" Roska laughed. "Only the greatest hunter can take the greatest prey. It is a testament to my courage and skill. There is not a greater hunter in the world than Roska."

"You sure don't have a self-esteem problem."

Roska seemed confused at the remark. "That has always mystified me about you, Nathaniel. You have the greatest skill, but you do not seek the greatest trophies. Instead, you are content to track down children and expendable city people who do not belong in the jungle any more than I belong in a bank. I, myself, care nothing for saving lives. And I do not hunt for money. I do not hunt for glory. And I certainly do not hunt to save the life of some fat fool who doesn't have the brains to stay away from a world that exists only to consume him. The weak should die. And the strong should live. And that is the simple truth of the matter." He paused before adding, "But I have proven all I care to prove. There is nothing left for me to conquer. Nothing left for me to kill that I have not killed. Except for you, of course. My most dangerous enemy. Your head will have a hallowed place in my trophy hall."

Hunter almost laughed. "I was never your enemy, Roska. I just wasn't your friend. I despise what you do, but every man has to choose his own path." He estimated they'd come at least half a mile and half a mile in this wilderness was ten miles in a city. "How far are we going? We're miles from an official trail. Nobody will find me here."

"I was told to keep you moving until the others arrived," Roska responded abstractly, "So I suppose we will just continue walking. Dante and his jackals will be here soon enough."

"How do you know Dante will keep his word to you?"

"I gave him some incentive."

At that, Hunter did laugh. "I see you don't know what kind of creature Dante and his friends can become." He continued laughing. "Dante's not going to keep his deal with you, Roska. After he kills me, you're next. Because Dante is not going to share his power with some kind of hired gun. When this is over, he'll have no use for you, and he'll kill you. Right after he kills me. I'm surprised that hasn't occurred to you."

"No man can kill me."

Suddenly Hunter stopped moving. He had been following a path uphill between clustered boulders. The site was unnaturally void of vegetation. There were only shattered granite walls and acres of boulders.

Hunter turned to face the Russian.

"Well," he said, relaxed, "I guess this is far enough."

Roska scowled, "Far enough for what?"

"*Lancelot*!"

Roska spun as a gigantic gray wolf landed atop a boulder directly beside him and was instantly baring shuddering white fangs. Then a large black wolf, snarling hideously, landed on a boulder on his opposite side and Roska whirled again, eyes and mouth open in shock. The wolves had taken attack positions with heads low, eyes blazing, fangs bared, front legs stretched out to grip the rock with all their weight on their hind legs. And in less than a second four more enormous gray wolves landed on boulders mere feet from the Russian. Then another wolf – a large silver male that Hunter had named Cisco – walked casually between Hunter and Roska snarling and snapping at the Russian with every step.

Roska slowly began to turn the rifle.

"If you point that gun," warned Hunter, "you won't get off a shot."

Roska's voice was tremulous. "Do you think this is the first time I've been surrounded by wolves, Nathaniel?" He tried to laugh. "Do you think this is the first time I have faced death? Ha! No! You underestimate me, Nathaniel! I have faced death a thousand times! This is nothing new! And it is well known that you will not kill an unarmed man!" He spitefully threw away his rifle and pistol. "These wolves obey you! They will kill only if you command them! Which I know you will not do!"

"It's not up to me."

Roska's face reflected confusion. "*What* isn't up to you?"

"Whether you live or die."

Roska pointed angrily at Lancelot with "They will not kill me unless you tell them to! Do you think I'm a *fool*?" His display of anger made the wolves lunge even closer, and Roska began to shift toward one and then another. He made a visible effort to calm himself before he gestured to the rifle. "Consider that a peace offering! I will go back the way I came! I will leave and you can do as you wish with Dante and his fools!"

"What about your reward?"

Roska's answer was bitter.

"Living dogs live. That is my reward."

Hunter took another moment to consider.

"You can go," he said coldly. "Take off your coat and boots."

"My boots!" grated Roska as he threw the leopard skin coat to the ground and removed his boots. "Why are you taking my boots!"

Hunter walked closer. "You speak of strength. Well, now's your chance to prove it. But you're on your own. And so are they. If you can make it to the road, you're a free man. But I don't think you'll make half a mile."

After gazing nervously at each snarling wolf, Roska focused again on Hunter and sneered, "Just because you don't use that rifle doesn't mean you're not murdering me. I thought you were better than this, Nathaniel. Between the two of us, I thought I was the only one who would murder a man for no reason! But I misjudged you! You *are* a murderer!"

Hunter stared stoically. "You come here, onto their hunting grounds, and threaten one of their own. They'll decide your fate."

"I haven't threatened any wolves!"

"You've threatened *me*. And they consider me one of their own."

Hunter expected it but he was still amused that Roska carefully turned his head and stared the way they'd come. The forest floor was littered with obsidian slices that would cut the soles of his feet to shreds inside a hundred yards. Then he'd be leaving a trail of blood that every predator within five miles would detect, and they'd all be stalking him. And Roska knew it, as well. Just as he knew that his chances of making it to the road were all but nonexistent. Frowning, he looked again at Hunter.

"Kill me," he said grimly. "When you've lived the life of a lion, you do not want to die like a dog." He squared off. "Do it."

Hunter gazed at Roska for a long time feeling the heaviness of the rifle in a way he hadn't felt a rifle in a long time. Then he slowly shook his head. And his words, when he finally spoke, held no compassion. He raised a hand to the fiendishly growling wolves.

"Their hunting season never ends because they're warriors, Roska. They fight for food. They fight for territory. They fight to defend each other. But they don't fight for trophies. Trophies are for fools. They only fight to survive, so all you have to do is survive, Roska, and you're a free man."

Roska gaped in silence.

Hunter bent and lifted the coat, his fingers gripping the pelt like steel talons. He straightened and extended his arm, holding the leopard skin jacket before Roska's astonished gaze. Hunter spoke like a judge pronouncing doom.

"This is the only trophy I will ever take."

CHAPTER EIGHTEEN

T he soldiers stepped widely back as they quickly opened the doors of the van and three monstrous shapes leaped onto the tarmac. They had stopped the truck at the base of Hunter's mountain, far from the cabin. But the largest of the misshapen creatures raised its head, sniffing, and turned to the others.

"He is deep in the woods," it growled.

Both soldiers leaped back at the words.

"*Jesus*!" one whispered, blessing himself.

As if they shared the same mind, the creatures ran swiftly toward the woods where they charged into the blackness enclosing the base of trees like an ocean of darkness embracing what death walked within its depths.

* * *

"I think I've got it!" cried Vernon.

Chaney bent, "What ya got, Vernon?"

Pointing at the screen, Vernon said excitedly, "The signal is reaching a laptop at this location, and I don't see it going anywhere else! It's some kind of school or something! Or maybe a bank or hospital! I don't know!"

Mack, who simply walked across the room, knelt. "Let me see."

The senior field agent studied the screen before he said, "It looks like an old school or … maybe a hotel. Four big wings around a central hub. Large parking lot. If it's abandoned, they could hide an army in there." He pointed at the screen with a single finger and traced a line along a road. "Looks like it's at the base of this mountain maybe eight or ten miles out." He stood. "All right, boys. Mount up."

With alarm Gantry asked, "How do we get to the vehicles? What about that guy out there with a rifle? The one that shot the bear!"

Chaney frowned, "He only killed the bear to lure Hunter into the open. He's gone. He's tracking Hunter and Hunter is leading him away from us. Just like he's leading the Scimitar away from us. He's taking them deeper into the woods so none of us get hurt."

"But won't they kill him like that?" asked Jeffrey, staring.

Chaney bowed his head as he paused.

"Living or dying ain't part of this, anymore. Hunter doesn't care whether he lives or dies. He means to end this. And if ending it means he has to die, then he'll die." Chaney lifted his rifle and cocked his head once before adding, "If I've learned anything from Hunter, it's that Nature always wins, in the end. And if Nature ends this with all of them dying, well, so be it. Mother Nature will have the last word."

* * *

Hunter sat behind a tall pine at the very edge of a ridge that no creature could easily climb. He looked up. The night was ablaze with stars, but there was no moon.

After quickly retreating to retrieve his belt, the Bushwhacker, and the Barrett with its explosive rounds, Hunter had returned to this towering cliff and kindled a bonfire at the base of it to cast surrounding rocks into a cascading sea of crevasse shadow. Some spaces were fully alight while some held a darkness so thick that it could be felt.

Hunter turned his face. It was unseasonably warm with almost no wind. Nothing was moving in the darkness. The night was still. It was like the forest itself was holding its breath as it watched this final conflict unfold.

In the stillness, Hunter's mind wandered …

He had begun this journey so long ago and he had, again and again, survived so many epic challenges that no one had expected him to survive. He had made the art of survival his greatest ability. But as he weighed the odds of surviving this battle, his single dominant thought was that all journeys have an ending.

He knew it would be a harsh life that only the strongest can endure. And he had known that if he needed help, no one would help him. He would live by his own determination, intelligence, skill, cunning, and strength. Or he would die. And there would be no grave. No stone struck to mark his last stand. He would die nowhere, and the forest would claim its own, and in a day his bones would be bleaching in the sun.

He had never expected anything more.

He did, however, have hopes for his spirit. He had studied the spirit world in so many ways. He didn't think himself smart enough to figure it out, but he did have the faintest hope that his own brand of faith was, perhaps, true. He knew it wasn't enough faith to move a mountain. But it was something special to him.

It was the only special thing he held.

Hunter looked down and, with a frown, wiped sweat from his palm.

It meant nothing to him. Fear would find expression one way or another. And, yes, Hunter knew fear. A man would have to be insane to not be afraid of what was approaching. But somewhere during a thousand life and death conflicts in the darkest jungle Hunter had learned that fear, as well as courage, could save his life. Whichever one he used was unimportant. The trick was listening to both and trusting his instincts. Despite what those with less experience tended to think, fear was a powerful tool if it was coupled with wisdom.

Hunter was certain they'd follow his scent directly to the base of this cliff. But he wasn't sure what they would do after that. He suspected they'd separate out of caution borne from experience because, without question, they would remember that Hunter preferred to hunt from a height. And if they retained even a shred of their human intelligence, they would approach along the crest of the ridge, and not the base, because that was how they'd been wounded in their last attack. And while they undoubtedly forfeited a measure of human intelligence in the transformation, they still had the cunning of an average tiger, and even tigers learned from their mistakes.

Hunter had killed the Scimitar in Alaska, and then England, because the bloodthirsty lust of the beasts had left them little more than utterly fearless predators obsessed only with the kill. They had disregarded caution. They had trusted in their own great strength and perfect instincts to defeat whatever puny weapon man could throw at them.

It was arrogance, not confidence.

They were not confident because confidence was for something that could recognize its own weaknesses. That was when confidence was needed most. But these maneaters did not recognize any weakness in themselves and so they needed no confidence. Nor did they know fear. The blood of the beast annihilated whatever regard a human being might naturally have for their own life because, in their minds, they simply could not be killed, and so confidence and fear were equally meaningless.

Hunter remembered how he had killed the first two Scimitar. Even when they knew they were defeated, and about to die, their faces revealed no fear. There was only rage, the obsession to fight, and the lust to kill, and kill, and kill. But it had been that unquenchable rage and the belief in their own unconquerable strength that had been their doom.

The bloody, fearsome images of Scimitar revolved in Hunter's mind as he'd set a series of traps at the top of this cliff. He had used all the grenades and detonation cord to rig a gauntlet that might slow down or even kill one of them. But since creatures like this did not naturally exist anywhere in the world, there were no trapper's tricks in his bag to guarantee success, which had left Hunter only with what his imagination could conjure.

Because these creatures were the physical personification of an unstoppable force, a hand-to-hand contest wasn't an option. And Hunter suspected that if it came down to the rifle or the prehistoric might of these creatures, the explosive rounds were all but useless. Without doubt they could survive every explosive bullet in his arsenal and still live to tear Hunter's heart from his chest. So, if his traps didn't take them apart piece by piece, any chance of surviving this fight were at best scarce.

A tremendous shadow moved past the terminator of darkness on a distant rock and, moving almost imperceptibly, silently slid from view. Hunter wasn't certain of what he had seen and so continued staring. But he saw nothing more.

Moving only his eyes, Hunter continued to gaze down. He didn't look for shape. He was scanning for movement because the red-green cones in a human being's eyes registered movement far before they would recognize form in the darkness.

If one Scimitar was there, the other two were there, too, and probably not far. Hunter doubted that they would divide their forces with one moving along the crest and one at the base. Such a tactic was probably beyond the grasp of a beast that believed it could kill whatever it encountered with its bare hands. But, just in case, Hunter had an explosive round chambered with the rifle aimed along the ridge to his right. If one of them approached along this narrow path, all Hunter had to do was pull the trigger.

He had seen that the rounds weren't powerful enough to drop one of them in flight. It wounded them. That much had been proven. But shooting any man-killing beast at close range, even if the shot would ultimately prove fatal, was useless unless you dropped the beast where it stood. If not, it would live to finish you and everyone with you.

Abruptly, the cluttered field below him fell silent.

All of them were here.

Enough.

It's time.

Hunter reached out and lifted a torch he had prepared. He used his knife and flint to strike a spark. He had constructed the torch from dry pine, rich with sap, so that it was instantly blazing with a light that couldn't be missed at the base of the cliff.

Suddenly all three shapes emerged from shadows, staring up. Even at a distance Hunter could see the great, jagged fangs and glowing red eyes. It was an altogether horrifying sight that would have terrified and paralyzed prey.

With a contemptuous frown, Hunter stuck the torch into a stack of debris at his back. In seconds the pinesap-rich bonfire was blazing to bathe the entire clifftop with light. Then, still holding the torch, Hunter dropped ten feet to a narrow ledge running beneath the crest of the ridge. He reached out to steady himself against the wall.

This battle would be fought on a tightrope.

Yeah, Hunter had to fight and kill every one of them. But he'd fight them where the terrain was their greatest enemy because no one and nothing was safe on this rock. Not them. Not Hunter. The ledge was barely wide enough for a foothold, and the fall was certain death because the base of the cliff was a sea of razor-sharp obsidian slabs.

Anything that landed on that field of butcher knives would be sliced to pieces before it hit the ground.

They might be bigger. They might be stronger and faster. But nobody's fast when they're balancing on a ledge barely a foot wide with a 300-foot drop waiting for them at the first wrong step. And it'd be difficult to bring that great strength into the conflict if they were using it to cling to the cliff.

Remember ... they fear heights ...

Fear will slow them down ...

Yes. All creatures, no matter how strong, feared falling because they knew instinctively that a great fall could kill them.

In deciding how to end this battle, Hunter had remembered a time when he watched a bighorn sheep on a ledge that an eagle was patiently circling. Where the sheep stood was barely wide enough for its hooves, but it was sufficient purchase. Then, suddenly, the eagle folded its wings and, like a lightning bolt, it fell.

The bighorn sheep was much larger than the eagle, so Hunter didn't anticipate a fight. But the eagle never meant to fight. It meant to kill. The eagle dove and struck, talons extended, digging into the back of the sheep. Then, with an effort that clearly took all the strength it possessed, the eagle lifted off the cliff and took the bighorn sheep with it. It only flew a few feet before releasing its grip, but it was enough, and the sheep fell a thousand feet to its death. Afterwards, the eagle descended and feasted on its kill. It had been a cunning way to kill something much more powerful than itself.

Still, Hunter had to lure them up here. He was hoping their arrogance and rage would overcome whatever natural fear they possessed of heights because he stood no chance against them in the forest. They were too fast and too strong. This cliff was the only arena that gave Hunter a fighting chance.

With a challenging roar Hunter hurled the torch so that it landed at the feet of the leading Scimitar. The creature stopped and stared at the flame before raising its face to Hunter. Even at the distance, Hunter saw starlight reflected on the bared fangs and felt the answering roar ascending the wall in a physical wave.

Hunter moved quickly along the cliff. He had no intention of remaining in one place and making some suicidal last stand. He was a guerrilla fighter. Like the eagle, he would use the terrain itself as a weapon. And after rounding a slight curve in the wall Hunter ducked into a narrow cut that gave him better purchase. It was little more than a small crack in the granite, but it was enough for what he had in mind.

He tied a vine to his belt; the end was anchored to a root set deeply into the wall. Even in the darkness of the cleft Hunter managed to rapidly finish what climbers call a 'high-altitude slip knot.' As more pressure was applied to it, the tighter it would become. And yet a climber could undo it with a single quick pull.

Hunter heard them scampering up the wall. He estimated three minutes before they reached the ledge. He unslung the rifle and didn't have to check to ensure that a round was chambered. Only an amateur would go into certain battle unsure about the status of his weapon, and it was a mistake that few survived. But Hunter was no amateur and he had already checked his weapons. He didn't need to check them again.

Faster than Hunter anticipated, one of the Scimitar reached the ledge and unleashed a guttural roar that congealed in the darkness. Hunter instantly heard it inching along the ledge, moving slowly and carefully, and he waited. Then it seemed to increase speed, gaining confidence in its ability to stay on the rock. It was sliding quickly along the shelf and when it was less than forty feet from where he stood, Hunter stepped onto the ledge, rifle level.

It roared thunderously as it saw him.

It reached out violently, claws clenching.

Hunter fired to hit the cord of C-4 that he'd laid along a higher ledge where the rock appeared unstable. The explosion was deafening, and the concussion was like being hit by a rogue wave. The creature instinctively ducked beneath the detonation and its feet slid from the ledge, but it didn't release its grip on the wall. Then Hunter raised his face to see rocks falling through the dark and the Scimitar also threw back its head, glaring up.

An avalanche of jagged chunks of stone hit the Scimitar in an unavoidable assault, and it swung helplessly, battered this way and that by rocks as it desperately tried to maintain a grip on the cliff with both clawed hands. It finally managed to twist fiercely into the wall, plastering its face against the granite even as a large plate cascaded down and struck its shoulder tearing one arm loose from its grip. It roared at the impact and even in the dark Hunter could see fear in its wide, red eyes as it glared up, searching for more falling rock.

The avalanche slowly began to dissipate but it remained off-balance when Hunter made his move. He leaped onto the ledge and ran toward it, ignoring all caution. It sensed the attack and raised its face. Its eyes widened at the unexpected, and even insane, attack. It only had one precarious grip on the wall and a single foot on the ledge as it drew back its free hand, preparing awkwardly for a desperate blow.

Hunter crashed into it on the ledge, strongly locked an arm around its neck, and slammed a foot against the wall. Hunter straightened his leg, violently throwing both of them from the face of the cliff and then they were falling. Hunter twisted away as the Scimitar lashed out, off balance, trying for a killing blow, and then the vine jerked Hunter's belt tight.

Hunter swung back into the cliff and rebounded in time to look down and he saw the Scimitar falling. Its fanged jaws were separated and its eyes were flared with fear as it descended 300 feet to the base where it vanished into black obsidian blades.

Hanging securely from the vine, Hunter continued to stare down anxiously searching for movement but saw none. The Scimitar had disappeared without a sound into the razor-sharp slabs, and Hunter knew it was dead.

Nothing, no matter how strong, could have survived that impact. Not even a man-eating monster from the bloodiest era of earth's past.

Hunter secured a solid handhold before jerking the vine loose from his belt. He gazed up to see the remaining two Scimitar glaring down at him from the ledge. He took a second to wipe what he hoped was sweat from his face and prayed that it wasn't blood although there was no way to be sure. Blood and sweat are both black in starlight.

Holding tight to the rock, staring up at two sets of malignant red eyes, Hunter bared his teeth in a snarl but said nothing. He felt no satisfaction in killing the first one – not even a sense of relief. But his killer instinct was fully alive and driving him back into the fight with a flood of the fiercest determination to fight to the death.

There were two more but now they'd be slower in their approach. From experience Hunter was aware that apex predators were also quick learners. If the other predators saw one make a mistake, they would be careful not to repeat it. And Hunter was certain the others saw how he'd killed the first, so they'd be far more careful.

He twisted and hauled himself along the perilously narrow ledge knowing he didn't have any time to waste. Although they couldn't reach him in this moment, they'd certainly find a way to descend to him. He glanced up again to know their progress and, almost unconsciously, recognized that the largest of the three – the one who was clearly the leader of the pack – was last in line. The closest was slightly less in scope.

Turning away, Hunter scrambled along the ledge as quickly as he dared. He couldn't move fast, but neither could they. He edged along the cliff until he reached the first exit from the ledge. The route couldn't even be seen from their elevation. It was nothing but a tiny cleft in the granite that ran upward to the summit. It was narrow and smooth, but a good climber could ascend it in seconds. And Hunter was a good climber.

Reaching the highest crest of the wall, Hunter gazed down and saw the creatures had almost reached the cut, themselves. With unexpected intelligence they had watched how he ascended the wall and were duplicating his every move.

Although they were only inches behind him, Hunter had to take a moment to catch his breath. He wiped sweat from his face and glanced over his hands to determine whether they were cut. He saw no injuries and he felt a wave of sincere relief because, in the wild, a broken leg was nothing compared to the handicap of injured hands. A man could always make a crutch, but if your hands are crippled, you can't do anything at all.

It was useless to fire down. Bullets stunned them, and that wasn't enough. Also, Hunter remembered that he might need all his ammo for his next trap.

Without waiting to see if they reached the summit – he knew they would – Hunter turned and ran swiftly through the forest. He reached the second trap and knelt to set the tripwire. Then he kept moving. He wanted them to follow his scent, so he made no effort to conceal it. He wanted them to know *exactly* where he was.

He realized the precise moment the beasts reached the crest because the surrounding forest so far from the cliff face fell still. All of a sudden, everything was silent and unmoving. Obviously, none of the denizens of this mountain knew what, exactly, had just entered their world, but they didn't want any part of it.

Hunter didn't blame them.

He didn't want any part of it, either.

CHAPTER NINETEEN

Chaney had expected a firefight at what turned out to be an abandoned hospital located nine miles from the base of Hunter's mountain. But as he exited the Humvee, he caught glimpses of silhouettes running into the distant tree line and realized that whoever was paying them for this stunt wasn't paying enough. They might be willing to kill for it; they weren't willing to die. No one was left to guard the store.

Lights outside the building, and throughout the parking lot, were alight so, obviously, someone had managed to get electricity working at this derelict ruin. Chaney entered the building, careful to use every light switch he found. He felt absolutely no impulse to go wandering around in the dark with a pack of bulletproof maneaters killing everything in sight.

After so many years of on-site inspections to guarantee no one was following the original scientist's tracks to recreate that first monstrosity, Chaney knew automatically what to look for. A quick search of the upper deck yielded nothing of substance until he reached what had apparently been substituting for an office.

A small laboratory burner was still alight on a distant counter, the blue flame crackling as it rose into shadow. There was nothing heating on it, but Chaney had the distinct impression that something important had been there.

He descended crumbling cement stairs to the basement. He had barely cleared the door when the entirety of the chamber confirmed every suspicion he'd harbored. Even more intriguing, or horrifying, a cage large enough to hold a gorilla had been painstakingly assembled against the far wall. Chaney walked to it and saw scratches on the lock.

It had been recently used.

Mack entered the room holding his rifle tight in his shoulder. He stared across the laboratory and asked, "Is this what it usually looks like?"

"It's a little low-tech," Chaney muttered, "but, yeah." He studied the machines. "It's usually a bit fancier. Usually there's ten times more than this. I guess they've got this Satanic stuff down to an art and just brought what was needed."

He lifted a wooden rack of test tubes. Three of the tubes were filled with a strangely swirling liquid. "Call your office and get us some people up here. I think this is the serum they use to turn themselves into those prehistoric freaks, and I'm not gonna mess with it."

"We should be wearing biosuits," muttered Mack. "A man could get killed just walking around in here." He lifted a cell phone from his waist. After he clicked it, he turned toward Chaney, "Hey! We've got a signal!"

Caution was prominent in Chaney's mind as he set the wooden rack back on the desk. All he had was a suspicion that this was the serum, but a suspicion was enough to leave it alone until a local containment team arrived.

Lowering the rifle, Chaney walked aimlessly across the room scanning random, scattered papers. He found a trash can and opened it expecting to see what one normally sees in an emergency room disposal unit, and he was right. The cylinder was filled to the top with bloody bandages and empty test tubes.

Survival instincts sharpened by thirty years as an FBI field agent made Chaney turn because the shadowed shape stepping out of a distant doorway seemed like a ghost. It raised a rifle, aiming at Chaney.

"*GUN*!" Chaney shouted as he threw himself behind a desk.

The intruder unleashed a deafening, blinding stream of rifle fire into the chamber that Chaney barely avoided by twisting across different planes of the overturned desk. Bullets tore cleanly through the thin wood panels to impact the cement walls and the barrage continued until the shooter was apparently empty.

Somewhere in the frantic twisting Chaney lost his grip on the rifle and he immediately reached for his service weapon. He ripped the pistol out as he erupted from behind the desk, gun level, and began firing as fast as he could pull the trigger. He sent a dozen rounds into the corridor and gazed through the smoke and instantly knew there was no body. He also didn't hear the sound of another magazine being slammed into his attacker's rifle.

Chaney's shots had missed, and experience told him his assailant was escaping. Then, as Chaney stepped around the desk, he stopped. Mack lay on the floor in a widening pool of blood. In one hand he still held his rifle. The cell phone lay on the concrete.

Chaney snatched up the phone to hear someone sternly demanding answers. Without answering, he shouted, "Shut up and write this down! This is FBI Special Agent John Chaney! FBI Number 35308! National Security Clearance Code Foxtrot 737!" He gave them the nearest crossroads. "Contact the closest biological containment team! We have a Level Four biological disaster! We need the Fire Department and contact this county's sheriff and get an ambulance out here *now*! We've got an FBI agent down! He's been shot! Send local SWAT!" He cursed. "*Damn it just send everybody! FBI agent down!*"

Chaney pocketed the cell and ran up the stairs. He didn't know what direction this unknown attacker had taken but the hospital was surrounded by empty fields. Anyone running across that expanse would be easy to spot. As he reached the upper level and ran out the door Chaney ducked as the first Humvee exploded in mushrooming flame.

The next thing Chaney knew, he was rolling across the gravel parking lot beating at his coat knowing that he was on fire. He wasn't. But flame from the explosion had enveloped him for a split-second – long enough for him to feel the flowing physical force of fire. Then, after a long moment, Chaney realized he wasn't on fire after all. Staggering up, he had to visibly look over himself to verify that he wasn't burning to death.

The compound was large. The few soldiers Chaney had with him were scattered along the perimeter searching for booby traps or enemies. No one had stayed behind to guard the vehicles, which was usually not done, anyway. But, in this situation, Chaney realized he should have thought of it before he went tear-assing through the building.

He instantly regretted his carelessness as a nearby truck roared to life. Chaney spun at the sound, raising aim, and then the truck was on top of him so that he was forced to dive from its path. It flew down the short drive and as it reached the highway, the remaining two hummers in front of Chaney also exploded. The detonations were only a split-second apart and from experience Chaney knew it was hand grenades. Breathless, Chaney pushed up once more from the gravel, grimacing at the scorching heat. He reflexively wanted to pursue, but no vehicles remained. They had come in three Humvees and whoever was driving that truck had destroyed them.

Stifling his rage as others came running, Chaney quickly descended the stairs again to find Mack sitting back against a cement column. He'd been hit in the chest, along the ribs. Chaney knelt and ripped open Mack's shirt. He released a tense breath as he realized Mack was wearing a bullet-proof vest, and the vest had held.

The bullet had been deflected by the mylar, but a ballistic vest doesn't protect the side portions of the rib cage, so after the bullet was turned, it had plowed through the vulnerable section of Mack's chest. Then Mack cursed viciously, lifting his rifle close, and Chaney knew he wasn't hurt too badly. He'd have contusions, a few broken ribs. But if he had the strength to get pissed off about it, he'd be all right.

"Son of a bitch!" Mack grimaced. "Did you get him?"

"No!"

"Damn it, Chaney! You let him get away?"

"I didn't *'let'* him do *nuthin*!"

Nodding at the wall, Mack said angrily, "What about those damn tubes? The ones on the desk! That bastard's formula!"

Chaney was instantly at the desk. He jumped behind it and searched.

The wooden rack was on the floor and all the tubes were broken. Serum was flowing in rivulets across the concrete. Chaney felt sweat freeze all over his body. Without hesitation he ran to Mack and began dragging him from the floor shouting, "Come on, Mack! Come on! We gotta get out of here! *Come on, Mack! Come on, damn it*!"

With an angry groan Mack staggered, protesting, toward the stairs and Chaney showed no mercy as he roughly manhandled the wounded field agent up the steps. Taking far longer than he wanted it to take, Chaney made it to the top almost carrying Mack in his arms. Then he kicked the door shut and turned as the Hostage Rescue operators, with Vernon and Gantry in tow, reached them.

"Quarantine this entire facility!" yelled Chaney. "We have a Level Four biological disaster! Nobody goes inside!" With great difficulty he somehow made it to the parking lot tightly keeping Mack's big arm draped over his shoulders. "Quarantine this whole damn parking lot! Nobody gets out! *Nobody*!"

Chaney hauled Mack to what he deemed a safe distance and fell across the gravel. Groaning, Mack lay beside him. Breathing hard, Chaney gazed at the building. Lights continued to burn like any other hospital. To an unknowing observer's casual glance, the ruin would look like nothing more than a harmless, derelict hospital.

No one would guess that the end of the world lay within it.

* * *

Hunter slid between two boulders that provided total concealment and sank back into shadow. He spent a moment with his head bowed, catching his breath and wiping more sweat from his eyes. He wasn't aware of any sharp pains, but that was no guarantee he wasn't injured. He'd broken an arm once in a fall and didn't notice it for three days. Then he raised his face, staring into the night. He didn't know how well they could see in the dark, but he knew they could see a helluva lot better than him.

A cat's vision was difficult to estimate or even understand, but Hunter understood they could see images even in the dark, and he'd dealt with that before. In truth, every advantage these creatures possessed had a mirror image in contemporary cats. They might be prehistoric, but they were still just cats and, at some time in his life, Hunter had dealt with their strengths and weaknesses with every other species of big cats, so it wasn't as if he were facing the unknown. He understood them well enough.

So far, these creatures had fought in a fashion similar to Smilodons – a type of Sabretooth tiger. Like Smilodon, they preferred to hunt from an ambush. But so did modern tigers, ocelots, bobcats, leopards, jaguars, cougars, cheetahs or lions. They all had similar traits because, in the end, they were all cats. They didn't want to chase prey but would if they sensed a kill. And they didn't work well together. By temperament and instinct, they hunted and killed alone. And Hunter had already seen that, although they were cooperating, it required great effort, and they weren't any good at it. They were held together by the thinnest of bonds. But while these beasts possessed all a tiger's strengths, they possessed none of its weaknesses.

For example, tigers fear fire. It was a weakness. It made them vulnerable. But Dante and his surviving colleague had revealed no fear of fire, so Hunter never considered using fire as a weapon. They'd probably just leap over it and keep coming. What was still human within them must be providing some measure of control. They also had no weakness that Hunter had discerned toward color, and a modern Siberian tiger was terrified of certain colors.

Hunter had set traps before that had normally been successful with tigers, but he knew none of them would work with a Scimitar. No. The only way to stop a Scimitar was to hit it with something so big that even that super-powered healing factor would be overwhelmed. It had to be quick. And it had to hit them all at once.

Leaning his sweat-soaked head back, Hunter closed his eyes. He took deep breaths, trying to slow his heart, which was beating far too fast. His throat was raw, and his chest ached even when he wasn't drawing labored breaths. And although he had no time to spare, he took another moment to bring himself down. He had to slow down his pulse in order to spring his next trap because he would literally be standing beside one of them when he struck, and he didn't want his racing heart to give him away.

Seeing nothing with a furtive glance, Hunter left the crevasse and moved along a solid rock wall. He didn't worry about running into one of them in the dark. He was following their progress by the sounds of the forest. Each area they entered went instantly silent, so he knew they were moving forward cautiously less than a hundred yards out.

Hunter leaned forward taking a deeper breath.

"Come on … Toughen up … Finish this damn thing …"

Ignoring caution, Hunter leaped up and covered the next quarter mile in less than two minutes, arriving at the entrance of a cavern. The opening was long and high like a half-moon and the cave itself was said to connect to other passages somewhere in Canada, but nobody knew for certain. It could be the beginning of a far-reaching system that stretched all the way to Colorado, or it could end right here beneath this mountain. Hunter had never really cared, so he'd never taken the trouble to explore it.

Strands of camouflaged detonation cord encircled the entrance. If Hunter could lure one of them into the cave then he could, at least, blow the det cord and contain it within the fallen entrance. It wasn't a perfect plan because there could still be some unknown, undiscovered way out of this cavern, but it was the last trap he'd had time to prepare.

In rigging it, Hunter had not only studied the entrance, but the cavern itself. Gigantic boulders littered the floor, and when he gazed up, examining the ceiling, Hunter had understood that it was what some call "a climbing cave." The ceiling was unstable. Rocks were constantly breaking loose to smash into the floor. And Hunter knew it wouldn't take much to bring the entire roof down to the ground. With that in mind, he had tactically run the detonation cord in such a way that he would use the cavern's natural instability to destroy it. It would be quick. And, once the ceiling came down, this one exit would be shut down with the heart of the mountain, trapping everything inside it forever.

Still, it wasn't a perfect plan.

Hunter couldn't conjure the perfect plan to destroy them. They were just too powerful. And to say he was operating with limited weapons and resources was an understatement. Besides a few grenades, detonation cord, and a rifle that was all but useless, all Hunter had was his wilderness lore, his skill, strength, courage, and instinct. But his experience and instincts told him that anything he could do to slow them down was good. And if the trap could hold one of them even for a few hours, it was worth the risk.

A sharp explosion lit up the night.

Hunter spun to see the light show as white smoke rose from the snare he'd set. He'd built it out of detonation cord by wrapping up the base of ten trees perched atop a narrow ravine. He'd used fishing line concealed within the hilt of his bowie knife to tie the trip wire to a grenade. He'd straightened the pin on the grenade so it could be pulled by the faintest touch. With any luck, a towering Ponderosa Pine would fall at just the right angle and crush one of them. It didn't matter that it wouldn't kill the beast. An injured predator was better than a healthy one. And anything right now that wasn't bad, was good.

At the very least, it'd slow them down.

Hunter continued to watch. Then an enraged roar rose above the canopy of trees, and he laughed, "Yeah … you're hurt."

He pulled out the last roll of detonation cord. The white strand was visible in the starlight but at this point they'd know where he was and wouldn't be in a "Search Mode." They'd be in a "Kill Mode" and that would impel them to overlook the obvious.

Hunter knew they didn't think too well when they caught the scent or sight of blood because no matter how powerful the synthesis was for this serum, it was still the blood of the planet's most murderous predator. The slaughter of tens of millions was in its cellular memory in such a way that the very molecules cried for blood. And no feeble means of scientific refinement can stop a Force of Nature.

Last, Hunter retreated into the cavern to where he'd stacked wood. In moments he had a fire blazing in the darkness. Then he returned and moved twenty feet from the wall to make sure the flame was visible outside the entrance.

It was.

"*Okay*," Hunter whispered, "*time for you to die ...*"

He wasn't putting all his irons in one fire.

He swiftly moved to where he'd taken too much time, he thought, to bend back a thick tree branch. He'd tied stakes to it so that, when it was unleashed, the stakes would kill a mountain gorilla. Still, he doubted that it would kill either of these monstrosities. They were just too durable to fall to a classic trapper's trick. They would be wounded, yes. It would even slow them down. But it wouldn't kill them. Then it'd be enraged and even more dangerous than it already was, but Hunter had no choice. At this point he had to hit them with everything he had – every weapon, every trap. He had to use every trick in his book in the hope that *something* might finally work.

Hunter set the last part of his trap by again removing the fishing line from his knife handle. He didn't set it earlier because he'd built it with a hair trigger and he didn't want it to be sprung by a wandering moose or elk. But it was too late for those considerations. He was clean out of time.

By now they'd be standing at the edge of the clearing cautiously studying the light of his cavern fire. They wouldn't rush in. They'd be searching for traps. But that is where Hunter had the advantage because they didn't really know what to look for. They had the instincts of a beast, but not the experience. They were amateurs at survival. In time, yes, they would grow wise to the wilderness. They would recognize a trap by sight. In time they might even rise to the level of their ancestors. But Hunter didn't intend to give them the time.

He lifted an armload of wood and walked across a short clearing between surrounding trees and the cavern entrance. Allowing himself to become visible, he walked slowly and casually. He entered the cave and lowered the wood onto the fire. The entire cavern was an ocean of pitch black and orange, wavering light.

From his elevated position Hunter watched them slowly creep across the grass outside the cave. They moved shoulder to shoulder – another mistake – until they stood fifty yards from the entrance. Finally, the larger creature struck the back of the other and motioned for it to approach the entrance.

Hunter saw that the dominate beast said something. Then, slowly, the smaller of the two began approaching the opening. It moved in a crouch, simian arms dangling low. Even at this distance Hunter could see its great, clawed hands clutching. Its mouth parted as it entered the cavern, and Hunter got a glimpse of a Sabretooth's fangs. Then it was a gigantic black silhouette inching forward. It often paused and the head swung left and right as it searched for a trap that it could identify. It stayed away from the walls. It walked widely around boulders that had descended from the ceiling.

Its caution was supreme.

Without consciously calculating it, Hunter knew this would be the most difficult part of the trap. He had to "somehow" get past the creature's superfast reflexes and senses and leave it in this cavern while he quickly fled the entrance. And that meant Hunter had to hurt it badly enough to delay any pursuit because he'd still need to ignite the detonation cord while also avoiding the largest, and last, creature awaiting him at the exit. At that point Hunter had no idea what he would do. He'd just have to trust his reflexes.

The creature was alternately a terrifying black silhouette or a flame-framed colossus as it approached. But even in the final few steps to the blazing fire, it didn't rush. In fact, it seemed to search closer as if the fire itself were the trap.

Which it was.

Hunter violently yanked the fishing line, pulling the pin on a hand grenade wedged between two boulders beside the blaze. The first grenade was tied to three more so that the detonation would have a multiplied effect.

In the wavering light Hunter, incredibly, glimpsed the chrome spool pinwheeling through the air and ducked. He had a fleeting thought about how the explosion could bring down the unstable roof and then it didn't matter because it was too late. The explosion sent a physical concussion wave at Hunter's low position that missed him completely in the barricade he had built, but Hunter couldn't escape the sound.

The solidness of the deafening sound was a new experience for Hunter, and he was aware he was screaming with both hands pressed hard over his ears. Hunter wasn't sure whether he heard the roar of the beast or if the sound of the concussion was all there was. Then the reverberating sound bounced off the decagon of walls and roof and hit Hunter with enough force to knock the breath out of him. Hunter hunched forward, sensing that full exposure to the noise would break every bone in his body.

Finally, he risked a glimpse into the cavern.

The beast was writhing across the floor lashing out blindly to strike anything that touched it. Hunter didn't know whether it was struck by shrapnel or the sound but didn't care. He leaped up and ran along the far wall hoping to escape detection. As he neared the entrance he didn't see the shape of the third beast and angled to his left – the one place he had a clear shot at the det cord.

He cleared the entrance and, before he could raise the rifle, he sensed something big rushing toward him from the far right of the cavern.

The last beast.

There was nothing to do but hit the det cord.

As the third beast reached the entrance of the cavern, moving faster than any man ever could, Hunter fired, and the detonation cord exploded directly beside it. Hunter had run the cord along the unstable roof, as well, so the effect was two-fold. It brought down the ceiling of the cavern in a gigantic collapse of granite and blasted the third Scimitar halfway across the grassy glade.

Hunter didn't stay in place to see if it'd been killed. He knew that one of them was, at least, trapped – if not dead. And the third *should* be dead, but something told Hunter that it wasn't. He rapidly climbed the slope adjacent to the cavern until he'd put a good hundred feet between himself and the third Scimitar and stared across the glade.

Still, it hadn't moved, but lay where it'd landed, and Hunter wondered if he was wrong. Perhaps this third and largest Scimitar had been killed by the horrific explosion. Perhaps the creatures weren't as durable as he'd feared. Perhaps, even, the concussion of the blast had disintegrated every bone in its –

A single arm lashed out to be slammed angrily into the ground, and with a groan the final Scimitar pushed itself up. As it rose, Hunter was once again impressed by its nightmarish shape. It stood, unmoving, with its back to the cave. Its wedged head was bowed as if in reluctant consideration. It did not even deign to cast a furtive glance at the cavern entrance now blazing with flame.

Hunter saw frustration in its stance and knew what it was going to do. He instantly shouldered the rifle and fired a shot into its back. The bullet hit it in the spine directly between its shoulder blades and it took a pitched step forward. Then it whirled, arms stretched out and fangs wide and distended, and roared.

Hunter quickly rammed another round into the bolt-action and fired. He knew the bullet wouldn't kill it but maybe it would slow it down. Because now it would do what every wounded animal does when it's hurt.

It would run.

With an uncharacteristic, human scream it turned and limped toward the tree line. Hunter took time for one last shot from the ridge. The bullet smashed into its back, knocking it to its face. But then it was instantly on its feet and exploded in a broken run for the trees. It reached the wall of darkness in seconds and Hunter lost sight.

Hunter descended the slope in a series of quick leaps and upon reaching the glade didn't even glance at the blazing entrance. He never removed his eyes from where he saw the beast fade into the woods. He paid only the faintest attention to the tracks as he neared the tree wall trying to pick up new distinctions that would make them easier to follow.

Hunter would need all the help he could get because this was a night track of a creature that preferred hunting in the dark and killing by ambush. And nothing was harder to foresee than an ambush in the dark by an apex predator that made the darkness its home.

Hunter chased its track through the night with surprising ease. The enormous creature was slamming branches and even small trees from its path with a destruction that seemed borne of madness. Only the most enraged beast would leave this kind of devastation in its wake and Hunter began to suspect that the mind of the beast wasn't driving it. Rather, it was the human part of its mind expressing this emotional rage.

Hunter could have quickly run it down for a final fight, but he was forced to slow and even stop at likely ambush sites. He had to take too many long moments to study the ground for signs of a prepared attack. He had to move very, very slowly past every overhang; they were the preferred locations for a Sabretooth ambush. And because of the necessary caution it took to execute a safe pursuit, Hunter lost critical time.

Hunter was ten minutes into the track, moving fast but with numerous stops to check the terrain, when he finally felt in his soul that he was closing on the Scimitar. He picked up the pace, ignoring the most likely spots for an attack. He was aware that such an alarming lack of caution and preparation was the number one killer of those venturing into the wilderness, but he was making a conscious choice.

Now, if the truly regrettable occurred, he'd die because he had purposefully ignored what his mind and instincts and experience told him to do. And he could live or die with that.

The nightmare shape erupted from behind a large Ponderosa Pine and struck Hunter before he even saw it move. It lashed out at the rifle and the first conscious thought Hunter had was that of the gun spinning like a cartwheel through the air – tore from his hands like a man would tear a toy from a child's grasp. Then a sledgehammer slammed into his chest to send Hunter sprawling across the forest floor. Instantly the beast loomed above Hunter and raised a monstrous arm to deliver the killing blow.

Shocked with fear, Hunter's mind raced frantically.

But he had no more moves.

He was out of moves.

This was it.

Then, as if struck by lightning, the Scimitar froze. It stood without moving. Instead, it was gazing above and beyond Hunter. Its eyes were flared so that the red rage was vanquished and the jagged fangs hung open in what was visible horror.

Everything told Hunter not to take his gaze from the Scimitar but, despite his fear, his caution, his instincts, and all his tactical knowledge, Hunter couldn't stop himself from twisting to see what had stopped the creature. And upon a boulder behind him was the silhouette of a magnificent black wolf. The wolf's majestic outline was framed against the stars, and it was glaring upon the Scimitar with blazing white eyes as bright as the sun. Then, with fangs of flame, the great wolf snarled.

Hunter cried, "*Ghost!*"

As Hunter whirled back, the Scimitar spun away and was instantly running, seeking escape deeper in the forest. Struggling for breath, Hunter rose and, as he cast another glance, Ghost was gone.

Grimacing, Hunter resumed the chase.

Quite suddenly Hunter felt wind between surrounding trees. It was unnatural and came from the forest and not the night. And it seemed to be moving in contrary directions, even swirling back on itself, when Hunter became aware of a subdued thunder.

He instantly knew what it was and ran, completely ignoring all ambush sites. He was aware of how the white trunks of Ponderosa Pines and aspen were flying past him but paid no attention. Any of the towering pines was a perfect spot for an ambush but Hunter knew that the creature didn't have an ambush in mind. It had chosen to escape, and Dante had prepared for this before he had transformed. Somewhere in these broken islands of trees, a helicopter had set down and it would be airborne as soon as Dante reached it.

Without being aware of it, Hunter was viciously sweeping back limbs from his face as he ran as fast as he could manage between trees. He couldn't see it, but he felt the ongoing draft generated by the helicopter's rotors. The pilot wasn't stopping the engine. He wasn't settling down. He was waiting for this last creature – and Hunter was *certain* that it was Dante himself – and then the pilot would instantly lift off leaving the others to die.

Up ahead, the forest began to thin, and Hunter beheld a lot of images at the same time or so swiftly together that he couldn't determine which was first.

He saw a long black helicopter in a glade with landing lights displayed. It was a military-model helicopter with no numbers displayed. Then Hunter saw the tall, naked figure of a human being standing just outside the bay door.

The man turned toward him as Hunter broke from the tree line, still running. In the fleeting split-second, Hunter saw Dante's face. His mouth was slack, and he was covered in sweat. He was gasping for breath as if he'd survived an exhausting run. His white hair was wild and disheveled. His teeth were bared as if the fangs remained.

Dante bellowed to the pilot.

The pilot extended a rifle barrel from the cockpit and Hunter dove to the side as rounds cut through the air with the crack of fully automatic fire. Hunter was up instantly running toward the trees, and he heard another blast from the chopper and then he was inside the wall of wood using every trunk for cover. He stopped fifty yards inside the forest and put his back against the trunk of the largest tree, breathing deeply. His throat and chest burned as he heard the rotors increase in rhythm and speed and a few seconds later the chopper lifted off. And Hunter knew Dante was in it.

The chase was over.

But not the hunt.

Hunter's teeth were bared as he watched the chopper disappear.

"No," he gasped, "you won't escape …"

CHAPTER TWENTY

Not bothering to move either swiftly or cautiously, Hunter made his way back to the entrance of the cavern. He studied it until he was convinced that it would take a truckload of dynamite to clear that avalanche. If the creature wasn't dead, then it was trapped. It'd take him a thousand years to move that rubble by hand. And it would take superhuman strength, which it wouldn't have in a few hours when the serum wore off. Then he'd just be a man trapped in the darkness of his own grave.

Buried alive.

At the thought, Hunter grimaced. He did indeed believe this guy deserved to go to jail for whatever international crime Chaney could conjure. But *nobody* deserved to be buried alive. And this guy wasn't the big dog, anyway. He was just a slave obeying orders for whatever Dante had promised him.

When he got back to the cabin Hunter would tell Chaney where to find this cave and that he'd have to bring a demolition team because the only way to clear that entrance would be with a whole trainload of dynamite. He'd also tell Chaney that there was no need to rush because the scientist trapped behind all that rock was very probably already dead.

A man can live months without food, but he can't live three days without water. And Hunter hadn't seen any water in that cave. So, no matter how quickly Hunter descended and brought back a team, it'd be too late to save him. And, at that, Hunter felt a genuine pang of regret. He had always hated killing a man, and none of that had changed.

There was nothing more to do here. He'd go back the same way he came. He was curious to see how far Roska had gone before the forest decided his fate. Limping slightly, although he didn't know why, Hunter walked to where he'd stashed his backpack. As he bent, he saw Roska's leopard skin jacket again.

With a bloody hand, he lifted it.

* * *

Hunter stood in the late starlight staring at a large patch of bloody ground. Without kneeling he could see that Roska made a defiant last stand, at the end. The ground was scarred from the violent marks of battle. Two dead gray wolves lay in the glade. Although Roska didn't have a rifle, he'd managed to kill them with his knife.

What was left of the great Russian hunter was scattered across the black loam as if to sanction it as some kind of animal graveyard. Hunter knew that was fanciful, but it sure seemed to fit. He saw no wolves and knew they had scattered at his approach. Even now, they were patiently waiting for him to leave. Then they'd finish what remained.

No reason to waste a good meal.

That was yet another constant with the forest. Nature wasted nothing. Everything lived by the death of the rest. What the wolves didn't devour, every other species would finish until the bones were white as snow. Nature was indifferent, implacable, and efficient. By tomorrow morning this glade, now drowned in blood, would be just another pine hollow with nothing but bones to mark what fell here.

Hunter scanned the surrounding walls of forest and saw countless green and yellow eyes staring at him from the dark.

"All right," he nodded, "we'll call this 'Roska's Last Stand.'"

Without rushing, Hunter reached the cabin at daybreak to find absolutely no one. He studied the ground and could see how they pulled out fast last night. The dew was coated on the gravel, so they must have left long before light. He bent his head and heard nothing, which meant they weren't close. The fowl were fluttering between branches and making their normal morning racket, so they weren't even in surrounding hills.

Leaning the rifle inside the door, Hunter walked to the HAM radio and turned it on. After several attempts, he finally managed to raise the Sheriff's Department, and the dispatcher excitedly informed him of all the "very dangerous things" happening at the old hospital. Hunter had to conjure an excuse to hang up as he received a report of every single official involved in "our big military rescue operation."

For a long moment, Hunter continued to stare down. He'd report Roska's death to Chaney. He'd report the death of the first two Scimitar. And he'd report the fact that Dante had escaped. Chaney deserved to know. Just as he deserved to know that this wasn't over. Dante had temporarily evaded him, it was true, but this hunt was *not* over.

Hunter had never made a hunt personal. That was a rule he had always followed because the second you get personally involved in a hunt is the same moment you'll make a mistake. So, the law was that, when you hunt, you hunt by intelligence and instinct and skill, and not with emotion and not with rage. But this entire conflict had been orchestrated to ensure Hunter's death, so he *did* take it personally.

He was breaking his own rule. And knew it.

But this *was* personal.

* * *

It required a police escort to negotiate traffic surrounding the old place, and then Sheriff Buford himself had to walk Hunter through an army of firemen wearing biosuits, deputies, state troopers, EMTs, linemen and the shotgun-wielding local militia, to finally see Chaney, who was standing alone.

As they neared the old building, Buford told Hunter of how Mack had been shot and already transported to a medical center. The sheriff also mentioned how Chaney had ordered Vernon and Jeffrey to guard the senior FBI agent in case he'd been exposed to any of the deadly toxins spilled in that derelict hospital. Finally, Chaney had ordered the Hostage Rescue operators to report to the ER to ensure all of them received much-needed medical attention although Chaney himself had insisted on remaining.

Flanked by troopers, leaning back against a car, and appearing perilously exhausted, Chaney was morosely smoking a cigarette. He saw Hunter's approach and shook his head as if he knew exactly what he was going to say. Hunter simply leaned back into the car beside him and didn't say anything. He just stared at the hospital where blue-suited technicians were carefully descending stairs carrying large steel containment cases.

"Let me guess," Chaney said wearily. "One of them got away."

"How'd you know that?"

"Because that's the most horrible ending possible. And since this whole damn mess has been horrible since the beginning, why change it now?"

Hunter asked, "If I tell you who, will you give me forty-eight hours?"

Chaney studied Hunter's downcast face. "You gonna finish it?"

"I'll finish it."

"Which one was it?"

"Dante."

Bowing his head, Chaney paused before he asked, "You do know he'll be human when you track him down, don't you?"

"No," Hunter lifted his face, "there's nothing human left in him."

"And the shooter from the cabin?"

"His name was Roska. He was somebody like me that —"

"*Nobody* is like you, buddy."

Hunter paused before he added, "Anyway, the wolves finished Roska. And don't worry about recovering his body. There's not any left."

For a moment, Chaney just stared into the cobalt blue sky. "The headquarters for Saturn Industries is one of the most heavily guarded places in the world." Then he seemed to understand Hunter's silence. "But he's not going to Saturn, is he?"

"No. I know where he's gone to earth."

"How do you know?"

"Because he's more animal, now, than human. And when an animal's wounded, it goes back to its liar. And that's where he'll go. He'll be in the most protected part of his house. A basement. A lab. Some kind of panic room.."

Chaney's face bent and he stared at the ground before, "Well, since we're talking about something that looks an awful lot like cold-blooded murder, let's agree. You can do it. Or I can do it. But it has to be done. And I'll handle the paperwork to keep both of us out of trouble." He waited. "You sure about this? It's a line you've never crossed."

"Yeah," sighed Hunter. "I'm sure."

Chaney looked away and was silent for a long time. Then, "All right. I'll give you forty-eight hours. But that's it. Then I'm gonna have to hunt Dante down with a couple of gunships and kill him whether he's human or not." He motioned toward the building. "This'll take a day to process and, after that, I'm turning this whole thing over to the army. But I'll be outside Dante's place when you get there. I'll text you the address."

Hunter pushed off the car.

"It's all I need."

Hunter walked away, head down. He was considering so much that it was all blending into a kaleidoscope of swirling, conflicting feelings all mixed with regret, fatigue, and the darkest sense of purpose. He had avoided this all his life. At times, yes, he'd been forced to kill animal and man. But he had never gone after a man with the single purpose of killing him. And then he remembered that murder was how all this began.

In the long trip through the security perimeter Hunter wondered where the man he had once been had gone. It seemed like all he had ever done was fight these creatures. It was strange because he had never wanted to fight. He had never wanted to kill. He had only sought to save life in an age that seemed to disregard the sacredness of life.

All that time he had spent risking his life saving people in the wilderness seemed like a gauzy, half-remembered dream from someone else's life. It was if he could no longer see the faces of those he had found, the gratitude of the animals he'd rescued. Even the feeling of defeating death so many times were difficult to remember. All of it seemed submerged by this terrible thing before him. And when he was finally through the wall of guns surrounding the hospital, he still wasn't sure if he could actually do it. But he had made a grave promise to himself that he knew he had to keep.

He had to finish this.

There *had* to be an ending.

So, there was no turning back.

Not for any of them.

Dante had tasted fruit from the Tree of Life and now he would never abandon his quest. And, eventually, as this serum had done before, the awesome temptation of immortality would corrupt human weakness so that it threatened every life on the earth. The beast would escape its cage again, and then this world would become a wasteland of death.

Hunter didn't trust the soldiers to do it. And, despite Chaney's determination, he didn't trust the rest of the FBI. It was too likely that laws or money or courts would prevent them from doing what had to be done.

Hunter's forehead hardened at the thought.

Yeah. He'd hunt Dante down. And he'd cross a line he'd never crossed.

His last hunt.

CHAPTER TWENTY-ONE

S cipio Dante closed the ostentatious front door of his sprawling Westchester County mansion. He was accompanied by a stern, middle-aged woman who carried a large black case. Two servants behind Dante secured and locked the double-wide panels and guards stationed throughout the opulent interior of the manor nodded with respectful regard as Dante walked silently through them.

Trailed by the unnamed woman protectively clutching the valise, the professor moved with the expression of a man using every ounce of will and strength to remain on his feet. He said nothing as he laboriously unlocked a black steel door at the rear of the house and entered a forbidden wing of the mansion.

That is, it *had* been forbidden.

Until today.

Embracing the valise, the woman followed.

* * *

At the base of the stairs Dante's companion turned on all lights for the vast subterranean complex revealing walls stacked with every medical machine available to science. There was a black cremator at the far end. With an expression of great pain Dante sat on a stool and spoke in a voice coarse and hoarse.

"Very carefully set the flask on the counter."

The woman 'very carefully' did what she was instructed to do, and Dante nodded, "Now you may go, but remain close. I may have need of you before tomorrow."

She ascended the stairs and there was the sound of a steel door shut and locked.

A hard voice echoed in the laboratory.

"You're not going to see tomorrow."

Spinning, Dante faced Hunter, who had stepped from some unknown concealment. Standing not twenty feet from the professor, Hunter didn't move. He simply stared as if he was about to commit himself to the flames. Slowly, Dante stood and began backing toward the counter that supported the flask.

"Make peace with God," said Hunter.

Dante's head tilted back as he regarded Hunter. "I thought you had morals against killing an unarmed man, Mr. Hunter."

"You're not unarmed."

Dante glanced nervously past Hunter's shoulder.

"Is your … friend … with you?"

"He's always with me."

"Our last encounter was … supernatural."

"He's natural. He's just not of this world, anymore." Hunter shook his head, "Do you know how much life you've destroyed with your madness?"

"I am a physician. Death is my profession."

"*Murder* isn't your profession."

"What's the difference!" snarled Dante. "I will be *free* from death!"

"Only God is free."

"Is death that important to you?"

"*Life* is."

Dante took another step toward the flask. "I see you count your dead. That is good. You *should* count your dead! We *all* should! Then you should count all your dead from

Alaska. All the dead from London. And all the dead from your mountain. And how many dead will you have, Mr. Hunter? Twenty? Thirty? *A hundred*? Add them up! What is the number? Good! So you know! And now I want you to think of *this*. I want you to add this number. If I fail to isolate and bottle the power of this creature's blood, then you can count my dead by the *millions*. Yes! *By the tens of millions*! Because I can save the lives of hundreds of millions – *of the whole world*! – if I can only distill this creature's power for rapid healing or for overcoming disease. For curing a thousand genetic maladies that have always been labeled incurable. Don't you see what we can accomplish with the blood of this creature? It is perfect in power!"

"Only God is perfect in power, Dante. And you're not God."

Dante straightened. "So you will kill me?"

"Yes."

"To protect the others?"

"To protect the *world*."

"How self-righteous of you."

"You've been wrong since from the beginning, Dante. That creature isn't immortal. It's just flesh and bone and will die like anything else. I know because I've killed four of 'em. But you're my last. This madness ends now."

Dante reached the counter. His left hand touched the flask.

Hunter casually drew the .44 and thumbed back the hammer.

"Is that the last of it?" asked Hunter as if it was incidental.

Dante hesitated. "Yes."

"Go ahead," nodded Hunter. "It can die with you."

Dante seemed to be measure whether Hunter would really pull the trigger. "How did you get in here? I have twelve men guarding the grounds."

"Ten," said Hunter.

"I see. How unfortunate for them."

"They're not dead," said Hunter. "I didn't come here to kill rent-a-cops."

"Of course not," Dante said and wiped sweat from his chin, his forehead. Then he added, almost breathless, "Yes … You've only come for me. I understand." He swallowed before adding, "What a pity … so much work … for nothing. But I must give you credit, Mr. Hunter, you certainly checked all the boxes when it came to –"

Dante whirled and snatched up the flask and Hunter merely watched as the physician greedily drank the last of the amber liquid and then Dante turned, wiping his mouth.

Hunter grimaced, "You have *got* to die."

Suddenly Dante convulsed, bent double. Groaning and coughing, he managed to stand in a crouch with a single arm over his chest, his hand pressing hard against his heart. The agonized groan that emanated from him was more animal than human. And, as the groan faded, Dante's altered voice emerged from his contorted stance.

"You could not possible know …" Dante groaned, "but this new serum … is much, much more powerful than the first. And so … it will kill me … or make me a hundred times more powerful." He lifted his face, and it was already shifting. He barked an agonized laugh. "I have gained eternal life, Mr. Hunter! I'm sorry you won't be joining me!"

Dante threw his head back and roared.

Watching in unexpected amazement, Hunter was too astonished to move. He had expected the transition from human to bestial to take a moment. But that wasn't what happened. Dante's alien alteration happened in less than a second. It happened so fast that Hunter barely understood what, exactly, *was* happening and then it was over.

In Dante's transformed Scimitar shape, he instantly towered over Hunter. His chest and shoulders had violently burst into gigantic slabs of shocking physical might. Then claws the size of a Grizzly's erupted from both hands and, when Dante clutched his fingers, the talons snapped like gunshots. His face elongated and teeth fell from his mouth as *tusks* erupted from his snarling jaws. His arms, human only a split-second ago, expanded and erupted in tight bunches of muscle until they rivaled the arms of a mountain gorilla.

Dante's eyes glowed blood red.

"*No!*" he growled, fang sharpening fang. "*I will never die!*"

Dante stepped forward …

Hunter's killer instinct blazed and he fired the magnum into a pressurized oxygen tank at Dante's side. Hunter was not aware of any distinct impressions after what was certainly a tremendous explosion. Not that Hunter heard, or felt, anything. He simply found himself staggering up within the orange light of fire and moving quickly from where he had been blasted. He didn't even wonder whether Dante might have survived the explosion. First, he had to check on whether he still had his arms and legs and wasn't bleeding to death.

Sliding down a long white machine in the roaring, burning atmosphere, Hunter was very much aware that he was leaving a tall smear of blood. He didn't care. It didn't matter. He had never expected to survive this, anyway. He'd come to kill Dante and expected to die doing it.

So very strangely in the moment, Hunter had no regrets. He had consciously made choices a lifetime ago and he would die with them. He had known at the time – when he had made the decisions – where they would lead. He had accepted the consequences then, and he accepted them now without regret, without sorrow, and without any heartfelt hopes for what might have been, for some are not created to know their dreams …

A movement somewhere in the white mist caught Hunter's attention and he stared but saw nothing stirring. But because he was conditioned to believe the worst,

Hunter suspected Dante had survived the blast completely whole or with the most inconsequential wounds, and he was searching for Hunter in this white, swirling half-light.

Hunter had automatically dismissed the professor's argument for continuing this experiment. Regardless of how many lives the serum might save, this experiment was over. That was Hunter's mind, and he wasn't about to reconsider. He did not reckon himself smart enough to decide the right and wrong of it. He had seen the death this creature left in its wake, and that alone was reason enough to end this.

Enough!

Think!

Hunter laid his head back against the cubical colossus of a machine and closed his eyes. He had his 45.70 rifle and the .44 but both were ultimately useless. They had been all but useless against the first-generation Scimitar. They were worse than useless against this monstrous, mutated version.

Suddenly Hunter was blasted forward as the machine was hit by what felt like a freight train. At the very last split-second Hunter thought he heard a muffled sound on the far side of the device and then there was an explosion with the rending sound of metal ripped from moorings and Hunter was rolling across the floor. He reached his feet in seconds and spun into the mist, vanishing should the creature be rushing forward.

Moving as quickly as caution allowed, Hunter made a silent path between machines, always pausing to listen and then look before turning into another path. He knew that if Dante could creep up on him once, he could do it again. So, either Dante could somehow see through this fog, or he had enhanced senses. He might even have acquired thermal vision in this nightmarish form, but Hunter doubted it. This new version of the serum seriously amped up the creature's powers, but it didn't create new ones. And Dante, even in this form, was just hard to kill. He wasn't unkillable. He could bleed …

'Life is in the blood.'

The thought struck Hunter out of nowhere.

He whirled, searching, and saw it.

Huge cylinders marked 'Liquid Nitrogen' were grouped along a wall. Hunter bowed his head, listening. Somewhere out there, Dante was prowling. Hunter could hear the distant, muffled footsteps. He could detect the mist stirring as if by an emerging ghost.

Reaching into his coat, Hunter withdrew a coil of detonation cord. He moved silently but swiftly to the nitrogen tanks and looped one end of the coil to the first tank. He repeated to wrap every subsequent tank until they were all strapped in the same coil. Now, when Hunter ignited the det cord, every cannister would blow at the same time and probably kill everything in this room. Then another thought dawned on Hunter, and he spun toward the cremator.

The huge cubicle laid within a protective steel shell separated from the room by over three feet of insulation. It was four feet above the floor. It was designed to withstand an inferno. It was far enough from the nitrogen cannisters.

It was a wild plan, but Hunter didn't waste a split-second calculating the odds. He'd probably die, anyway. But he'd stand a better chance locked in that cremator than he would stand out here when those tanks exploded because everything in this room was going to be frozen at four hundred degrees below zero.

Yeah. Dante was tough. But he wasn't *that* tough. The blood in his veins would instantly turn to ice and his flesh would freeze him where he stood. And not all the savagery in the universe would be strong enough to break him free.

Science had created him.

But Nature could destroy him.

Hunter finished wrapping the last cannister when he glimpsed a shape to his right and spun to see Dante do the same. In full display, framed by white as if he were emerging from the gateway of a darker universe, Dante stood gigantic and glaring. His monstrous hands clenched tight, and the hideous jaws separated.

He roared and charged.

Hunter hurled the rifle aside and was instantly running. He took six steps and dove into the cremator reaching away with his hand clutching the detonator. Then he hit the button to shut the door and punched the command to detonate.

The door slammed shut as the cylinders exploded.

Hunter caught a glimpse of Dante as the cylinders erupted with the force of a frozen volcano, submerging the colossal Scimitar in the Ice Age that had once held it. Hunter didn't know whether Dante had been killed by the blast. He had no idea whether he was going to survive this, himself. He lay inside the cubicle listening to the outer shell freeze with a sharp crack. But as he waited, he felt no change within the oven itself. The grate upon which he rested didn't freeze. And then the minutes began to drag with a deep, profound silence.

Hunter blinked, for the first time sensing that he might stand a chance of getting out of here, after all. He didn't put much hope in it, but a small chance was better than none. And now there was nothing to do but wait until the nitrogen dispersed.

Folding hands over his chest, Hunter assumed the stillness of a dead man. He slowed his breathing, conserving what little oxygen the cremator contained. And, lying in total darkness, he began to calculate.

It was august, so the nitrogen would gradually warm. No longer pressurized and contained, the nonmetal element would spread until it became the same temperature as surrounding air.

Hunter knew nothing for certain, but he sensed that waiting for six cannisters of liquid nitrogen to reach the same temperature as the outside air would take far longer than he could afford to wait. Even if he was right about the gradual warming, he'd run out of oxygen long before he could safely leave this metal coffin.

Blood and sweat drenched Hunter's clothes and, as he began trembling with residual adrenaline, he slowly became aware of a dozen sharp wounds. He knew he was hurt, but there was no way to know how bad. And there was no way for him to even wrap his injuries. In the narrow confines of the cremator, he could barely move. He couldn't sit up or remove his bloody clothes. All he could do was endure the pain.

And wait.

"Damn," Hunter whispered, "this is a bad one ..."

He tried to estimate how long the oxygen in this soot-lined grave would last, and he guessed he had about four hours. Of course, Hunter reasoned, he could be wrong. He might run out of oxygen long before that.

From experience, Hunter knew that symptoms indicating hypoxia were different for every individual. Some revealed no symptoms at all before dying from a lack of oxygen. Others began desperately gasping when they first felt faint. Others began sweating before they collapsed. And some famous mountaineers had been talking up a storm on the North Face of Everest when they suddenly turned blue and fell on their face. So, not only did hypoxia hit each individual differently, it could hit the same individual in different ways.

Hunter had suffered hypoxia several times during week-long alpine rescues, and he knew how his body had reacted in the past, but that was no guarantee that his body would have the same reaction in the future. Hypoxia was, as one physician had told Hunter, a "silent killer" because it killed before the victim even knew they were dying.

Hunter had no choice but to lay here – at least for now. He wouldn't wait so long that he was certain that he wouldn't freeze to death from a liquid pool of nitrogen, but he'd stay as long as he dared. An hour passed, and then

Hunter thought he perceived muffled sounds on the far side of the thick carbon steel.

The lid of the cremator was suddenly slammed open.

Hunter instinctively ducked but didn't know why. There was nowhere to go. He couldn't even raise his head to see what had happened. Then the metal grate he laid upon was pulled into the surprising brightness of the basement. Only then did Hunter notice dozens of firemen moving about the demolished ruins.

He turned to a friendly voice.

"I said I'd give you ten minutes," smiled Chaney. "But after the explosion we had to wait an hour for this mess to clear out."

Without speaking, and after taking a careful breath, Hunter rose. He stood and noticed the floor was covered with steaming foam. Everywhere throughout the complex firefighters were moving with calm, unhurried precision. Only then did Hunter see that a large part of the wall to his right had been completely blown away leaving the garden in view. Mist from the nitrogen was moving lazily before being swept away by the morning wind.

Hunter grimaced at the residual cold; it felt like the same cold he had known when he'd been submerged in a hurricane ice-storm – a cold that encased each individual part of you so that your legs and arms felt like they were entombed in a glacier. It was the kind of cold you could still feel years later when you might be standing in the sun.

"Where's Dante?" managed Hunter.

Chaney turned and pointed.

Standing gigantic and monstrous at where the liquid nitrogen had erupted, Dante was frozen through and through. His fangs were still separated as if even in that halted form he would yet devour the world. He looked like a monument to the power of evil.

With a frown, Hunter raised the .44.

He fired.

The bullet struck the towering shape and Dante's bestial form exploded into spinning, shining shards of ice that rained across the chamber with the sound of an unstoppable iceberg smashing into an immoveable cliff. As Hunter stared, he saw rivulets of blood in every flashing, slicing, sliver of ice. Not moving, Chaney watched until, finally, the last fragment landed to lie still on the stone. Then, wearily, he swept sweat from his face.

Without a word Hunter lowered the gun.

They stood in silence until Chaney finally said, "Yeah. That's the way it should be." He paused. "It's the same way the first monster died ten thousand years ago."

Hunter grunted, turning away.

"The monster is man," he said.

Hunter walked through the demolished wall and into the garden's iridescent flowing peace. The sky over the river was steel blue above a scarlet sea stretching to the horizon. And as Hunter reached a place where he was separated from the rest, he felt a strange chill and turned to stare back at the fortress he had quit.

A ghostly white mist rose from the broken walls.

"For dust you are," said Hunter, "and to dust you shall return."

EPILOGUE

I t was fall of another year when Chaney took it on himself to travel to Hunter's cabin so high in the Montana mountains. He reached the crest by sunset and saw nothing moving. The place had been long abandoned. Any sign that anyone had lived here was gone.

Something flickered at the edge of the woods, and Chaney turned, staring. He walked up the slope until he reached a site that seemed more silent than the surrounding forest. There was nothing to mark it as special, but Chaney had the impression there was something sacred about it. And then he saw a slight movement.

A magnificent black wolf stood beside a post staked at the edge of the wilderness. The great wolf, eternal as night, simply stared at Chaney with the patience of the dead. It was as if he was here, had always been here, and would always be here.

Chaney whispered, "*Ghost ...*"

At the top of the post, something fluttered in the wind.

Chaney walked forward until he saw that it was a leopard skin jacket. It had been struck to the post as if to return what remained to Nature. Then a thought fell upon Chaney, and he turned to ask Ghost if there was truly life after death.

The wolf was gone.

Wind stirred where it had stood.

Chaney sighed, "I guess I'll never know ..."

At the base of the stake, Chaney suddenly saw something shown to him in the dust. He brushed aside the dirt and found a gray, weathered Scimitar fang. Hunter must have injured the abomination worse than they knew that night.

The once terrifying fang was scorched and torn as if it had been exposed to the unendurable wrath of an angry god. It felt weightless and hollow as if whatever evil had possessed it in this world had been annihilated by a force as far beyond its defiance as the stars beyond the earth. And Chaney sensed that all the lives claimed by its cruelty had been somehow lifted up, resurrected, and restored. It was as if the ultimately meaningless strength of flesh and bone had met the resistance of what is, alone, perfect in power, and the conflict had left the Scimitar fang scorned, damned, and destroyed.

And when Chaney closed his fist on it, the fang crumbled into dust.

THE END

www.ingramcontent.com/pod-product-compliance
Lightning Source LLC
Chambersburg PA
CBHW070621300726
48975CB00006B/1885